Dedalus European Anthologies
General Editor: Mike Mitchell

The Dedalus Book of
Estonian Literature

D1615240

The Dedalus Book
of
Estonian Literature

**Edited by Jan Kaus
and
Translated by Eric Dickens**

Dedalus

Dedalus would like to thank Traducta, The Estonian Translation Fund in Tallinn and Grants for the Arts for their assistance in producing this book.

Published in the UK by Dedalus Limited,
24-26, St Judith's Lane, Sawtry, Cambs, PE28 5XE
email: info@ dedalusbooks.com
www.dedalusbooks.com

ISBN 978 1 903517 95 6

Dedalus is distributed in the USA & Canada by SCB Distributors,
15608 South New Century Drive, Gardena, CA 90248
email: info@scbdistributors.com

Dedalus is distributed in Australia by Peribo Pty Ltd.
58, Beaumont Road, Mount Kuring-gai, N.S.W. 2080
email: info@peribo.com.au

First Published by Dedalus in 2011

Printed in Finland by Bookwell
Typeset by Marie Lane

The Editor

Jan Kaus was born in Estonia in 1971.

He is a novelist, essayist, scriptwriter, critic, poet and translator from Finnish into Estonian. He has published eight books, including the novels *The World and a Few* (2001), *You* (2006) and *A Moment* (2009), which have been translated into six languages.

He has been the chairman of The Estonian Writers' Union (2004-2007) and is currently the literary editor of the cultural weekly "Sirp".

The Translator

Eric Dickens was born in 1953. He grew up in England and went to the University of East Anglia, where he studied Swedish and European Literature. He has lived at various times in The Netherlands, Finland, Poland and Estonia. He now lives in Sweden.

He is the editor of *The Dedalus Book of Flemish Fantasy*.

Translator's Acknowledgements

Apart from Jan Kaus who compiled the anthology and wrote the introduction, I would also like to thank Ilvi Liive of the Estonian Literature Centre (ELIC) who provided photocopies of texts I did not have to hand, and thank my checkers Tiina Randviir and Inna Feldbach who drew my attention to shortcomings in my translations, not least where I had simply misinterpreted the original. Literary translation is teamwork, so the translator does not deserve all of the credit for a successful rendering.

Contents

Upheavals in the Borderlands: Jan Kaus.................................9

Maiden of the North: August Gailit...................................... 13

Flash Photography: Karl August Hindrey............................. 37

Bread: Eduard Vilde.. 57

On Lake Peipsi: Juhan Liiv..66

Bird Cherry Petals: Friedebert Tuglas...................................71

Grandfather's Death: Anton Hansen Tammsaare...................86

Night of Souls: Karl Ristikivi... 96

Eight Japanese Ladies: Arvo Valton.....................................120

Uncle: Jaan Kross... 128

An Empty Beach: Mati Unt.. 156

The Collector: Rein Saluri... 205

The Rococo Lady: Maimu Berg..212

Chance Encounter: Eeva Park...222

Stomach Ache: Peeter Sauter... 234

Nuuma Aljla: Madis Kõiv 267

Aspendal the Rainmaker: Mehis Heinsaar........................... 282

Afterword...297

Author Biographies...299

Upheavals in the Borderland

Jan Kaus

When I was born in 1971, Brezhnev was still alive and the façade of the monster called the Soviet Union more or less intact. When my adulthood started to take shape, the monster was finally gasping for air and starting to disintegrate, sinking into the depths of history. This meant, that the course of history shaped my consciousness directly – but I am not the only Estonian to have this kind of experience. So let me share some thoughts about the connections between Estonian literature and the national consciousness.

Our history, especially our recent history, consists of several drastic and often sudden upheavals, which have all influenced literary expression. One can even say that these upheavals form a certain historical continuity. With regard to the 20th Century, the most serious upheaval, which has still not been properly understood (and which has been one of the central themes for our most internationally known novelist Jaan Kross), was the violent and still very traumatic end of the independent Estonian government in 1940. In fact, this peculiar upheaval masks other upheavals (the first Soviet occupation 1940-1941; the Nazi occupation 1941-1944; and the second and much longer period of the Soviet occupation). The final large upheaval so far came with the renewed independence at the end of the 1980s and the beginning of 1990s. This has led to several smaller upheavals as well. One very rapid, unexpected and still evolving upheaval is the entering of the Western mass-culture into Estonian society, the birth and childhood of the dream of continuous consumption.

So, the meaning of the book as such, especially a book of literature, has to endure the upheavals as well. Changes in society are firstly changes in meaning and states of mind. In Soviet society, literature played an important role in bringing and holding the Estonian identity together, which was not the main goal for the Soviet Estonian government. Quite the reverse, the government was ordered to propagate the Russian language in Estonia. Any national feeling was considered to be dangerous nationalism, an expression of anti-Russian tension. Maybe this is the main reason, why Estonian literature created the ability to talk "between the lines", as the readers of the same nationality acquired the skill to read between the same lines. This served the purpose to maintain the consciousness of the Estonian identity despite the everyday Soviet reality. The writers from my generation often have great difficulties in imagining the significance of the Soviet Estonian Writers' Union, the role of publishers, editors and, of course, the all-powerful, but mostly narrow-minded, censors during that period. This was a totally different reality, which required a totally different language – or system of languages. As only one Estonian language existed, it had to have different meanings for the censor and for the common Estonian reader. The literature from that epoch was full of hidden meanings. This practice made it possible to achieve beautiful and poetic results and should be remembered, when reading, for example, the short story of Arvo Valton, where the ugliness of the machinery, which in every-day life was accompanied by the rhetoric of the industrial heaven on earth, is in deep contrast with the pure clothing of the fairy-like creatures from the "outside" world. The public compulsion to form a homogeneous mass was quietly resisted in the writings of that era, thus the loneliness of the individual was simultaneously perceived as inevitable (Mati Unt) and desirable (Rein Saluri).

Nowadays, in the aftermath of the latest upheaval – the end of the Soviet state and hopefully, a Soviet way of thinking – the need for the hidden meanings has vanished. Nowadays, everything is in the open. Art is everywhere, artistic expression can be even brutally sincere – this is the aesthetic method of several writers who started to publish during the final years of the Soviet Union – Eeva Park and Peeter Sauter, among others. Nowadays, a contemporary writer can say anything and the only censor that he or she has to deal with is the inner censor of the individual or literary circle.

Strange times are connected to strange places. During Soviet times Estonia was considered almost as part of the Western world; an interesting, but also strange, almost foreign place. In the streets of Tallinn or Pärnu one could have found a vanishing whiff of the "Golden" epoch of the interwar years, when Estonia tried to be a part of a "free" Europe. And, during the last two decades, the borderland of what was once the Soviet Union has been turned instead into the borderland of the European Union. Therefore the concept of geography is always quite problematic for an Estonian.

But what can one say about the feeling of time and history? This is the story of a nation of peasants, whose "national awakening" did not take place until at the end of the 19th Century. One of the most important Estonian poets Juhan Liiv also wrote stories and his book *Ten Stories*, published in 1893, is considered to be the first Estonian collection of short stories. So, long after Shakespeare and Milton, Cervantes and Lope de Vega, Villon and Rabelais, this tiny nation discovered its Western identity (with the help of Baltic German culture). Eduard Vilde, who wrote his classical novels and plays at the end of the 19th and at the beginning of the 20th Century, was actually the first Estonian writer to travel around Europe and experience the European way of life. But at the same time it is almost unbelievable, that approximately one hundred years later, at the beginning of the 21st Century, the German literary scholar Cornelius Hasselblatt has written a 900-page long history of Estonian literature, which still is waiting to be translated into Estonian (and English). Furthermore, before the destruction of the Estonian state in 1940, Anton Hansen Tammsaare created the poetical cornerstone of the nation, an epic description of human life behind the back of God, *Truth and Justice* – a five volume novel about the Estonian state of mind, the eternally unattainable and unjust truth, and the almost always unobtainable justice. And if some of Tammsaare's contemporaries could not appreciate the absence of metaphysical truth in his work, they could easily find the mysterious, romantic and playful worlds of August Gailit, or the gentle childhood memories of Friedebert Tuglas, or continue to travel around the world with Karl August Hindrey, a truly international gentleman. And this multiplicity continues in the present day – some reflect the harsh conditions of reality, others create fantasy-worlds full of unlikely possibilities (Mehis Heinsaar) and some are walking the lanes of memory and history (Madis Kõiv), and, of course, some may try to reflect, create and walk in the same story (Maimu Berg). The upheavals of our history have of course divided our literature – the protagonist of the brilliant novelist Karl Ristikivi, an author who had to escape to Sweden during the Second World War, strayed from his homeland. But he nonetheless describes these feelings in the Estonian language. This endurance of the language through the literature is the success story of a nation that quite often portrays itself as suffering greatly.

Estonia is still a country looking towards the West, but has many of its roots situated in the East – maybe not only in the Soviet sense, but also in the Finno-Ugric sense. Let me remind the reader that the Eastern border of Estonia has been described by Samuel Huntington as a part of the line between the East and West. So, the identity of the modern Estonian is a controversial and difficult one, and at the same time, a member of an enormously enterprising and active people – and this identity is maybe manifest in the inability to shake off the collective ghosts of the (recent) past and the need to act and react actively in contemporary life. And, of course, literature always reflects identity, giving the latter its mirror – the world of words.

Maiden of the North

August Gailit

1

And now, my good friends, may the young pipers cease to play, may the offspring of the raven hold their peace, press their beaks under their wings, Old Oode himself will tell you a tale, a tale of the voyage of King Sangar and his jester Pimpa to an unknown land, which is situated in the far North and is filled with strange wonders and powerful spells. There is neither falsity nor untruth in my tale, which really happened and is true, I travelled with them, saw for myself – what a firmament, what measureless lands!

I am old now, hard of hearing and poor of sight, I am no longer good for anything, I can only watch, as I sit on a rock, how the clouds in the sky graze the Sun, and how shadows course swiftly across the meadow – I have chased these shadows all of my life, but all that I have got in my palm is pure dung and a drop of stinking sweat, nothing more. My life is now over and ruined like sodden foot-clouts: former meadows are now verdant forests, erstwhile rivers have become river beds, in the place of former cities and bastions you will find but a few mossy stones standing in the thick brushwood. Oh, my good friends, great storms have arisen across the land, great disasters have wrecked our pastures, neither places nor men from before remain, everything is once again stunted and laid waste, the famous paths of the heroes are no longer trodden by the living. Life trickles like a snow-glutted spring, men have fled to the marshes, abandoned children shriek in the huts, dense tracks of enemy feet cover the meadows, there is no longer the bleating of lambs in the forest, no longer horned cattle in the byre, the horse no longer whinnies in the meadow, but the owl hoots in the darkness and in every place the embers of ruined houses glow – oh the heavens and the miserable lands of the continent!

But there were once other men and other deeds!

A bear would be slain with bare hands, the beast would be thrown over one's shoulder like a bread bag, and with a couple of wolf cubs under their arm the men would go joyously through fields and woods, cudgel in hand, the hum of a song on their lips. Men were strong and had stamina. Not even our enemy dared come into this land, and were he to stray into it, the evil bastard, he would be burnt and drowned. Some would fall on the battlefield, others perish in the marshes or bogs, ripped apart by wild beasts, frozen like a bull in open country, or fled crawling on all fours, dust swirling behind them. There were not enemies enough in our land, men would travel to foreign climes to kill and for trials of strength and to bring back tons of gold, cartloads of furs, shiploads of plunder. Each and every man had chests brimful of pearls, embroidery and glass beads, tobacco pipes, beads with small bells, and other splendid things. And when they came from the heat of the battle singing songs, vaunting and swaggering, the land trembled and the forests swayed!

But most powerful of all was King Sangar, a spruce tree among bushes. He was a young and strong fellow; he would take a bull by the horns and press it down before his feet in the dust as if it were a feeble bug. His sword could only be lifted by ten men, and a hundred were too few to shift him, it took a hundred to hold the man still. And he had soldiers as plentiful as herring in a net, in each hut, shack, hovel, or farmhouse there were men as plentiful as the trees of the forest, with weapons as plentiful as cut brush. By the cliffs at the sea coast stood the citadel of the King, and its walls and ramparts were so high, its ditches so deep that even the flight of an eagle would not suffice to see all. And the port was filled with ships, whose countless purple sails threw shadows on the sea and the heavens into shadows. And at the right hand of the king stood I, old Oode, oh ash and dust and the bones of a sinner!

And there were other men for the King to command, for instance that jester Pimpa, a wretch like no other on Earth. He was a travesty of a man, maybe spawned of a goblin and a dog-snout mother, who, on seeing his appearance, even they, had thrown their offspring into the bushes in shock and horror. Soldiers, returning from a famous battle had found him mewling and whimpering in the bush. One took him for an imp, the other for a monkey, a third however tied him to his back to show the King: if he was useless as food, maybe he could be put in a cage to entertain children. So that is how the jester came to the King, and he was more animal than human. His arms reached the ground and he was bow-legged as a yoke. This monster was hunchbacked, and his bald pate shone like a full moon, whilst his red lips reached round to his ears on either side. The chap's face was completely blue and his huge eyes would roll and be ablaze. He wore jester's garb, round his head hung small bells, he held a lash in his hand as would a dealer in bulls. But he was of submissive character and compassionate by nature, and never did anyone any harm. He would wander around like a beast and amuse both the King and the people.

Maybe each bug, beast or monster – when the time comes – will seek out its own kind, what wonder is it then that such a creature was born to this Earth. But what was a wonder was that this ugly wretch had a daughter called Ane, who bore no resemblance whatsoever to her father. She was small and bashful, was happiest during sea voyages, wandering in the woods, or hiding in the nooks and crannies of her rooms away from prying eyes. And she was strange, this child, like a deer caught in the woods, a bird pushed into a cage, always fearful, trembling and fugitive. She only felt free when alone, especially at night; then she would walk through the endless rooms, laughing, playing pranks, or singing weird songs, ones that had never been heard before. The songs were unusual, like puffs of wind before a storm, mysterious, soothing, as if within them lurked covertly a breath of the coming of great turmoil and gusts of passion. That is how the woods would sing before the coming of the storm and the meadows would sound like gentle hands strumming the zither. If any stranger chanced to hear her singing, and seeing her childlike comings and goings, Ane would grow serious and sad in an instant, and would not raise her eyes before the sun was again about to set. Then she would liven up again, the colour would return to her cheeks, an inexplicable joy would seize her limbs and when dancing she would spin like a top. "Witchcraft and sorcery," was what I said, "witchcraft and nothing but." But the girl threw her arms around my neck and said it was no witchcraft, no sorcery, merely the joy of life, which was so good! Look at her, with a dog-snout for a grandmother, a goblin for a grandfather, but life is so good, as if she dared say such things to a stranger!

I do not know in what kind of forest she grew up, and on what highroads she learnt her song. Above all she loved her jester father and looked after and cared for him, as if he were any normal human being who was there to be loved. And she was pretty this girl – and many a soldier, crowned with the glory of victory, wished her as his own, though she was the daughter of a lowly jester, and utterly poor and pitiable. But the girl wanted no one, despised even the strongest of men. I asked whether she, the crazy one, yearned for the King himself? But when I had uttered the name of the King, she began to weep, wept for a whole day and the next, but when all her tears had been gathered in her lap, she was joyful again. Such was the daughter of the jester, who went by the name of Ane.

But then a new spring arrived, the dulled waters of the sea became green again, the woods began to sway in the wind, sprout buds, and birds came from the south, and all the groves, the forest, and heath land were filled with such creatures. The birds would twitter and sing, and human hearts began to beat more gladly. Bears left their winter lairs and would move about going deeper into the forest. Werewolves would return home – even though the woods and paths were flooded by the water from the melting snow, and it was difficult to proceed.

But King Sangar, among the strongest amongst men, was sitting idle and planning no campaigns. That spring, many bewitching tales were circulating about a maiden living in the north. But the tales were like the winds: no one knew whence they came and whither they were bound. They would move on the ground, raising the dust and leaves on the roads. And so it was that the tales of the Maiden of the North would go from mouth to mouth like a tankard of beer.

It was said that beyond land and sea, beyond woods and marshes, where the primeval forest and the heath land came to an end, among snowy wastes and icy cliffs, there was said to be a famous realm, that belonged to the Maiden of the North, Illali. Her castle was said to have been built of mother-of-pearl and diamonds, its roof consisted of the Northern Lights and myriads of stars, and clouds like white flags were supported on tall towers. Bliss and silence were said to hold sway there, sadness was alien to the realm, and pain unknown.

The King listened, took it all in, but said not a word.

However, the tales swelled like dough in the trough. And Illali's beauty was spoken about, to which the heavens would dim, the waters would ebb into the sea, and the flowers would wilt in shame, as if struck by the frost. Illali's shoulders were said to be like a pair of swans, her eyes like jewels, her mouth like a spring, at which no man had ever bowed down to drink.

The King raised his head and asked:

"Oode, are all my ships ready?"

People were as if starstruck, they no longer did their work, did not feel their cares, they drank, ate and sang about the beautiful Maiden of the North. Whilst singing away, the cowherd forgot his herd, the ploughman his ploughshare, the soldier his sentry duty, and women would leave their children unsuckled, girls their hair uncombed, the hammer would no longer ring on the anvil, nor would the axe echo through the woods, nor the clatter of wheels on the highway; all that could be heard was a shepherd singing in the meadow and a soldier on the rampart. Even the herdsman would appear before his door, sit down and raise a chant about Illali, his eyes raised to the heavens like soaring birds.

Then said the King:

"Oode, my friend, order the sails to be hoisted up the masts,

I wish to sail far out into the open sea!"

Even Pimpa the jester put a rose on his breast, took up his zither – and when the sky cleared and the moon came out – appeared on the ramparts of the castle and sang about his own betrothed, a distant maiden from the north. The people gathered around him and hooted with laughter at the strange tale of the ugly jester.

The only one who did not sing was Ane, she was silent and sad.

"What's happened to you?" I asked.

"Soon you will set out to sea with the King – take me with you!" she cried.

Her eyes blazed like those of a wolf cub and her arms were outstretched towards me.

"No, my child," I replied, "women are a danger and a burden at sea. You could not cope with the storms, nor put up with the cruelty and coarseness of the seamen. Our voyage is long, you would grow weary before we arrived. Only old sea-wolves, used to winds and storms, can take all this in their stride."

"I want to see this much-praised maiden for myself," cried Ane, "I just don't believe in her beauty. You are blinded, dazzled, merely repeat what others sing about. I can see misfortune approaching, the bards have lied! Take me with you."

She would not give up, clung to my side. But I grew stern, hardened my heart, and shrugged her off.

2

Preparations for the long voyage commenced.

Four ships were made ready, fifty men on each ship. New sails were fixed to the masts.

When we were ready, a shaman and wise men were invited to the shore at Randla. And there were plenty such men and they all foretold a good voyage and a joyful return.

When we had revelled enough, we raised the anchor. In the lead was the King's vessel, three others in its wake with provisions and weapons. Even Pimpa the jester came along, to keep the King amused on the long voyage. Gradually the cliffs disappeared, we were surrounded by the shimmering blue ocean. Looking down over the men at the oars, I saw one poor boy amongst them. He was weak and listless, and could hardly lift his oars.

"Who's that kid they've brought on board?" I asked angrily.

All eyes turned towards the boy.

When no one answered, I replied:

"He has come here unwanted, maybe we should throw him overboard!"

Two strong men rose up from their oars. But then the boy crashed down on his knees before me and began to weep so piteously before me that in that weeping I recognised Ane.

What should I have done with this rascal?

And so commenced our voyage. Our sails bore us onwards, blown by the wind, then subsided, and the men sat at the oars. Silent stretches of water glittered around us, the endless heavens were arched above us. The days passed like moments, the nights were starry and the crew laughed and joked. Foamy waves storming at us were few, and we rode them like seagulls. The sea was silent, the sails hung limp around the masts, and the men sat at the oars. The blue water foamed around their powerful strokes, a long gyring gull stayed at our stern. The setting sun shone in the faces of the men, they were both joyful and playful.

The moon rose in the black sky, songs were heard from the most powerful throats of the sea wolves. Only Ane did not sing, she was silent and wordless. On one occasion the King asked: "Who is that boy?" and I replied that it was a relative of mine, who wished to see distant seas and lands – he will no doubt grow up into a strong and clever man, bringing joy to us, not shame. So the girl remained unrecognised, slept along with the men, ate their provender, did their labour, and never did I hear either complaint or discontent. The sun had burnt sores into her shoulders, but her lips would smile at me. She was a dogged soul.

Days passed in this way as well as a countless number of

nights.

Then suddenly a short wail was heard, like a brief hoot. The masts cracked and the sails shook. Whirlpools arose in the smooth sea. This all lasted but a moment, then the strange silence and peace enveloped the seascape as before.

But then clouds arose, the sky grew low and grey. Puffs of wind like urchins began to churn furrows in the sea surface. It squalled, and floundered, and seethed, growing ever stronger with each moment. The attack was now in unison, sweeping along waves and beginning to spread them across the restless surface of the water, till this all straightened into a concatenation of snow-tipped hills. They left one, picked up the next, stormed on to the third, turning the waves bigger and bigger. They made deep crevices, tossing our ships hither and thither. The vessels rocked and quaked, the masts creaked, the sails strained.

Joyful faces grew grim, strong shoulders hunched over the oars. Brown beards were wafted in the wind. The oarsmen tied themselves to their benches, so that the swelling waves would not snatch them away. But there was no complaint.

As night approached the storm rose, one I have never seen the like of. We plunged down then rose up on the crest of the wave, again and again, unceasingly. The winds whined, the waters churned, the night sky was pitch black. The men grew weak and saw death approaching.

"This is witchcraft," they yelled and shuddered, "witchcraft and the incomparable power of evil!"

But on the evening of the second day the winds abated, the waves diminished, the clouds flew apart like startled birds. The men's heads were raised, joy sparkled in their eyes, their shoulders straightened like trees after a storm.

But our joy was premature, worse travails and spells were yet to come!

We entered a bank of fog.

The farther we sailed, the thicker it became. The crew members could not see the man next to them, and their words were smothered as they left their mouths. Day resembled night, grey, ice-cold fog moved about us. We could no longer see the sea or the sky, we were as if thrown into a chasm. Our position and direction vanished, we were lost as if in an endless swamp. The onset of day and its parting were no longer marked, all was darkness.

Blocks of ice floated past us, we heard them collide with our vessels. The sails dropped water, the sheets were wet. A grim silence settled all around us. The men froze and shivered. I could hear their complaints. One oarsman said:

"Where are we sailing to, can anyone say? Time passes, yet we have not arrived anywhere. The power of witchcraft has us in its thrall, we have been brought here to die. I am beginning to think that all the talk of the Maid of the North is a pack of lies and trickery, nothing more!"

Another replied:

"We are not being led to battle, we are being lured as dogs are to follow in the footsteps of some woman. Or does anyone actually know where this maiden, chosen by the King, is to be found?"

I jumped up and went up to the crew, unable to control my ire. But they were not afraid, they snarled at me and through the fog I imagined I could make out their marauding eyes.

Days passed, a huge uncountable number, but the fog did not retreat from around us. The wet sails hung limply, the crew shivered at the oars. They rowed slowly and reluctantly.

The King sat motionless at the helm.

"Witchcraft!" bawled Pimpa as he stumbled along the deck. "Witchcraft, may bears maul me so I can escape this horror!"

And he ran up, now to one, now to the next oarsman, and yelled in his ear:

"Sea-wolf, are you not ashamed to die along with a jester? Tense your muscles, show your strength, ahead are sunshine and blue waters!"

And the oarsman would awaken from his paralysis.

We were lost in the fog for a long time, hope began to fail us. But then suddenly we felt a breath of wind. A while later we could again hear the splashing of the waves. The wet sails picked up the wind and the sheets tautened.

Then we again saw the foamy sea.

We cast anchor, waiting for the other ships to catch us up. But long days passed, and the ships did not come. Only on the fifth day did we see one of our vessels, but its masts were broken, its sails slack, the sheets of the sails had been cut through. And there was not one man aboard ship.

The faces of our crew grew grim. They stood there as if condemned to death.

Then said the King:

"Oode, give the men their swords and shields, a heavy battle lies ahead of us. We have arrived at the waters at Saare, the waters of the sorceress Kikikraa. These are her tricks and her crimes. What was foretold was not the truth – bitter days lie ahead. Kikikraa has wrecked our ships, killed our men, she is lying in ambush. She does not wish for us to arrive at our destination, she herself wants to be my bride?"

But the days passed, we rowed slowly into the wind, the ships of the sorceress were nowhere to be seen.

The wind got up, the sky was covered with clouds.

The waves rose like mountains and turned towards us. A biting wind gusted between them as if whipping up dogs. I ordered the sails to be furled, for the men to sit at their oars. But the storm snatched the oars from their hands like splinters. The men looked on helplessly, their eyes and beards wet with the spray of the sea.

"Stay at your posts!" I shouted and handed out new oars to the men. These oars too flew like birds into the air.

Blue thunderbolts soon rent the clouds. The stormy attack howled ever more loudly.

The crew was exhausted, their senses blunted. Their faces had grown grey and sleepy, their eyes wandered.

We no longer had any aim or direction. One moment we would be heading north, then would veer abruptly around in a southerly direction. We encountered no ships as we sailed, we were moving through dead waters. We looked restively around us, looking for the horizon, but all there was to see was boundless stretches of blue water. And the days passed, countless in number, while the winds tossed us about at will.

The barrels of drinking water had been polluted by seawater, our food supplies were running low. The chins of weary men were now all stubbled, indifference was reflected in their hungry faces. They no longer worked their oars, we were it seemed doomed to perish. A couple of men threw themselves overboard, but we did not try to save them.

Then suddenly we saw some ships ahead of us.

Their sails were filled with wind and they moved like spectres.

The King shouted:

"These are Kikikraa's vessels!"

The men reached for their swords.

3

It may indeed be true that old Oode has seen battle in his lifetime and smitten his enemy so that the land around thundered. It may be true that he has mown down men, so that by the end of battle there have been heaps of corpses in the valleys like mountains, with nowhere left to stand or for the eye to roam. But the likes of the battle that now commenced this old man had never seen before. This was a thrashing and bloodletting that lasted the whole day and well into the night and even longer.

When the vessels of the sorceress of Saare, Kikikraa, with their black sails had arrived next to ours, boarding lines were thrown across and the sorceress's soldiers began to swarm towards us not as mosquitoes would or chaff, but it was as if a black thundercloud had arisen swiftly in the sky. And the sorceress's men, were most peculiar, the likes of which I had never clapped eyes on before – tall, lithe, and wearing the silvered horns of elks on their heads, cloaks made from polar bear fur around their loins, while their faces were swarthy, drawn and lifeless. And many they were, it was impossible for a mere mortal to estimate their number, and all the sorceress's ships were filled with such riff-raff. And old Kikikraa herself led these vultures, cawing and standing like a crow on the bridge of her ship.

Our men were weary from the long voyage, but the eagerness of the King gave them vigour. They forgot their exhaustion, began to howl like dogs. They mowed down the enemy in large swathes as you would hay, felled as you would trees, firm of footing, strong of muscle. Their morose, grave, heads jutting forwards like bulls, their eyes bulging in their sockets, as they stood their ground amidst the slaughter.

Even Pimpa, unable to raise a sword, was leaping about like a magpie into the lines of the enemy, yelling, whirling about, pulling at their legs and tossing the enemy overboard into the sea. The soldiers of the sorceress had no doubt never seen such a creature, they regarded him as a wonder, and were unable to decide whether to stab at him with their swords or kick him aside like something getting in the way of the true slaughter. So the jester whirled in the fray, bawling enough for ten men, guffawing for a hundred. He was of no mean use in this battle, spinning like a top, tossing men overboard, and stabbing at their cudgels with his knife.

But best of all was the King himself, his battleaxe like the lightning of God. The vile slaves of Kikikraa certainly forced their way towards him, but the King swung his stronger weapon, and brought them low like mere insects. The man had his job cut out for him, you could see his strength and skill. Anyone that his battleaxe reached, was cloven in two like a log, each half landing in a different place. Sangar knew no respite. When he wished to take a rest, little Ane at his side would snap, like a puppy:

"For Illali, fight for Illali!"

"For Illali," said the King, rallying again, and the enemy would fly about like shards and slivers.

It was a slaughter, it was a battle! The heavens grew red, the sea grew pale. The clouds rose into the sky like red fabric, the wind began to shudder, the waters to wail. The waves rose, eagerly snatching at their prey, rushing onwards at speed.

Our ranks began to thin out a good deal. Quite a few were struck by an arrow or a poleaxe, and lay groaning on the deck, they would attempt to rise once more, panting, but their heavy heads would slump at the advent of death. A few men fell in the sea and plummeted down to the depths, curses and execrations on their lips.

And the enemy showed no signs of yielding.

Great numbers of soldiers swarmed forwards, they were countless and endless like the clouds beyond the sea. We had certainly mown them down, had certainly fought them in a manly way, the ships and the sea was full of their corpses, and yet they came on, more and more in number. Our soldiers weakened, the lines thinned out, but the slaughter saw no end. Then I shouted:

"Kikikraa and her horde have bewitched us, we are lost!"

"For Illali, men, for Illali!" yelled Ane.

"For Illali!" replied the King, panting.

"We are lost," said Pimpa now. "The forces of Kikikraa will not lessen in number!"

And the battle became ever more bitter, more savage. As if intoxicated, urged on by blood lust, the men hacked away.

Kikikraa screamed from the bridge:

"Forward, men!"

Like a fresh wind blowing across the ranks of the enemy, ever greater numbers swarmed over onto our ship. They neither yelled nor raged, did not even groan when dying, merely fell as if under a spell.

Evening came, darkness fell across the waters. The wind blew black sheets of cloud into the sky. The waters grew turgid. All that could be heard was the swish of the battleaxes, cries, curses and Kikikraa's shrill shrieks. In the darkness, you could not tell friend from foe, as men were led onwards and fell screaming to the deck. The struggle was conducted with the last strength of the soldiers as they sensed the end of the battle was nigh; they fought on in the darkness.

Then someone shouted:

"The King has been taken!"

And indeed, the moon flashed between the clouds for an instant and I saw the King was bound up. He struggled and yelled, but could not escape his fetters. Those still on their feet, tried to force a path through to the King, but our poor forces had thinned out. We were melting like a chunk of ice thrown into a cauldron. One after another they fell dead, weakened by the loss of blood.

Then I heard Ane calling:

"Oh misery, the ship is on fire!"

The scoundrels had set fire to our ship, the sails had caught fire, the masts were aflame and burning like candles. A pillar of black smoke rose up into the heavens. There was no escape, we had been dealt a fatal blow. I too was ready to fall on the tip of my poleaxe, but before I could do so ropes were tied round my throat.

We were caught in the darkness like chickens, we were fettered like foals, hobbled. And strong hands seized me, heaved me into the air and I landed right at Kikikraa's feet. Here, the King and Ane already lay. Even Pimpa the jester was brought here tied up. I too fell down, poor soul, next to the others.

Then the anchors were raised, the black sails caught the wind and the vessels began to move forward swiftly in convoy. Our ship was like a blazing pillar in the sea. As I raised my eyes, I could make out, by the light of the moon the shoreline quite nearby – was this a spell or an optical illusion? We had been so far out at sea, without ever catching sight of land. Kikikraa had led us into the fog and turned the prow of our ship away from the cliffs.

The vessels landed.

On a cliff, high and rocky, stood the castle of the sorceress of Saare. Around the black towers flew flocks of jackdaws and ravens. The sky was black with these shrieking birds.

We went up a steep stairway. Heavy doors were opened before us. We entered a space that was full of light and the wonders of witchcraft. As if huge fairy-tale gardens stretched out before us. Large weird trees were full of red and black flowers. Their stench was poisonous and soporific. The ceiling glowed like the evening sky. White maidens brought food to the table in silence. Around the garden stood musicians who played so hypnotically that we stood there in fear.

To the left was a throne, on the throne sat a queen, young and alluring.

"Come closer," she said, "do not be afraid. May you be my guests and partake of my dishes. You have made a long journey, taken part in a great battle, it is now time to relax and make merry!"

"This is Kikikraa!" cried Ane in sudden fear.

The filthy crone had changed herself into an alluring queen, pearl necklaces glittered like snakes around her neck. Was this not the old sorceress herself, full of trickery, trying to beguile us with flattery and kindness.

"Why have you brought me here?" asked the King. "I am on my way to the north, to a distant and unknown land, I am awaited there, not here!"

"You will stay here!" smiled Kikikraa. "No power can save you any longer. I wish to marry you myself, to be your bride!"

"Be damned, old harlot!" cried the King. "You will never be able to break me!"

"I shall break you!" bawled the sorceress. "If not with good then with evil!"

She rose from her throne, made a gesture and immediately wind, dust and ashes whirled into our eyes. When we opened them again, neither the fairy-tale trees nor the garden were still there. We were standing in a dark room, and instead of food there was only dried manure. Kikikraa laughed at us. Grey hair fell across her wrinkled face. Her eyes glowed like coals.

"I will break you!" she repeated, with a sneer.

Then we were tied up, taken down into the deepest dungeon, thrown onto the floor, now the company of rats and mice.

4

There are dangers, there is misery, death and destruction, but all of these are ephemeral and insignificant compared to the dire state in which we now found ourselves. In our dark dungeon the days passed, many days, many months, many years. We grew old, infirm, our previous life seemed but a distant dream. We would move like ghosts in the night in our cramped dungeon, laments and curses on our lips. We lost our human face and feelings, asking ourselves frequently why we were here. Time ran on, stormed onwards, we merely crouched in the darkness and grew ever older. Now and again we were tossed a loaf of bread through the hatch, were given water in a jug, a dull light came from above, the only scrap of light we ever saw. We were wretched in our piteous state, we longed for death and oblivion.

Pimpa the jester was perpetually yelling, the King lost hope, even I began to mutter, only Ane was happy and chirped like a bird. She kept us going ceaselessly with her song about the Maiden of the North for days on end.

"Just a short while more," she said, "only a brief while, and the doors of the prison will be opened and the fetters will be removed from our ankles. A short while more, and we shall be free, we will set sail again, plunge oars into the water. It will not be long now, no more suffering awaits us. The strength of the sorceress will soon ebb, she too will be reduced to dust and ashes. The Maiden of the North will heal our wounds, lessen our dangers, change our lives into beautiful fairy-tales. Her castles are full of sunlight, her open spaces full of flowers. She has mercy as plentiful as the waters of the ocean, kindness like the sun in the sky. We are suffering only so that our reunion will feel all the more wonderful, we are being tormented so that our joy shall be more complete. So do not weary, do not break!"

"Not break!" groaned the King.

"Nonsense!" said Pimpa the jester. "I reckon that even the sorceress will suffice for a woman. Although she is old and ugly and a heap of bones would be more alluring, we would at least be released from this ghastly dungeon if we were to do a deal with the sorceress. So I think that once the wedding is over and her wishes satisfied, could we not find a suitable poison for her?"

And he fell before the King.

"Listen to me, your majesty!" he yelled. "Take the sorceress as your bride and save me. The rulers of realms may die, famous generals perish, kings die wretchedly, but a jester must live! What is life without jest? Whole nations could die out and the gods grow sullen, should a jester die. Human fate depends on a jester, as a jester guides the thoughts and deeds of gods and men. A jester is like a grub at the root that gnaws for years at a time, till the tree falls as if struck by an axe. A jester is vital for everyday life as the world rests on his shoulders. Your majesty, spare your jester!"

"Be silent, cur!" I shouted angrily.

Pimpa started blubbering and bawling.

And that day too passed, like so many others.

Then came Kikikraa. She sat down next to the King and said: "Have you been humbled at last? Maybe you've stopped dreaming about the Maiden of the North. Why try to avoid the inevitable when it will not help? Maybe you do not yet recognise my power. I can give you realms to rule over, lands as far as the sky curves down to the earth. I can give you riches and power, so that you would become king among kings. I will give you power over the winds, power to hold sway over the sea. People and animals will hearken to your word. You can build golden castles straight from sand, bewitch slaves and soldiers made of coal. I will teach you the language of the birds, no secret or wisdom will be hidden from you. I will also give you immortality, so that you are on an equal footing with the gods. That is little, maybe you wish for more?"

"I want the Maiden of the North!" said the King.

"What nonsense, she doesn't exist!" Laughed the sorceress. "It is all a mirage and an illusion. Mere hot air, nothing else. All there is in the far north is tundra and icy lands, nothing else. No plant grows there, no bird flies there, the winds merely blow across a dead wilderness."

"You're lying, you're tricking me!" cried the King.

"Are you still being stupid and pig-headed?" laughed the sorceress. "Do you want to stay here and suffer? Well then, stay here until you break!"

"I shall not be broken!" bawled the King.

But the sorceress was already gone, all that could be heard were her mocking sneers.

"It's all just a mirage and an illusion," echoed Pimpa, sobbing.

The patience of the sorceress soon came to an end. She could not break us with ill-treatment, now she tried cunning. One day a love potion was sent to the King, an item of witchcraft that would confuse the human brain. We did not know what the jug contained. But before the King could put it to his lips, the jester had drunk it down.

His life up to now had been what it was, he had always suffered and been aggrieved, but what now followed was much stranger. The jester no longer sat still or kept his mouth shut. He cried and bemoaned the trials of love and longing, and his voice was relentless like the whinings of the wind. Now he would be savage and wild, banged on doors and walls, he was recalcitrant, threatening, scoffed, even once fell to his knees, was helpless and pitiful, begged, wept and wheedled.

"Kikikraa, my darling," he whispered, "you are the most beautiful of women and fairer than a goddess. Your eyes are like the blue skies and your lips like a field of poppies. Wherever you tread, flowers spring up and springs gush forth. Birds twitter around you and sing praises. I know that I am but a wretched jester, there is no creature more loathsome than I, but the bird cries from its darkness, so why should I not extend my hand? They may say about you that you are a sorceress and ugly and that your soul is filled with evil and crime. Only I know that your mercy is boundless and your goodness without end. I wish to hold your hand and strew flowers before your feet!"

This and other things were uttered by this misshapen being, rendered quite imbecilic by the love potion. Our admonitions and friendly advice were to no avail. He had no wish to listen to us, regarded us as his enemies, who were only trying to insult his loved one. He was quite out of his senses, so strong was the sorceress's strange potion.

I, poor wretch, therefore saw the days pass, my ears rang with the shouting. The jester yelled for one woman, the King for another. I tried merely to listen and keep my wits under control. Is it not true that when two jesters are in action, someone needs to keep a cool head and hold their peace?

"Illali!" groaned the King.

"Stop mentioning that name!" shouted Pimpa. "It hurts my ears like a knife, and everything within me struggles to get out. What is the Maiden of the North compared to my Kikikraa – a muddy track through flowering meadows. Poor me, cursed by the gods, why must a wretch like me put up with constantly having to hear the name of the Maiden of the North!"

The sorceress arrived, a number of maidens in her wake. The whore came to behold the results of her potion. When she heard the King utter the name of Illali, she was startled. All the more so when she saw how Pimpa threw himself at her feet.

"What does this jester want of me?"she asked angrily.

"I love you," shrieked the jester, "forgive me, but I love you!"

"Scum!" yelled Kikikraa and ran out of our dungeon. But she was no longer able to avoid the jester. Day and night he would call for his loved one and the cries reached the ears of the sorceress. She hated this wretch, became irate and uttered curses. Like a goblin she flew through our dungeon, emitting fire and ashes. She beat the jester, clapped him in irons and made him lie with his mouth pushed to the ground. But not even now did the jester give up. Whether awake or asleep he would talk of Kikikraa and the low arches of the dungeon would resound with his chatter and cries. This was disgusting to the sorceress. Even she could no longer stand the declarations of love of this wretch. She no longer found peace from the ravings of the jester.

And so she came into the dungeon, emitted fire and pitch from her mouth, was wild and filled with ire.

She croaked once, croaked twice, but when she had croaked a third time, it was like a violent thunderbolt, and the ground trembled beneath us.

When we had come to ours senses and raised our eyes, neither the sorceress nor her castle were anywhere to be seen, there was neither a dungeon nor were we in fetters. It was a still moonlit night, we were on the shore. The waves rolled towards us, behind us in the darkness deserted plains stretched out. On the distant shore the lights of fishermen's huts twinkled. Silver clouds drifted across the black sky, they too seemed a miracle, after our long captivity.

Casting my eyes over my companions, I could not recognise them. They had become old and grey, their backs were hunched, their limbs covered in rags. Only Ane was her former self, joyful and young, although her face was a resinous yellow.

"Free, free again!" cried the King.

"Kikikraa, my darling, where art thou?" asked Pimpa, coming round.

But presently we lay down on the sandy shore and fell into a heavy slumber.

5

We built a new ship, hoisted new sails. It would not be honourable to return home after only doing half the journey, honour would be derived from sailing onwards, obeying the orders of the King and hiding our private sorrows at the bottom of our kitbags. The longing of the King bore us on wings, as did his love and faith. We had to find the being who had enticed us into undertaking this long voyage.

Again we saw storms and more tranquil waters. Again the name of the Maiden of the North rang out. We saw shooting stars and thought of her as our fortune. Only Pimpa continued to sigh for Kikikraa, but who listened to him, or cared about him now! The wind bore us along, through seas and endless expanses of water.

But in the end we did reach the shore, heaved the ship up the cliffs and continued our journey on foot.

These were quite different lands, different landscapes. Out of dark chasms rose the Northern Lights like golden rain, glittering and effulgent. The plains were covered in yellow mists and through these the sky shone like an apparition. The hills stood in ranges and at their tips were crowns of fire like wreaths on a head. There were no bushes or trees, black birds would fly silently, not even the whirr of their powerful wings could be heard. There was no hay here, nor did flowers bloom, dogs of fire ran like globes across the land, each one effulgent in colour and light. Caves hewn into the hillsides were few, that was where the giants lived, compared to which we were dwarves. We stopped, rested, asked the way.

"Ever onwards," came the answer, "your way goes ever on and on, until you reach your destination!"

So we rose and continued on our way. We did not count the days, nor were we discouraged by hardships. We moved across the empty landscape, crawled along steep walls of rock. Even the Northern Lights were left far behind. On finding a spring, we bent down for a moment, quenched our thirst, and moved on.

"This is not the realm of the Maiden of the North," said the King sadly.

"Nor is Kikikraa here!" sighed Pimpa.

We came to a halt, once again asked the way.

"Keep on going, to the left," came the answer, "veer to the left, then you will reach your destination!"

We veered to the left. Winter came, we got stuck in the snow, we slipped on the ice. Summer came, we continued our journey with new vigour. But the blue vault of the sky receded before us, shining as if there was no end to the earth nor start to the heavens. We grew weary, we grew old, the blood flow weakened in our legs, but we did not stop. And when we asked yet again, the answer came:

"Illali's castle is to the right, just keep on walking bravely onwards."

"I don't believe them any more!" cried Pimpa. "They're lying to us and sending us astray. No, no, Kikikraa is somewhere entirely different, somewhere else completely!"

He stopped, looked ahead with his sad eyes and said: "Look, there is Kikikraa!"

We tried to hold him back, forbade him from leaving us. But Pimpa merely held his head firm, no longer turned his eyes to the south, and broke into a run. Even Ane followed him sadly with her eyes, but remained with us.

"That's not Illali!" said the King, he too disappointed. "We have been chasing the wind. The wind has blown us back, we have found nothing but empty shadows, there is nothing else!"

He had grown old and hunched, his eyes had become dim and lifeless. Deep wrinkles had formed on his face.

"There... there Illali does exist!" shouted Ane. "We have simply erred on our journey and have not been able to find her! A little more patience, a little more journeying and her mother-of-pearl castle with the golden towers will be radiant there before our eyes. Onwards, we must press bravely onwards!"

"I'm tired," replied the King, "I don't wish to go anywhere any more!"

"Only a day or two," begged Ane.

And so we trudged on. We reached forests, swaying grimly before us. Huge trees rose up into the clouds. Sluggish rivers traversed these forests, black and without a glimmer. No man or beast lived here any more, even the sky was white and cloudless. The sun and the stars were far behind us, a dull gleam came from beyond the hills. Here there was neither day nor night, simply a gloomy twilight. Our voices sounded strange, like gurgling. I gave a shout and listened, but there was no echo.

Then the forests and rivers came to an end. We had come to the end of the world. A high wall rose up to the sky, at its upper edge it disappeared into the darkness. Here the realm of the dog-snouts commenced.

We stopped resignedly and turned back once more.

"There is no Illali!" the King exclaimed. "We have been pursuing the wind, following empty shadows!"

We wandered around aimlessly. At times we stopped, put our hands to our mouths and called in unison:

"Illali!"

The valleys replied sadly, as if in mockery:

"Illali!"

Time passed, we reached a snowy plain. The sun shone over the expanse of ice, the sky was blue and clear. We stopped, saw someone running towards us. We recognised the jester.

"Pimpa!" I shouted. "At least we've found you!"

But the jester ran swiftly past us, without even glancing in our direction.

"Now I know where Kikikraa lives!" he shouted in joy.

And the day came when the King could no longer rise from his bed. He sat in the snow like a snowman, and remained there, weak and despondent. Ane rubbed his frozen hands, tried to urge him on with talk of the Maiden of the North, but nothing helped now. He looked at us blankly, a curious smile on his lips. Then he stretched out his hand to Ane and cried:

"It is you, it is you I have been seeking! Happiness stood at my side, but I could not recognise it!"

The poor wretch said something else, wanted to take Ane's hand, but death came and cut him down.

We dug a deep grave in the snow, buried our King amidst the plains filled with driving blizzards. A cairn of snow was raised. Blocks of ice were brought to the grave.

When we had mourned for three days at the graveside, I said to Ane:

"Maybe that's enough weeping, enough sadness, we have a long road ahead."

I took Ane by the hand, but her hand was cold and fell like a log from mine. She too had died, so as to be able to wander with her King and seek out better lands and more blessed climes.

I buried her too, next to the King, and added another half cairn of snow to this joint grave, and I mourned for another three days, then carried on my way.

Years passed before the shores of my native land rose up before me.

Thus ended the long voyage to an unknown country, where there were strange miracles and powerful sorcery.

Oh, you miserable wretches, you may now remove your yellow beaks from under your wing, you have dozed and snored enough during the telling of this tale. Old Oode may have told you the tale of the attempts to grasp at shadows, but you have heard nothing, the words have gone in one ear and out of the other, the substance has dissolved, the words rose into the air like smoke. And so, my dear wretches, there are no more men and deeds – everything is once more logs and splinters and wretched slaves.

1927

Flash Photography

Karl August Hindrey

Gradually, individuals began to emerge from among the four hundred travellers returning home on the *Leopoldville*.

In Matadi already, they had swarmed to the vessel from the interior, from Dima, Tanganyika, below the Equator, from the Kasai province, which were left behind like some mysterious, feverish obscurity. The ship was about to set sail before evening, which pressed, foggy and smoky as always, down from the parched hills over the small twinkling lights of the river port below. These individuals stood far apart, diffidently, growing chilly in their own loneliness, despite the heat. Once again, Africa thickened its suffocating veil over the Congo, spreading blackly like oil and sinking rapidly over the ocean.

Chains had rattled and clattered, large crates had been banged down on the deck of the vessel by crane or dropped into the hold, the sound of footsteps on deck had fused into a monotonous and nerve-shattering string of sound, where the barefoot thudding tread of the negroes were knotted together with echoes of the hard and heavy soles of the whites as they rushed forward. Even in your locked cabin you could still hear people dragging things about, shouts of command, and the to-ing and fro-ing in the corridors, on the stairs, on the quay, and on the deck above your head, and you were waiting impatiently for that quiet that would follow the wail of the ship's siren. A lull, since they are still at Boma, with Banana ahead, from which yet more passengers and goods would arrive. One night in Boma, and then whether you get away from Banana before nightfall will depend on the amount of goods in the barges, which they want to empty into the *Leopoldville* and then drive out the last

37

malaria mosquitos from their yawning holds. Quinine buzzes in your ears like the pristine drone of Africa, which the depressing sun has set singing.

Gradually, individual travellers began to stand out from the four hundred voyagers bound for home. Only by Banana, sailing towards the open sea along this muddy, yellow river, still some hundreds of kilometres from the coast, which was still the River Congo and hundreds of kilometres further off shore would remain the stubborn and powerful Congo, as it bored its way into the crystal blue distance of the Atlantic Ocean – only in Banana would passengers begin to take on distinct forms. In its restlessness, swarming pell-mell and always changing, like a hostile and strange throng, it did not allow your gaze to alight on it. But little by little, several groups began to emerge, several types, and as the days went by, individuals would emerge from these groups.

The clergymen and the ship's officers were already becoming distinct from the mass of ordinary passengers, on account of their uniforms. In as much as this involved Catholic priests. The Protestant missionaries slowly made their presence felt by their quiet, taciturn behaviour, while those working for the government of the Congo and the staff of large companies, the businessmen and the commercial travellers, constituted a far larger group whose members only began to emerge as individuals later on.

The first from among the clergy to stand out was a fair-haired, crew-cut Dominican friar, whose aura of masculinity dominated the promenade deck which ran along the whole length of the covered space from the stern to the radio station. He was standing, feet spread apart, in front of a group of nuns who were resting in armchairs, some already ill and very tired, yet were listening with grateful smiles to this manifestation of the male sex in a monk's habit. Other Dominicans, older men with long beards, were equally manly with their loud voices and avid thirst, especially the prior from somewhere out in the forests of the Kasai, who thumped his hairy fist on the table, demanded more cognac, and was glancing around him with his big rolling eyes like a commander and a conqueror. But this was a man among men at the table. The other one, the younger one on the promenade deck, still needed to assert himself, still required admiration, as he gestured with his hands and explained to the nuns about wild beasts, ailments and medicines, waterfall adventures and the tricks of the natives. They were grateful and silent, and looked up at this lively hero in fond and modest admiration.

The ship's officers were not worth a glance. Such men belong to every vessel, like an impersonal pleonasm, although you would sometimes see the younger ones bustling around on the anchor deck like sailors, and you couldn't help but noticing the unpolished nature of the first officer, a rarer species of sea dog for such an obscure vessel, although common enough in the Congo fleet. They would wear their uniforms as if they were something too ceremonial for them, too new. The only one, besides the captain, who had the air of an officer was the Russian radio telegraphist who had ended up here after the turmoil of the Revolution.

When I had been on my way here to the dark realm of the Congo, I had asked the ship's captain, out of sheer curiosity, whatever I considered to be worth knowing or interesting. I had asked whether people in the Congo kept domestic animals and cattle.

"Animals," he laughed with his watery whisky eyes, "animals? More than necessary. Large, very large beasts. You'll get to know them all right! Real brutes." And he pulled an angry face, raised his glass rather oddly with his right arm, clumsily somehow. Seeing the look on my face, he said: "This here arm was bust by one of those brutes, down Stanley Pool way. That beast was a black one. But the white ones are larger, much larger."

I now started looking, searching among the whites present there, whether any outward sign would denote dramas having taken place, ones that had occurred in secret there in the distant forests and in the parched hills. But all the faces seemed pretty ordinary, although the first class passengers here were mixing with second class passengers in a way I had not seen before. In first class a colossal woman, very dressed up, would cause the nuns to lower their eyes, who would, in her resounding beer voice, laugh at the unambiguous jokes of some young Angolan Portuguese. She could well have hailed from the red-light district of Antwerp, but out here in the Congo she was the wife of an important government appointee. And returning to Europe second class was a Scandinavian zoologist, who had fallen on hard times during a research trip and came shyly into the first class bar, as if anyone would have banned him from there. He would clutch the one glass of cold beer he could permit himself. He was the friend of a river captain that the Congolese government was sending back as superfluous and pernicious, and it was on account of an intrigue involving a young lady that his superiors had desired him to leave. Though he did want to sue in the courts. These were hardly brutes, and the captain maybe the victim of such brutes. But the third one there, who always sat on his own, was deep in thought, gazed out over the sea, his neck resting on his arm, and said nothing. What was known about him, nevertheless, was that he was one of two men that an enraged negro had shot at. The second man had already been rotting for a month in the hot sand of the Congo, while his companion's arm had mended sufficiently for him to travel, probably on account of an impending trial. A couple of thieves, who were in second class, to the chagrin of other passengers (there was no third class) had been sent home to be punished. They did not contribute anything to the great tragedies of Africa over the three week long voyage to Antwerp, except for the disgrace of becoming déclassé, and this was reflected by a ban on drinking wine as they sat at the same table as the plaintiff. This group accentuated an imaginary third class, in which sinners and paupers travelled.

In first class there were men whose eyes allowed you to imagine that they could turn nasty, but those eyes were worldly enough and they were able to laugh often, very often. And they were by no means always malicious and irate. That little rotund gentleman in first class, who had sat next to me at the start of the voyage, the man with the thin imperial and watery eyes, who looked like a moth-eaten example of thrift in his threadbare pullover, out of whose sleeves poked delicate wrists, and yellowed hands with twitching fingers, who seemed to be the type to creep in under the fence, an unobtrusive soul, a quick creature who did not want to stand out, silent, yet tenacious and dogged. "I've been out there for sixteen years," he sighed as if relieved. "Sixteen whole years! Now it's enough. Finito. Now I'm going home." People had frightened him, he had fled from their presence. He had fleeced the negroes, quietly, slowly, doggedly. And swindled the whites politely, then slipped away from their anger, like a weasel. Now there would be enough, sufficient, really enough to live like a rich man back home. But he no longer understood how to do so. He would buy himself a gramophone and drink two glasses of beer a day. But that was all.

Nor was there any reason to count the gentleman who had gone out to inspect the mine belonging to his syndicate, along with a European demi-monde lady, as one of the brutes the commandant had mentioned. Or include a couple of young civil servants who were, after a three-year stint at their employer's office, going back to Europe on leave, with an eagerness to buy the kind of things that earning a largish sum of money instils in one. The ship's shop emptied noticeably of all manner of fancy goods and sweetmeats, of which there had clearly been a shortage out there in the brush and shrublands of Africa.

No, there was no longer any Africa to be found anywhere here. And the more the remarkably cool breezes of the Equator blew over the glittering spring-like waters, the more people divorced themselves from the baking heat and the peculiar, feverish and unrelenting atmosphere of the black portion of the world.

And then there were the children, those little mulattos.

They were represented in both first and second class. There were olive brown, terracotta hued ones among them, even those that were almost white, under whose skin, like a delicate crust, the dust of Africa seemed to have whitened, like a delicate ashen network of black corpuscles.

But this hue emanated a smouldering strangeness, aroused protest. The fact they were children did not offer them any peaceful happiness or help them to participate. Their play was that of children, their crying was that of children, their mischievousness and shrill cries, their need of warmth and love were childlike. But their skin colour got in the way. As if something was embodied in them that nature had not intended.

Anyway, the governor's wife from one of the largest government departments somewhere in the deep south would take one or other of the little dark-skinned children onto her lap in her motherly way. She would point out to her bouncing little white boys that other children too wanted to ride their bicycles along the boards by the railings. The demi-monde woman would stroke their heads and let them bounce on her knee, maybe with a vague or conscious desire for a child of her own in her heart and soul. Or people could also walk with them, holding one in each hand, as did the young handsome doctor, limping on account of his gammy leg, an elegant lion of a man to mere children, but also so that others would see his lack of prejudice and cordiality. But when he had played with them for a while, he would appear at the bar and shrug his shoulders: "What a pity! Poor creatures!"

They were indeed poor creatures. They had no mothers with them. None of them had. Mothers had not been brought along, they had been left behind somewhere deep in the hinterland and had suddenly been deprived of everything, were without children, and without their white god and master.

At the same time, I never saw the father of any child of mixed blood, except for one. Were they perhaps seasick in their cabins, or did not want to acknowledge their offspring? Only one of them would always stroll with his little boy who resembled his father a lot, both because of his physical appearance and his gentle behaviour.

The two of them would saunter, always in silence, always alone, the broad-shouldered Nordic type with his taciturn face, and the little, almost white boy with his black curly hair, from the middle of which a parting had been drawn, the reminder of a different taste. Had his mother parted the hair in this way, and the boy had not wished to change it? Was this some ideal for inducing orderliness on the part of the father originating in some Scandinavian village? But the father did not look the type, his thinning hair had no parting in the middle, but was combed straight back from his brow.

When the father occasionally stood at the bar or read in the smoking room, the quiet little boy would play with others, always peaceably, and with his gentle eyes looking on when the other children, the white or black ones, were doing something he was not part of. His round limbs, clothed in a sailor suit, were soft, from being well fed and well treated. He would hop from one to the other of his well-shaped legs, more on one than on the other, when the direction of the game or the attention of others demanded. And in his eyes, always that trusting gentleness. It was as if no one had ever said an unkind word to him. But in that trustfulness, there was something submissive, more perhaps than in good-natured, gentle-hearted children.

I addressed him once, as he stood near my chair, with both his fat little hands with their well-shaped fingers behind his back, raising now the one, now the other foot from the floor.

He looked at me with his deep, dark eyes, came closer out of politeness and answered freely and respectfully. I asked him whether he liked the sea, whether he had already been to Europe, whether he could already read, I asked pointless questions, as he was clearly too young to have travelled before, or to be able to read, probably only five years of age. He said that his father was taking him to school, and that his father had promised to buy him a gun and some pet rabbits, that his father was going to show him some horses and rails on the street, and that he wanted to buy mittens, as it sometimes snowed in Europe. Father this, and father that.

I kept on asking him about the future, to avoid leading his thoughts back to the past, which could maybe give rise to sadness.

And then his father came along, made a slight, stiff bow in front of me and his son's hand stretched out in his direction, and the hand of the man and that of the child found one another in a movement that they both seemed to have been born to, so assured was the gentle way they found one another. And then they both walked alongside the rail, in silence and harmony.

By the time the lights of Dakar glittered over the black water, when the *Elizabethville*, had approached her sister vessel as it glittered along from the other direction, and noisy greetings were exchanged from deck to deck between those arriving and those leaving the Congo, when night once again made its velvet wall-like presence felt beyond the lattice of the rail, I had become friends with Ördal. While developing prints, we had on a couple of occasions asked the advice of the man in front of us in the queue, in my case when I asked him how much developing fluid was necessary in his experience, he had then shown me his own prints, as I tended to show mine less to him as his bravura began to dominate. He had made photos of wild animals at night as they had quenched their thirst at the water's edge, or stilled their hunger on dead prey. He had made these photos, with his gun in one hand, his camera in the other, by flash.

"It was pretty ghastly at first," he related. "Because although the animals had been blinded by the flash of the magnesium, you yourself were as blind as a bat afterwards, and you imagined that the eyes of the beast would recover more quickly, especially in the case of the big cats. But later on, I observed that lions and panthers were nonetheless so startled that they didn't attack." And he showed his plate photos, made at quite close range.

I asked him how he had hit upon the idea of doing this in the first place.

"Well, when I arrived there," he continued, "like the majority of white Congolese or Africans in general, I had turned my back on Europe. Going out there meant taking a risk, and people talked about the graves, sleeping sickness, malaria, quinine and mosquitos. So lions and rhinoceroses didn't present much more of a danger. By the way, it is trickier with the latter beasts. They will come at you from behind like crazy locomotives. And what should you busy yourself with, if your brain is constantly boiling and glowing in the heat of the sun, when you have grown tongue-tied from the childishness of the blacks, and the futility of trying to order them about, before you yourself end up thinking like a child.

I once got a black to take a telegram for me, when I was living near Dima, telling the syndicate that the building in Makalungu had burnt down and that the quartermaster had been badly injured. My boy, a good faithful chap, did the couple of hundred kilometres on foot all the way to Dima, but happens to meet a friend, his blood-brother on the way and they talk until nightfall, since talking to a blood-brother is the very first duty and pleasure one has. Then they roll more cigarettes from the telegram and my boy comes back a couple of days later and asks for a new piece of paper – the white bwanas have been very angry that he'd rolled cigarettes out of it and had beaten him. Luckily he did know the details of the Makulungu case, so that the necessary measures could be taken. And when you have to wrestle with such matters, from one hellishly scorching day to the next, when you yourself are like a flaming stove ready to explode, and it doesn't cool down even at night, when you can no longer get to sleep, when you then hear the roars of wild beasts, then you look for something that can steer your mixed and chaotic thoughts in one direction. So I started to take pictures of the animals, first smaller scavengers like jackals, then the bigger ones. You gradually get used to it."

"But what if there'd been an accident?"

"At first, I didn't really care. Later, once my son had been born, I grew more cautious, but as I said, the danger wasn't too great. And it had become my passion. It's a really breath-taking experience, when you get on the plate moments that would otherwise have remained secrets forever shrouded in night. If a wild animal doesn't know it's being stalked it lives a normal life; its train of thought is linked with every muscle, organ, the rise and fall of the juices, all these end up on the print in a flash. Here, I'll show you a few pictures."

And then he showed me lions, explaining the characteristics of each one, which were to be seen on the prints in a convincing and often surprising light.

"They've now got ahead of me with their movie cameras. But flash photography is still much sought after nowadays. I've sent photos to newspapers in Europe and America. They accepted them gladly, and I still send them. For the fee I've received, I've got them to send books and newspapers. And I've got plenty of reading done."

We had passed Tenerife. The sunshade was taken down. Instead of its shadow, a broad swathe of light washed over the deck of the ship, your chest felt liberated, the view ranged over wide open spaces, while in purely tropical climes showers would wander across the sea and wash over the deck leaving gleaming patches like metal. It was as if Africa had disappeared completely, and yet we were not yet beyond its reach. The snobbery of the Congolese, and their great efforts not to appear to be seen as a jungle people meant that they would now dress for dinner in black dinner jackets instead of white ones, the sun helmets would vanish from the decks as well as the white clothing, and instead stylish European suits appeared. Also for reasons of climate. Those who had spent a longer time in the Congo would feel the cold.

Even Ördal appeared to be suffering from the drop in temperature. He appeared less frequently on deck, would do a couple of swift rounds of the promenade deck with the boy, then vanish back into his cabin. He seemed again to be self-absorbed, probably even more so than previously. His face showed a restive, bitter expression, but I attributed this to the cold.

After dinner, he came up to me in the saloon and asked if I would play a game of chess with him. "The boy's asleep," he said tenderly, somehow apologetically. He seemed to be becoming absorbed by the moves of the game, then grew rather absent-minded, ordered a whisky for himself, and I did likewise. He drank his up quickly and ordered another. I followed suit and said, laughing:

"Here's to Europe as she approaches."

He knocked over his king.

"Lost anyway."

He rested his head on his hands and looked down into the bubbles rising from the soda water. His otherwise soft features had hardened, his brow was grim, his grey eyes angry with suffering.

"Here's to Europe? You can say that again."

We fell silent. It was obvious that he wanted to say something about Europe. I didn't dare rush him with a question.

This broad-shouldered man had changed, and was still changing further before my eyes. From being a gentle-natured, somewhat listless individual up to now, he had become impatient and agitated, someone whose restlessness was seeking a way out; something that had been suppressed was trying to push its way out, and I could see how he was forcing himself to breathe steadily. Or maybe the alcohol had affected his heart?

Suddenly he looked at me in a hostile manner, with barely concealed anger.

"I know you think that I can't take my whisky. I also know it's a sign of the watering down of a manly spirit, even somewhat vulgar, when men start telling private matters as alcohol softens the brain. I also know that the other man will let drop, with slight superiority, phrases of sympathy, and so on, like giving alms." He drank with quite a thirst and raised his voice:

"But I have to talk to someone. I haven't talked for seven years. Who was there to talk to? That woman out there," and he pointed in the direction of the stern, "who had bitten the earth when I took her child away? In previous times I used to talk, there in Europe," and his hand pointed abruptly towards the bows, "I used to talk at length, broadly and deeply." His voice was all acid mockery.

"Flash photography. My son," he looked challengingly at me, "yes my son, he may be a mulatto but he's still my son, my son cries in his sleep. Children always cry for their mothers, mostly in secret. Their pain is so sacred that they don't want to show it to anybody. And my son also cries secretly, that tough little boy, he was already crying on the train back in the Congo, later on board ship, although all the new impressions will have made him dog tired. He would have cried even more if he had seen his mother there by the riverside as we left. I absolutely forbade her to see us off, the river was half a kilometre from where we lived. I am a bwana, a lord, a god, I can forbid someone from doing something, and they must obey without question, without thinking; people must take poison if

47

I order them to, walk across glowing iron, drown themselves. Half a kilometre to the river, where I cajoled the trusting and happily smiling boy to come along, saying we would now be going on a little trip. His mother couldn't cry in his presence. But when the blacks had already rowed away, she ran down from the house, her arms in the air, down to the shore and screamed. She fell down and bit the earth. The boy asked who was screaming. I stood in front of him, he didn't see. But the day before yesterday in the night my boy shrieked out like a small panther, then said "mummy" and sat up in bed. When I turned on the light, huge tears were flowing like a string of pearls from his frightened eyes."

He drank and grew weary. He then began to speak quite quietly, monotonously, since his dreamy gaze was once more directed at the bubbles rising in the soda water.

"That cry was a flash in the night. And those dropping tears. I've seen such tears in Europe too. That was long ago. Between then and now seems like a period of my life that can never be restarted... That mother's cry on the banks of the river, her cramped fingers that drew lines in the earth. I also had such flashes back in my native land." He laughed quietly as if taken pity on himself from some superior standpoint. Then he looked at me somehow begging for forgiveness, and said:

"Now comes what you of course feared and rightly so, things you mostly see in books: a broken heart, Africa, a broken life out there too. Or death at the hands of savages or torn to pieces by beasts of prey. The last did not happen in my case, as you can see I am ordering another glass for myself. Yes, in my home country I also used flash, everyone did, some with greater skill or passion than others. But I had a special talent, I was to become a writer in order to enrich society with my achievements. But when you come across someone who, on the one hand, constitutes a compliment to yourself, a compliment without whom life is no longer liveable, yet on the other hand possesses qualities that vex you and cause problems for whose resolution you pant and gasp for breath, then there is no longer any opportunity for literature."

He played with the stem of his glass, rolling it between his fingers, drawing up memories and thoughts from the slowly bubbling liquid. He continued in hurried snatches:

"In short, it's all nonsense, absurd. It was a snapshot using flash photography. She was sitting among a group of young people, the flash had made her shut her eyes. But around her waist rested the arm of the young man sitting behind her. You may say: so what? But I knew that she had been with this group of people just once before. I had known her for years and she had always explained to me, and I saw so myself, that she would never allow such familiarity which is so widespread and goes by the name of camaraderie. She was rather, in my imagination, adverse to intimacy, to touching another person's skin, with its living system of nerves, which by leaving the skin untouched wants to see and feel a respect for sanctity, and felt in a touch violence and an unwanted and rough violation of exclusivity or rights, that one allowed oneself. But there was that arm around her waist. There, the young man whom she hardly knew...

No, please don't start thinking the usual and banal thought – there wasn't anything between her and the young man, nothing about to happen, no special sympathy between them. But it was in that very fact that the whole misfortune lay. How did that arm end up round her waist? Well, it could have been a clumsy, chance gesture, just as the picture was taken. But I also came across this snapshot quite by chance. She didn't want me to see it. She didn't even want to show me it, although I had seen the photo in the hands of others, but she said that the arm had not been round her waist. She maintained that it hadn't. She had never ever lied to me. Why was she lying now? Or wasn't she? Perhaps, as the flash went off, she didn't even feel that arm. Perhaps she found this photo embarrassing. All the more because she had been quite cutting to a girl some while back who had allowed herself to be photographed in the group with her arms around a young man's neck."

"Quite a likely reaction, psychologically speaking," I interposed.

He looked at me quite seriously, now immersed in what had

been a long forgotten episode, and said with resignation:

"Maybe. But why had she always maintained that the gentleman, who had had the young girl's arm around his neck, was very congenial to her?" Ördal now said slowly, stressing his words:

"But what if she had some subconscious reason to be angry because the girl had her arm round the neck of that specific young man?"

We fell silent for a short while, I cleared my throat in order to say something I wasn't yet sure of, but he continued, listlessly brushing aside any criticism he imagined I was going to make:

"The light of the flash makes shadows and dark patches which were previously unnoticed, suddenly dimly discernible. What does anyone really know of anyone else's secret desires, especially when they have not emerged from the subconscious? What do they know of another person if they do not want, for whatever reason, to reveal themselves? And then, in a flash, all those instances came to mind where she had let people get too near to her, where she had exposed herself to situations, where things had been interpreted wrongly, and where she should have fended people off. What did it really mean when she said and seemed herself convinced of the fact that she did not tolerate an excess of intimacy and familiarity, when she was perhaps only thinking in relative terms, only comparing herself to women her own age and the freedom and licence of her surroundings? Had such occurrences shaken her so little, or so deeply that she had regarded them as bagatelles with regard to mutual trust, or were they too wounding, so that only when speaking about them later could she ask, in surprise whether she had actually said so earlier? Was her surprise genuine?

He drank avidly, and the tempo of his speech increased.

"We've both read Tolstoy's *Kreutzer Sonata* so we know how a flash of intuition works, and where and how far it can lead. We know furthermore, when we look indeed at ourselves how little one person can guess about another. We've read our Strindberg and know how mysterious molecules, atoms, vibrations, emanations, and whatever you term them with any scientific exactitude, make a man feel, get an inkling, when a woman has been unfaithful to him, so that mutual contact is broken between them. The low urge to detumescence of a student or a soldier is to be discounted in this context to the same extent as someone whose restraint has been weakened by drink, or the urge for pleasure in someone without inhibitions, the urge to rule over natural people who have lost their culture. Those driven by the fever induced by the sun and the heat to lose one's will to be a gentleman, as happened with me out there. And you should know that I am the son of a clergyman, one of a line of ministers of religion that emerged from the peasantry, who have been bred to be cultivated, and who have all tried to utter the axioms: "one body and one soul" and "love will never die", against which prevail all our physiological and psychological knowledge. We now know how one person can be greatly influenced by another, both mentally and physically, so that they can become very afraid. When Tolstoy's merchant says in the carriage that a man can, a woman cannot, because women accept, he is only partially right. A woman can accept a good deal more, but also in the fabric of a man another person's essence can enter by way of the pores. Then we see and feel, how, with their presence, their emanations, or passions, another person can poison the minds of others like a plague. Then we with joyful liberation feel the high purity of another person, which makes them clearer and calmer. Why do we speak so much then of coarse germs, growing powerfully under the microscope? It is said to be scientifically inexact in the case of that English mare, whose one forefather was a zebra but whose descendants were all zebroids, despite the noble English blood of all the sires. But science is right to doubt, science has still to wait for the results of further experiments, this chapter is not yet at an end. And what can I do with a woman who has the spores of others in her blood that speak against me and against which I rail. Finished. The end. It is an entirely different person, with only the face of the one before, the same face maybe only to our dull and inadequate eyes. But blood has its smell, my corpuscles will begin to seethe and I will be ill at ease and my nerves will be inflamed."

Now I began to dispute his zebra theory:

"You've got more than enough material out there to surmount that quite erroneous theory based on the chance games in nature of the English zebroids. There must be countless numbers of them on the black continent, those women who, later on, marry a black again. So all subsequent children could very well be of mixed race, some of them, at least."

"How do you know it's not the case? They do exist."

"Going back to their former husbands or representatives of their race."

"It's not that easy to find those whites out there in the bush," he said, waving his hand. "And I have not been talking about usual or quite ordinary occurrences; only about rare possibilities that can happen with very special examples of a race, where the bodily constitution has been on a winning streak, since the average mass wouldn't give such clear results. In the case of the mass, there is no memory in the blood, if I may put it that way, not a strong enough memory, at any rate. In the way that the strong have strong memories. I can very well imagine some Genghis Khan or Alexander the Great amongst the countless millions of bacilli."

He spoke with a supercilious impatience, rushing forward, as if wishing to rid himself of the topic that was nonetheless so self-evident that no child would fail to understand it, and would not ask questions or dispute it. And he sank again into rumination.

"How was it possible," he then asked, rolling his cigarette between his fingers, and staring at it, "for me to take a black wife, that is what you are of course asking yourself. Because you have already heard that there were inhibitions, strong inhibitions, within me. Africa, you will say, the heat, befuddled brains, a weakened will, a climate that leads to a breakdown of morality. All of that, of course, for sure. Such would not happen on Riddarholmen in Stockholm. But she had something that reminded you of Riddarholmen, or at least some woman or some imagined ideal from there. She lacked that kind of sex appeal to the extent or in such nuance as you see in European women flaunting it like an auctioneer's poster... oh, let's drop the subject. But black youth is no different to youth anywhere else, a little more excitable than ours with regard to dances and games, but when I saw how one girl always hunched up in fear, wary of attempts to touch her, and only then was she able to smile again when she was able to sit calmly at a little distance away from the others, when she looked at me once, liberated and grateful at my noisy intervention, then I discovered in her something I did not think existed in my native land... And moves me to such an extent, fills me with such agitation when I see an organism, consisting of countless cells, curling up against attack, against a stranger. Suddenly trouble, alarm, signals, and whoopings in those cells, thousands of corpuscles and strong soldiers are ready to do battle according to the age-old commands and laws handed down from generation to generation. I like that kind of soldier, his war cry is also there in the labyrinth of my cells, my corpuscles keep an eye like allies on this soulless battle formation. But look at others, look for instance at the Italian woman here on this ship, who sings in the evening and during the day wiggles her hips, she's always in a state of alarm, but in the opposite sense. Here there are no soldiers rushing into battle, defenders, here there are those who invite hospitably to a feast, mixing with former guests and those of mixed blood and of the original race. Those who once long ago were perhaps themselves foreign adversaries and inimical to them, shield before them and sword in hand, pushed into the tightest of corners, have been tamed by superiority or general merriment, they have lost their strength and flexibility. Or look at that English engineer from the High Itur out Tanganyika way – he gets up and goes each time the Angolan Portuguese take a seat near to him. In him there is an immediate revolt of the tiny proud devils of which he is made up, every fibre in him is in opposition, every capillary carries forward the alarm signal, although his outward appearance is tranquil and indifferent as you like."

He had grown very pale and was massaging his temples. "You will also have read about blood transfusions. Read that people suddenly used to die right in front of their doctors when pumped full of foreign blood. Sometimes they died, sometimes the procedure succeeded. Until it was discovered that there are four blood groups. And these should not be mixed, otherwise death will come instantly. But in all of these groups there are some special natures with special propensities. When someone who has bled dry gets blood from their own group pumped in, do you imagine it will not influence the individual who gets blood added? Will his inner person not change under the influence of this new blood? By the way, there is this to consider... in the Congo the whites are afraid of the bites of blacks... Their teeth are supposed to be poisonous. There are several whites running around with only one arm. A negro has bitten them. Foreign blood is poison. I believe that. In my home country I even despised blood from a southern country, I have been able to see southern women and enjoy them from an aesthetic point of view, but no warmer feeling have arisen in me with regard to them. But now I myself have grown more like a southern person than I ever imagined I could. Ha, Jewish matchmaking poetry, got from the Rose of Sharon, the Jericho rose is something that I have ignored, but I now have a child with a negro woman, a mulatto, a mulatto!" All of a sudden he shouted: "And my blood has been poisoned, I have foreign spores inside me!" He looked me angrily in the face, with his white face.

"You are not taking into account the law of regeneration," I said. "It will all vanish in time."

He continued to look at me with distrust, although his face then softened gradually and he leaned back wearily.

"Do you really think so?" He was like a sick child, to whom you had to say that it would get better.

"Vanish in time," he repeated, "vanish in time." We fell silent for quite a long time, I did not want to disturb his thoughts as they grew more tranquil. Behind his brow, the spasm was subsiding, he became quite gentle.

"I think I'll blurt out something more to you," he then said sternly. "Then you'll get the full picture. Vanish in time?"

Then he straightened up.

"Maybe it really will vanish. Everything foreign out of the

blood! Her blood too." He nodded towards the bow, in the direction of Europe. "She has gone and got married... Her husband is dead... Maybe an organism can expel from itself all that is foreign and hostile. But it will take a very long time. Maybe sometime before death... That would be good... You see, it is a variant on the theme of love will never die and one body, one soul." He smiled wryly. "But that woman back there in the Congo wasn't completely black. She speaks pure Kiswahili like the boy. An old Egyptian race, which reached further south in Africa through migration. But foreign blood nonetheless. In my homeland up north they don't hate coloured races. But they do not mix with them, keep themselves pure on account of racial instinct. Which has vanished in me."

He rose and stretched out his hand.

"My son will end up calling out for his mummy. That's what I fear. That's what I will always fear."

At Cape Verde it grew stormy. Neither Ördal or his son appeared on deck. In the dining room they sat far away from me.

But the Bay of Biscay was calm this time. Ördal again walked diligently with his son around the promenade deck, both of them in warm clothing. When the little boy had gone to play with the other children, Ördal came up to me and said soberly:

"Before, I had to put the boy in school in Belgium. I had to stay there, in order to travel back to the Congo. Now I am taking the boy to my native land... To Ebba... I haven't fallen for that theory that everything will vanish in time, the heat down there doesn't allow you to think things through. I have perhaps thought only and always about my native land... about everything, in fact. In the end there isn't... well, her husband has now been dead for five years... The boy looks a lot like me. Ebba is good with children. She has none of her own... We are such good friends, old pals. Someone to talk to... Perhaps it will turn out that way... And the boy will be exotic, in the snow, on skis he can make a sensational photo. What? They won't reproach him for anything, will they? I don't think so either. Although he does love the saxophone and the drums and the castanets. Have you noticed how he listens? The blood or memories of sound from his native land."

In Antwerp he came to my cabin before disembarking.

"The ship leaves tomorrow already. You know, I am afraid, maybe, of what she will look like now. I'm afraid of stretching out my hand and taking hers. Imbecility, eh. Live well. Have a very good life."

And then I saw him going down the gangplank, amongst the crowd with the boy over his shoulder like a burden, not a heavy one, but one that has to be borne with affection.

1932

Bread

Eduard Vilde

I had arrived in Como from Milan by the afternoon express. I hastily wiped the dusty sweat from my face and neck with a wet towel in the hotel, before rushing out back onto the street. My heart beat rapidly at the thought of the lake, admired by many, whose beauty I would now be seeing for myself for the first time. But before I had managed to make my way through the narrow and higgledy-piggledy streets of the small Old Town, something else caught my eye. There were flags flying on many of the houses. On one of the broader streets leading to the lake there were balconies with coloured tapestries, filled with waiting people. The pavements grew busier and more bustling for every minute that passed. I wanted to ask someone what was being celebrated, but all at once the sound of a band sealed my lips. At that very moment a procession nosed its way round the corner. It flowed along the street like a red river. From the blue air I did, however, pick up a name that answered my unspoken question. Como was celebrating Garibaldi Day.

The greybeards at the head of the procession, with their red doublets and red caps, marching behind, to the singing of the choir, under the tattered battle colours – one with an empty sleeve, another with a wooden leg below the knee – these were Garibaldi's volunteers, a unit from among his famous "Expedition of the Thousand" in the War of Italian Unification. Behind the red head of the procession, came a reddish body of people, consisting of the guilds, private citizens and servicemen of this small town. And me, an onlooker filled with curiosity. When the procession had done the honours at the richly decorated memorial to the heroes, it headed for the lake, onto whose shore opened a square lined by hotels and restaurants. Its north-westerly corner, however, sank into blue, which reached from earth to sky, and from right to left the lake was squeezed into a frame of dark green. I stood and looked on as the procession wound its way, like a spurt of blood, into the heart of the bluish-green distance. The garish clash of colours stirred my imagination.

I felt my body growing lighter, my mind fresher and in my breast something stirred, as if I had just swallowed a gulp of vintage wine. The red procession described a slow circumnavigation of the square, then made for a garden restaurant through a grand portal, and beyond this both the head, then gradually the tail, of the procession disappeared. Soon afterwards, the garden and the hall of the restaurant resounded with the joyful singing of patriotic songs dedicated to Garibaldi. A dance soon began in the hall. There were chairs in front of the restaurant near the open windows through which you could watch the dancing taking place inside the hall, and these chairs soon filled up with spectators. I too found a place at one of the small marble tables where a gentleman was already sitting alone. The waiter brought the wine and I began happily to examine the two vistas right in front of me, which were full of life and colour: Lake Como on one side, and an Italian celebration on the other. I have to admit that my gaze tended to fall more on the dance hall than on the lake. A number of willowy and slender young girls' figures which flitted with the agility of eels, flashing like lizards, in the arms of men over the floor, afforded me such pleasure that I soon forgot about the blue lake and the paradisaical shore around.

And the flushed faces, the curly brunette heads, the glint of metal, the red flames of flowers and the glowing roses like coals, in the thickets of hair, slipped past me, image after image, quenching my thirst for beauty, youth, vigour and desire. It was a long time since there had been so much warm blood flowing through my heart as today...

Suddenly someone gave a sob behind my back.

I turned around. My gaze fell on the gentleman, all alone, with whom I was sharing a table. Yet this gentleman was looking with amusement through the window into the hall. And the neighbouring tables were ringed by laughing faces. My ear must have deceived me.

A couple of minutes later – my eyes were once again enthralled by the Italian maidens – there was a slightly louder sob.

As if from a dry, narrow, burning chest, this cramped, broken tone forced its way out.

When I looked again, I was no longer fooled by the tranquil face of my table companion. It had to be him who had sobbed. I looked at him with as heartening expression as I could muster, so that he could do nothing else but answer. Not with words – I could hardly demand such – but with his true face. He should not dupe me any longer.

He answered. And candidly. With a smile. But with a smile that was a silent sob. And shaking his head, he mumbled something in Italian or French, which I interpreted from his tone of voice as saying: "I do apologise! Please don't let me disturb you!".

I did not feel the right to disturb him any longer, so I looked away and again at the multi-coloured throng. I was put out. But as I did not wish him to notice that or, as he did not appear to take any notice of my discomfort, I continued to play the role of avid observer of the dancing. And conquered any temptation to again look in his direction.

But I now had the feeling that his gaze was focused on me. Covertly but constantly. This went on for a couple of minutes, then I heard him move closer, and a question reached my ear:

"Excuse me... Do you think that Como women are pretty?"

I said that I did.

"My wife was much prettier!"

He said this and swallowed hard.

I now felt the right to look him in the eye once more. What I saw was a pair of eyes seeking conversation. And apart from conversation, these dark, moist glittering eyes sought compassion, with a measure of naiveté and trust.

I could not refuse him as much. Looking at his youngish, pale face, with its thin strip of a beard, and a somewhat too long and straight nose, which did not exactly add anything to his intellect, I asked as sympathetically as possible:

"Your wife – she was prettier...? In other words..."

"Yes, much prettier!" he blurted.

"In other words, she's passed away?" I finished my sentence.

"No, run away."

Saying this so lightly and drily, he looked past me, and focused his dull gaze on the whirl of the dance. I now saw that his eyelids were red and slightly swollen, as tears were welling up in the corners.

I waited in silence, to see if he would speak again and what he would say about this disaster, once he had his grief under control. His lips, under a thin, pointed moustache quivered nervously, then he began to speak again. In a hushed voice, slightly nasally, he said:

"You see that slender young girl in the reddish-brown dress, round whose waist that cavalry officer in his blue uniform is now putting his arm? The one who's just looked over her shoulder, is nodding and laughing... White teeth – coal black eyes – but rather dull hair... You see her? Now... she looks a little like my wife, in terms of her height, movements and posture... She's slim all right, but really too thin, angular and sharp. My Ninette wasn't. My Ninette blossomed, glided, burgeoned, despite her slimness... You should have seen her, sir! You would have seen her perfect build, her figure, her grace... You should have seen her dancing or simply walking across the floor, crossing the street..."

The speaker's eyes were ablaze: the bliss of remembrance seemed to have wiped away every drop of sadness. He had moved so close that he could have touched my shoulder with his chin.

"And her face, sir – Ninette's face!... That girl over there in her reddish-brown dress – her face is nice enough, but no more than that! That one in the red bodice is actually prettier – you see which one? That one, who's sitting between two of Garibaldi's soldiers, and is now raising her glass to her lips... Look at the soft line of her jaw, with its little double chin... her chubby cheeks with those roguish dimples... But she lacks Ninette's eyes. Large as chalices, deep, laughing eyes, between glittering lashes... When she looked straight at you, a warm glow would surge through your body, and your heart would begin to pound!"

He took a quick gulp from his glass, as if in a great hurry, a good swig of his wine, and spoke even before he had managed to swallow it all, and continued, his mouth still wet:

"But I'm missing out something... Neither of these two girls have beautiful hair. It's thin and ordinary, a brownish black... There's only one out there that has really black hair – that one – the young woman with the yellow fan, panting so vigorously... See the one I mean? That fair-haired man is taking her back to her seat... But Ninette's bluish black hair... yes, bluish black, sir ... with a touch of blue at the roots whenever bright light shone on them... long and thick and draped over her body like a robe... "

"Was your wife Italian?" I asked, when his flood of words had subsided somewhat.

"No, she was a Frenchwoman... From the south of France."

"And you yourself?"

"Also French..."

"But you speak German very well."

"I can also speak Italian and English... I started speaking to you in German as there was a German newspaper sticking out of your pocket... But I am – I must apologise, sir – being very impolite! Please allow me to introduce myself: Georges Lebaudin, the Montpelier representative of Armand Clarette & Company, the leading firm in town, one of the leading ones in the département and in the whole of southern France – only deals in brands that are fine, traditional, guaranteed and eminently respectable... Here you are, sir, please be so good as to accept..."

His right hand had made an automatic gesture and he handed me two items: the visiting card of Georges Lebaudin, Esq., and the price list for Armand Clarette & Company's wines.

He had handed the latter to me probably by mistake, but he

didn't notice that; instead, after I had presented him with my card, he simply put it in his waistcoat pocket, and continued his tale:

"I've been travelling in wholesale wine for four years now... A very good position with regard to salary, commission and travel expenses – no problems there whatsoever, but hard, a tough job, sir... Just imagine: only a few days holiday: a couple of weeks at most, after travelling for two or three months at a stretch. The clatter of the train has hardly left your ears, your feet have hardly forgotten the rocking on board ship, and you're back in your compartment or cabin... And then that never-ending hotel life! From one hole to the next. And spending money everywhere. What's the point of a good salary, if you have to dispose of it when on your travels?"

"So you were always away from your young wife?" I interposed.

"Oh God, of course! That is the lot of a commercial traveller! Always alone, always apart, always longing and the boredom..." He let his voice drop. It became gentler, moister, as his eyes had again begun to glitter. "And Ninette lived life to the full. She loved company. She had something to show for herself... Such a young voluptuous beauty – but she wasn't blind – or made of stone... she knows when she's being looked at, feels pleasure... And if the seducer is sly and smooth..."

"You think your wife got into the claws of such a man?"

"It's as good as certain... To run off on her own – there would have been no reason at all for her to do so... After all, our life together was a happy one... He swallowed audibly, his lips quivering.

"You don't know who seduced her?"

"Well. There are several possibilities, but I'm not absolutely sure..."

"Your enquiries in Montpelier gave no result?"

"Yes... I mean to say: God knows... I had enough time for enquiries. This all happened four weeks ago. I had just arrived back from a six-week stint – Holland, Germany, Denmark... And when I got home the nest was bare... The first two or three days I was simply dazed – stupified – incapable of thought... could not go anywhere or ask anyone... I just couldn't believe it... And when I began to ask around a bit, then came orders from above: tomorrow you're back on the road again."

"So you left?"

"Couldn't be helped! And now I'm here... While travelling I do what I can. I assume that they too are on a trip. It's the holiday season. And I can't imagine that Ninette would have run off with a pauper. That's pretty well certain. She likes nice clothes, jewellery, fun... I gave her what I could, but... such a beauty and when the temptation becomes too great..."

"So you're searching for her while travelling, Mr Lebaudin?"

"Yes... I often make detours from my business destination... It's a waste of my time, costs me money, but I don't care... Luckily, my job is taking me this time somewhere where I imagine I could find them. In early April I was on the Riviera. Now I've been travelling to Rome, Florence and Milan via Naples and the nearby islands, where I had no business to conduct, then I came here and when the northern Italian lakes have been done, on to Switzerland and the Tirol... I'm hoping, sir, for a little good luck."

"But, if I may ask, what are you trying to achieve by finding them? Are you thinking of asking your wife to come back or do you want..."

Mr Lebaudin showed me the butt of a revolver hidden under his jacket.

"I want to see the robber's blood... I long to take his life... I have sworn that he will have seen Ninette's face for the last time once I've caught up with them!"

"But in doing so, you'll ruin your own life."

"I simply don't care!"

The bluish line on his brow seemed to have thickened, the blood had left his lips, leaving them white.

"You're not thinking of punishing your wife just as harshly?"

He seemed slightly numbed by the comment.

"I don't know yet... That depends on what happens and what the situation dictates. How she responds to me at the time..."

"You could perhaps even forgive her a little, Mr Lebaudin."

"Yes... no... I really don't know... not now, sir! At first I thought of doing them both in... But on second thoughts... Look, she isn't really that bad... And if she were to..."

Suddenly, Mr Lebaudin's voice died away. His mouth remained open, his eyes opened wide, as if he were emitting a soundless yell. The next moment he had jumped up from his seat.

"What is it, Mr Lebaudin?"

He did not reply. He stood there next to me transfixed like a pillar of salt. His pale face had grown elongated and narrow.

I peered more closely at the crowd, towards where his eyes were staring with boundless astonishment.

From the lake, some twenty or thirty paces away, a happy couple were approaching – an almost boyish young gentleman and a slightly older woman. Both were wearing bright fine quality walking clothes: the man was wearing a stylish Panama hat, while the lady beside him was sporting a small promenade-hat decorated with blue ribbon, carrying a red silk parasol which formed a background to the hat. They were in lively conversation, and the woman was laughing so heartily, that she doubled up, thus releasing for an instant her partner's arm. But she soon linked arms again, raised her little bud of a mouth again and talked to her admirer until his reply made her laugh again...

"Ninette!" the words slipped out of my mouth.

"Young Clarette!" whispered Mr Lebaudin.

"Young Clarette? Your boss's son?"

Georges Lebaudin did not reply, but I detected an affirmative answer in his expression.

A moment of paralysis ensued.

Agitation sealed my mouth, froze my limbs, stopped my heart.

The couple approached, along the front of the restaurant, looking for a free seat and, passing the entrance, moved slowly towards our table. They were so absorbed in each other's presence that they were unlikely to spot any specific face among the crowd.

Now they were some seven paces away... now only three.

I saw Mr Lebaudin's right hand move...

Now young Clarette and his mistress were passing our table...

Monsieur Georges Lebaudin raised his right hand and lifted his hat...

1908

On Lake Peipsi

Juhan Liiv

When the chill of midwinter becomes a sharp frost, the ice-bound Lake Peipsi rattles its chains. From its mute bosom, silent in the captivity of the ice, explosions can be heard resembling reports when large cannon are fired, and in the boundless stretches of snow blue cracks appear. The blue water can be seen by those standing on the shore, at first as a wide ditch, then as the eye roves further out, the blue thread narrows and finally disappears, like a hair growing from the grey bald pate of the horizon. These are rifts which the frost has made in the ice. The astonished visitor will, despite the biting cold, stop on the banks of the river of rivers. Listen! The bangs and panting then a growl, as if Kalev were riding a sleigh drawn by six horses across the ice. This is Old Father Frost from Finland, who is rolling along at the front, before the North Wind, his ice sleigh following. But no, this is a still heap of ice, piled up by the autumn storms. One crash is heard and immediately by the onlooker's feet a barely visible crack will appear, straight across the lake like an arrow. Soon, however, it will broaden and in a few hours will be a wide fissure.

Such cracks have taken the lives of several people. Woe to those driving across that encounter a crack when far out on the lake, a gap that the horses cannot jump and night is approaching. Quite often these cracks have trapped people crossing the lake and fishermen for a night or two, and also – when an animal detects the crack too late to halt – the horse, vehicle and driver are swallowed up. These are cracks only to be found on Lake Peipsi!

Even more feared on Lake Peipsi is when the ice is breaking up in the thaw. Then, it is difficult to trust it, but hard not to rely on it. Although sometimes the ice just won't budge. "This year even George won't get his share out of Peipsi!" says a man from the shore, when Peipsi is still frozen over very late and Saint George's day is at hand. On other occasions it simply doesn't consult the calendar at all. When the winter has not been particularly severe, when there is a southerly wind, coming from the depths of the River Ema, like a sleeper awakening from the slumber of death, its huge chest rising up overnight and all of a sudden rattles its chains and its angry roar can be heard all the way to the fishing villages announcing the fact that it has broken its fetters. In the morning the blue water flows and chunks of ice are thrown up onto the shore.

Woe to those who go fishing on such a night, even more so those who decide to cross the lake under similar circumstances!

One March morning twenty years ago two Estonians proceeding on foot were standing on the eastern shore of Lake Peipsi, near the Russian town of Gdov, and were deliberating. The men were from Lohusuu, Jaak Kirsimäe and Rein Ristiotsa who had, while still on the other shore of the lake, heard a couple of weeks before of the lands beyond that lake. In "Russia" it was possible in those days to rent a small manor house for next to nothing, and the men from Lohasuu and Kodavere knew no other Russia than the part immediately across Lake Peipsi. There was both fear and homesickness on the sombre faces of these two men as they looked towards the Estonian side of the lake, where their relatives waited. A warm wind, the southerly bringing the thaw, and the wet and brittle ice on the lake did not bode well. The ice on the lake was expected to break up soon, and this is why both of them were hurrying to complete their business – should the lake become ice-free what should they do in a foreign land without any money, and amongst a foreign people? And indeed the state of the lake seems very dubious. What should they do? They stood there for half an hour looking over towards their homes, and at one another, and neither wanted to be the first to broach the subject.

"Let's go, Rein!" says Jaak looking up to the sky. He finds this hard to utter.

His companion looks enquiringly at him – not on account of what he had said: he too wants to say the same – but if only his companion would only look him straight in the eye, that would be a comfort to him.

"We'll drown, Jaak."

"If we drown, we'll be doing so in the name of God, Rein."

And again the two men survey the open stretch of ice. The route has been marked out and they are good walkers and will therefore be home by nightfall.

"I'm going, Jaak."

"Me too!"

"Whether we drown or not, Jaak."

"Life or death, Rein. My wife's stayed behind, she could die there and I might never see her again, if I wait any longer to cross the ice."

Courageously and holding onto one another's arm, Jaak and Rein set out on their journey. The strong southerly wind is blowing from the side and thick clouds cover the sky, but they had set their minds on this, tensed their walking muscles, and the land recedes behind them more and more. Everything seems to be going well. The overcast weather does not frighten them, and by lunchtime they have crossed to the middle of the lake. The ice is indeed covered with water, but is completely unbroken.

Now thick wet snowflakes begin to fall. The wind gets up and whips the snow into the men's eyes. They can hardly get their bearings, or make out the bundles of twigs that mark the path towards the naked trees on the far shore. The men begin to get a little worried, but trudge on relentlessly. They estimate by the time it has taken that they are beyond the halfway mark by now, but it is terribly hard work with this vile wind blowing. It tears at their clothing, snatches at the flaps of their coats, as if it were angry, that they did not want to give in to its power.

Over there – what's that – something can be heard in the distance. Jaak and Rein stand stock still and listen, and indeed, there in the distance, across the sheet of ice, water is flowing! The lake is thawing. The men cannot yet see any cracks, but what is happening there is familiar to them: the water is frothing, the chunks of ice dancing and with a cracking sound waves are breaking off chunk after chunk of ice; oh what a disaster!

"We've had it, Jaak!" yells Rein, who takes his cap off and recites the Lord's Prayer. "Keep going, Jaak!" he then cries out.

The men hurry forward, the noise grows louder. The ice is groaning and shaking beneath their feet. Keep going, keep going, quick, quick!

The men stop for one brief moment. They take off their belts and knot them together, and when this is not long enough, they cut their bread bag into strips, tie them together with the shoulder strap, and carry on. They both wind one end around their arm. If one should fall in, the other can pull him out; the ice under their feet will not remain solid for long. This is all happening in great haste. They both promise to look after the other's wife and children, if one of them should survive. Keep going, keep going! The rumble increases, the wind has now become a true storm, the snow comes as if in sackfuls. Oh God, oh God!

"I'll give a chandelier to the church, if I get out of this alive!" yells Rein.

Oh, God, oh God!

Jaak does not reply but in his heart he promises never more to beat his wife if God spares him, nor add water to the linen to cheat the merchant by making it seem heavier, nor let his horse eat hay on the sly at night in his neighbour's field, or doze off in church, or adulterate the grain with chaff: none of this sort of thing any more.

Were any true man of God to look for a brief moment into the hearts of these men, he would certainly have been joyful.

"Hurry up, hurry up, oh God, oh God!"

"Oh, God, oh Jesus!"

If they are given one more hour, then they will be saved. The ice can now clearly be heard to be cracking – only one more hour! Land cannot be far away. Hurry up, hurry up...

Water is seeping up from under their boots, there is now so much on the surface of the ice. Already they can see the black silhouette of Lohusuu church, but also that the water keeps on coming!

Still about five versts to go...

The ice is juddering, groaning, cracks are appearing. If only they were given another half-hour; oh God!

One verst...

The ice is sagging under their feet – they can feel it clearly, that it is becoming mushy and slushy, but it still holds – one more powerful wave and it could disintegrate! Only one word is on the men's lips, only one: God.

Half a verst...

The men are hopping from one block of ice to the next, more than once does one of them have to pull the other out of the water, life and death are still wrestling.

Still?

"Well I'll be damned. Land at last, bloody hell!" shouts Rein, up to his knees in water, as he has just fallen from a block of ice. "Jaak, damn it, my feet are already on firm land!"

"A chandelier is a chandelier," thinks Rein and presents the church with a small candlestick.

When a week later Jaak has to take his linen to the merchant, he adds a little water to it in anger: "Taxes are high; what difference does it make if the merchant gets one or two roubles more or less."

1892

Bird Cherry Petals

Friedebert Tuglas

The old bird cherry trees dozed motionless under a windless sky. From their branches, however, petals fell unceasingly. They fluttered down slowly, delicate and sad, withered as if borne by the sorrows of vanishing. They fell, quivering patches of sunlight, onto the grass between the trees.

Leeni's eyes dreamily followed this play of light and shade. Her bright auburn hair was covered more and more by the petals as by a white wreath.

She had laid her dolls under the bird cherry tree to sleep there – three in a row. And with her half humming a song, half in thought, the fairy-tale continued. They would grow up, the three golden-haired daughters of the king. They would sleep in the enchanted wood, they would sleep in the enchanted castle: a sleep of a hundred years. And the sons of the king would wander, seeking the flowering fern, to find the track to the castle...

All motherly love and tenderness were united into one lullaby.

But now she was tired and languid. The air was exhaustingly hot, filled with the scent of the earth and flowers. And this, in turn, enfeebled her thoughts.

She was still worried about her children. In recent times they had grown so torpid and lifeless. They did not appreciate motherly love, appreciate her care. She had taught them to walk and speak. But they could not even take one step without her help, and their childish wishes she could only read in their blue eyes. She would have wished that they had smiled just once for all to see, stretched out their arms to her in joy and marvelled at the fairy-tale. But no, they would have to go through life deaf and dumb...

Let them at least dream: dreams as beautiful as this world of springtime. Let them dream of their mother's love, worry and longings! Because even if they may be deaf and dumb the world of dreams was always open to them. If they could not manage to do so when awake, may they at least laugh and dance in their dreams...

Leeni sat with her hands on her lap, her narrow thoughtful face raised. She filled her lungs with air, then sighed deeply and remained gazing there.

A slice of the secrets of nature opened up before her. Mildewed tree branches rose, forked and gnarled, full of cracks like the wounds of life's struggle. Up above, the branches had grown into a tangled mass, abundant and sinuous like knotting snakes. Above them was the canopy of leaves and blossom, full of jagged gaps. While down below, in the moist heat, shoots were pushing forth, creeping across the ground, climbing up the trunks, gasping for light and air. Beyond all this, beyond the charred fenceposts of the garden, and through the cobwebs, the vaulted sky, the fields and the edge of the wood...

Beyond the kitchen garden, everything was silent and dead. Only in the raspberry bush a small bird was chirping and further away, the bell round a sheep's neck tinkled. But all of this was so quiet and monotonous, as if repeating in their own way the beating heart of the Sunday countryside.

Leeni shut her eyes. She was overcome by a dreamy sleepiness, happy and sad at one and the same time. She no longer saw or heard anything but a yellow glow through her eyelids and the distant tinkling of the bell.

Then suddenly, as if caught in her sleep, the laughter of people and the rustle of grass underfoot. She woke up with a start, but could not be bothered to look round. Because from their voices, those approaching were already familiar: her sister Marie and the farmhand Kusta.

Why should Marie be laughing so forwardly and coquettishly! This hurt Leeni's ears. No, not even here could you find peace for your dolls and your thoughts. They were always turning up, talking and laughing!

Dry branches cracked and the bushes rustled. Now they had already passed the bird cherry trees by now. Leeni could still catch sight of her sister's brightly coloured skirt through the branches, as loud as its wearer. And now they were already sitting on the ground, as the branches no longer cracked. All that could be heard was whispering and laughter, laughter and whispering...

Leeni stretched wearily. Oh! – her chest hurt from sitting such a long time. She stood up and for a moment yellowish-green coloured spots danced in front of her eyes.

The orchard could be seen over the brushwood, filled with old mossy apple trees. Next, a row of grey beehives, with clods of earth on top. Then rowan trees again and beyond everything else, the drawbeam of a well like a huge threatening arm of a giant hand against the sky.

Then Leeni spotted Kusta and Marie. They were sitting on an empty hive, their backs against the fence. Marie had her hands in Kusta's hair, was ruffling and smoothing it, leaning her breast on his shoulder. Kusta had a large sandwich in his hand. He ate it greedily, laughed between bites and had his other arm round Marie.

There they sat, and Leeni watched them.

And at once her dreaminess and weariness had vanished. She was as awake as they were. Why was her heart beating so, as she crouched there in the bushes! Like hammers pounding in her breast. But now she was already right behind them.

But in all truth, how did this all affect her? Let them sit there, let them laugh. She would play with her dolls and go back to them. Or should she emerge from the bushes and pass them coolly, as if nothing were the matter. And what was the matter? Only that a boy and a girl were sitting on a beehive and laughing!

But for all that, her heart was beating so! She stood holding her breath among the blossoming branches, her quivering lips open.

Kusta stopped eating and wiped his face with his sleeve. Then suddenly he took the girl in his strong arms and pressed his

73

lips against hers. They stayed like that for a moment, their heads thrown back, their limbs taut. And Leeni watched them, her eyes wide open.

Aah!... Now she understood, now she had grasped the whole matter!...

Her legs began to shake. Her first thought was to flee, run away from what she feared... something shameful... but what was also so exciting and forbidden...

But the very next moment curiosity rose in her again. Leaning against a bird cherry tree and hiding her glowing face in her hands, she froze on the spot, full of fear and shame.

She saw, through her trembling fingers their heads pressed together, and Marie's winding bob of hair, like writhing snakes. She saw her sister's head bow down and put her arms around Kusta's neck. They laughed silently, hiccoughing with every limb and muscle. And then Marie's choked whisper could be heard:

"But you really can't go on ogling Maali any more, you just can't!"

"I'm not ogling her, I'm not..." replied Kusta, also in a whisper.

"Like you'd like to gobble her up, like she was something special for you!"

"She's not..."

Their chests were pressed together. The boy's head was inclined towards the glowing face of the girl. Then another whisper:

"She's not young, she's not pretty, and she's as poor as a church mouse. What is it you see in her, or she in you?"

"Nothing... Nothing at all..."

The tiny bird was still chirruping and the air was just as sweet and close. Leeni's head was going round and round from the fragrance and the hot whispering.

Oh, how nice it would be to be away from all of this – far, far away!

She stumbled through the bird cherry copse. She passed her dear little children, the king's daughters. The shadows were receding and they were now in full sunlight. Soon it would tan them as brown as Moors.

But she forgot her little children. Let them dream that their mother is tired, that she wished to cry and complain and had no idea what to do next! Let them dream how her little heart was beating in pain and shame!

She left the garden, crossed the yard, and went into the meadow. A long path led between the winter rye and a field of clover. Overhead, the endless space of sky was blue. And under this, between the sprouting crops walked the little girl, her head full of bitter thoughts.

Ah, grown-ups, grown-ups! She felt pain, felt shame for them. She had the feeling that by getting to know their secret she had somehow become part of it. She had the feeling that she should tell her father and mother everything and ask their forgiveness on her knees!

Ah, grown-ups, grown-ups! How mysterious are their thoughts and deeds. Yet they laugh loudly, scorn everything that is childlike and gentle. Because they laugh at her and her children. They say: "You're a big girl now and you're still playing with dolls! Time now to find yourself a husband and yet you're playing with dolls!" They have no understanding of her love and joy. They know nothing of fairy-tales!

Oh, why do they have to tease her, hurt her with all their words, all their deeds! Flowers lose their fragrance when they pass, and the bird cherry petals turn black, when they cast a glance at them.

All at once she burst into tears, loudly and bitterly. Crying, only crying was all that was left for her to do – crying for everything that was beautiful and delicate, what there was in life and what people neither saw nor wanted to see! Marie and Kusta no longer mattered. It was now a universal worry that she was bearing in her breast.

But at the same time this worry itself grew more beautiful, almost like a fairy-tale in its own way. She saw her surroundings again, and the tears dried up in her eyes.

The only thing to do now was walk and walk – with rye on the one side, clover on the other – between them the path disappearing off into the distant sky. She had to walk and walk – only the fields and the sky, the sky and the fields!

But that sky was like a blue sea, across which long white sails floated. Over them poured the sunlight, falling between them like a golden shower of rain. And the soft soil, rough and porous, sucked this in, drank it up, itself pulsating with birth pangs. Here the little tiny leaves and buds were stretching out their heads, growing almost visibly. In the steaming soil beneath, tiny insects moved about, bright red like clots of red velvet. Under every tiny leaf, every blade, there was something sitting, swaying on each stalk. Along the stems wondrous creatures were climbing, slowly moving their barbed legs, their mouths agape, their eyes popping as if out of their minds.

The air was like honey and the earth like a sleeping child on a sultry summer's evening: it was dreaming and had grown delirious and ran its gentle fingertips along the cord of the cradle.

Now Leeni was already walking along the path through the ridge of hillocks, which wound its way between the bushes, and no one knew who had been the first to tread it. It was as if the hornets had picked it out and the midges trodden it down through the moss!

She walked along, feeling an overwhelming joy at everything she saw and heard. Both at the rustling heather under her feet, and the chattering squirrel in the tree. She had forgotten where she had come from and where she was going. All she wanted to do was walk, and she had but one feeling in her heart: she wanted something, but did not know what; she was happy and sad at the same time, and she didn't know why.

If someone now crossed her path – no matter who – she would laugh and cry with them for joy. And they would run pursuing one another down the slope into the valley. Oh how the air would whistle past her ears and the birch twigs would strike her in the face! And the flowers would flash past like a string of pearls!

And all at once she broke into a run. The earth seemed to sink beneath her feet. How her heart pounded and her breath struggled in her chest! But she was now running ever faster, as if someone were urging her on, on a thousand wings. Ever onwards, eyes closed, into the opening void.

Under the trees she sank down onto the turf. The blood throbbed in her head pounded like hammers in her chest. She looked up with her throbbing eyes, unable to think. All she saw was a few wisps of cloud like the ridges of snowy hills.

She resumed her journey until something twinkled among the bushes. It was a stream, winding its way beneath the ancient ash trees and alders. Where the path narrowed, making progress difficult the stream might be tamed, like a shadow. When it however threw itself down into rock pools, it was inscrutable and gloomy. It could play coquettishly in the rapids, then suddenly paw its way into the banks, flooding trees and bushes alike. And so it proceeded between fields and woods, until it quite forgot the pranks of its youth and would wander gravely through the water-meadows, down to the sea.

Leeni had known all this as far back as she could remember. She was herself a part of this landscape, where every blade of grass understood her, every tiny head of the dropwort would bow towards her.

The path broadened out, and through the branches, thrust steeply upwards, a red, sandy incline came into view. This was the deepest pool in the stream, black and purulent. On the opposite bank it changed into a foul bog, where bulrushes and reed mace grew.

At the high edge above this pit sat the herd boy Vidrik, a fishing rod in his hand, with one eye on the bobbing cork on the shining surface of the water.

"Vidrik!" cried Leeni joyfully.

But the boy hardly turned his head towards her, then thundered angrily:

"Can't you keep your trap shut! It was just beginning to bite at last, and now you've gone and frightened it away!"

And he spat into the water in irritation. The dog that sat at his side bent down on hearing the plop and watched the saliva spread out across the surface of the water.

Leeni sat down, tired and sad, next to Vidrik and also began to watch the cork.

Vidrik was an odd boy. His thinness, his face filled with wisdom with its half-closed eyes, and his tranquil way of speaking and clumsy gait. In all of this there was something of an old man. When he remained silent, it was as if he did not notice, what was happening around him, while he was pondering the things of the world. And when he laughed, it was as if to say: look, here I am laughing, but I am laughing at the foolishness of other people!

He didn't seem to care that he was short and thin. Nor did it matter to him that he would be looking after the cattle of two households in the summer. This would usually end in a quarrel and they would simply send him away.

These quarrels had nothing to do with him being worse at his job than other cowherds, or that he was given too little to eat. No, these misunderstandings arose because of the thoughts going round in the boy's head. Because of thoughts! Why did these idiots not want to understand that he too could have thoughts of his own? But they always ended up dismissing him as soon as it became clear that the herd boy was cleverer than the farmer himself. Once he had even worked as a cowherd for the church manor. But they threw him out by the end of the week. Because even regarding the Holy Bible he had strange ideas!

Did they think that they achieved anything by throwing him out and sending him on his way? They achieved nothing! He left full of the sad awareness that the world didn't know what it was doing. He would carry his pair of bast shoes under his arm, under his other arm a bag, the shaggy dog Eku walked at his heels. And so he went. But in the bag was a loaf of bread as hard as stone and three books. In two of them was written about the firmament, steam engines, the countries of the world and kings. The third was handwritten – on blue paper, and no one else had ever seen what was written there.

Some pages were even secret ones, written in blood – brown letters full of terrible secrets. There were fragments of The Seventh Book of Moses, words about treasure, a list of the unlucky days of the year. It was full of witches' crosses like some mysterious graveyard.

Now he was sitting hunched up, his body resting on his thin arms, his bare legs outstretched like black tree roots. And next to him sat his dog. He was old already. His eyebrows and muzzle were white and time and the trials of life had removed his coat from his flanks. You could count his ribs and see his heart beating. He was deadly thin and terribly serious. His head hung between his sharp shoulders, his lips were ajar, there were bitter lines at the edges of his mouth.

Leeni soon became restless watching the motionless cork. But the eyes of both Vidrik and the dog were nailed to it. The slightest tremor would send a tremble through them too. Holding their breath they bored their eyes into the cork, as if the whole happiness of their lives depended on it. They both understood the rustle of irises and the play of the water in the same way.

Amidst this tense waiting the cork suddenly vanished beneath the surface.

The dog jumped up, he glanced at Vidrik's face then uttered a low growl.

Vidruk jerked the trembling rod and the bait came up out of the water. But there was no fish on the hook.

"The bloody devil!" swore Vidrik, and Eku lay down, full of shame and anger, his hairless ears drooping. "It's been lurking here for an hour: neither bites nor goes away!"

But when he wanted to spit on the worm and throw it back into the water, he saw that the fish had bitten after all, but the hook had vanished along with the bait. Now Vidrik got really angry.

"Bloody scarecrow, bloody bugbear, bloody nameless savage!"

He stopped, as if expecting an explanation from the fish. But it did not reply to such abuse. He spat and started all over again, slowly and reproving:

"Who do you take me for? Do you think I'm stupid, daft or just backward? Or do you think that the world only exists for your merriment, as your plaything?"

But the fish did not answer for all that.

"Better you never existed! You should have been born as a frog or a leech! May the Devil take you and your offspring!"

He fixed a new hook on the end of his line, snuffling slowly like an old man. And while doing so he said, already more quietly, like a man who knows that although he has been cheated, the cheat has gained nothing from it:

"What I'd like to know is where you are planning on going with that hook stuck in your gut. You're finished, you'll end up as carrion! You'll push your head deep in the mud and die there! You think I'm joking? Well, plenty of others before you have tried, but..."

He spat contemptuously into the water.

Leeni was watching the boy, her eyes wide open.

She had never really looked at him before. She had been afraid of his seriousness, the look in his hollow eyes, the laugh on his wrinkled face. She now observed him as if for the first time.

And Leeni saw how Vidrik ripped a large earthworm in two and stuck one half onto the hook. Then he spat on it, threw the line into the water and said in a threatening tone as if dealing with whole legions:

"Now, we shall see!"

And then both of them watched fixedly – the herd boy and his dog – the bobbing cork. And once again silence and sunshine reigned over the stream. Only the silhouettes of the boy and his dog were outlined among all this beauty like bent, burnt logs.

And suddenly Leeni felt sorry for Vidrik, inexpressibly sorry. How lonely and unhappy he really was! If only someone would treat him kindly! If only someone would make him laugh or cry heartily! And Leeni said to herself, unexpectedly and in a half-whisper, leaning her head towards the boy:

"Vidrik, why do you always sit here on the banks of the stream?"

But he replied in an irritated, rude voice:

"Well, where else have I to go?"

The boorish Vidrik did not even turn his head! And for a moment there was a stifling silence again.

"Vidrik... would you like... shall I fetch you a sandwich?"

She said this in a muffled voice, as if begging for mercy!

"A sandwich?" Now the boy did turn his head and looked enquiringly at Leeni. And following his head, the muzzle of the dog turned, the same expression on each face. "Well, why wouldn't I want a sandwich?"

Leeni jumped up. She was suddenly filled with joy. She cried clearly and loudly, as if singing in some children's language:

"*Piópile pisiin! Pimipina pitúpilen pivárspiti.*"

When Vidrik looked at her bewildered, she repeated, running already:

"Stay here! I'll be back soon."

She ran non-stop until the thatched eaves of the farmhouse could be seen through the trees. There it was as silent as before. Her sister Marie was leaning on the garden gate, her weary eyes half-shut, with three globe flowers stuck in her hair.

"Well, where are you running from?" she asked without enthusiasm.

"Me... I was down there in the meadow... you know, where Kalevipoeg's huge boulder is."

She just had to tell a lie! As if someone were commanding her to.

"There's lots of globe flowers and primroses down there..."

"Oh yes?"

Marie's sleepy eyelids flickered, the wilting globe flowers drooped over her forehead.

In the cool shade of the granary there was the smell of mould and mustiness. A row of cobwebs hung down from the rafters of the empty corn store. Between the beams the sun shone in and the dust danced in the golden sunrays.

But Leeni was no longer paying attention to anything. She

stood on tiptoe and took from the shelf a broad loaf like a shield. The tough inside rolled around the long knife. She cut off a hefty chunk of bread and with a shaking hand spread a large pat of butter on it between the descending sunrays.

The lawn of the farmhouse was deserted as before.

Now all I have to do is run off without anyone spotting me. But what if they should see me? Let them see, let them know. But then again, no, no... This must remain a secret.

She slipped out past the windows, ran across the garden and stopped beyond it, panting for breath.

In the bird cherry petals, in the heat of the full sun, her children were resting. The poor things were sleeping their restless sleep, they waved their sweaty arms on account of delirious visions. They dreamt that their mother was passing them indifferently, only throwing them a swift glance, her head filled with other thoughts, her heart full of other worries. They dreamt that she smoothed her hair as she passed, tugged a few strands down over her forehead and that she pushed a carnation into her hair.

But don't let her children think that their mother had forgotten them. It was just that she didn't have the time right now. Did they not realise that Vidrik was hungry? And did they not realise that he was lonely and unhappy?

Their mother would, of course, come back sometime, stroke their hair, pat their faces and sing about the sons of the king!

Leeni slipped into the pasture between two broken fence-posts, along the dog track and continued along the path between the open fields. The sun stood with its reddening face in the sky, from the earth a warm fragrance rose. Its blue haze could be seen across the breadth of the sky.

But Leeni rushed on, ever faster, shaking with excitement. What bore her along was the joyful thought that Vidrik was waiting for the sandwich. She almost felt as if Vidrik had asked: Leeni, you know I'm so hungry, so very hungry... And as if she had said impatiently: Well, I suppose I can bring you something out of sheer pity.

The stream was already winking in front of her.

Vidrik was sitting where he had been on the bank. He was cursing, watched by his loyal Eku, the damned perch that had bitten through the line and was still teasing him as stubbornly as before, full of satanic spite. Vidrik could see clearly how the fish was circling the bait, knocking the float with his tail and if it could have laughed, he would have heard its hellish sniggering.

For only an instant was there a glimmer of pleasure in the corners of Vidrik's eyes when he saw the sandwich. He took it, broke off a piece for the dog, spat once into the water and began to eat greedily.

Leeni sat next to him, staring intently at his mouth. Oh, how he ate! It was as if he had never seen anything in his whole life apart from bread made from chaff and watery potatoes. Or as if he had not eaten a morsel in three days.

The girl's face was flushed and her ears glowed. Poor Vidrik, poor boy! He's no more than a shadow, sorrowful and alone, all he does is think and dream. Why have they been so distant from one another! If only they shared all their thoughts and moods! For he shouldn't think for a moment that Leeni doesn't suffer in her life, that she has no worries. She too is someone that nobody understands, or sympathises with her aching heart!

But that heart was beating right now, as if it wished to leap out of her chest.

Aah... Now Leeni slowly put her hand on Vidrik's tattered coat and leant her head gently on his shoulder. Aah... Now one should be silent, otherwise your heart will burst through your ribcage.

Before her darkening eyes there was a patchwork of the sky, a red hill and the black water, her breast was full of despair and shame, as she leant against the boy, trembling with anticipation.

Now something miraculous will happen, as only occurs in fairy-tales. It will arrive like swans in springtime or when the bird cherry tree bursts into bloom overnight.

Blue dragonflies hovered over the stream and a green frog sat on a water lily leaf peering up at the sun with narrowed eyes.

83

But Vidrik did not notice anything. He chewed and swallowed, with deep creases on his forehead. When he had finished eating, he pushed another worm on the hook and again threw it into the water, calmly and cold-bloodedly.

Leeni's hands slid slackly onto her lap.

Oh, how her head ached! Her chest was full of fire, and her eyes could no longer make anything out.

She covered her face with her hands, and without her even realising, the tears started to flow through her fingers, gently at first, then in ever greater amounts. And suddenly she was convulsed by sobs.

Vidrik turned his head towards her.

"Oh dear. What's the matter with you now?"

Leeni turned onto her stomach, the tears streamed down her cheeks and she moaned plaintively:

"Vidrik... you don't... love me!"

But at that very moment Vidrik shouted:

"Shhh! It's biting!"

The fishing rod arched and out of the water a large perch with glittering scales came writhing onto the sunny bank. Vidrik grabbed it by its gills and noisily smashed it against the ground. The dog leapt around the fish as if performing a Red Indian dance, drops of saliva on its grey muzzle.

"Bloody great!" yelled Vidrik victoriously. "Who do you think you're tricking. You thought you were the cleverest creature on Earth – you! You don't know half as much as you think! Leeni, look how angry it still is!"

But Leeni no longer saw anything. Her eyes were blinded by tears. She stepped slowly along the path towards home, so slowly, that it was as if she had suddenly grown old and the joy of life had vanished for ever from her heart.

Again the fields are green as are the tops of the trees against the blue sky. And once again she was in the garden.

The ground was now white with fallen bird cherry petals. The petals covered the costumes of the dolls and the locks of their hair.

And the dolls dreamt:

Tiny bells are jingling in the air. Ah, the princes are out riding! They are galloping up the castle hill, their cloaks on their shoulders like eagle wings. The musicians come in their wake, their heads bared, cornflower wreaths on their brown hair. And the zithers are playing plaintive love songs amongst the ringing of hooves.

Now the castle gates fly open and the sons of the king enter. The red plumes drag along the ground as they doff their hats. And now one of them asks, falling to his knees:

"Are you then the enchanted daughters of the king?"

And they reply in bashful voices:

"We are."

But – oh, why do they suddenly turn their backs, their faces full of laughing mockery?

"Ladies, look at yourselves in the mirror!"

Down on the castle road sparks are flying under the horseshoes and again the zithers groan with new paeans to love.

Aah – the sun has burnt the faces of the king's daughters to the colour of those of Moors!

Leeni fell to her knees before the dolls.

A slight breeze stirred the tops of the bird cherry trees and the last petals of the blossom fell to the ground. The last ones – now there were no more left up there. The trees were now a dark green. But beneath them the ground was white as on a quiet winter's evening. And on this carpet of white knelt a little girl, a withered carnation in her hair, her chest pounding with pain, like the heart of a victim being sacrificed on an altar, and whose sacrifice the gods have not accepted.

1907

Grandfather's Death

Anton Hansen Tammsaare

One morning, grandfather did not rise from his bed. When his daughter-in-law asked him what was the matter, he replied:

"Nothing at all."

"So, why aren't you getting up?" she asked.

"I'm going to die," grandfather replied.

"How can you be dying if there's nothing wrong with you?"

"Let's wait and see."

"But who'll weave that basket from the twigs that you brought back from the woods yesterday?"

"The twigs," said grandfather, and fell silent for a short while. "You can put the twigs on my coffin."

"You surely don't intend to make baskets in the grave, do you?" asked his daughter-in-law, smiling.

"What else is there to do there," grandfather wondered.

"Well, you've certainly earned a good rest," she said, rose from her chair and left the room, as if she had some urgent errand to attend to.

A short while later, six- or seven-year old Uku entered and said:

"Granddad, are you really going to die?"

"Your mum told you, eh?" asked grandfather by way of a reply.

"Mum told dad, and I heard, and I came to see."

"How I was dying?"

"Yes, granddad."

"Aren't you afraid of death?"

"Why should I be frightened, death's not coming after

me?"

"Don't you be too sure about that. Sometimes he comes after the likes of you. Comes and knocks on the door, knock, knock, knock, and asks whether a certain apple of his mother's eye lives there."

"Are you the apple of your mother's eye, too?" asked Uku.

"What's the point of talking about my mother's eyes, when I haven't really got any eyes in my head myself?"

"How did you manage to see when you were walking in the woods and picking up those twigs?"

"I've got my walking-stick," explained grandfather.

"Does your walking-stick have eyes?"

"How could it be otherwise. My stick has eyes and ears."

"When you die, will you leave me your stick?"

"You've already got your own eyes and ears."

"But when I'm old and go blind like you, granddad..."

His mother came back into the bedroom, interrupting their conversation.

"Do you want something to eat?" asked his daughter-in-law. "Food'll drive away all thoughts of death."

"Why bother driving them away now?"

"So you really are thinking of dying?"

"What d'you mean! I've been groping my way around blindly with my stick, these past ten years or so."

"Where have these thoughts of death come from so suddenly?"

"From a tomtit, my dear daughter-in-law, from a tomtit."

"What d'you mean, a tomtit? A tomtit isn't a bird of death, like a jackdaw or a cuckoo."

"My bird of death is a tomtit."

"Where did you bump into one?"

"Yesterday, in the woods, it started knocking away at the peak of my cap."

"And how d'you know it was a tomtit?"

"From its chirp, what else. It taps a bit with its beak and

cries out."

"And that's supposed to mean death?"

"Well, what else could it mean for someone like me? Do you expect the birds to come and peck out my blind eyes?"

"So where were you when the tomtit arrived?"

"I was resting my legs, sitting on a tree stump."

"Then maybe the bird didn't know it was you, and thought you were a tree stump yourself."

"Of course it thought I was a tree stump, a rotten tree stump. And that's what I am, the tomtit came to remind me with its beak. It's God's bird. I myself had forgotten. Now I won't forget again."

"You never take any notice any more of what people say, granddad, so why should you take this little bird so seriously?" she asked.

"The bird didn't say anything, it did it in another way. It went knock, knock, knock with its beak. As if it wanted to drive in a nail."

"Not all nails are coffin nails."

"I don't need any other nails any more, my dear daughter-in-law."

They fell silent for a while, then she asked:

"Will you die happily, when death comes?"

"What else?"

"No regrets about departing?"

Grandfather did not reply, simply moved a little in his bed.

"So you do have regrets," said his daughter-in-law, a moment later.

"Sort of," grandfather agreed.

"What is it you actually regret?"

"Life is so beautiful," said grandfather.

"Really?"

"It's getting more beautiful every day," replied grandfather.

"But your eyes can't see the beauty any more."

"That's what's most beautiful about it."

"You say you're dying and now you're cracking jokes about

your blindness."

"What jokes?" asked grandfather. "My eyesight has tormented me most of all, throughout my life. I was always running, always hurrying, in order to see this or that. Never had peace in my life, neither night nor day, I was always rushing around. But now I grope my way along with my stick, I stop and listen."

"And that makes life beautiful?" asked his daughter-in-law.

"Beautiful and peaceful. A bit more, and I'll no longer be hankering after anything."

"But you get satisfaction from your pipe? You've still got it between your teeth."

"Sure, between my teeth, like I've got my stick in my hand. With one I grope my way along, the other I puff at, though from day to day I'm growing less and less interested in puffing at my pipe. You have to imagine the peace and bliss that fills you when all you desire is a crooked stick and a pipe! But I don't know, why God should have arranged it so that by the time you can live happily, then it's time to leave. You've made great efforts to get this far, so that the jaws of life no longer snatch after you, and then it's time to depart."

"Maybe not yet."

"Oh, it'll come..."

The daughter-in-law put the shirt, onto which she had just sewn buttons, onto the table and again left the room. Uku had presumably been lurking outside, because as soon as his mother had gone, he slipped into the room.

"Granddad," he said immediately, as if afraid of his mother returning before he had finished, "will you leave me your stick when you die?"

"I want my stick with me in the coffin," replied his grandfather.

"So you don't want to give it me?" asked Uku. "Then sell it to me, granddad. I'll buy it off you. I've got plenty of money."

"How much money have you got?"

"Not quite sure. But at least three krooni."

"And you'll give all of it to me if you get my stick?"

"All of it."

"You know, Uku, such a stick like mine can't be sold for money."

"What will you sell it for, then?"

"You have to make this kind of stick yourself, or earn it by living a long time."

"Sell me your pipe, then," wheedled Uku.

"My pipe!" said his grandfather, with astonishment. "Death won't be able to find me, if I sell my pipe to you."

At that point their conversation was interrupted, as Uku's mother returned and Uku himself felt that he was not wanted. The main thing was that there was no point staying around if he couldn't talk to his grandfather about what his heart desired most, as Uku was used to having private conversations with his granddad, and not when his mother or anyone else was present. But his mother did have an inkling that he and his grandfather were up to something, so she asked:

"What's the boy doing prying around in here?"

"He's bargaining for his inheritance."

"What inheritance?"

"Well, I do have my walking stick and my pipe."

A short period of silence ensued, then his daughter-in-law asked:

"Did he get what he wanted?"

"Not yet. I've still got a few companions in this life."

Again there was silence in the room. Finally, she said:

"You're not going to die just yet, granddad."

"Why not?"

"You're still worrying about your companions in life."

"A pipe and a stick are also good companions in death," replied grandfather.

A few days went by. Grandfather lay there as before. He didn't cause trouble, but nor did he want to eat, just sipped some cold water now and again from a mug, fingered his juniper walking stick and kept his pipe between his teeth. He did once stop it with tobacco, but didn't light it. When he did speak, he always talked with his daughter-in-law about his joy for life right now, why he had to depart, while with Uku he would talk about the stick and the pipe, which were going into the grave with him. No amount of wheedling on the part of the boy helped, his grandfather staunchly refused to part with his last two companions in life. When Uku, in his desperation, turned to his mother for help, hoping she might change his mind, she said to the boy:

"Grandfather's not going to be dying just yet, if he's clinging onto his pipe and his stick."

"Granddad says that Death wouldn't be able to find him if he didn't have his pipe and his stick," the boy explained to his mother.

"That's just a joke," said his mother soothingly. "Dying people don't crack jokes."

But his mother's words were of no comfort to Uku. His whole mood was so affected by the walking stick and the pipe that he would rather have heard tell of his grandfather's death than that he was going to remain alive, when he would at least get one or other of the objects, if not both.

The third day, grandfather lay as before, his eyes towards the window, where his daughter-in-law was sitting sewing. At that moment a tomtit flew up to the window and with its tiny beak went knock, knock, knock against the pane. Her hands stopped working, as her eyes were now watching the tomtit.

"Can you see my tomtit?" asked grandfather.

"This one's yours then?" she asked back.

"Whose else could it be. A pretty green colour under its belly."

"How can your eyes make out the fact that it's green?" asked the daughter-in-law, her heart quailing.

"They can today," he assured her. "I can also see is that God's little bird flew away for a while, but returned, and is having a look to see whether it's necessary to knock again, or whether this is enough."

She listened to grandfather, watching him intently, forgetting the tomtit entirely. She would have liked to say something, but she couldn't find the right words. She left the room perplexed, and left grandfather to his little bird of God. Once outside, she said to her husband, granddad's son:

"He probably really is going to die, he says he could see the tomtit at the window."

"Maybe he just heard it knocking on the window pane."

"No, no! He saw it fly away and return quickly."

"My mother always said that blind people get their sight back when they are dying, and deaf people their hearing, so in his case, perhaps..."

"Yes, maybe..."

When he had heard the old saying from the lips of his parents, Uku ran immediately to his grandfather's bedroom. Because if he really was dying, this would be the very last chance to persuade him to change his mind and leave him his pipe or his stick or both.

But when he entered the room and started to talk to his grandfather, he didn't reply. The boy thought that he'd perhaps dozed off, but then he noticed that his grandfather's eyes were open. This made him realise what kind of sleep it was when your eyes were open. Granddad's eyes were also so strange, like those of a sheep when his mother would bring in its head in a basket, in autumn.

Uku ran like lightning out of the room to his mother and father, yelling:

"Mum, oh, mum, granddad's gone and died!"

"Don't be daft," his mother replied. "Only just now, I..."

"His eyes are like a dead sheep's eyes!" said Uku.

"Shut your gob!" bawled his father.

"You shouldn't say things like that about your granddad," scolded his mother.

These last words were said on their way to the bedroom. When they arrived, they found that grandfather had indeed departed, as if he had followed the tomtit's invitation, made by that little bird of God. There was nothing more to be done but to shut the dead man's eyes.

But when Uku was alone with his mother, he asked right away:

"What's going to happen to granddad's stick and his pipe?"

"We're going to put them neatly in the coffin," his mother answered.

"If only I could have the stick," sighed Uku.

"What would you do with granddad's stick?"

"Well, his pipe, then."

"My dear boy, what on earth would you do with his pipe?"

"Granddad won't be doing anything with it any more either, now that he's dead."

"Sometimes the dead need things that the living don't," explained his mother. But Uku couldn't understand this and thought his mother was just making excuses. So he never left off asking for his grandfather's pipe and stick, and in the end, his mother felt she had to have a word with her husband about it. But he said something that was impossible to argue against:

"If grandfather wanted his pipe and his stick with him in his coffin, then they will have to be there."

With those words the whole matter was now settled. But Uku never gave up hope that something would happen so that his mother and father would change their minds. Maybe something would happen as it had done with granddad, when the tomtit came to announce his approaching death. No one had ever said that a tomtit had anything to do with death, but now he had seen and heard that it was all true. Why shouldn't the same kind of miracle occur with granddad's pipe and stick: everyone said they were in the coffin with him, but then one of them suddenly wasn't, and stayed with Uku.

Even on the morning of the funeral Uku was still expecting some kind of miracle to happen, he waited and circled his grandfather's coffin. In the end he couldn't help but ask his mother, quietly, almost in secret:

"Has granddad got his pipe in his pocket?"

"Yes, yes," his mother assured him. "It must be there, I put it there myself".

But suddenly Uku felt, that if he were to feel whether the pipe was there with his own hand, it would not actually be there, as if by some miracle. So he ran after his mother, and managed to say:

"I want to see if it's there."

"The pipe, you mean?"

"The pipe..."

"Have you gone stark raving mad, you and your pipe!" cried his mother, but none the less took her son by the hand and said: "Well, go and feel for yourself whether granddad's pipe is in his pocket, if you won't get any peace otherwise."

So Uku, along with his mother, stepped up to the open wooden coffin, where she said:

"Look, there's granddad's stick in his hand, should he need it in the next world, and his pipe is in his pocket, feel for yourself, then you'll believe it's actually there."

They all stood in a group around the coffin and the candles were burning brightly, when Uku stretched out his hand over the edge of the coffin and put his hand in the pocket where the pipe indeed was. When he had pulled back his hand, he felt suddenly that all his hopes for a miracle had been in vain. If there had been no miracle today, how could one ever happen in the future? The tomtit had brought tidings of death to his grandfather, but it wouldn't be possible now to take the pipe from his pocket, it would have to remain there.

And Uku went and hid so that no one could find him and shed bitter tears, as if he were the most upset about his grandfather of them all. But were anyone to have asked him why he was really crying, he could hardly have said that it was because of the pipe and the stick, and that while his granddad not only had his stick, his pipe and his miraculous tomtit as well whilst he, Uku, who was still alive had neither a stick, a pipe, a tomtit, nor any miracle. His dead grandfather had something to go to the grave with, whilst Uku had nothing with which to live. Because what he did have right now neither interested him nor made him happy. He would give anything for his granddad's tomtit, that would knock at the peak of his cap in the woods and then at the window of his home.

1939

Night of Souls

Karl Ristikivi

The following is an excerpt from Karl Ristikivi's existentialist novel
Night of Souls, *first published during his Swedish exile in 1953. A
nameless young man enters something resembling a concert hall in
Stockholm a little before midnight on New Year's Eve and finds himself
in a labyrinth of salons and staircases, meeting people from whom
he feels alienated. In the last section of the novel, the protagonist is
called to bear witness, seemingly in a dream, to instances of quite
ordinary people having committed one of the Seven Deadly Sins.
This is conducted as a trial scene, similar to the one experienced by
the old man in the Ingmar Bergman film* Wild Strawberries, *which
was first screened a few years after Ristikivi's novel appeared. At
the time, Bergman was married to the exiled Estonian pianist Käbi
Laretei, so it is not inconceivable that Laretei may have conveyed
similar exile feelings to her husband, something which is also in
evidence in the particularly depressing film* Shame.*

The passages from Night of Souls *reproduced here come from the
middle section of the novel where the protagonist is seemingly in
limbo, physically and mentally, belonging nowhere, lacking friends
and acquaintances, or a roof over his head. This echoes Ristikivi's
real-life experiences when he was fleeing to Sweden via Finland
during WWII.*

AT THE BORDER

If I am now to try to give an account of the following events – if they can be termed events – then I must apologise right from the start that this cannot be a full one. Under the strain of what preceded, the sharpness of my senses had become much blunted and a certain obtuseness had overcome me, as always is the case with exhaustion. I almost have the feeling that I am writing about someone very remote from myself, someone I hardly know and whose life story I am only familiar with through third-hand accounts. Someone who has gone far away, so that I can no longer meet him to ask how it really was. And I do not wish, by way of my imagination, to add or embellish, as I have already mentioned before. That would still be a sham, even though excuses could be found to give that sham grandiose names. I have decided to stick to the truth, though it may not be the whole truth, tedious and grey – yes, even if in the next instance it can be seen as untrue. We do after all know how our senses as well as our memories can fail us.

Anyhow, I heard the door slam shut behind me, locking as it did so. I knew it was locked since I turned and tried the handle but could not open it again. I had by then already begun to vaguely suspect that it was not the right door and that it had only been left unlocked by accident.

Just then, I heard the distant ringing of bells and the thought flashed through my mind that now, out there in the city, the New Year had begun. Or at least the Old Year was coming to an end. But it was so far away that it left me quite unmoved. I had nonetheless steeled myself against that ringing, which was something I have always feared.

I even received the impression that I counted the strokes and heard that there were twelve. But carefully considered and with hindsight, I could well have been imagining this.

Even more embarrassing was the fact that I would have to give an explanation for the rooms through which I had been walking.

I had lost interest not only in what had been occurring behind my back, but also what was going on around me. This can best be compared with how a sick patient resigns himself to his condition, satisfied with the mere fact that he is not in pain.

That much had changed compared with my previous life. (Yes, I have said it now and cannot take it back, even if I wanted to do so. For I know all too well that too much has been said and can lead many in the wrong direction, searching for an explanation and or conclusion where I did not intend to explain or conclude. But be that as it may, let us term it so for simplicity's sake, knowing at the same time that one word can have very many meanings.) I had been wandering around, mostly observing and listening, taking in impressions and distilling feelings out of them. I had almost always felt a forbidden joy, a thief's joy at this, that I had simply wandered into this serendipitous situation by accident, where I was empowered to see, hear and feel. Now, all had changed, perhaps only within me, but in conjunction with that, all that surrounded me also appeared to have changed. Nothing new, however, had come to replace the joy of acceptance, and this gave me a paralysing feeling of emptiness.

I do not know precisely how I arrived at this small room, which was divided in two by a counter and above it wire mesh. Behind the counter sat an oldish man wearing some kind of dark uniform, and who had pushed his hand out through a small opening.

"Your identity papers, please!"

I had no papers of any kind on me and said so. He smiled regretfully, but also with slight distrust.

"How can that be? You must have some papers. Otherwise I cannot let you through."

"Very well, I can always go back..."

I turned round, in order to leave by the same door, but there stood a soldier who was half-barring my way with his rifle. He said nothing and I concluded from the cornflower blue roundel on his cap that we would not understand one another's language.

I went back to the counter. The official had, however, shut the window and was still sitting where he was before now sorting some pink-coloured cards, while a cardboard notice by the window said: "CLOSED".

Someone touched my shoulder. It was a middle-aged man, small in stature, wearing a worn and patched grey *Wehrmacht* uniform, who shook his head in an irritated and weary manner, saying:

"Under no circumstances can you remain here. You'll have to go on!"

I tried to explain: "I can't go anywhere, I haven't got any identity papers," even I was aware that this was a feeble and naive excuse which would have no effect. The soldier at the door looked at me with a mocking smile on his lips; he seemed used to such scenes. The official at the counter pushed the last cards into a drawer, locked it and went into a back room accompanied by the jingling of a bunch of keys.

"Could you at least give me some advice as to what I ought to do now?" I said again, addressing the man in *Wehrmacht* uniform. I believe that he even found it difficult to understand my poor German, let alone grasp my situation.

"Forbidden! Forbidden!" was all that he repeated, in the way you talk to children, idiots and foreigners, and he pointed at the sign on the wall which said simply:

VERBOTEN!
INTERDIT!
NIE WOLNO!
AIZLIEGTS!

And lower, above the spittoon:

ÄLÄ SYLJE LATTIALLE!

"Please show me, then, where I can go. Take me along – oh, never mind!" My former torpor was already beginning to retreat before my anger. It mattered little what he did, if I was not allowed to stay where

I was. That is to say, it was not entirely a matter of indifference, since in spite of myself I was glowering at the soldier at the door.

The man shrugged his shoulders. He twisted his head and looked at his uniform jacket from which all his stripes had been removed.

"I am not permitted to do anything. You must leave, or else..."

"Or else?"

"Or else you will have to solve the problem yourself," he said with resignation. He seemed to have lost hope that I would ever understand anything, and he was right in thinking so.

Then suddenly another man rushed out of the back room behind the counter, he was quite similar to the previous two – small in stature, middle-aged and with a puckered face. But he was wearing some kind of French uniform, either police or customs, and he came up to me waving his hands and giving a garbled explanation of which I understood nothing apart from the fact that he kept repeating the words: "*Interdit!*" and "*Défendu!*" When I did not react, he turned to the German and began to abuse him in fluent German. Although his words sounded anything but pleasant in tone, the German grinned on hearing his mother tongue.

"How come, you speak such good German?"

"I'm from the Alsace," said the Frenchman. "I am, at any rate, a loyal citizen. Nothing can ever happen to me."

The German looked sadly at his own uniform, again with such a strange movement of the head that it looked like a cat licking the fur on its chest. But then he gave a wry and ambiguous smile.

"Nor me. I only follow orders. But what are we going to do with this man?" What he said was the usual reply, but not without a slight tinge of humanity.

The Frenchman shrugged his shoulders and spat on the floor. He could afford to do that, since no one could expect him to understand the sign which was written in Finnish.

Suddenly the phone rang twice, long and shrill, this was clearly a long-distance call. The first official came half-running out of the back room and snatched up the receiver. I could not hear what he said, but it could not have been much. Then he opened the window and pushed out his hand.

"One hundred and three!" he yelled. "One hundred and three!"

There was no one else in the room apart from myself whom he could have been referring to, so I went up to the window. The official handed me a cardboard number token and nodded to his left.

"Go and wait in the waiting room until your number comes up!"

The German had already gone to unlock the door, reluctance written all over his face. Then he positioned himself in front of the door like a guard and stretched out his hand.

"*Ausweis!*"

Was this whole business going to start all over again? I had no identity papers and had said so on several previous occasions. Then I remembered that I had an old identity card in my pocket, dating from the time of the Occupation, and half-defiantly I pulled the worn scrap of card out of my pocket.

The German looked at it and shook his head.

"*Ach du liebes Kind!*" He handed it back to me, still shaking his head.

"But you issued it yourselves," I explained defiantly.

"That doesn't mean a thing now. It's out of date."

"But it does show my number – you just saw yourself how I got it."

He sighed resignedly and moved aside slightly. I could wait no longer, it was now clear that I would never receive permission. So I pushed my way past him, and stepped into the waiting room. It was clear that this would offer no solution to the problem, nor was it sure if this was a step forward.

But that was of no importance in the present situation.

IN THE WAITING ROOM

I should have been able to guess this earlier. How would I have been able to avoid waiting, that night? On looking back – and looking forward is something I dare not really do – the waiting was like some kind of interplanetary space.

For that reason, I haven't remembered anything more of the waiting room than the fact that it was, as expected, large, grey and depressing. Space and time were here in some sort of harmony regarding their dimension, one accentuating the length of the other. There have been so many such rooms and in the end they all resemble one another.

Although the room was a large one, there was nevertheless nowhere for me to sit down. It was so ingeniously filled by other people waiting that I was unable to find anywhere to sit without disturbing someone. And that I did not wish to do, did not perhaps even dare, for that matter. These people bore no sign of the well-disposed nature, or at least polite indifference, which I had encountered earlier in the building. They looked at me in a hostile manner, though I could in no way have been abrogating their rights, since we all had a queue number.

In the best seat at the corner table sat an older gentleman who was engrossed in his copy of *Svenska Dagbladet*. He had sat down in such a way as to block access to all the empty chairs in the corner, and I felt that he would on no account move up sufficiently to let anyone through. This he would not do since he could not tolerate the proximity of other people, any nearer than five paces away. This much I had managed to learn about him, at least on previous occasions. For him to be sitting and waiting here so patiently was by no means a mistake, since he was a most upright and dutiful person who never demanded any privileges for himself, and would not let the scales of justice be tipped in one or other direction. Next to his chair lay his walking stick with which he carved out a passage for himself when walking along the street, and he had placed his hat on the pile of magazines on the table so that no one would come and read one, although it was unlikely that anyone would take an interest in such typical waiting-room reading material.

The long wooden bench along the opposite wall had been occupied by a stout older lady who had spread out her bags and packages all over it. Her distrustful eyes watched everything as if under fire and sitting there in the middle of the bench as she was, she managed to puff herself out like a hen trying to protect all her dear ones under her wings. In so doing, her eyes had begun to squint somewhat in an attempt to keep as large an area under fire as possible. I do not, of course, know how long she had been waiting here, but she had clearly also been waiting everywhere else and was trying somehow to make up for lost time. She was now knitting feverishly, since this was something she could do without looking, as habitual work does not need to be checked by looking. She was terribly busy and no doubt a good mother, as demanding of herself as she was of others.

From time to time she threw scornful glances at her immediate neighbours, who had made themselves at home after a fashion. These were a young couple, a boy and girl – they could not yet have been married, since they were too young. They were clearly not used to having to wait, but had made an attempt to put up with the situation, by being oblivious to it. They had taken two extra chairs to rest their feet on, and they were so engrossed in one another that they hardly noticed what was going on around them. At any rate they did not notice that they had in effect occupied more than four chairs, since it would have been rather indecorous to try either to get past them or sit in their immediate vicinity – like forcing one's way into somebody else's bedroom. On the other hand – why should they waste their precious youth waiting, especially since they no doubt loved one another.

But not only the older lady threw them reproachful glances, but also a lady a good deal younger who was sitting against the wall straight opposite them. Next to her there was a vacant seat and I considered this to be the only one to make for so I initially made an attempt to reach it. But she turned her head abruptly in my direction, and, the reproachful look still on her face, she raised her hand as if in defence.

"This chair is reserved," she said. "I'm waiting for a friend."

It is possible that she had become embittered by the long period of waiting, but I still suspected that she was not waiting for anyone, nor had anyone to wait for. I have already mentioned the fact that she was young, in her twenties, and by no means ugly, if only she had not have been so embittered. She not only looked spitefully in the direction of the young lovers, but I soon noticed that she looked in the same manner at everyone else waiting here.

Among these was first and foremost a family of four who were first in the queue, and were the noisiest of this otherwise silent group of people. This is not to say that they spoke a lot, or at length, but they ate. They were eating the whole time with the gusto some people do when on a journey. It has to be said that they were the jolliest of everyone here, probably on account of the fact that the father of the family took a hip flask out of his pocket now and then and raised it to his lips. He offered it to his better half, but when she stretched out her hand he pulled back the bottle with a laugh. His wife did not become annoyed at this, instead she burst into laughter, it was only a joke. Otherwise, they had made life comfortable for themselves – the wife had taken off her shoes, while the husband had hung his jacket over the back of an adjacent chair and was sitting in his shirt-sleeves. There was only one interruption to their eating – this came when their smaller child, a chubby little girl of around two, suddenly felt the opposite urge and pulled an enamelled potty from her mother's suitcase. Everything occurred as naturally and quietly as if they had been at home.

Another person who felt himself at home here was a man on the other bench who slept all the time. I could not really decide whether he was young or old, for he was sleeping, his back turned to the outside world and his coat pulled up over his head. It could only be seen indirectly that he was quite tall. And it hardly made any difference whether he was young or old – when sleeping, a person can be of any age, normal time means nothing to them. This is one of the most pleasant ways of spending one's time in the waiting room, provided, of course, that you are not going through the same tedium in your dreams.

"You can't half sleep, you sodding louse!" I then heard somebody say. The deep, slightly hoarse voice seemed familiar. Next to me stood a middle-aged, stoutish man with a red face and thinning hair. It was an ordinary man in work clothes, I thought I detected a faint whiff of alcohol, although he was a good five metres away. I looked hastily away, since I feared that he would spot me and that a quarrel would ensue. I had met him several times on the street, in the tram and in cheap canteens, and on each occasion he would pick me out to vent his anger on.

He was the only person not sitting down. He kept moving around, approaching someone, then someone else, never coming too close, instead scowling at them in a hostile manner, when he came within a few paces. For the most he said nothing, only muttered something indistinctly. His vocabulary appeared to be very limited, two-thirds of it consisting of clichéed swearing. For this reason I could never understand why he was angry. Perhaps he had been subjected to some indignity, but he never spoke about it and it was not impossible that he had forgotten it. The source of this seemed not even to be such a common human feeling as envy, assuming he was not simply envious of people only because they existed. It did indeed seem as if other people restricted his freedom, he walked among them like a lion in a cage and felt himself driven into a corner. And not only by living beings – it seemed that even inert objects got in his way – he kicked at every chair and brandished his fist at the wall, the door and the windows. Of course this room was depressingly ugly, but I could imagine he would also kick at flowers in a flower-bed and raise his fist to the moon and the sun. Because I do not believe that his mood was caused simply by this long and tedious period of waiting, I had met him before. (For instance one Midsummer Night in Helsinki, before the war and other unfortunate incidents, when I began to realise that it is a crime to be a foreigner.)

I do not wish any longer to stop and consider all the people waiting with me. Waiting is, in itself, hard enough. In this, at least the behaviour of the last man was justified as he obviously felt like a prisoner. Prison is usually intended as a punishment. But innocent or not, we all have to sit and wait at some time or other in our lives. We are bound by time and space, and are more or less cut off from, or kept from, all the normal processes of life. Someone waiting has as little freedom as someone in prison.

It is easiest of all to wait when it is only a question of time and we know what will happen and when it will happen. In such a prison we have more or less retained the freedom to do as we please. We can pick up a book or a newspaper and read it. Or, if there is nothing to read, then the majority of us can go up to the newspaper kiosk and buy something. We know when the train will leave, and can therefore divide up our time of waiting and make use of it within the limits provided.

What is more difficult is if we do not know if the train will arrive in five minutes' or five hours' time. Or not at all. In this case, we have arrived at a type of waiting where it is a question of yes or no, of right or left. The letters on the page begin to dance and the food goes round and round in your mouth. Then you lose the strength in your hands as if they have been gripped in invisible handcuffs. The death cell is then but one step away.

People have written books about prison, but never about a waiting room. I am therefore inclined to believe that being in prison is easier. Writing a whole book about a waiting room would prove too hard, just as hard as reading one there. For this reason I will shorten my own period of waiting and allow the sister of mercy to arrive, who holds in her hand a list and is running her eyes down the row of names with the attention for detail of a proof reader.

"Is there anyone here who has not yet been to see the doctor?"

I should have been able to anticipate this. Always, sooner or later, you have to go and see the doctor. The doctor decides whether you are admitted and if you are let out. And a doctor is only human and finds it difficult to decide, so he mostly decides the opposite, just to be on the safe side. If he is not so human as to err in his judgement.

AT THE DOCTOR'S

All hospital nurses somehow seem to move at a marching pace, the corridors of a hospital have stone floors and their shoes never have rubber heels. Their dry and rapid steps differ both in weight and tempo from those of soldiers and are even more impersonal, the skeletons of footsteps.

The glass door opposite was opened. A stocky middle-aged man stood there in his white smock and was beckoning impatiently.

"If the doctor is in a hurry, then his assistant could always conduct the examination," said the sister.

"No, that won't do. This matter is far too important. And the armed forces are very demanding, a number of cases of cheating have come to light recently. At any rate, I could not take the responsibility upon myself, if I were not present."

The nurse stood aside and allowed me to enter.

"Ahaa," said the doctor. "We have an old friend here. Well, how are things?"

Do not get the impression that this was a friendly question. I had seen this doctor on numerous occasions so it was not surprising he recognised me. His appearance had not changed significantly since I saw him for the first time at primary school. I will have changed as little in his eyes. He had a smooth, pink face, a shiny bald pate of the same hue, steel-framed spectacles and a warty nose. He walked ponderously, his head pushed forward, and one received the impression that he could not see anything at all. He is the first person I have ever seen who was always wearing spectacles, and for that reason I long held the belief that spectacles tended to ruin a person's eyesight. (My grandmother also saw badly when she put on her glasses, she always had to look over them to see who was going past on their way to church.)

When I had taken off my jacket and shirt, he let me sit down. He too sat down and began sorting slips of paper like a professor preparing to put his questions to a candidate at an oral exam. The room was small, hygienically comfortable and smelt of *eau de Cologne* and ether. It was more like an average study than a surgery. There were even paintings on the wall, run of the mill modern landscapes, neutral decoration which you would hardly even notice if you did not happen to be forced to look at them.

"You visited a sick young man," he then said unexpectedly. "You didn't have my permission to visit him."

"No – I wasn't aware that I needed anybody's permission to do so. And he was at home, not in hospital."

"He was, but you weren't..." he said somewhat ironically. "But leave it, what's happened has happened and there's nothing we can do about it."

"I would like to ask how he is. Is there any hope for him?"

He shook his head slowly and looked at one of the pictures on the wall.

"Or do you fear he will get worse?"

"I wouldn't like to say anything one way or the other," said the doctor. "It wasn't a good thing that you saw him. Now you are thinking about the matter all the time, and that isn't necessary. It only makes my job harder. For that reason I don't want people seeing or knowing anything. It makes everything more complicated. For that reason I have always envied vets."

He rose and came up to me. He began listening to my heart and lungs with a stethoscope in the usual way. He turned my eyelids inside out and had me open my mouth.

"Well, and how are we keeping ourselves?" he then asked.

"I don't have any special problems. The usual emigré illness, as they say."

"Come, come, now you are going too far. I was asking about your symptoms, not the diagnosis. We doctors make the diagnoses, that's our task. Yours is simply to tell us how an illness manifests itself."

I had no idea what he was driving at, and whether his aim was to declare me fit or unwell. I did not even know which of the two would be in my best interests right now. I have learnt as much over the years so that I realise that it always turns out the opposite to what you had expected – if I need a clean bill of health, then I'm declared quite ill, if not an invalid, whilst if I feel ill and want help then they can never find anything wrong with me.

Just in case, I complained of the usual ailments – sleeplessness, headaches, digestive disturbances... He listened to me in silence, his head cocked slightly to one side, his hand playing with his stethoscope. I could see that he was hardly listening, that he was thinking about something else entirely, which he was then going to ask or reply.

"Yes, yes, yes..." he then said when I had finished. "That's as maybe. But don't you have anything more personal, for example..."

"Is the doctor thinking of dreams?"

"No, no, not dreams! When it boils down to it, you can't do anything about those. Everyone dreams the most worthless dreams, at least they say they do. And it's always the same – they see themselves back in their native land and are trying to escape from it, all over again. Such dreams mean nothing at all. They're like popular songs which everyone goes around whistling, even the least musical ones among us... Don't you ever see anything else, anything at all?"

"I do, actually. Very often too. I see dead people."

"Dead people? What do you mean? Corpses?"

"No, the living dead. I'm thinking of people who are dead or are most probably dead, I mean to say, have disappeared without a trace. I then see them alive and I am surprised and glad. It was therefore only a dream that they had died or disappeared."

"But that's the same old story. Those dead people are only a symbol for your native land."

"Couldn't the opposite hold true?"

"How could you think like that. You clearly just want to contradict me. Everything can be stood on its head, but that doesn't tell us what this upside-down thing may mean."

"I think that my native land could well be symbolic for a dead or vanished person. Someone whose return would cause us unpleasant problems. Hence wanting to flee again."

"Ahaa, that's not such a foolish thought. Suppressed wishes – that's not entirely impossible..."

He went back behind his desk thoughtfully shaking his head and sat down. For a moment I remained undisturbed with my own dreams.

I have never fled from that shore in a small fishing vessel. I do not believe that it would have been possible to do so. But in my dreams I have done so on a number of occasions, everything always occurs in exactly the same way as in previous dreams. It is a dark sombre evening, so silent that you have to row extremely carefully. But the oarsmen are so practised, they have been rowing across this stretch of sea for decades and know it as well as their own shingle-strewn strips of field. They have died long ago. They, who are alive, although unaware of it, have been abandoned on the shore. The water is a deep green as it was on the very first day which I can ever remember, very long ago.

I have never departed that way. But I can see the shore from that direction, bare, deserted, dead. Only in very early children's memories was it green, later it was perhaps a figment of the imagination. In actuality it has always been old, faded and dried out. Not only the grass, but also the hardy juniper bushes have finally withered to yellow. Grey limestone which looks as if it is growing upwards, poking up through the thin turf like the spine of some starved creature, like rafters of a deserted house poking through the roof. The biting sea air gusts away across the increasingly barren flatlands, taking with it the last grains of earth from between the stones.

An empty, dead shore. It is hard to believe that it could ever be brought back to life. It is hard to believe that reality could ever efface this dream. Even the sea retreats here, the muddy seabed dries up and cracks, it hurts to walk here barefoot. Where would I have got hold of such heavy, iron-studded boots, with which I could step again onto this shore? And would I have the heart to walk with iron-studded boots along a shore which has been my mother, though she is now dead?

The doctor was sitting writing something in a book with black covers. "Dead..." he said. "And what happens then? How do your dreams end?"

"They always disappear off somewhere, go away. And then I grow afraid that what is only a dream in a dream will become reality. I do not want them to leave, but I cannot do anything about it. They of course grow somewhat hazy and distant, I see them from far away. They are sad, as people leaving always are..."

"Not everyone leaving is sad, some are in fact extremely happy. Isn't it more that you always wish them to be sad?"

"Maybe..."

"I do not know what I should think about your dreams... Don't you ever dream anything else, something more normal?"

Dreams about the lift could not come into question, my friend Stanley had already used that subject. But trains and buses would perhaps do.

"Ahaa! And of course you always get there late..."

"Not always. Sometimes I have to wait, even a good while. It is worse when I get on the wrong train, or miss the stop where I have to change trains."

The doctor snapped the book shut and flung the pencil onto the table.

"I really do not know what I should do with you. I don't like your dreams. You simply should never go to sleep. You should spend more time outdoors, in the fresh air. I believe it would be best if I were to prescribe some forest work for you. At any rate, your present state of health precludes me from recommending you to be accepted."

He rose and went to the door, then turned suddenly and came back.

"I will, nonetheless, give you the opportunity, but only at your own risk. This is happening from purely scientific considerations in order to see how it turns out. I'll prescribe you a pair of spectacles, such strong ones that you'll be able to see normally with them. But be careful with them, they'll easily ruin your eyes completely. And as I said, I will not take any responsibility. Do you agree to this solution?"

"I agree, doctor," I said meekly, but happily.

"Then come this way!" he said and led me into a dark ante-chamber where the only thing lit up was a screen with letters and numbers. It was impossible to read what was written there with the naked eye and my first test pair of spectacles did not improve matters much. But as time went on, I began to see a little more clearly, I even began to comprehend the connection and meaning of what had at first been meaningless groups of letters and numbers.

"You do, of course, know that you should not commit to memory what you read here, let alone tell anyone about it," said the doctor. "It is a military secret."

This was the first time that I heard that this examination had anything to do with the army. It pleased me no end, but at the same time I felt a great fear that I would not pass the test. And yet the doctor's warning had exactly the opposite effect – I now tried to remember the number I read. I succeeded in this at first and later had the opportunity of looking it up in the phone book. But whether the number was so secret as to be ex-directory, or whether it was all a trick and mockery, I do not know, since I never did find it. And by now I have, of course, managed to forget it ages ago.

It has often occurred that I have been tricked in this way, or have managed to fool myself. Something I am told is very important or which I feel myself to be so, proves later to be quite irrelevant and unimportant. And at the same time I allow more significant matters to slip my attention. I have now given up entirely trying to grasp what is of significance and for that reason I am knowingly defenceless to any accusation of only describing unimportant matters.

When I had put on my clothes once more, I was led out into a new waiting room, where I had to wait until some tests had been made, as was explained to me. It was here that I noticed for the first time that under the white smock of the medical orderly, the green of military-uniform trousers could be seen. He passed me, some test tubes in his hand, and gave me a surprised and, to an extent, sympathetic glance.

"Stupid man!" he said. "He had the opportunity to go free and did not want to take it. I really can't understand him."

The young man in the grey hospital dressing gown who had been sitting in front of me, looked at me with a much more astonished and quite disparaging stare.

"He must be out of his mind! It's never happened before. Everyone wants to be free, don't they?"

"From what?" I asked, but they presumably considered my question so stupid, that it did not require an answer.

"How could it be possible that he was given a choice?" asked the young man in the dressing gown. "Such things happen once in a hundred years."

"Then you've still got a century to go," laughed the orderly.

"Oh, I've nothing to worry about. I'm an old hand at the game, they won't catch me. I know all the countermoves, I have treated the matter with scientific thoroughness. Once I'm out of here, I'll write a book about it. And I'm telling you, the book'll be a bestseller."

"Is it a question of honour to be declared unfit?" I asked with a slight schoolmasterly emphasis.

"It's the stupidest kind of pride," my companion said. "What kind of honour would it be for me to play the corporal in the village?"

"At any rate, I have nothing whatsoever to lose," I said, trying to excuse myself. "I have nothing to do out there, I haven't even got a home to go to."

"You always find somewhere. Me – if I could only go, I'd even go barefoot, in the middle of the night... But you clearly don't know what to expect, you are new here, after all. You don't happen to have been along to the recruitment commission?"

"No. Not that I remember, at least."

"Of course, volunteers have to go to see the doctor first..."

Since he had been here no longer than me and yet was more knowledgeable, I tried to probe into what was going on, as I myself was completely in the dark. But as soon as I started posing questions, he clammed up.

"Don't ask me, I don't know anything, and I don't want to know anything. None of it's any of my business. I just want to get out of here and go back. It doesn't matter to me whether what's happening is stupid or sensible, pointless or extremely meaningful."

He had walked over to the window and pulled back the curtain. To my surprise I saw that there were bars across the windows, and I began to better understand my companion's longing for freedom. But I also began to understand the irony of those bars with regard to my own situation – a strange way of thinking, preventing people from escaping whom they nonetheless intended expelling. It was as always; you can come in freely, but are no longer at liberty to leave.

Then suddenly the door opened abruptly and a short man with a sour face entered the room.

"What's that man doing here?" he asked pointing in my direction. "That man must go before the commission without delay!"

"Who? Him?" asked my companion with surprise. "And still nothing for me?"

"You could be waiting a long time!" said the sour-faced man. "You can't just go around letting such men go just like that!"

BEFORE THE COURT

They were standing in the middle of the room arguing, two policemen and three soldiers. The soldiers were wearing Air Force uniforms which meant that at first I could not tell the difference between them, since the colour of the uniforms was roughly the same. But their views were quite different.

"He's not yet a soldier," said the older police officer.

"He becomes a soldier as soon as he signs up."

"But he hasn't yet been accepted. And as long as he hasn't been accepted, he remains under the jurisdiction of the civil courts."

The younger policeman added: "He comes under the civil courts, in any case, if it is a question of an offence committed before he starts his military service."

"What sort of offence? What's he accused of?"

"It's not for the police to give an opinion on that. We simply deliver the summons."

"A summons is not the same as an arrest warrant..."

"Who's said it was? No one has said anything about arrest."

"Then he has the freedom to choose whether he wants to appear before the court or not."

"A court appearance is compulsory. And besides, he hasn't yet been accepted, nor will he ever be accepted, for that matter. As far as I remember, he would have to produce a certificate of good behaviour for that to happen."

"You talk as if he has already been found guilty."

"In our eyes, every suspect is guilty."

"At any rate, there's always the Foreign Legion," said the soldier who had remained silent up to now. He was a tall young man with a shock of fluffy blond hair, a broad face and the smile of a country lad.

"Ask him if he'd go along with joining the Foreign Legion," said the police officer sarcastically.

"Of course, and here he comes," came the familiar music-hall cue. "Let's ask the man himself."

The three soldiers approached me and we shook hands in a friendly manner. When the blond soldier uttered his name – Christer – I must have looked a little taken aback, since he burst out laughing.

"Listen, I'm no ghost. I've never been dead. I just happen to have the same name."

"It's just that I don't know how you could already know me," I said, trying to find a polite excuse for my consternation. "I

115

have never had anything to do with the Air Force."

"Nor me," said the second young soldier with ginger hair and the eyes of an inveterate crook. "But it's not for that reason. The reason is simply that the uniform is nearer to civilian dress and therefore easier for a newcomer to wear. Though I feel it's a pity I don't have a tie, and it'll take time before I get the right back to wear one. But it doesn't matter – at first there's always something to regret. Christer says so too and he is almost a veteran by now, at least compared with me."

The third young man was a good deal more reserved, but this could have been in contrast to the unexpected familiarity of his companions. In fact, it was just him who had defended me *vis-à-vis* the police most resolutely and skilfully.

"I'm sorry that I couldn't manage to do a better job of defending you," he said. "Unfortunately our powers have their strict limitations."

"Does that mean that I must nonetheless be handed over to the police authorities?" I asked, affected by his dry, formal way of speaking.

"That was just a misunderstanding," said Christer, trying to set my mind at rest.

"Maybe, but experience has shown that it's hardest to solve problems which are only caused by misunderstandings."

"I can tell you this much, that it is a civil court, and at least that's better than a court martial," said the third soldier.

"But what am I being charged with? I don't even know..." I did not finish the sentence. My conscience was far from being technically clear. I had entered the building, not in the manner of a criminal or with any intention of deceiving anybody, nonetheless in a kind of unlawful manner, although I did not know precisely what my infringement of the rules consisted of. And this recruitment business also sounded somewhat dubious. I had not consciously expressed any wish, nor had anyone recruited me. I had simply used the misunderstanding that had arisen, and that could in itself be a criminal act. I did not really have any right to appeal to anyone's defence counsel or for assistance. Even if only metaphorically speaking, I was here under false pretences. It was not inconceivable that all these kind and friendly people were taking me for someone else, and their attitude would change abruptly if they were to find out who I really was.

But I did not bid them farewell, and this at least gave me slight hope as I left with these policemen.

We walked along the corridor again, up or down the stairs, I cannot now remember which. I had wandered around here so much by now that my head was beginning to spin. I cannot describe the route we took, nor is it very important to do so, at least for now. All I remember was trying not to keep in step with the police officers as if this would in some way betray me. (I have heard or read somewhere about a deserter who worried about the same problem.)

The courtroom was situated on the third or fourth floor, where exactly it is hard to say since, as I have pointed out earlier, I had lost my bearings. The room was large but had a low ceiling, was quite shabby and dirty, something I had not at all expected in this building where almost everything bore witness to traditional opulence. The dirty plaster of the walls was cracked and had fallen away in places. The once white ceiling had turned unevenly black with smoke, presumably from the oil lamps once hanging there. The only light now came from naked electric light-bulbs which were in the larger half of the room, intended for the general public. At the front of the courtroom, above the dais, the light was nevertheless somehow softened. The worn floorboards, once yellow in colour, could very well have done with some scrubbing, though they would hardly become any cleaner for it. I had never seen such a floor in this country, nor such seats – which are called Viennese chairs, I think – which had been laid out in rows. Every place had been filled by members of the public, whose impatience was evident from the incessant creaking of chairs. And the people were different to those I had encountered so far that evening, save my companions in the waiting room. They too were somehow poor and worn in appearance and judging by the stubble on the men's chins they too had not been able to nip off home for, if not ten years, then at least ten days.

To my surprise, I was not led to one of the chairs intended for the accused, but a place had been reserved for me on the front row of the public gallery. In my initial relief, I did not observe the fact that I had been seated between two fat old ladies with garlic on their breath, who were seemingly old friends, since they managed to talk the whole time, though I did not pick up any of the meaning of the words which flew past me.

I have never been in a courtroom before, so I cannot say to what extent this room resembled a real one in the way it was set out. I fear that experts will find much here which does not fit, so I will not make any attempt at describing details in a realistic manner. It reminded me more of a university lecture theatre with its somewhat raised podium and blackboard covering the whole wall behind it. Very likely that the room was usually used for some quite different purpose and was only being temporarily used as a courtroom.

The raised portion was nonetheless bordered by a red carpet as with the altar of a church and looked worn, giving the rather strange impression that people had knelt there. The judge's table was, however, covered in an appropriately green tablecloth and was entirely empty, if we disregard the judge's crossed hands which were resting upon it. The judge himself was an old man with white hair and a weathered pink complexion and who seemed to be asleep. To his left at a small table sat a bespectacled young man with a long pale face, who seemed snowed under with papers which he was, with irritated zeal, trying to put in some kind of order. A thin girl with a swarthy complexion and wearing a grey shift was constantly looking for new documents in cupboards and carrying them to the clerk's table. To the right the prosecutor and the counsel for the defence were seated conveniently at the same table and were chatting amicably. I could not work out who was the counsel for the defence, or who was the prosecutor.

Further to the right of this table was a part of the room which had been cordoned off and here sat twelve people: the members of the jury as I know from reading crime novels. I had caught glimpses of all these people throughout the evening, but I was not closely acquainted with any of them.

I did not have any further time to devote to studying the gentlemen of the jury – this term is, in fact, a misnomer since almost half of them were women. Now the judge appeared suddenly to wake up, he opened his eyes, though he hardly saw anyone, certainly not me. For that reason I received the mistaken impression that my case had not yet begun.

"Bring in the first witness!" he said. His voice was unexpectedly soft and well-modulated.

1953

Eight Japanese Ladies

Arvo Valton

The young Japanese ladies were enchanting in their brightly coloured kimonos, with their childlike faces and modest behaviour. On seeing them, Georg came to a halt. He looked at them all together and felt that something was happening inside him.

When he had recovered a little, he bowed to them stiffly. He had to show them around, so he pointed in the direction of the gate of the industrial plant.

The watchman at the gate, who never called anyone "sir", asked:

"Where are you taking those butterflies?"

Georg had not yet recovered his power of speech and did not reply to the old man. He let the Japanese ladies through the turnstile. This was something incomparable – those pure colours and lithe movements, against the backdrop of the grey, smoky industrial plant. The Japanese ladies, with their large bows on their backs really did resemble butterflies. Though maybe even Japanese angels would have wings there instead of waistbands, thought Georg.

They walked across the muddy yard of the plant. Georg carefully picked out a route that was higher and drier. In front of the acid works there was a large slushy puddle that you simply couldn't avoid. The workers in their rubber boots walked straight through the slush with no problem at all. Georg indicated that the Japanese ladies should stop, rushed towards the ore storage area, pulled a plank from in front of the acid works and made a gangplank. The Japanese ladies smiled at him. Georg crossed the gangplank first. In the middle it bent slightly; the muddy water washed over his feet. The charming Japanese ladies in their ankle-length kimonos followed Georg, one by one. They were brave, those eight dancers.

First of all, Georg led them into the acid works. All according to plan. During the tour he would have to follow the route of the production process exactly. He pointed to the reactors, the pipes, the cooling aggregate and the large deposit cistern. Disgusting acid fumes seeped through the inadequate insulation. These irritated their noses and eyes. How badly these yellow fumes would affect the beautiful childlike eyes and delicate complexions of the maidens! Georg would rather have taken them swiftly past all of this, but he was not allowed to. He had to show them everything. Those were his orders.

That morning, the managing director had asked him to come to his office. Georg had gone to see him with slight trepidation, as a call from the boss boded ill for everyone. Not always, but most of the time. The boss had told him that a Japanese girls' dance ensemble would soon be visiting the plant and that Georg would have to show them everything. This was part of the cultural entertainment that the town council had arranged for them. And no one at the plant could speak Japanese, but as Georg had some grasp of Spanish, he'd been chosen. Because, although a knowledge of Spanish would not be of the slightest use to the Japanese girls, it would none the less be better for Georg to give the guided tour, rather than some other individual that didn't even know Spanish.

The managing director had taken the town council's directives concerning the guided tour of the chemical plant very seriously. At all costs, he ordered Georg to be very thorough, and told him that the progress of the guided tour would be checked at several stages along the route.

As they at last left the acid works and were walking along a sloping gallery in the direction of the ore foundry, they indeed ran into the managing director. He scowled at the Japanese ladies as if they were exhibits and said to Georg with grim gravity:

"We have to show them what this plant can do."

At that point, Georg felt a measure of relief. They would not be worried about being checked for a little while now. The Japanese ladies were also feeling better now they were in the fresh air. They were joking in Japanese and laughing, though Georg couldn't of course understand a word of what they were saying. He looked eagerly at these beautiful beings and felt quite clearly that he had fallen in love with them. With all eight of them, as to Georg they were all one face, one entity. It was impossible to tell which of them was the most beautiful, as all of them were. And modest, noble and loveable.

He had heard a few things about Japanese ladies before, but had never imagined, that they would be so gentle, would have such pure complexions, such beautiful eyes and perfect movements. He had heard that Europeans were eager to find wives from Japan and that there were special prohibitions against taking Japanese wives to foreign countries. Now he could understand why. He himself would gladly take a few: all eight, if possible. And Georg stood there daydreaming for a moment. How the Japanese women would learn the local language and have pretty children, his wives would be eternally faithful to him and his friends would be envious of him. Georg's patriotism would be consoled by the hope that the Japanese ladies would soon become part of the community, and the blood that they gave to his children would not be that of an enemy.

However, the reality of the chemical plant brought Georg swiftly and painfully down to earth amongst the acid fumes and dust that could cause silicosis. He felt he had no moral right to fall in love with the Japanese ladies. If only, in secret...

Georg escorted the young ladies down a wobbly staircase to the iron ore depot, where dumper trucks growled and where the steady movement of an excavator sunk its heavy claws into ore that was wet and dank, lifted its load above the tipper then opening its jaws so that stones and dust fell with a rumble onto a grate and a man with a sledgehammer would smash lumps of rock that were too large to pass through. The Japanese ladies said something among themselves and pointed with their fingers. They seemed somehow impressed by the excavator. Or was it the athletic figure of the ore crusher, whose naked upper body was dripping with sweat.

Georg decided they had seen enough of the ore, and took the young ladies down another flight of stairs, where the ore storage area opened up to a bucket conveyor. Then they climbed up to a higher story, where the conveyor took the ore up in order to send it sorted by size along short conveyor belts into several storage basins, after which they had to descend once again, into a hot dusty area filled with huge, elongated drying drums.

In the drying area Georg showed the Japanese ladies the furnace, into which the searing flame from the pulveriser shot, he pointed at the movement of the ore. He couldn't explain a thing to them, but he had to show them.

When they again climbed some stairs near the end of the row of drums with the dried ore, they saw the chief engineer. He was sitting on the stairs, wearing heavy-duty overalls. As the panting Japanese ladies passed, he glowered at them.

On the next level Georg took a short break. There were still five high stairways ahead of them. Georg looked at the weary Japanese ladies with love in his eyes. He wanted to convey his feelings to them. But he had no idea how to do so. He looked at them meaningfully – all at the same time – but felt that this was not enough to convey his feelings.

The young ladies had no doubt managed to pick up something from his gaze, they smiled and made an onwards and downwards motion with their hands. Clearly, they wanted to escape from here. But Georg shook his head sadly and pointed to the stairs leading upwards. Now it was the turn of the Japanese ladies to shake their heads, but Georg was unable to abandon the production process halfway. He didn't know when or where he was being checked. This was not important for him now, it was imperative, as self-evident as life itself. All that was important now was Georg's feelings, and he wanted to show them. He gently touched the hands of the Japanese ladies, and this made his head spin. This touch was something special, but according to the rules of physics, nothing unusual was taking place. Yet Georg now felt how imperfect the laws of physics were for the explanation of things in this world.

123

The Japanese ladies interpreted this Occidental touch in their own way. Presumably they decided that this represented a plea for them to ascend the stairs, and they did what the nice young man wanted. The group moved up the stairs passing by the ore elevator. At the top, the machinery separated the dry ore, which had been ground into smaller pieces into the various filter basins. They then went down once more. There was such a dreadful amount of dust in the filter areas, that you could not see anyone standing more than three paces away. Georg was worrying about the obedient Japanese ladies' kimonos. He led the dusty Japanese ladies onwards along the length of the row of cyclones, past the pneumatic pipes. Then they descended again and walked along past the waste basins, where an old woman in a padded jacket let the sand run into the tippers. Then the tedious walk continued along the row of concentrators, up to the hideously noisy grinding mills, where the enriched ore was ground down into very fine particles.

At one corner of the grinding mill area there was a room for the workers, where they could take a rest from the din, although they could not stay there for long, as there was always something going wrong with the mills. Georg looked at the control room and saw a patch that had been cleared in the dusty window glass. When the dismayed Japanese ladies, their hand pressed to their ears, had passed it, the door opened a fraction and someone shouted into Georg's ear:

"They've got to understand that our plant is one of the most powerful in the whole world!"

On account of the din, Georg didn't understand what was wanted of him. He followed the young ladies into a side room, where it was relatively quiet. This room had several doors and the girls pointed questioningly in their direction. They seemed to suggest an exit. But they led to a labyrinth, and with the best will in the world, Georg did not really know whether it was quickest to cross the yard towards the exit, because the row of machines was by no means at an end.

Naturally, Georg felt sorry for the young ladies. They were, after all, dancers and wouldn't grasp the significance of even half of the machinery here in the chemical plant. But they had to be shown everything, those had been his orders, and besides, Georg was very keen to be in their presence as long as possible. He hoped that he would have the opportunity of declaring his feelings for them.

The Japanese ladies followed Georg gladly into the next number of halls as they were hoping that these would now lead to the open air. In one hall, where there was not a soul to be seen and you could hardly breathe, Georg wanted to tell them what he felt. He stopped them and said:

"I love you all."

Hoping that they had perhaps heard the more common version, he now said:

"I love you."

The Japanese ladies, who were dishevelled and tired, looked at him with dull eyes. No, they clearly didn't understand what he meant. Georg dredged up phrases from school and released them all in one great gush:

"*Yo-te-quiero-ich-liebe-dich-i-love-you-j'aime-toi-ya-ljublu-tebya-kocham-cię.*"

Then, his invincible tirade over, he looked at them all. They stared at him with astonishment. They did not understood why this previously silent and gesticulating young man was suddenly releasing this flood of words over them. Georg, however, felt sorry that he had never had the opportunity to learn these words of wisdom in the Japanese language.

Somehow he had to make himself understood. Georg wanted to try something, but suddenly in the next hall a worker came in, so he waved them on to the next. What he didn't need was for someone to see him expressing his feelings for the foreign ladies.

Georg took the Japanese ladies to the next stairwell and started climbing. The ladies, however, stayed put and did not follow him. When he looked towards them, they pointed with their fingers and shook their heads. They obviously did not want to climb the stairs. But this was no longer of any importance for Georg. He saw that there was no one else by the stairs. This would perhaps be the last opportunity he would have to give an indication of his feelings. He dropped on one knee before the young ladies and put his hand on his heart.

The young ladies looked at him quizzically and said something among themselves in Japanese. They sighed and began submissively to climb the stairs. No doubt they thought Georg was pleading with them to follow him. Maybe they even thought that Georg would get into trouble if he led them out of this tiresome industrial plant.

They tripped down a long gallery, where a conveyor belt was taking the pulverised concentrate into the main basin. And so followed chemical reactors, mixers, cyclones, settling tanks, conveyor belts, elevators, basins and worst of all more stairs. All the way to the very end, the warehouse where the end product was stored.

The Japanese ladies were unhappy, covered in scratches, and the next day they had a performance. They were constantly hoping that the very next door would lead out into the fresh air. But Georg himself was not aware of his own tiredness; his bubbling feelings were keeping him alert. And yet he still had not had another opportunity to express them as there were people looking on everywhere they went.

In the end, it was all over. Georg did not even make an attempt to take them through into the administrative department. Once out in the open air, wild horses could not drag them back inside.

It was a mournful scene as they walked across the muddy yard of the industrial plant back towards the gate. They were limping, dragging their tired little feet, no longer caring about their sandals and dusty kimonos, and were simply stepping indifferently through the mud and slush. They crossed the yard like battered butterflies. But Georg loved them for all that. And even now, he was thinking, with the end in sight, how he could pick out one woman from amongst them. In his dreams, of course, as he could not wish for anything more.

And then it happened. One of the young ladies dropped her fan in the yard. Georg bent down rapidly and picked it up. He pressed it to his breast and would not let go of it. The young lady stretched out her hand uncertainly, then looked at the rest, they gave her advice in Japanese and her hand dropped back and she bowed her head in consent: she would leave the fan with Georg as a memento.

This was his chosen one from among the eight. He looked at her for the last moment and the young lady remained in his memory forever: delicate, lithe, tired, dusty, her kimono nonetheless still bright, with beautiful eyes and a sad Oriental gaze.

As they were about to depart, the managing director turned up, elegant and important. He held out his hand to the Japanese ladies' hands, but by way of tradition, they only placed the palms of their hands together, and made a slight bow.

The managing director asked Georg:

"Well, what d'you think, did they get a good impression of our plant?"

Georg defiantly said nothing and sadly watched the departing coach.

1968

Uncle

Jaan Kross

This tale needs to briefly be set in context for the reader to appreciate it to the full. The story is semi-autobiographical. The author Jaan Kross (1920-2007) was himself a law student at the outbreak of World War Two. The narrator Peeter Mirk is Kross' alter ego, the protagonist of several stories and novels.

Subsequent to the Molotov-Ribbentrop Pact signed in August 1939 by Soviet Russia and Nazi Germany where Europe was divided by Hitler and Stalin into two spheres of influence, Soviet forces occupied Estonia in 1940, sending many Estonians to the Gulag. The German Nazis pushed out the Soviets in the summer of 1941. In 1944 the Soviets returned, this time until 1991. During the German occupation, Kross was imprisoned for several months, suspected of being an Estonian nationalist. Ironically, when the Soviets took over for the second time, they sentenced Kross to eight years in the Gulag – for Estonian nationalism – a "child's sentence" by the standards of the time.

On that occasion[1], I came across Mardimäe Manor quite by chance. Or, to cavil at the well-worn cliché – what do we mean by the word "chance"? It could also be claimed that I stumbled upon the manor along an unbroken chain of preconditions, the chain itself beginning Lord-knows-where. Nowadays, we would

---

1 In the main part of the story, in June 1940, the narrator Peeter Mirk is visiting Mardimäe Manor during the second Soviet occupation.

state in our fashionable cosmological jargon: it all began with the Big Bang itself. Then, in August 1945, there was a clear feeling that the chain led back to the spring of 1944, that is to say when the order had arrived in Tartu from a certain adviser to Herr Litzmann[2] at the General Commission in Tallinn to swiftly pack together and transport, in part to Tallinn, in part to country manor-house cellars, such-and-such valuable collections housed in the University Library. Those items most valuable from a German cultural (and, consequently, global cultural) point of view were to go to Tallinn, those of lesser importance to the stone cellars of suitable manor houses throughout the Province of Tartumaa.

The order had come to set to work the appropriate librarians, as well as assistants assigned by the Vice-Chancellor of the university. Carpenters had begun (swearing as always) knocking together crates, heads of department (anxious as always) bustling about and directing operations, bibliographers (critical and whispering as always) making inventories and packers-cum-bearers (sweating and sniffing as always) lugging piles of books and manuscripts down creaking flights of stairs. Each, of course, according to his nature. Perfunctorily and smoothly, assiduously and laboriously, thoughtlessly and twitteringly, inquisitively and mutteringly. Some hurried, others dawdled, some made sure the order was carried out to the letter while others again tried to find the easiest way of wriggling out of it. For there were two, even three attitudes to the order, and as many reasons for carrying it out.

Some wished to do everything correctly. More rapidly or more slowly but above all, correctly. Others were indifferent to results as long as they got the mark notes and penni coins[3] at the end of the day to pay for their food ration coupons. A third group which formed after much cursing and whispering among themselves, a group which

2 The surname of the German governor, Litzmann, caused great hilarity among Estonians, since lits is the Estonian for 'whore'. Wagon Lits has become a similar butt for jokes.
3 During the German occupation of Estonia, 1941-44, the currency was modelled on the German Mark and Pfennig.

grew even larger during the thin cigarettes and dishwater coffee of the lunch break, well, this third group began to hatch their own plans.

Why should the most valuable items be packed in the first place? To save them from air raids? All well and good. But not only for that reason. To also send them out of Estonia at the first opportunity! And why the hell should they help to organise that? To rescue them from the impending battles in Tartu. Fine. But encouraging their theft?! No! The order the librarians had received was a monolithic order from a monolithic robot. Like the majority of orders at the time. Any attempt to sabotage it could in itself prove deadly. But a deadliness which may, in fact have spurred people on rather than scared them off. Lord knows. The order came from Berlin to Tallinn and from Tallinn to Tartu like a vehicle speeding along on caterpillar tracks. Armoured, targeted and utterly indifferent. Like the majority of orders at that time. Resistance to the order shot up like so much grass (weeds, they would have said in the other camp). Victorious grass. Which existed under the ever present risk of being trampled into the mud, but which sprouts again and grows over everything. The result: the contents, numbers and addresses of the crates became all jumbled up.

Where what ended up, whether in Germany, Tallinn, Haapsalu or in the manor houses of the Province of Tartumaa, was not clear to any of those involved. Even now, in August '45, with Estonia again under Soviet rule, no one had a complete overview. But one thing was clear: some of the crates, about two or three lorry loads, had ended up at Mardimäe Manor, that is to say what had by then become the present schoolhouse. And now that the order had been given to return evacuated books to Tartu, these too had to be returned. Lorries drove out to that end, from various institutions in Tartu, the University included, to seven or eight places that week. So the chain of book collection split off in seven or eight different directions in order that chance could have its share.

Anyhow, we had shown the head of the school our authorisation papers permitting us to remove from his cellar all the books stored there. The crates of books had been brought together after taking them up from the cellar of the manor house, i.e. the schoolhouse, and had been heaved up onto the back of a lorry. All three of us, the driver August, our faculty lab assistant Volli Priipõld and myself had shaken our clothes clean of dust and cobwebs. Volli Priipõld had even gone so far as to strip down in the bushes near the house, throw himself into the manor pond, which was sheltered from view from the house, and swim a few lengths. The driver had gone off to the village and would be back in time for departure at six. Priipõld dragged a comb through his wet hair, put on his jacket and said:

"Let's drop in on the Comrade Director."

"Whatever for?" I said reluctantly.

"Haven't you noticed?"

"What?"

"I know him. In fact, he's my brother," grinned Priipõld."My elder brother, but still..."

The headmaster, or as we now say, the Secondary School Director, Priipõld's brother and consequently Priipõld himself, lived in three uncomfortably high-ceilinged rooms with plastered walls in the left-hand wing of the old manor house, now the schoolhouse. During the recent war, or God knows, perhaps during the previous war, they had installed a stove in the third room, so that the room formerly belonging to the lady of the manor had been downgraded to becoming the headmaster's kitchen. Or been ennobled to the status of the kitchen of the Director. Take your pick.

Priipõld Senior was slightly dozy, prematurely podgy, somewhat tedious and badly shaven, but in relation to his surroundings, as soon became evident, he had an almost womanish attentiveness about him. Teacher as he was, he did not at any rate try to lecture his brother, fifteen years his junior. He showed us to the table in his uncomfortable dining room without delay and his wife, a gymnastics teacher but a shade unkempt and looking rather more like a kitchen maid, served up a plate of fried eggs and pig's ribs, while Priipõld senior, winking at his younger brother, produced a bottle of moonshine.

"The pupils are off for the summer. Nobody'll drop by. Let's take a nip with our dinner. To make the news from town more palatable".

We had been eating for ten minutes and had taken our first swigs of our host's firewater, an almost bearable drink incidentally, and had begun to break the ice by telling stories. The Director spoke huffily about the insuperable difficulties he had in getting proper repairs done to the schoolhouse. It all boiled down to the fact that just about every other matter was regarded as more important at the Education Department than repairing school premises. The Director shot an inquiring glance at Volli, apparently received an affirmative glance back from his brother who did, after all, know me well enough, and went on to vent his anger on the Education Department with whom he was on a bad footing: "Look, for you university people things are, I hope, very different. But at the local Education Department they are already drawing up plans for pupils to help with the peat digging this coming autumn – for the good of the rural economy, you understand. Instead of organising some firewood to heat the school buildings with, through the Ministry of Agriculture. To hell with them..."

"Oh," groaned Volli, worldly-wise, "don't you go imagining that the Council of People's Commissars itself lugs firewood to the university – ha, ha, haa – a row of People's Commissars, briefcase tucked neatly under their arm each with a cubic metre or so of firewood, placing neat stacks of it in the University quadrangle. We have to find our own and haul it ourselves. Just like you do. Just like you."

We had probably not yet embarked upon our second glass. The Director's better half with her yellow dress, her smooth, dark hair and a face which seemed to exhibit a greasy tinge of sunflower oil, had popped out to the kitchen for a moment. The Director raised his glass, winked at me and grunted to his brother: "Here lad, take that glass too... Linda never touches hers anyway." There was a knock, and the dining room door swung open slightly. A woman's voice said in embarrassment:

"Oh, I'm sorry, Linda isn't in here, then?"

"She's in the kitchen," said our host, "but come in anyway! We've got guests."

"No, no, that's all right. I only wanted a word or two with Linda." And the door swung shut.

I had seen the profile of the woman who peeped in so hastily for a matter of some three seconds and I very much doubt if she had spotted me at all. We downed the contents of our glasses and I then asked:

"Who was that?"

"Our new Estonian language teacher, Hilda Malm or Hilda Meigas as she's now known," said Priipõld Senior.

"What do you mean 'new'," remarked Volli, "she's been with you for all of two years."

"In the autumn she'll be starting her second year," his brother conceded. "Damned good she is too. We're very happy having such a teacher. Coming to such a backwater school as ours with a degree in her pocket. Sometimes one person's misfortune can be another's good luck, so to speak."

"What misfortune?" I asked.

"Well," said Priipõld, "isn't it a misfortune for a young university language-graduate to be a widow – an officer's widow – and of an officer who fought on the wrong side? She gets jobs offered to her all over the place. But once they start looking at her curriculum vitae, they won't touch her with a bargepole. Only just managed to get in at Mardimäe. I got summoned to the Education Department on her account. Did I know who I was dealing with? And I said: Of course I know who I'm dealing with: a very good teacher. Whose husband, admittedly, was in the German Army. But in her case, you have to consider a number of mitigating circumstances. That, for starters. And secondly: he is, after all, dead. The Head of Personnel turns his leaden eyes on me and asks: what mitigating circumstances? I said: his background. The lad was unemployed during the bourgeois era. He'd left grammar school. Joined up. And found that he could get fed and clothed there. By serving in the army, I mean. And within the space of a few years, the clever boy had become a lieutenant. A bourgeois lieutenant, admittedly. The Head of Personnel then said: that's all very well. But he did get the opportunity of becoming a Soviet lieutenant. Any honourable man, any thinking individual, would have given his life for the new regime which was so kindly disposed towards him. But what did he go and do? D'you think we don't know? He broke his word as an officer! Went over to the Germans at Velikiye Luki!"[4] And Priipõld continued: "At the time I was genuinely in ignorance of that fact. Hilda had never told me. All I knew was that he had been killed fighting on the German side in early '44 somewhere in the Kriva Marshes. Linda has a chit issued by the Germans to that effect. Anyway, I then said to the Head of Personnel:

'Well, after all, he no doubt got the bullet for changing sides, but that doesn't mean his wife and kids...'

'For changing sides he missed his bullet,' said the Head of Personnel.

'OK,' Priipõld had said, 'there's no need to fire a second bullet into the corpse. If his widow can do a good job at our school, she should be left to get on with it. Or would you rather that one hundred and fifty children have to make do without a mother-tongue teacher for an indefinite period to come?'

'Well, if you are prepared to take personal responsibility for Hilda Malm.'"

"All this happened during our Christmas break," the Director clarified, "after I'd seen her working for six months or so, and so I said: 'OK, I'm prepared to do just that.'"

And I thought, that is to say I, Peeter Mirk, thought: so this podgy and stubble-chinned Priipõld was not making himself out to be any more humane or enterprising than he actually was. He

---

4 Velikiye Luki. One of the bitterest memories of the Second World War for Estonians: young Estonian men were conscripted into the German and Red armies and ended up killing one another in this battle in western Russia. (See also the note about the Narva Front and the Blue Mountains.)

probably did take the responsibility for the new teacher. For Hilda, Hilda Meigas did get permission to work as a teacher. It would never have been allowed otherwise.

"And you really are satisfied with her, then?" I asked – so that he would once again confirm the fact.

"Oh, without any shadow of a doubt. A perfect catch!" cried Priipõld, so that you could almost suspect him of having a certain masculine interest in his teacher. And at the same time he lowered his voice in a slightly coquettish manner, glanced hastily in the direction of the kitchen door, then back at us:

"And not only in the classroom, you understand! Not only with her boys and girls. There's a literary circle and other things, even peat-stacking on the farm. But also – as you might say – in private life. Oh, my word, yes. You see she's no longer that young or pretty. Over thirty, if she's a day. And she's had her trials and tribulations, hasn't she, what with her three kids? Even on her teacher's salary it hasn't been easy for her to feed and clothe them all. And then, last autumn you know, they sent along this new boss to run the community centre. A nice, handsome chap. A serious lad, and a real talker too if needs be. And what is most important – a bachelor. So that the village girls all vied with one another curling their hair and getting all dressed up. And they keep tripping off down to the community centre... But tough luck: it was Hilda Malm who managed to twist that man around her little finger. And one month ago they went and got married. Much to the chagrin of the village girls, I might add."

Priipõld Senior laughed with such gusto that it freed him of any suspicions of personal interest. I then asked him:

"So your teacher has an easier time of it, nowadays?"

"Why shouldn't she? The head of the community centre does, admittedly, work for a pittance. But it means a few kopecks more at any rate. And the main thing is: she's got a decent man, a hearty man, a man with golden hands around the house. And they've now managed to get some pretty good accommodation for the five of them. Slap bang next to the community centre. The old boss's house."

"And how do the children get on with their stepfather?" I enquired.

"Well, the two smallest ones hardly remember their real father at all. But Jaak is ten now. Already finished Standard II last year. He takes things as they come. If your real father's six foot under, it's surely better to have a stepfather for the boy than a gaping hole in the family."

After finishing the fried eggs, we ate some of Mrs Priipõld's rather tart apple kissel. I declined another after-dinner glass politely and rose from the table:

"My dear friends, thanks very much for your kind hospitality. I'll leave you now to discuss family matters. For a while at least. No, no, please. I'm going to take a walk around for a bit. I'll return at six for the trip back."

I left the schoolhouse and walked in the direction of the village and on the way it all came flooding back:

When I took up my studies at Tartu some eight years back, I rented a room which my cousin Elga had found for me on my mother's instructions. In the apartment of a recently deceased doctor's widow in a very ancient building on Luts Street. One month later, I received a letter from my mother in Tallinn: "My dear Peeter, you must move out of that room at once! I simply cannot understand how Elga, such a well-brought-up girl, could have been so thoughtless. It turns out that Dr Kolts, in whose apartment you have been lodging, was a doctor of venereal diseases! And your present room was the doctor's surgery! The very thought disgusts me – quite apart from any danger involved – as to what sort of people have sat on those worn chairs or threadbare sofas on which you may be sitting or even sleeping!"

Well, I rather thought my mother was tackling the problem in too radical a manner and that she was getting a bit carried away with all her hygiene stuff, as usual. But I cannot conceal the fact that the letter did arouse my unease about those worn plush and leather armchairs. So after a period of looking around for somewhere else, I finally moved into a new room on what was then Rüütli Street. This room I found all by myself. The landlady, a Miss Saar, was the daughter of the owner, and a student of medicine whose mother was said to be staying for a while with relatives in Riga or some such place. After a couple of weeks, and with Mrs Saar still in Riga, my mother came down to Tartu from Tallinn to pay me a visit and to have a look at my latest accommodation. She was satisfied with my room. But as we were getting ready to go into town to have dinner, and my mother was arranging her hair in front of the mirror, her eye (and then mine) fell on a letter on the hall table waiting to be posted. The address on the envelope was in Miss Saar's hand: 'Mrs Alide Saar, Harku Prison'. Miss Saar blushed furiously and admitted that her mother, a midwife by profession, was serving a sentence for performing an illegal, and no doubt unsuccessful, abortion and would be in prison for another year or so. That was enough for my mother: "Can't you find yourself a landlady who isn't in prison? And you would have to go and find one who is in prison on account of a crime. No matter, no matter, what sort of crime it happens to be, but that it should result in a prison sentence..."

So in order to put my mother's mind at rest, I moved out of the Saar apartment as well. Then Andres Kolk, a former classmate and at that time a fellow law student and students' fraternity pal of mine came up to me one day in the café, and said: "Peeter, I hear you're looking for a room. My landlord has got one going free. Professor Tahkna. The very same. Old fraternity member, mathematician, and a pal of my dad's. I've got a room there, the other is free. Do professors rent out rooms to students? Well, obviously they sometimes do. And you want to know why? Very simple. Päts[5] relieved Tahkna of his Vice-Chancellorship. And of several other offices too. Because he is

5 Konstantin Päts (1874-1956) was leader of the right-wing Agrarian Party and became President of the Estonian Republic. In 1934 he staged a *coup d'état* to prevent the ultra-right, pro-Hitler, Vapsid from obtaining control. Deported to Siberia in 1941, Pats spent most of the rest of his life there, although it is thought that Khrushchev sent him back to Estonia in 1954. But he was incarcerated in a lunatic asylum and soon sent back to Siberia to die.

a Tõnisson[6] man. He's still allowed to continue as a professor. But he lost one hundred and fifty crowns a month. And the apartment is too expensive for him on his present salary. But he does not want to move house. He's got his library, his paintings, his stuffed animals. Too much hassle. Stuffed animals? He also hunts. Anyway, I got the room at his place through my dad, and he's prepared to rent out the other room too. To another member of the students' fraternity, of course. Whom he can rely upon not to turn the flat into a gaming house or any other kind of house!

So I rented a room and became a boarder in Professor Tahkna's elegant apartment on Tiigi Street. And there was nothing about this landlord or his family that my mother could possibly object to.

Old Tahkna himself was actually a likeable old stick who smoked his one after-dinner cigarette every day with mathematical regularity. Mrs Tahkna gave domestic science lessons from time to time, but her teaching duties were not particularly burdensome. So she managed to keep at least the dining-table area of the rather stark Tahkna residence impeccably well provided. Although such things used to interest me less back then.

The Tahknas had two children. A son and a daughter. Grammar school pupils. At some point it was mentioned at table that there was, in fact, a third child, their eldest daughter, Hilda. Who lived with her husband and child or children on their own somewhere near Tallinn.

From the few sentences that ever slipped out at table, I received the impression that the Tahknas had some kind of problems with this daughter. In the jollier and more down-to-earth Mrs Tahkna this fact was hardly noticeable. Though such things tend otherwise to be more noticeable in mothers. In this case, however, I observed a certain twinge of annoyance pass over the thin Ancient Roman face of Old Tahkna himself at any mention of Hilda's name. Until, some time later, when I had become more pally with the two youngest

6   Jaan Tõnisson (1868-19??). Liberal leader, Päts' foremost rival. Editor and legal expert. Deported to Siberia. Date of death unknown.

Tahkna children and more or less received an explanation from them. Hilda's sister, Karin, who was a sixth former said very little. In all matters concerning her elder sister she was the soul of discretion. But her brother, Peep, a fifth former, was a happy and quick-witted blabbermouth. He explained, without my having to prompt him:

"Anyway, you see, dad's disappointed with Hilda. Why? Because his daughter didn't become the first Estonian female professor of mathematics. And because she didn't become anything else either, for that matter. Hilda left grammar school to read languages at university. That was bad enough in itself. But then getting married two months later. For love. And to a son-in-law who dad just can't stand. Dad's an academic snob. He would have liked a son-in-law who was, if not a full-blown professor, then at least a *Privatdozent*. An academic at any rate. But Kaarel was a mere cadet at the Military Academy. By now, he has in fact risen to the rank of first lieutenant. But in dad's eyes that's not worth a fig either. On one occasion dad said right out that a lieutenant, even a first lieutenant was, in his opinion, a nobody. And a general, a complete nonentity."

"But Hilda," I asked, "what does she think of her life?"

"She doesn't think she's in love," said Peep, gloating. But then added with almost adult gravity: "But dad's attitude saddens her, of course. Though not to the extent of making her unhappy. She and her Kaarel and the kids are – how shall I say – happy. Or how else should I put it?"

And twelve or eighteen months later, I saw this all for myself. In as much as external signs are tokens of proof. Kaarel and Hilda were visiting the Tahknas along with the children. As far as I could make out, this had never happened previously. Before the wedding, Hilda had brought her fiancé along to meet her parents. What had occurred on that occasion I never did manage to find out. Hardly anything on the surface of it, no doubt. But the slightest note of scepticism in Old Tahkna's voice or the slightest sidelong glance from the old man's owl-like eyes would have sufficed for Kaarel, and especially for Hilda. For since then, Kaarel had not set foot in the Tahkna apartment. Hilda had turned up on one or two rare occasions in their eight years of marriage. So the visit in April 1940 was, by family standards, something of an event.

And that was the first time I saw them and, in Kaarel's case, also the last time.

At the time, Hilda was twenty-six years old and, as I then saw it, past the flower of her youth. A tall, slim woman with light-brown hair and high cheekbones who gave the impression of having squinted at the sun a lot because, at the sunburnt corners of her eyes, a halo of small creases radiated. And her grey eyes were unexpectedly clear, set as they were among all that sunburnt skin. As for Kaarel, he could easily have been his wife's brother judging by his appearance. Only that his slightly Donatello-like profile made him seem a good deal more handsome than his wife was beautiful. The devil knows. Together, the impression they made was striking.

Despite any differences, they were of the same ilk. But not as yet with that slightly pathetic similarity of those who have been married quite some while. Nor any longer in that way which is born of the first discovery of one another and can, for a short while, assimilate quite different souls. Their similarity had something quite fresh about it and yet was already tested and solid. Hilda wore a very simply tailored costume of heavy beige material and Kaarel cut a somewhat ascetic figure in his black Estonian naval lieutenant's uniform. With their slim figures and long-limbed movements there was a quiet, barely detectable and yet almost triumphant symmetry. They sensed and comprehended one another in half-glances. The reciprocal harmony of their demeanour seemed independent of the world around them.

At that time, they had two children, the four- or five-year -old Jaak, who began romping around with me, and a bouncing two-year-old boy whose name did not spring to mind as I walked down to the village from Mardimäe.

But the reason for the Malms coming over to see the Tahknas was not only to let the grandparents see the little boys. The reason was that Hilda had, for the last eight years – and this, I imagined, without the consent of her parents – been studying as an external student and had just passed her university finals. And had thus graduated as a philologist, and as far as I could make out, had become an expert on folk poetry. And, in a rather off-hand way, she placed a typewritten copy of her dissertation on her father's bureau.

We had just risen from the dinner table and had stepped into Tahkna's study. I had, in fact, been dragged there by little Jaak. And, after some hesitation on my part, I felt that it was nevertheless within the bounds of etiquette for me to enter the study, taking into account my status as a boarder, and thus on the periphery of the family. Anyhow, Hilda had placed her dissertation on her father's bureau. Kaarel was sitting on the leather sofa opposite with his younger son on his knee, and I was standing behind the armchair, trying to prevent Jaak from clambering up onto my shoulders, so that I could see what was going on. For it seems to me that I already knew then – or perhaps not until much later, God only knows – that this moment was of great significance for Hilda and her husband.

Old Tahkna slowly stubbed out his after-dinner cigarette in his ex-Vice-Chancellor's crystal ashtray. Pursing his thin lips slightly, he eyed his daughter's dissertation. I knew what was written on the title page. Kaarel had informed me before dinner. There was, of course, the name of the author, Hilda Malm. And the title: *The Magic of Numbers in Estonian Folk Poetry*.

Stiff-necked, bird-faced, or if you like, Voltaire-faced Professor Tahkna eyed his daughter's work. He picked it up. He flicked through the seventy-odd page document with his left thumb. In a voice a bit too sonorous for his slight frame he said, with a slight smile, whether benignly or honed in sarcasm it was hard to tell:

"I see. So Mrs Malm intends to impress her dad. With the word 'Numbers'. Ha ha ha. But I have to say: numbers have no magical significance, if that is what you are driving at. They used to have, once upon a time. But not any more."

I do not know whether the thought struck me then or five years later on the way to the village from Mardimäe, or perhaps now, over forty years later, but be that as it may: it is a crying shame that intrinsically kind old men, such as Tahkna, are so inept at covering up their disappointment... I could not utter this thought to anyone, at least not at the time. And no one there said a thing. Hilda may have smiled a little. Kaarel dandled the toddler on his knee. Jaak pulled at my hands trying to get me to lift him up onto my shoulders, which I finally did. And Mrs Tahkna said with such artlessness that it sounded patently insincere: "Dear friends, why don't we all have a nice cup of coffee, with some of those lovely fresh cakes from Café Werner?"

That same evening, the Malms left for their place out at Suurupi, or wherever it was.

And events began to run their course. Or continued along their predetermined one. Towards the end of 1939, Prime Minister Eenpalu,[7] whom Old Tahkna considered to be a stammering police constable, had been replaced by Uluots.[8] Uluots struck ex-Vice Chancellor Tahkna as an inefficient bungler of classical proportions. At any rate, Tahkna's antipathy towards the new Prime Minister did not seem significantly less than towards his predecessor. What Tahkna thought of the Barbarus[9] government, I never got to hear. For in the spring of 1940, a few weeks after the Malms' visit, I moved out of the Tahkna apartment. I did hear, a year later, that Kaarel had joined the communist Estonian Territorial Corps and – no doubt owing to his impeccable class background (son of a lumberjack and a servant girl!) – had been sent East at the outbreak of the war. Hilda had moved in with her parents along with her two sons. Soon afterwards, the front reached Estonia and Tartu suffered its first bombardment in which half of Tiigi Street burnt down, leaving the Tahknas and Hilda roofless and destitute, apart from a couple of bags of belongings saved by chance. They moved from Tartu to somewhere

---

7 Kaarel Eenpalu (born: Karl Einbund) (1888-1942): Prime Minister from May 1938 to October 1939. Died in Kirov, Russia.

8 Jüri Uluots (1890-1945): Prime Minister 1939-40. Died in exile in Stockholm.

9 Johannes Vares (1890-1946). Modernist poet and puppet Prime Minister under the Soviets. Unclear whether he was forced to commit suicide by the NKVD. Pen-name: "Barbarus".

in the country called Palupera where the Tahknas' summer house or cottage was situated. I am not quite sure which. And until the late winter of '43, it seemed as if they had vanished from the face of the earth. Until I bumped into Hilda. In Tallinn, outside Café Kultas. She was wearing Mrs Tahkna's threadbare black winter coat. She looked very pale, very thin, but her eyes glowed with a strange excitement. By some miracle Kaarel, who had been given up for dead: executed, lost, or fallen in battle, had turned up at their home only a few weeks previously! He had gone over to the Germans at Velikiye Luki. And from there through a German filtration camp...

"And why ever by that route...?"

"God only knows..."

I invited her to the tiny café in the House of Art some fifty yards away and we went inside. Over her steaming rye-flavoured dishwater, that went by the name of coffee, she began to talk:

"God only knows... But perhaps, as an Estonian lieutenant whom the Communists didn't shoot, he would arouse the Germans' suspicions per se. And if this lieutenant had then served in the Red Army, he would become suspicious thrice over. And going over to the German side would double that again."

"But now, at least, he's home," I remarked.

"Was home," replied Hilda. "They gave him one week's leave. But yesterday he already had his Legion papers in his pocket. I saw him off yesterday, at the Baltic Station, on his way to the Leningrad front."

I said: "Lord Almighty – surely he didn't come home just for that, just to save *Neues Europa*? He came for you and the kids, for Heaven's sake!"

"Nobody cared about that," said Hilda in a whisper, glancing around her in the way that had already become second nature to us. "They told him: having come from there, and being a commissioned officer – there was simply no other choice."

"And now?"

"Now he's at the front," said Hilda. "He was hoping to get a couple of days' leave in a month or two." And suddenly Hilda's eyes flashed with the same excitement I had seen during the first moments of our encounter. So that I couldn't help thinking, almost pityingly: your husband is coming to visit you in two months' time and your poor soul is already glowing with anticipation... It would be quite a different matter if you were to use those two days to flee to Finland... But I could not, of course, say so aloud. For who was I to advise them? Kaarel was ten years my senior and had already seen something of life, or been swilled through one or two copper pipes as we Estonians say. And because of his rank at the naval base, he must surely be in contact with those who were organising trips across the Gulf of Finland. I asked her:

"And how are the Tahknas at Palupera?"

"Freezing," said Hilda, "and dad's ill."

"What's wrong with him?"

"We don't know. They say it's a peptic ulcer."

Our coffee was already cold as the heating was poor in the House of Art. People were not only freezing out at Palupera, but here in Tallinn too as well as all over the country. We got up and went out onto the snow-covered Freiheitsplatz where we shook hands. I then said:

"Give my regards to your father and mother. And Kaarel. When you write to him or see him."

She smiled with sorrowful lips – yes, that was my very thought, with sorrowful lips – the title of the recently published collection of poems by Marie Under,[10] and slipped round the corner onto Harju Street. And I heard nothing of them for another year. Then one day in early March 1944, I happened to hear something, again via my uncle, that is to say Dr Veski, at a small dinner party held by the narrow social circle of old student fraternity friends which I happened to be attending. The conversation touched, among other

10   Marie Under (1883-1980). Perhaps Estonia's most accomplished twentieth-century woman poet. Her collection *Mureliku suuga* (*With Sorrowful Lips*) appeared in 1942 during the German Occupation. She was elected an Honorary Member of the PEN English Centre in 1937 along with fellow-Estonian Friedebert Tuglas. Fled to Sweden in 1944, where she died.

matters, on how long the Narva Front[11] would still hold. Someone broke in:

"Haven't you heard – the Tahkna's son-in-law, you know, that first lieutenant, his name escapes me, has been killed in the Kriva Marshes?"[12]

"Killed, killed. They're getting killed all over the shop. Estonian lads," added someone. "And the most evil thing of all is – fighting for both sides."

A third said: "Malm, that was his name, the Tahkna's son-in-law. First-Lieutenant Malm. Yes, it's true, I'm afraid. I met Tahkna's daughter in Tartu. Tried to comfort her. Said the usual things, you know, about who can tell what happens during wartime. But she showed me the chit she'd received from Divisional HQ. Yes, it's gone pretty badly for the Tahknas. Old T. was under the knife only a couple of weeks back. Stomach cancer."

But all manner of shocks and unexpected turns of events, including death in battle, were so commonplace in those days that the death of Lieutenant Malm, who was after all almost a stranger to me, did not shake me unduly. For one painful moment I thought about the Tahknas and Hilda, chiefly Hilda. Painful, because it seemed that in losing her husband Hilda was losing more than any other woman in the same situation. And painful too was the fate of the Tahknas. For all the bitterness in their relationship with their son-in-law and their daughter, Kaarel's death must have come as a crushing blow under the present circumstances. And I thought with special sorrow about them all out there at Palupera while I myself was, in comparison, undeservedly healthy and had a roof over my head, for the time being at least.

And I have to admit: at that time I had too many other

11 Narva Front. The turning point of World War II from the Estonian point of view. From late winter till autumn 1944, the German and Soviet armies first clashed at Sinimäed (The Blue Mountains) Narva. Around 200,000 soldiers and others were killed in these futile battles. By September 1944, Soviet tanks were entering Tallinn as "liberators".
12 Kriva Marshes: Krivasoo (Est.) or Kriusha (Russ.). A place near the River Narva which forms the border between Estonia and Russia.

things hanging around my neck for me to become preoccupied with their fate. Among them, my own constant battle, trying to dodge conscription into the Leegion. Every six weeks, I took a double dose of those bloody tablets for a whole fortnight, tablets with which they corrected lazy thyroids in cretins in lunatic asylums. Any person with normal thyroids would get a pulse of around ninety on swallowing these pills and would have clammy skin and break out in bouts of sweating, and a hammer tap on his knee would send it jerking God knows where. His sleep would be a mere catnap and his outstretched hands would tremble without any further tricks having to be employed. In such a state, I went back after two months to the University Polyclinic to get my papers. There they nipped my nostrils shut with a clothes peg, shoved a length of rubber hose into my mouth and measured my oxygen intake. The reading had to be over 150%. Otherwise, it would mean immediate drafting into the Leegion. On three occasions the Recruitment Commission sent me home after such a rigmarole.

When Tartu had suffered its second and more deadly bombing at the end of August 1944, and the Germans had retreated from the city, things began to move at such a rapid pace that hours seemed to encompass weeks or even years. By the beginning of October, I was back in Tartu and the University, which by some miracle had more or less survived the bombing intact, gradually began term among what I remember as sleet falling on still smoking ruins.

At the start of the New Year, underground radio announced that my former Dean of Studies, Professor Uluots who, according to the broadcast, had acted as Prime Minister standing in for the President and who, according to Tahkna was an inefficient bungler of classical proportions, had died on 9th January in Stockholm. Old Tahkna died that very week at Palupera, indeed, as it seemed to me, on that very day. At any rate, of that very same ailment, stomach cancer. The thought struck me and so I asked myself: how profound did differences between these men need to be for such parallels to have been rendered impossible? This dissonance – one, the

Chairman of the Estonian Patriotic Union[13] while the other, a devout Tõnisson man – was patently not enough. Or perhaps it is so that all differences are insufficient to ward off death. And are thus equally devoid of relevance.

A month later, I saw Mrs Tahkna – Comrade Adèle Tahkna – sitting in the front room of Café Werner amidst the smoke and fug. I went up to her to offer my condolences on the death of her husband. It seemed to me that the lady was wearing the same skunk-collared winter coat as Hilda had been wearing the previous winter. But her dignity was not diminished by mourning. Even when I added: "All the more, as Kaarel's death must have come at a difficult time..."

"Yes, what can be done," said the old lady opaquely, and pressed my hand with hers which had, I observed, become callused from the well-chain, the bucket-and-yoke, and the snow shovels of Palupera. Then she looked at me from under her pre-war black velvet hat, her hair streaked with grey, and smiled:

"But Peeter – if I may still call you by your first name – our home has not been visited only by the Grim Reaper. Life has peeped in on occasions. In fact, Hilda has given birth to a daughter. Last November. Poor Kaarel still managed to come home last April. Then went back off to the front and was killed. Straight away, on the third day, it seems. So little Helle will be all of two months now."

And it was typical of Mrs Tahkna that she gave me ample opportunity to count the months on my fingers so as to dispel any suspicions I might have harboured about Hilda. I had heard how they lived in a house with thin plank-and-sawdust walls, in a barely heated room, eating potatoes grown in a corner of the Tahknas' garden. And I thought, being then too young to appreciate the joys within a family of any additional living being, that surely, under such circumstances, another child was something they could have done without... But against all expectations Mrs Tahkna, seemed to rejoice in the child,

13 Estonian Patriotic Union: after the 1934 *coup d'etat* by Päts, the Patriotic Union was the only legal political party. Its nominal leader was Professor Uluots, but the *éminence grise* was President Konstantin Päts himself.

and politeness being what it was, I complimented her on becoming a grandmother again and asked her to pass my greetings on to Hilda. Congratulations and condolences, at one and the same time.

And for another eighteen months I again heard nothing. Until Hilda popped her head round the door of the Priipõlds' dining room, some one-and-a-half hours before. But had clearly not seen me.

As I walked down to the village, I thought to myself: I do not have the slightest reason for not dropping in on Hilda and her new husband. Perhaps I would not have visited her – or her and the Tahknas – at Palupera during her father's illness or after his death. Since I was not particularly close to the family and my presence would hardly have brought any comfort to them in their hour of need. As for Hilda, I knew nothing of her attitude to the conventions of polite society. By entering into her first marriage she had totally flouted them.

But to Mrs Tahkna, and I felt in my bones, my presence would, at any rate, have been embarrassing: for I would then have to have seen the family of a former Vice-Chancellor in their present state of indigency. But now Mrs Tahkna wouldn't be there. And for Hilda, things must have gone relatively well. Whether relatively or extremely well rather depended on what sort of fellow her new husband had proved to be. Or not so much what sort of fellow he was, but more Hilda's attitude towards him. Whether he was a man she could put up with in her state of widowhood and who could be counted on to lend her a hand in some small way in bringing up the children and dealing with everyday problems. Or a serious and sympathetic man whom she could even grow to love. Or was this the new love in her life towards whom I should feel, despite my strictly neutral attitude, a twinge of intolerance in the name of Kaarel's memory? My visit would, no doubt, come as a complete surprise to Hilda and if not exactly a thrilling surprise, then at least a slight diversion from their humdrum backwater-village existence. And the visit would afford me the opportunity of getting a glimpse of her new husband. The man Priipõld Senior seemed to regard as a likeable lad. And my whole visit was, of course, of no significance and my meeting Hilda, mere chance.

After asking someone the way, I found the community centre in the middle of the village without any trouble. In a village where everybody knows everybody else, it sufficed to ask a passer-by where Meigas, the head of the centre, and his wife lived. I was directed to a small cottage with vertical slatting behind an acacia hedge, and whose ochre paint, applied in times when pride in one's home still counted, had not yet been weathered by the years of war.

I knocked and the door was opened by a boy, ten or twelve years old. A fair-haired, serious boy with the intense gaze of someone from before this epoch of accelerated history, in other words, still a little boy. I would, of course, never have recognised him on the street. But given the place and time, it was quite obvious who he was and I said:

"Hello. You must be – Jaak, am I right?"

"Yes." But he, of course, did not recognise me. I asked, and was startled at the maybe inappropriate wording of my own question:

"Is your mother or – your father – at home?"

But the boy did not clam up in any way, merely corrected me, so that it was me who felt a slight embarrassment:

"Mother... and Uncle. Yes, they're home."

I said: "Would you be so kind as to call them. I'd like to have a word with them."

"Mum's in the garden. But Uncle's in the house," said the boy.

He turned and went from the porch through the living room to the hall which presumably led to the back door of the house. As he passed a door on the right-hand side of the hall, he opened it and said into the room:

"Uncle, there's someone to see you. And Mum too."

I heard the boy as he left the house by the back door and went into the garden. And how he called out: "Mum!" At the same time, Hilda's new husband came from the right of the hall, half turned and began to approach. During those fifteen paces it took him to reach me, I eyed him and thought: interesting how women, I don't know how often, but sometimes at least, remain faithful to their ideal type... It was, of course, not Kaarel. But it was a tall, slim man. Even taller than Kaarel had been, and even more wiry. He was also a good deal older and with his short pepper-and-salt beard looked even older than he in fact must have been. He was wearing an indigo tracksuit and slippers, having presumably left his muddy boots on the back step.

It seemed to be as I had – well, I can't exactly say feared, but which I had, on the one hand wished, for Hilda's sake, but which, given the background, disquieted me: this man was the new love of Hilda's life. I naturally shook hands with him nonetheless:

"My name is Peeter Mirk."

He shook my hand rapidly and firmly:

"Kristjan Meigas. Oh, Peeter Mirk? I've heard your name mentioned by Hilda."

I said: "Quite likely. I was once in digs at Professor Tahkna's."

"That's right. It was in that connection she mentioned you," said Meigas, his white teeth flashing in a smile. "And how did you happen to find your way here? But do come in, won't you."

We entered the living room. He showed me to an old armchair and sat down opposite.

"Do you smoke?" He offered me a "Karavan" from a pre-war lilac-coloured packet. "This is what we puff at, out here. We're lucky to have even those."

We smoked, and I told my story: about the books stored in the school cellars and the lunch at Director Priipõld's. And how Hilda had popped her head round the door. And the news I had heard from Priipõld. That Hilda and Comrade Meigas... I avoided repeating the bit about the disappointment of the village girls.

"Well, I see you already know all there is to know," said Meigas with a twinkle in his eye. "Somewhere and somehow we all manage to find someone. If we do. Oh, but here are the others."

Hilda came in with the children by the back door and I immediately understood that my hunch had been right: her new husband simply had to be the new love in her life. Hilda had, of course, aged a good deal. I saw her now in the cold light of day. But in some strange way, her bearing, her sprightliness and her litheness of movement – I can't exactly put my finger on it – overrode with such force the fact that she had faded somewhat, and she in fact gave the impression of having grown younger.

Jaak remained standing by his mother with the dignity of an older brother. The little girl – this must have been Helle – was holding her mother by the hand. But the middle child, a boy of some seven or eight years, whose name I had never known, rushed up onto his stepfather's lap with a vehemence too childish even for his years: "Uncle! Uncle! Uncle! Make me a windmill! Go on! Please! Go on!"

Meigas said: "Urmo, listen" – and he said something into the boy's ear and took him onto his knee so that the boy quietened down and sat silently on the man's knee. I had risen to greet Hilda. Hilda stepped over to me and looked first at me, then at her Meigas with an excited, almost agitated glance:

"You're – Peeter – aren't you? I didn't recognise you at first. So many years ago." And then, to Meigas, with definite agitation: "You've been talking? How, I mean – and what about?"

"As you can see, we're certainly having a nice chat," said Meigas rather jocularly.

And I said: "The usual things. I was explaining to Comrade Meigas how I became acquainted with his wife. And how I happened to be at Mardimäe."

Meigas said: "Hilda, stop worrying. We've managed to get to know one another quite well without your help. That we have. But I think it's time for a cup of coffee."

Freshly roasted coffee was not exactly a common commodity in such regions in the summer of 1945. So little so, in fact, that we drank it with a certain ceremonial reverence. During coffee, I got to hear that

Mrs Tahkna had moved back to Tartu from Palupera. To rent a flat along with a friend from her schooldays, herself recently widowed. Karin had got married to a Komsomol leader at the university. Peep had fled to Finland to escape conscription back in 1944. And was God knows where by now. "And I've managed to get a job teaching local schoolchildren," said Hilda, "and have found myself – a husband – out here. As you can see. Well, it has all happened so recently that – that as you can hear, I haven't yet managed to teach the children to call Kristjan 'father'. But if we ask them to do it, they do. Though otherwise they still tend to call him 'Uncle'."

Hilda had put the little girl to bed in the adjoining room and had cautiously tiptoed back in to us. The three of us were sitting in old armchairs, borrowed from somewhere or other, around a low table. Jaak had brought in a stool from the kitchen and sat listening to our conversation while sipping milk out of a white jug and offered his stepfather a match to light his cigarette with. Meigas struck it and said:

"Thanks. But it's better not to play with fire."

Urmo squirmed in and out among our chairs jumping up into his stepfather's lap and clambering down again. Which made me ask, the question being addressed more to Meigas than to Hilda (partly out of the wish to taunt the likeable, but still rather cocky, Meigas a little):

"Are your children still Malms? Or has Comrade Meigas given them his surname?"

Meigas said, puffing at his cigarette: "Mmm, at present they're still Malms. We'll see. Depends on how things in the world turn out."

I sipped my coffee and refrained from asking whether it might not benefit the children to finally stop being Malms and become Meigases. I refrained because that would no doubt only have boosted Meigas' ego. Hilda wouldn't have taken offence. She was looking at her Meigas far too lovingly for that. But Jaak could quite well have been hurt. In spite of having offered his stepfather a light. For the filial piety of such orphaned boys can sometimes be a very touchy matter. We carried on chatting and I asked in passing where Comrade Meigas had been working before he came to Mardimäe Community Centre.

"During the German Occupation I was in Harjumaa Province, staying with relatives. Farm work. In '41 I did the same work as before, as a land surveyor. Here and there."

"And what does your work here at the community centre consist of?"

"Oh, we arrange the agitprop sessions, where necessary. Run the folk-dancing circle. And we try to persuade the old musicians to come and play. And for the lack of anyone better to do the job, I even repair the odd instrument myself."

Fair enough. More or less what I had imagined. And in due course I rose, thanked them for the coffee and said farewell. Half-an-hour later Volli Priipõld was asking me, in the lorry in front of the schoolhouse, where I had been. And I told him: for a walk. We drove back to Tartu, and for six months I forgot about the whole Mardimäe business.

The first morning after the New Year recess, which had replaced the Christmas holidays, Volli Priipõld came into the office stamping his boots and shaking the snow off his coat, which he proceeded to hang up on the rack, and took his seat at the desk. I could see from the look of numb perplexity on his face that he had something on his mind, but I didn't start prying, for I knew he would come out with it in the end. And, sure enough, at the first suitable opportunity he said:

"What a crying shame! You remember, in August, at my brother's, when we were eating lunch, that his Estonian teacher peeped in at the door – a tall, fair-haired woman?"

"Yes I remember. What of it?"

"And then we were told that she was the widow of some officer who had fought on the German side, and had recently married again. To the boss of the community centre. And Ruudi, saying how the village lasses were astounded that such a nice chap and a widow with three kids could... D'you remember?

"Yes, yes, I remember. Go on."

"Well it now turns out," said Priipõld in a half-whisper, although there were only the two of us in the room, "this chap, this new boss of the community centre, was, in fact, the former husband of the teacher woman.!"

"What are you trying to say? You mean Kristjan Meigas was Kaarel Malm?"

"Precisely. How come you know their names so well?"

"Your brother happened to mention them."

"Bloody good memory you've got – anyway, they've gone and arrested him. He'd changed sides at Velikiye Luki. Afterwards became a German Oberleutnant. Obtained false papers for his wife about his decease at the Narva Front. It's the talk of the whole of Mardimäe. They dragged Ruudi in twice for questioning: why didn't you know about this?! Why didn't you give him up?! How could he have given him up if he didn't even know?"

I said: "And if he had known – even then..."

"Well, that would have been his lookout," grunted Volli.

I asked: "But the – teacher woman? Have they arrested her too?"

"Not as yet," said Volli.

And Hilda remained free. Free, and was not deported. Though she was forced to become a cleaner at a tractor station. It is almost incredible to relate, but it does seem that the interests of the three children were taken into account. But I never saw either her or the children again. And Hilda saw her own husband (this I heard from old Mrs Tahkna, who has now been dead these fifteen years) – Hilda saw her husband on one more occasion. About a year after his arrest. Somewhere on Toompea Hill in Old Tallinn, on the street, outside that same building, I believe, where nowadays young theatre enthusiasts flock around the bronze bust of Voldemar Panso. Yes, in front of that very same building. When Hilda had been waiting a couple of hours in minus twenty-five degrees Celsius, Kaarel was brought out having been sentenced to twenty-five years in a labour camp, then five years of exile. He smiled a wan smile, before being bundled into the back of a lorry and driven away.

1990

An Empty Beach

Mati Unt

SUNDAY

was the day our food no longer smelt or tasted of anything, and the evening was empty and my wife and I decided to go to a restaurant, not least because we had the trip out to the western islands in front of us the next day, this being the last important part of our summer holidays. In the restaurant I said nothing despite the cognac, I looked out of the window at the sea and tried to remember some insignificant detail, a fleeting impression of the sea from the window in this same restaurant, when something was flapping in the wind, but what exactly it was I couldn't remember, and besides now (1967) there was nothing similar to be seen that could remind me of what I saw then (1965). I couldn't remain seated, but then one of my wife's former schoolfriends came to our table, and they started nattering and didn't pay me the slightest bit of attention, not even the former schoolfriend, though this was the first time we'd met, and so I just couldn't take it any longer and rose from the table, excused myself and went over to the bar. I sat there, eyeing my own face in the dull reflection of the glass cupboard behind the bar, ordered a brandy and tried to think logically, naturally, vitally, like a human being, soberly, in a way only I myself would think, weighing up all the circumstances, anticipating and despising compromises, but I was thinking entirely in English, a language I don't know very well at all: OUR METHOD IS LETTING GO and then I thought: ESTONIAN CULTURE IN OUR HANDS (Andres Ehin). Then someone nudged me in the ribs and asked if it was me. I said "yes" and a tough man with a crew cut began to accuse me of everything that had happened in Estonia over the last thirty-five years. I'm not yet thirty years old, but I saw in the man's gaze a cold metallic threat. At the same time, a woman was singing behind a partition, a woman singer, without restraint, in an ugly manner, and she sang and sang and sang and sang and sang and sang and I didn't let the man go on and said, mechanically: if your time ever returns, you'll shoot me against the wall of a shed in my home village, it's your way of thinking and you can't alter that fact, you're just not interested in freedom, nor power, perhaps you've never have been particularly interested, no doubt you've never been interested in what's going on in your native land, and the main thing is that you've got a full stomach, isn't that the case? All you want to do is kill, but you can't really manage to do that properly, and you're only prepared to take it out on old, pathetic people, women and children, and that type of violence just happens in a squalid way, without elegance, watching the clock and fearing the dawn. You lot are all afraid. Even my father asks me why I bother writing at all, aren't I afraid of upsetting the government, which has given me my school education, aren't I afraid of upsetting the management of the collective which pays me a hundred and ten roubles a month for doing nothing. And yet I still wear some SS officer's leather winter gloves which he left behind in our yard when he had spent the night there. You're all cowards, you included, but if there's a group of you together you'll shut your friend up for good, like you used to do with poor peasants. The man eased up a bit, began to dispute with me, described ontogenesis and phylogenesis, the rule (or rules) of life, I shook his hand and he shook mine with vigour like some conspirator or other, some fellow airforce pilot, some lecturer or reporter. And then I went back to my wife, whom I first met two years ago and whose parents live here in town, and I sat down next to her, and her schoolfriend rose as if she were afraid of me and went off. I asked whether my wife would like anything more to drink, she didn't but I did. We sat there a while in silence, then we had one dance, looked at the other dancers and listened to the soloist

MONDAY

and then we left the restaurant walking home under the soughing lime trees and arrived at the snow-white house where my mother-in-law lives. We entered the house and I had a wash in the bathroom. The mirror was misty and I wiped it with my hand. I saw my face in the wet glass, so incomprehensible yet familiar. I went into the living room. As it was the height of the summer season and the house was half full of paying guests from Moscow, we had to sleep separately: my wife on a narrow divan and me on a camp bed. We had to talk quietly so as not to disturb the old Jew sleeping in the next room, whom my mother-in-law called the German toad, and so as not to wake my mother-in-law herself, as the door was ajar and we could hear her breathing. Helina combed her hair before going to bed and looked at me fixedly and without desire. Then we lay there apart in the dark and in silence. When the silence had grown intolerable, I got up, sat on the edge of her bed and without touching her started saying that she would be mine, although no woman would permit herself such things, maybe only a nymphomaniac, and I thought I'd mention it, just in case, but she shook her head, and when I continued, she started to cry quietly. After that, I went back to my own bed and decided to pretend to be asleep, but I just couldn't, my heart was pounding, it was stuffy, I got up again and started talking: how crazy and beautiful too, was your idea to go and visit your lover with me! I've of course always been for free love and universal brotherhood, a new and better world, but I had never expected that this new and better world would come so close to me, that it would arrive unannounced, come SECRETLY and LIKE A THIEF IN THE NIGHT, its lips slightly parted, like a wolf. My wife then said in a hushed and humble voice, that she would do anything I wished, and if I didn't want to go to the western islands then we wouldn't go. I had got what I wanted, but I now began to argue that it was too late to change our minds and we now had to go. Had to go. TO THE WESTERN ISLANDS. The tickets had been bought. My wife insisted that we could always get our money back, she clearly wanted, at that moment, to live with me and be happy. But I said: we've got to go, all my previous reluctance was just stupid. You have to take life as it comes, life is tough, powerful and tender, as writers say, me among them, life is worth living, each of us his own life. And I rejected all my wife's advances, her rare attempts at reconciliation, in order to improve everything and smooth over what had happened. I sat by my wife's bed until three o'clock in the morning. Then I put on Helina's dead father's pyjamas. They were too large for me, recently washed, ironed and fragrant. Helina's father had been ailing for a long time but then (1964) he was brought to the mainland in a hopeless condition. The crisis came very quickly and by the second evening the doctors said that he would not make it to the next morning. Helina's father lay in a coma and it was impossible to communicate with him in any way. That night Helina went to the hospital to keep her mother company. I walked her there. The whole of nature was full of signs of foreboding. When we came out of Helina's place and were walking under the trees thick with hoar frost, a shot rang out and hundreds of jackdaws rose above the town. THE BIRDS FLEW ACROSS THE SKY. My heart fell, we walked swiftly along the slippery pavement. I don't know what had happened to me, but suddenly I stood still, took Helina's hand and pointed with my free hand at a window. There was a red light burning in the room, and on the windowsill, a tiny black DOG was sitting completely still. Helina's tense nerves snapped on account of my gesture and she broke into a run, dragging me behind her. I could hardly keep up with her, wanted to kiss her, but she turned her own dry and chapped lips aside, looked downwards and I recited lines by someone or other, that death is a house for the night on an open plain. On the Riga road I began to retch, I'd been up two whole nights and had smoked non-stop, and now it was beginning to take its toll. Helina just couldn't wait, but ran on to the hospital, and we only met up again the next day, and Helina told me that her father had not died in the night, but had, by the way, died just as we stood talking by the steps of the building which, before the upper storey of the university had burnt down, used to be part of the physics faculty. At that time (1964) we were not yet married, but now (1967) lying there in Helina's house, wearing Helina's father's pyjamas, we had already been married for three years. And we were still MARRIED the next morning when we arrived at the airport. The contents of a wastepaper bin were burning, and the grey smoke brought tears to your eyes. The phlox were in bloom just in front of the whitewashed main building, where a plane stood in a distant meadow, into which we climbed and which rose into the air and flew and flew and flew, until it landed describing a wide arc down onto an airfield that resembled a field for grazing cattle. When we got out of the plane, there was a strong wind blowing from the sea and as we walked across the open space towards the border guards, the hat of some woman we didn't know flew off her head and rolled along crushing some dog daisies. I ran after the hat right in front of the border guards, I picked it up and just then the importance of the trip struck me. But there was nothing to be done, we'd arrived. The border guard didn't even look inside my passport, my shaking hands and evasive glance didn't arouse his suspicions, he even smiled as he handed my passport back. We followed behind the others and stepped into the waiting room. There, the windows under the high ceiling jingled on account of the strong wind, local women were sitting with milk cans, but Eduard was as yet nowhere to be seen. We sat down on a bench. We were now in the border zone, Eduard's home region, on the WESTERN ISLANDS. Here I only had a right to vote in an advisory capacity. I looked at my wife, who looked totally calm, though her nostrils quivered slightly. I stood up, walked around the room, one shoulder slightly lower than the other and read the timetable. How many routes are there that I will never fly, though no one forbade me, especially local routes, but I'm used to only travelling where I have business (or not?), and in the end you get used to the same routes, and that's all there is to it. Then a door opened and in stepped Eduard, greeted us with a broad smile and I went up to him and I held out my hand first, as if I wanted to demean myself in front of the island women, wanted to demonstrate the equivocal nature of my situation. I do of course read more into things than it is worth doing. People have often held that against me. Even a trip to Võru will give me material for conversation as well as the excitement both a week before and a week after the trip itself – as if the end of the world is nigh and I'm talking about my trip to Võru, a provincial town, I'm speaking as if I were Hemingway, off on a trip to Madrid. I see hidden danger everywhere, apocalyptic predictions, archetypical symbols. I once cracked the joke that my career was to SEE MORE IN THINGS THAN WERE WORTH SEEING, that's the only thing I can do really well, and it is with this kind of exaggeration and mystification that I feed my family. No, no, the joke didn't go down well – no doubt everything was bad and who could I sell it to? Eduard and I went out of the waiting room into the bright sunshine and here, on the western islands, there was someone from the mainland: at the edge of the road sat a man, who had translated Beckett plays, and I greeted him. Then the bus came, but I didn't feel at ease on the bus. Every time a stranger looked at me, I was forced to lower my eyes. The passengers preferred Eduard. There was not one of them that wouldn't have thought that Eduard suited my wife better than I did. All of them thought the two of them to be a couple, and me their guest. Each one of them would have laughed, had I told them my true status. Society gave Eduard the right, society regarded my claims as groundless. And unfortunately they were, too. I had not got one ARGUMENT whereby my wife should be mine, not Eduard's or somebody else's. I could have said that I loved her but no one would have believed me. My story would not have matched my appearance and my expression – my hands were resting slackly on my knees, there was not enough passion in my eyes. My thoughts were somewhere else entirely and I felt ill at ease on that bus. And so on: the whole journey on the back seat, the arrival in the port, fruitless attempts to buy some hunter's sausage, another bus, which took us another five kilometres, an ancient oak grove, and Eduard's comments about it. And then the OLD WOMAN at whose house our stay had been arranged, her beautiful period farmer's house with its rag mats and runners, embroidered pillow slips in a high stack at the head of the bed, the tapestry with a picture of a castle, lots of flowers. And I said a lot about the flowers, I spoke eagerly about them, praised the pelargonias, the asparagus and the cacti, showed an interest in their propagation and fertilizers, their growing conditions, for the simple reason, that Eduard was sitting with us at the same table, before dishes laden with tomatoes and cucumbers. Every moment was precious to me, at least I would have given that impression to others, I presume I gave a decent, friendly and hearty impression, perhaps as friendly and hearty as Eduard, in whom such qualities were self-evident. I talked and talked and won the old woman's heart, but everyone apart from the half-deaf and good-natured old woman had already seen through me. Then we were taken up to the LOFT, actually an area above the barn, which was filled with hay at the back. We spread out our blankets and sheets right by the door, just above the ladder. From the ceiling hung a naked one-hundred-watt bulb. The sea was about three hundred metres away, across a hot road. In my bag I had a spare shirt and socks, my swimming trunks, a thick jumper, a raincoat, a camera and some film, shaving cream and a razor, a toothbrush and toothpaste, soap, a towel, a pencil, two jars of aspirins, one issue of a Finnish magazine containing Hans Magnus Enzensberger's introduction to *The Museum of Modern Poetry*. My wife's bag, on the other hand, contained Mishima's play *Hanjo* which described a mentally ill girl, who has been waiting for years for her lover, whom she hopes to recognise by his fan. In the end, the boy turns up one day, but the girl recognises neither him nor his fan. The boy runs away in despair, the girl however comes under the influence of a tormented ageing woman artist. In the book there is a review in Estonian: "*Hanjo* presupposes, indeed demands inner intensity, the necessity for the audience to be on the same wavelength as the author, and together to arrive at the social core, to the understanding of the conceptual content. This concentration in the audience is achieved by the actor R., when he sits and expresses his views and opinions (reading the newspaper, etc.). Then a tautness of thought, inner wealth and the power to convince are felt. Honda was losing the verbal duel with Yoshio (actor A.), the unexpected trains of thought do not come out in bold relief and the whole scene has a tendency to drag." Meanwhile,

Eduard was waiting for us outside. When my wife had composed herself (what an expression!), we went to the beach. It was an empty beach, I had never seen anything like it before: water smooth as a mirror, green, not one living soul around, only the empty summer house of a cosmonaut up on the hillside. We felt awkward and started playing to overcome the uneasiness. The game was very simple, but it is almost impossible to describe fully and comprehensively; I've tried, but it would be easier to draw. Two people join their hands under the water and with their free hands take hold of those of the third person. This third person slides their legs forward under the water and swings himself over the joined hands. Then people change places, and everything starts all over again. My push-off failed, I went headfirst under water and my legs kicked helplessly above the surface, when my wife and Eduard were looking deep into each other's eyes. I struggled until they let go of my hands, then came spluttering to the surface, and refused to play any more. Eduard too no longer wanted to play, and suggested a swimming contest. The sea and sky had merged on the horizon as the sun was beginning to set. The three of us swam out to sea, with more or less the same result. I put my head under the surface and looked at my green arms, drowning there: LOOK, HE'S BROUGHT THE HEBREW MAN TO US IN ORDER TO LAUGH AT US, HE CAME TO SLEEP WITH ME AND I CRIED OUT LOUDLY. Then we got dressed by the shore, my wife behind the bushes, we, the men, right there on the sand, the two of us, NAKED, without peering at one another. Our shadows were very long, shadows were rushing from all quarters; I hadn't brought along my camera to take a snapshot. I asked Eduard how his summer had been, and Eduard replied that he had been haymaking on his parents' farm. I made the suggestion that we could build a bonfire on the beach the following evening and bring along some vodka. Pity we couldn't get hold of any hunter's sausage. Eduard knew where in town they sold one type of pretty thin and fatty sausage, which could also be fried over the fire, and promised to bring along about a kilo of it. Then my wife came out from the bushes, wearing her dress, walking barefoot across the sand. We walked Eduard to the road and he left, his silhouette rippled in the hot air over the asphalt. We watched him walking, I was holding my wife's hand. A cat crossed the road, clouds stood motionless in the burning sky, we went up to the loft, switched on the one-hundred-watt bulb, lay down to rest. I switched off the light. I touched my wife, put my hand cautiously on her body and moved it like a frightened schoolboy, but my wife knocked it away, silently, without a sigh. We lay there in silence, motionless, next to each other, the hay rustled beneath us for no reason, as if there were snakes in it, but no, it was simply the stalks breaking under the weight of our bodies. Right in front of me was the door to the loft and between the cracks the dusk was already too red for summer and I fell asleep and

TUESDAY

we were walking with a friend in a mediaeval city; it is an autumn night, the streets and cobblestones are shiny from the rain. I am talking with the friend about morality and marriage. Suddenly a shot rings out, and with an unpleasant thud from somewhere a soldier's body falls down from the balustrade onto the pavement. We turn our heads, and right next to us stands a man in a dark shiny coat, blows into barrel of his revolver, then puts the weapon into his pocket. Without paying us any attention, without even noticing us, he passes by, while we stand there frozen in fear, his expression is frighteningly serious and natural. We step onto the street only when the sound of his footsteps echoing in the narrow streets of the old town has died away, and we start walking, but from somewhere, now far away, now nearer, shots can again be heard. Soon we see three bodies, all soldiers, piled up, unexpectedly killed, one has his white face pointing up to the sky, the rain trickles into his open mouth; again, faraway shots, clear, they are coming more frequently, morning is nigh, a dull morning light is approaching. And we, our heads hurting and suddenly sobering up, rush out of town: morning will reveal everything and we will be held responsible. Hurry, hurry, says my friend, but the cobblestones are slippery, our legs do not want to take us away from this place of death. Someone is already opening a window, someone who only slept for a short time. – In the morning my wife went into town to register with the militia. I sat alone at the water's edge, ON THE EMPTY BEACH, I splashed around in the shallows, the weather was fine. I collected seashells, put them on a log sticking out of the water, and watched them grow dull as they dried. All at once I saw, that from far away, from where the town should be, a smooth, high, impenetrable BANK OF FOG was approaching. One end of the bank tailed off into the sea, the other into the woods. The fog was approaching rapidly and I stayed sitting where I was. The nearer the white mass got, the more my heart began to quail. In the end the cloud swallowed me up entirely. The sun and sea disappeared, I was alone, my body was covered with cold foggy sweat. I could hardly hear the invisible water splashing against the invisible rocks. I did not move, did not get up. I sat there without glancing at my watch and then a yellow light began to return, the air warmed up and the cloud left me alone. The bank of fog left as silently as it had come, along the waterline but now, moving with the sun, it was no longer grey as when it was approaching, but snow white. I bided my time. I wrote magic formulae in the sand. The time I spent sitting here passed slowly, time flowed and I wanted to kill it, this time would never return, it came from off the land and the sea, and went back whence it came. The sun was scorchingly hot. I began digging a hole in the sand beneath the shallow water, in order to be able to hide in it; I worked with both hands, I worked like an excavator, the sweat ran onto my lips, the sand seeped back into the hole, but in spite of it all my work progressed and I hunkered down in the hole so that only my head stuck out above the surface. I looked around me. The empty beach. No particular features. Anonymous space. Could be anywhere in the temperate zone. A white sheet of paper, a white beach, a bright beach. I have arrived here via the neck of the womb. On a dolphin's back, without Eurydice, in a carriage, by helicopter. From the distant future, from the Middle Ages, from the village of Linnamäe, from a Cro-Magnon cave, from the capital, from a pub crawl. I myself am a blank sheet of paper. Yet Eduard, large, hairy, on the divan with my wife in the flat right now, a brute of a violinist, the man I will never become, and the indefiniteness I now experience on the beach transforms them in their embrace into indefiniteness, which is not in the slightest any more consoling. On both sides, to the right and to the left, the water's edge disappears beyond the horizon. This mad and lovely self-torment! This inadequate behaviour! When the sea pours from my palms, when the sky pales – who could then still keep hold of his wife? Here, in Estonia, which, as is generally known, borders the Gulf of Finland, which is part of a broader area called the Baltic. In my mind's eye, however, a length of indecent film was running continuously, a film showing my wife (?) and Eduard. Postures, touches, all sterile when it came down to it. Ah, what delicious self-torment, what a lovely masochists' summer holiday! The sun burnt my pate, the water sloshed lazily, as if in a dream, I walked on the beach, back and forth, humming a mournful song. Then my heart began to pound again. I grew afraid. I grabbed my things and made for the main road, as if a monster had appeared on the horizon. To the road, the road! But there was no one there either, not even an animal, not even a car. I had the feeling that everything had left, fled, escaped after receiving certain unexpected information, been called away, in an organised fashion, following a bulletin on the radio, but I had been left behind. I sat at the edge of the road and read Enzensberger. The following had lived in exile: Rafael Alberti, Bertolt Brecht, Luis Cernuda, Jorge Guillén, Juan Ramon Jiménez, Else Lasker-Schüler, Antonio Machado, Saint-Jean Perse, Nelly Sachs, Pedro Salinas and Kurt Schwitters. Sergei Yesenin, Attila József, Vladimir Mayakovski, Cesare Pavese and Georg Trakl had committed suicide. Robert Desnos had died as the result of time spent in a concentration camp, Miguel Hernández was tortured to death, Nazim Hikmet was a political prisoner for 15 years. Jakob von Hoddis was killed during a euthanasia programme, Max Jacob and Osip Mandelstam died as prisoners, Federico García Lorca was shot dead. Then my wife turned up in somebody's car and said that she'd gone on a walk with Eduard around the old Teutonic Knights' castle, and I asked her what they had been doing there for so long, and my wife said that it was pleasantly cool there. I asked whether Eduard was coming to our place that evening, as we'd discussed the previous day, and she said that he would be. And I thought for the first time: why don't the three of us start living together, or even four of us, and in the evenings Eduard could play his violin for us and we could sing sentimental songs? We'd go to work with Eduard, come home tired in the evening, our woman would be waiting for us with a warm meal and would look after the children we had in common. But this great democracy, this great love of humanity is still far away, that can't be helped, what is needed is a new race of human beings or at least firm measures to better the race, but until then we will think like this: Eduard has to be killed (a hole in the hull of his boat, run over with a car, by breeding germs from an isolation hospital, falling through deceptively thin ice), Eduard has to be tortured (by conversations, glances, pins under his fingernails) and Eduard had, of course, to be loved. For Eduard – he is, after all, me. I am Eduard, the Eduard of this world, and Eduard is me. The same malignant cancerous cells. Us. You two, You. One huge one-faced you. Us. You. You, that can do anything you want, and that you are doing, and everything you do is an injustice, but HE WHO DOES WRONG, LET HIM CONTINUE DOING SO AND HE WHO IS A DIRTY BASTARD, LET HIM BECOME EVEN DIRTIER. AND I WILL COME SWIFTLY AND AVENGE ALL ACCORDING TO THEIR DEEDS. Once this spring, when my wife had gone off to Tallinn, I invited him round to my place. He came and we drank liqueurs together, which made my hands sticky. I wanted to like him, because I liked him. His tragic gaze was downcast. We talked about many things, I talked about the days I'd spent happily with my wife in Valgametsa (1965), I showed him pictures of our wedding. I told him about my problems, my complexes and my persecution mania. He was, of course, indifferent to everything I said, and that was his right. But those nights when I waited till dawn for my wife to return (if you can call it waiting) had secretly united us. We formed a trinity, we were linked in some mysterious way, we shared one woman, we shared the same skin, the

The Dedalus Book of Estonian Literature

same tone of voice, the same womb, we were intimately acquainted with the same mental and physical reactions. I could have kicked his face in, pushed him into a hole in the ice, slit his throat, but we were now inseparable. We would no doubt have understood each other even better, were there not something invisible that united us both – my beautiful, well-educated wife. When he had to leave, I saw him off. I wished him a quick goodnight and shut the outside door. He stood there outside in the darkness. I stood by the door and listened. He had not budged. We both held our breath, all that was separating us was the thin wood of the door, us, two solitary souls that Satan was tempting and sundering. In a room upstairs, negroes were singing. I tiptoed back up the stairs, wiped the table clean, got my bed ready and went to sleep without putting out the light. From the wall, a photo of my wife looked down on me: turned, looking back, into a pillar of salt, petrified, and yellowed in her frozen smile. Now (1967) we were walking, the three of us, along the empty beach, we built a fire surrounded by bricks, drank vodka and chatted: about strangers, their relationships, how these relationships fell apart and reconfigured, about character traits, parapsychology and other subjects. Eduard and me took it in turns to go swimming, as my wife was afraid of being left alone at the bonfire. Our fire was the only one on the whole beach, you could see it from a long way off in the dark night, and it could have attracted wild animals, tramps and criminals. Eduard stayed by the fire, but I went into the dark sea. You had to go out a long way, the water only got deeper very gradually, there was the rush of the sea around me, I couldn't make out the waves, as the sky had suddenly become overcast, all I could see was the shadows of the waves, as they came towards me from out at sea, their monotonous rush became unbearable, I had the feeling I was in the path of an approaching express, I instinctively looked landwards, through the junipers a faint light glimmered and so I went on. The wind was very warm, strong and pressed my naked body back. Then I grew afraid that I would not be able to return to the fire, where the two of them were sitting and chatting. And when I looked behind me again, I couldn't really see the fire any more. Had they now put it out,

168

my beacon, or had I veered off so that I was now on quite a different beach, or even in the restricted zone? Anything was possible and THE SEA was rushing past, you couldn't see the stars. At any moment, a searchlight could be trained on me, a pale, pathetic and thin-skinned being amidst the primordial, black sea. I took a dip in the rushing water, but didn't start swimming, everything was so uncertain, I thought: if I start swimming now, the bigger waves would hide the last landmark from me, the shoreline, about a kilometre away, still faintly visible. I won't be able to get back, I'll swim out to sea, sink to the bottom, into the realm of slave vessels overgrown with moss and cold-skinned nymphs. Suddenly feeling afraid I started swimming back and the black waves pursued me, lashed my back and urged me on. I reached the shore and made for the bonfire. They were sitting in the firelight and I eyed them a while from among the juniper bushes. Their mouths were moving, but I couldn't hear a thing. The fire battled with the wind, blowing hither and thither, the HOLY FIRE, and they were still on either side of it. My wife was poking a stick in the ashes and nodding at Eduard's words. I combed my hair and went over to them. We still had plenty of vodka and we again started talking about people: about a girl, the daughter of an executive, who had once been kind to Eduard, but she had disappointed him later on, we spoke about Eduard's parents, about Eduard himself and how he had managed to survive a bout of severe diphtheria during his childhood, about Eduard's job at the radio sound archive, always about Eduard, never about my wife or me. Eduard never asked us anything, all he did was answer our questions, as if we were before some committee or other. We had abandoned self-love, I neither loved my wife any more nor myself, and she no longer loved me nor herself, the only one we still loved was Eduard, we mollycoddled him, thought about his difficult childhood, his aching soul, his mind of a child, his music, his violin. I again thought that I couldn't refuse him my wife, I had to conquer my egotism. I still had a flask of vodka in my back pocket, which I had kept secret from the others. I excused myself, stood up, and went away from them and the fire. Among the juniper bushes I took out the flask and drank half its contents. Then I sat down on the moss. I am a more or less healthy young man, haven't got a particularly strong constitution, but I get drunk relatively slowly. I felt I had to do something, I wanted to sing. I stood up again, watched them, helpless in the firelight, while I could watch them from the darkness with others (which others?), shamelessly, audaciously. Eduard's head of a violinist, his wilful chin, my wife's seriousness. I went back to the fire, and thought that now it was my turn, my show. I began speaking and they listened, my wife felt ashamed at everything I said, she smoked and stared into the fire. I want you to be happy, Eduard, was what I said, I want your violin to sing of our night together, the three of us, that your violin tells everyone on this Earth, how love has been perfected. Why, asked Eduard irritably. Why, why, I replied, and couldn't be more trite, IT'S THE DUTY OF YOUR VIOLIN, WHY ELSE THIS SOUND BOX, THIS MONSTER MADE OUT OF THE BELLY, THE VENEER AND THE STRINGS, WHAT'S THE POINT OF HAVING IT IF IT DOESN'T SPEAK OF THE HAPPINESS OF MY WIFE? That's an insult, said Eduard, controlling himself admirably, I want you to apologise. No, I am not apologising, go... you pimp, I kept on. Eduard hunched up, there were tears in his eyes. My wife looked at me like a wild beast and covered her face with her hands. Eduard was moaning quietly, and began to speak, almost in a whisper: it's natural... completely natural... there's no getting away from barbarians... I know, that's just how it is...the light flickered over his young, yet somehow senile face. I knelt down at the other side of the FIRE and silently begged for forgiveness. Then the sea roared again and the fire crackled. I don't want to die. Even now I am counting the years I have left to live. That may seem weird to you, but not to me. I'm not afraid of a heart attack, a car crash, a ship sinking and so on, I am afraid that the situation could alter and my neighbour could shoot me by the barn in my home village. Why? For no particular reason, obviously. Just in case. Or someone my age could betray me and sell me down the river tomorrow. Someone my age, someone I started studying literature with back in 1962. We became people who were aware on the crest of the social wave, and we had the illusion that we were brothers, a great illusion, which I have harboured for some ten years now. I have become compromised here and there, right and left. And now it's all over. BECAUSE YOU CAN NEVER FORETELL DANGER. BECAUSE IT NEVER ANNOUNCES ITS APPROACH. BECAUSE IT'S BETTER TO KEEP SILENT THAN TO CRY OUT LOUD. BECAUSE YOU SHOULD NEVER PUT OFF UNTIL TOMORROW WHAT YOU CAN DO TODAY. BECAUSE YOU CAN'T PUT BEAUTY INTO A CAULDRON FOR FOOD. Because an individual is, when it comes to the crunch, a burden on mankind. By now, I was again exaggerating. My wife stared at the ground. And Eduard stared at the ground. The fire blurred before my eyes into one red oval. I sipped my vodka, but didn't offer Eduard any. I carried on speaking. I'm not afraid of death. I'm indifferent to it. I'll try to use the years I've got left as best I can. But how is that possible in your presence? I want to go to Paris, Greece and Japan. I want to be with every woman I ever meet. I want to always be drunk. You say that I seem ten years older when I'm drunk? Look, I'm telling you I am really ten years older, but when I'm sober I manage to catch up with myself and look younger. Being a village lad, someone who never polishes his shoes, doesn't wash his hands properly, can't do table talk, I want to rise in society, though to tell you the truth, I don't know what that really means. I ought to lose five kilos in weight, I want to be as slim as Eduard. Is there something wrong with you, asked Eduard looking at me attentively, maybe we ought

WEDNESDAY

to go home? No, I said, there's nothing wrong with me, I'm just tired: so tired of flying, tired of life. What is it that's making you so tired, asked Eduard? I gave a start. You, I replied, you're so rich: I've given you everything: my wife, my unborn children, our death together in old age. You haven't GIVEN me anything, Eduard pointed out, I have TAKEN it. I wanted to know how far she'd go along with what I was saying, she the pure soul. He himself was

171

speaking now, I couldn't get a word in edgeways: you have to GIVE
THINGS UP, you have to DIE, as this is SACRIFICE, a very
INDIVIDUAL act, which others CAN'T REACH, and is therefore
over the BORDER. I couldn't follow what he was saying any longer.
Was Eduard speaking or the juniper bushes, the sky? Maybe life had
passed me by? Why don't I understand anything any more? Help me
with vodka and sleeping draughts, make me a bed among the flasks,
because I am sick unto death of others and myself. You are right to
laugh, boy, your brain's filled with *putanitsa*. You what, asked
Eduard irritably. *Putanitsa*, I replied, it's the Russian for a mess, a
muddle, and it also means that no one would care a damn if I were
dead. Well, you're managing to cling on, said Eduard soothingly,
taking pity on me. No, I'm not managing to cling onto life, I yelled,
I'm simply too drunk, I'm tired, I'm fed up with your company, I
want to go to sleep, I hate both of you. Poor chap, said Eduard, how
paranoid. My wife patted my shoulder. To calm me down. Don't be
petty, she said, aren't I allowed to be happy? Oh yes, I said back, I
may look like a snotty-nosed brat, but I do understand this much: you
want this evening to end badly, and if that's what you want, you'll
get it. My wife had already climbed up into the loft and the hay was
rustling. I took hold of Eduard's collar, shook him, pressed him
against the wall and raised my fist, ready to hit him in the face. But
then Eduard said something very natural and heartening and my
arms dropped of their own accord. I then pushed him into the nettles
by the stack of firewood. GRAND THÉÂTRE DE LA PANIQUE, is
what I said, something is now going to happen, maybe excessive, no
way out, and why is it you want to steal my wife, I asked, my wife,
who I'd have abandoned ages ago, if you hadn't come between us,
but now you're forcing me to love her again, sincerely, even though
I don't want to. But you do, honest to God, said Eduard,
incomprehendingly, as if to calm me down, but me too, Eduard that
is, love her too. Are you some sort of jet plane, some sort of cloud in
the sky, some sort of radiator, or kitchen cupboard, that you dare to
love her, I asked. I love her, said Eduard, as if he had stomach ache
or as if his heart ached on account of me; she, Helina, is the one who

will decide. You're a Judas, I spelt out, one great big handsome Judas, why don't you wear a beard, a thin white beard? Now the GRAND THÉÂTRE DE LA PANIQUE commences, I repeated and red blood flowed to my head like a rush of water. I had stepped over the threshold of tolerance into the realm of black despair. From a dark sky the first raindrops fell. I suppose you have friends, I suggested, who can arrange to get imported lingerie for my wife, my wife likes everything foreign. You're being vulgar, he replied and turned away from me. I whirled him round to face me, touched his face and felt the tears on his cheek. Marina, I whispered and went into the garden without looking back, Marina, take me away from here, I can't cope any longer. I tripped up beneath a cherry tree and fell headlong onto the wet grass. I burst into tears and bit the earth. You're humiliating me in front of my wife, you are too good a person, she's got good reason to love you, I yelled, my mouth filled with soil. He hauled me to my feet. This is JUST TOO MUCH, this is what you wanted, you wanted me to blow my top, I cried, pushing him off, and walked towards the main road, which led to the North, over the sea to Helsinki. In my pocket I had a diary with addresses in Helsinki: an aesthetician, a radical author, and a linguist, with whom I was secretly in love. They were of course asleep by now, I should have phoned them. Then I felt the hot asphalt under my bare feet. No need to phone: a car was already coming my way, in front of which I could throw myself. I went straight towards it, and startled the driver who started shouting. I took no notice, I was sure he wouldn't be able to brake in time. But Eduard, who had run after me, pushed me aside at the last moment, and the car screeched past. In the direction of Helsinki. But I had one more chance, so I decided to take advantage of it. I have written this up in my diary. "I had made preparations for several days running. First of all I dropped some scraps of paper containing a mixture of phrases and numbers involving the restricted zone. After that I managed at length to get hold of a small radio transmitter, with which I would every evening send quite meaningless signals into the ether. I was sure that they had already picked up the transmissions and they were simply waiting to see what to do next. I was sure that my game would be taken seriously. My latest actions had been incomprehensible and melancholy. No one would believe that I could be a loyal type of person. My name had already been noted long ago. And suddenly, things fell into place. When interrogated, provocative questions would be put to me about anti-Communist authors and I was asked whether I wanted to go and live abroad. No one would understand my real reasons, not even my wife. I now decided to conform to their expectations. I took a map, drew a red line from the shore into the sea, and wrote 02:20 next to the line. I dropped this map on the route that the border guards would take on their rounds. I went to the local shop and bought a Swedish-Estonian phrasebook, deliberately buying it very openly. These preparations had to be enough. Then I sent out a new signal and started off for the restricted zone. Everything went well: the soldiers spotted me immediately and began to shout at me to stop. I ran quickly onto a dune, where I was clearly outlined against the backdrop of the sea, and began to wave my arms, so as to give the impression that I was giving a signal to a launch waiting out there in international waters. That was my farewell to life. A poor university degree, an unfaithful wife, cyclotymic oscillations be-tween joy and despair, no clear conception of national pride, bad teeth, getting lost like a child, the protagonists of my books weird bastards. The sea glittered at my feet, the slimy creatures and fish were asleep, not the waves though; the SEA was my primeval home, from which I crawled up back onto the sand, millions of years ago. A shot rang out, then another, a bullet pierced my chest and I fell onto the rocks, down from the cliffs, onto the seaweed, into the mud, as if I were as dead as a dog. In my pocket was a letter of apology to the head of the border guards for having caused my native land such pointless trouble." My throat went dry. I lay there on the ground where I had fallen. Up in the loft. I went downstairs. It was a cloudy morning and the mobile shop had come to a standstill on the main road. There were a few local men standing at the back of the vehicle, drinking beer and swearing. I too bought a beer. Somehow a morning paper was pushed into my hand and I read it. I read that twenty students had been arrested in Spain, an Israeli barracks had been blown up, military exercises were being conducted in Bulgaria and in Chicago, 6,000 guardsmen had been mobilised to quell the riots among blacks. My head was really aching, my temples throbbed at every step. EDUARD was with us again, grim, serious, business-like. I couldn't understand how he'd got here. I asked him where he had spent the night. Why do you ask, he said, giving a start, I spent the night with you two up in the loft. I see, was what I said and offered Eduard a beer. He refused. I got the feeling that he was angry with me somehow. I should have talked to him and apologised, as it was hard to bear looking at the tragedy in his large violinist's eyes, a sad limpness, and his delicate violinist's hands, the leaden heaviness of his long violinist's legs. But I was fed up with Eduard, and I hadn't got a good rest. So I left the others without a word and went for a walk in the woods. The sun began to come out. I sat in the moss and wrote four reminiscences from the past in my diary. First: "Once, long ago, several years back, we were travelling together in a bus through the autumn rain, which covered the windows like a curtain. The mud squelched under the wheels, it was the end of the working day and the passengers were standing there tightly-packed, you could smell their wet clothing. Your hair brushed against my face. More people got on, the bus roared away. Suddenly everyone could hear a clear woman's voice: – Wait... Did you regret ever meeting me? Were you thinking of someone else, when we were together? – I was startled but then realised that the voice was coming from a small aperture in the bus roof, hidden by a piece of black fabric – No, not for a moment, replied the man, not only when we were together, but even when I was alone, I thought of no one else but you. – Were you jealous of me? When you were with me, was there ever any reason for things to bother you? Were you fed up with me, the woman now asked. – No, never. – The bus stopped. More people got on, the noise they made muffled the woman's voice. Then the bus drove on and again the woman's whispering could be heard, so that the passengers remained silent in amazement. – Kiss me here, and here... and here... (noise). You know how I regret not having a child by you, my darling... What pleasure that would give me... – The theme tune, growing ever louder, smothered the woman's last words. Our stop was next. Pushing my way past the wet passengers, stepping on toes, and exchanging curses we reached the doors, while the violins were playing, then the doors opened, and we emerged from the stuffy belly of the bus into the chilly October rain." Second: "Once, before we were married, the three of us were walking along the riverbank, in the vicinity of the port. You, my friend Konrad, and me. Konrad's black leather coat, rustled in the wind, we walked along the rails, it was night, no one was about among the sheds and cranes, but there was a large shed lit up in the distance, where you could see, through the wide open doors one single machine working away, and its pistons, transmission shafts and flywheels hummed monotonously, without anyone supervising it, or paying any attention to what it was doing. I said: you're walking on one rail, me on another, and we're holding hands. We're not supporting each other, just maintaining each other's balance. I wish our whole life could be like that. – You had tears in your eyes. Konrad kept silent. Later, on a suburban street, in the half-darkness, under the cover of the trees. A lorry parked under the old linden trees, full of cattle bones, the leaves falling." Third: "Our first hike was to Vapramäe, we got off at the observatory and started walking along the spring road, joyful in the sunshine. When we reached Vapramäe, we saw something that shocked my wife: the road was littered with mating frogs that had been splattered by lorries. In those days, I still didn't understand what made those creatures crawl along the road, where death culled them in the middle of their Dionysian festivities. I had to take long strides to avoid treading on the squashed mass of bodies and in the end we couldn't take it any longer and we climbed up a bank by the roadside and crossed a field of stubble left hehind by the harvest of the previous year. Far from that place we lay down to rest. It was early spring, I spotted a lark hovering in the sky and singing. We didn't look at one another, we didn't touch, not even with our fingertips. Down on the road, heavy lorries were rumbling along, their tyres made slippery by organic matter." Fourth: "One day you suddenly fell ill in the palm house of the botanical gardens at the university. You were carried to a bench under the palms and as you writhed with cramp, you held my hand. In the aquarium fat black axolotls were swimming around lazily. When you began to recover, we went for a walk along the banks of the River Emajõgi, making our way through the slush, the city drowning in a bleak fog, and you said that you would soon be dead. You also mentioned that you wanted to become a sociologist. I invited you round to my place that very evening, so that you would become mine. I knew that this would reduce your pain. My rented room had no curtains; through the window the landlord could be seen plastering the outside wall and I built a barricade of books on the windowsill, there weren't enough and so I piled my suits on top. Only now was our bed hidden from the landlord doing his plastering outside. But it was shrieking and creaking something terrible. I whispered beautiful fairy-tales into your ear. I had never before slept with a virgin. I had only read about such things in reference works." Now I have to describe our intercourse, in detail, not in order to shock anyone, simply because literature describes everything, and why shouldn't I then describe the sex act, maybe even more successfully than describing war or an alder grove. But suddenly, I no longer wished to write down descriptions. I jumped to my feet and ran out of the woods. Eduard had gone away. My wife was reading the newspaper. By the sea. By the grey sea. I put my head in her LAP and she stroked my hair. I opened my mouth, but she shut it again with her finger, summoning silence. The sun began to come out again. My headache abated and I took off my clothes and went for a swim. Apart from us there was no one around; just the two of us in the whole wide world. We romped around in the water, splashed one another and I took over a hundred snapshots of my wife – most of them with a foreshortened perspective, with the huge sky in the background, so as to remember the occasion. I sang and danced in the water, imitated someone or other, and my wife, completely tanned, burst into laughter at my antics. I sank to my knees and read love poetry. I felt good that we didn't have children. That would have thrown our relationship into even more

177

confusion. I love children very much, but I could not see that my wife could or should give birth. I remembered how she once took someone else's Russian child onto her knee, a dark-haired and naughty child. I couldn't take my eyes off them. She reminded me of the MADONNA. A good job I didn't say so out loud! Then the day began to come to an end, evening was approaching, we lay there on the beach, we began to feel chilly and pressed ourselves down into the sand. My wife was reading the paper. The sea was now like a mirror – an ominous sign of what was to follow over the next couple of days. I took some sand and scattered it over my wife's skin. Fine grains of sand slipped into her pores, hardly noticeable before, now visible in the low sunlight, and I thought that here, on the empty beach, dreading the fact that summer was coming to an end, we were capable of loving to distraction every cell in the body of every living creature. Everything was so fleeting, so bleak and beautiful and I said: "Time simply moves on, this SUMMER will never return, this BEACH will be covered with bushes, this BENCH will rot away, this cottage will BURN down, you will rot away just like this BLADE OF GRASS or this ANT, but where will your pure BEAUTY, that quality so praised by Baudelaire, vanish to? You are ONE of many that the EARTH has given birth to and will take back. When we had just got to know one another, this at first meant that I was in search of human values and had reached you and YOU became my highest value, and especially your LOVE fulfilled that role I had long been looking for, the role of the PRINCE, to use the terminology Paul-Eerik Rummo used in his play. I was convinced that the skin and lips of this woman, picked out from MILLIONS, had something ETERNAL about them and particularly this erotically tinged beauty would fill the aching gap that I had been given by way of my genes. I am now looking at your skin, now, as it begins to grow chilly, now, when I don't know what will become of me, where I will be living and what I will be doing next year. And I understand that you are simply a PIECE OF LIFE that I am holding onto, as we are two magnets, so close to one another that our force fields touch, but you are no better or more important than that CLOUD, there in the sky. I love you. But you do not differ from the world, you belong to it. I am the lover, not a gambler, I'm an unskilled labourer. I am a knight, not a clown or a martyr." I did not say a word more and that evening we went to sleep early. I dreamt

THURSDAY

that I was falling from the parapet of a skyscraper. The next morning we went into town to do the shopping and went to see a costume drama by René Clair in a half-empty, whitewashed cinema, along with Eduard of course. But we took the bus back to the beach without Eduard. I went up to the loft, despite the fact that it was hot sunny weather, I lay there on the hay and read a letter from my wife through again which she had left for me once when she had gone off somewhere with Eduard, and which I carried around in my back pocket: "You are a good man and I get the feeling that you understand me. What has happened to me now is beyond my understanding. You are very dear and good to me and I remember fondly those beautiful days there have sometimes been between us and I hope even now that they won't come to an end. But since I met Eduard, it's as if I've become another person. I hated him at first, he seemed such an arrogant and horrible type. But now I have the feeling that we were friends in a previous life. I keep on crying and wonder why you and me can't be like brother and sister – we get on so well together. I just can't help it, I must have gone mad. I dreamt that I was being crucified, and then the Day of Judgment arrived. This means that my road in life is predestined. I also dreamt that I was a goddess bathing in a vat of blood. My subconscious was helping me do what I, of course, would never be able to do. Please forgive me. I love you both." You love us all, you accursed Latter Day goddess, was what I was thinking morosely, I pushed the letter deep into the hay and hid my head in it too: the blood you dreamt about, where the harlot was sitting, a host of people and pagans and tongues. And the woman you saw is a great city, belonging to a grand realm holding sway over the kings of the Earth. Down below, a car horn sounded. I now remembered that I was to go to a student meeting that evening as part of the summer camp. I buttoned up my shirt and descended the ladder. The driver was smoking nervously and started the car as soon as he saw me. We drove off. At the meeting, I said my usual spiel: (that not all art can be understood by everyone; theatre is an encounter [Grotowski]; the new generation has been born into a tragic world; I am not a proponent of emancipation; easel painting has had its day; even if the term "collective unconscious" is not precise and scientific, it is at least poetic; a writer must be honest, love should be free; my first novel is more or less autobiographical, but searching for prototypes is a perverse way of going about things; I have been to the German Democratic Republic and Poland, but I don't remember anything special about them; play (*Spiel*) brings us back to ourselves (*Selbst*); my literature teacher aroused my interest in literature; rumours that I am a homosexual are unfounded, although I do not hate anyone for making such hints; I can't say anything about my future plans). The student brigade leaders invited me to drink some vodka behind the bushes, but I refused and went for a walk with Marina. She asked me, with rather a wry smile on her lips, whether my wife knew we were likely to meet here. I said she would hardly suspect anything, she was in love and had too much to do. I told Marina that until I'd actually arrived at the camp, I didn't know whether I would meet her there, but I had come in the hope I would, and if she was not there, I'd have gone straight back to Tallinn the next day. We walked along a narrow woodland path, she in front, me behind, we exchanged hasty abrupt phrases, we were seized by a kind of awkwardness, as if the month we had been apart had turned us into total strangers, and we both had to force ourselves to remember why we had been together, why just us, why that combination. Marina asked with feigned malice, whether my wife was still being unfaithful to me. I lied (why? out of pride? or lack of trust?) that the word "unfaithful" (an empty expression, a non-word) was perhaps an exaggeration, in our language, in our mind, we tended to think of something different (I said "different" although I was thinking of sexual relations), and not how my wife and Eduard were carrying on. Their relationship was too platonic, too cultivated. They had gone for walks, sometimes Eduard would play the violin at his place. Once I rode past them in a taxi quite by chance and saw by the light of the headlights how they had their arms round one another as they walked down the middle of the road. I let the taxi drive some two hundred metres ahead of them, let the taxi go off and waited for them in the middle of the road, but at the last moment I went to hide behind a big rowan tree. I heard their voices, but couldn't make out what they were saying. I didn't start following them, I walked slowly back towards the town centre, picked up a taxi on the corner and went after them. They had reached our house and were kissing. I got out of the taxi, walked past them without saying anything and went up to my room on the first floor. I waited for about ten minutes before my wife arrived. That's how it is – they had kissed, but that was all, they were educated people, really cultivated. Marina believed me and asked whether I wanted anything more, but I didn't reply, didn't want to seem base. Then Marina said that I looked out of sorts, tired and pale. I was afraid that Marina thought me unhappy, that I was worrying too much about my marriage, and I said that I had had a great deal of work to do that spring. Had gone through a lot too, but that wasn't everything. The woods were sparse, we were no longer ill at ease, and Marina was telling me her news. Many people are said to be anxious about our marriage, especially Konrad. Drop it, I said. Let's not talk about my marriage. Now you're here, so why think about others. We reached an old barn, its roof covered in moss. All around us the completely ordinary inland countryside, an alder grove, slightly softened by the mists of a summer night. I was happy that we couldn't see the sea from there, in all its showiness. Marina leaned against the wall of the barn. The mosquitos were eating her up. She killed one on her forehead, smearing herself with blood. I went up to her. She had long hair and I

FRIDAY

took her HAIR and draped it across her FACE. You could no longer

181

make out her eyes, nose or mouth. Everything was smooth and dark. She could no longer see me and I pressed my mouth against her hair, but my lips could find no raised or sunken places under this rough carpet, the contours of her face had vanished entirely. I slid my LIPS along her hair and felt my heart beat stronger. Gradually, as if pretending to be searching for something different, proceeding as if in a state of absent-mindedness, I began to part her hair, until my lips discovered the softness of her LIPS, although there was still a mass of tickly hair in between. Nevertheless, a kiss was possible. To put an end to the pretence, I brushed the last hair out of her mouth, she put her ARMS around my neck and we began to kiss. She pressed herself RIGHT UP against me and I responded in the same way and we wanted to melt into one. Surrounding us were the woods, a BIRD shrieked shrilly now and again, there had to be a MARSH nearby, since the grove was clammy like in a cellar. I felt my CIRCULATION start again. I slid gradually down her body, until I was KNEELING in the long dewy grass. Kissing her tanned, rough LEGS, I felt I no longer wanted to do anything else, and bit her knee. She made a faint moaning sound and bent down towards me. I was in the darkness of her WOMB, I kept silent, had not up to then said a single word, or used her pet name. I felt that I would never start talking to her. Still kneeling, I took hold of her, rose to my feet with her in my arms, and took a few steps. Her eyes were shut, her face relaxed, her lips pouting. I carried her to the barn and laid her down on last year's hay. Only now did she open her eyes and looked at me with an insipid, tired smile. When we started to embrace, I felt I wanted to pierce her right through, to the other side, into the ground, reaching through the earth. She muttered disjointed words, and afterwards I was bathed in sweat and covered in bits of hay, I wiped off the sweat, but it returned, and then I realised what was going on: an area of low pressure was forming that evening, and the evening damp rising, bad weather was on the way. I brushed off the bits, looked over to the door, and the light struck my eyes. In the sky above the grove stood clouds, pink underneath. I hate summer nights. The whole of summer is ephemeral at our latitude, its beginning also means its end. And the fact it grows light so quickly gives rise to the thought that a crime has been committed and you've been caught in the act, so you have to flee, that you are late. Lovers and hooligans find their refuge in October, November, in the rain and mud. I said to Marina, that I would come and live at their camp, and that she should tell the others that my name is Peep, let me stay at the camp till the end. Later, when this gave rise to discord, as I was ignoring my social responsibilities, I could lie that I had been bitten by a rabid dog and that I had been given an injection at the last moment, and that I had been lying down for some weeks now. You left your things back there, said Marina. Don't care, I shrugged my shoulders, let them stay there. The only thing I miss is the camera with around a hundred snapshots that I made in the shallow water during the day. I've got iconographic material on all my friends, even former ones, and I should also have pictures of my woman. If there are no photos from those days, then those days don't exist. You can write anything you like later on. Only a photo is the real thing. A little while later, I lit a cigarette and asked Marina, what she'd been doing and why she hadn't written to me after we'd parted in Tartu. Where would I have written to, and what about, Marina asked, where and what about? She buttoned up her dress and began to comb her hair. I suddenly felt superfluous, went to the window, lit a cigarette and watched the morning grow lighter with horror. The thought suddenly struck me that my wife had achieved her old intention to take up violin lessons again, something she had broken off during her childhood, that Eduard had brought his violin and that they were playing in my absence some sonatas, some *divertimenti* (God, I know nothing about music), playing the violin in the loft and the sweet duet could be heard right across the dewy fields down to the sea, and they were playing with impunity, like crazy, panting, but on they played, and that was the end, and I had been defeated yet again. They had a world which I could not enter, where discussion proved futile, and my only way in would be to learn to play the violin, although I lack an ear for music. And even if I had, I couldn't play with impunity. When you play the violin, you are no longer human, merely a violinist, and everything beautiful is destroyed, played away to nothing. Before me lay the hinterland of Estonia, tall grass, cow pats. I stormed into the barn, to Marina, took her by the shoulders and told her everything. Our eyes were up close, I could see no expression, only two small, round, bright blue, translucent globes, they were eyes, but I could not explain anything to them, nor they to me, it all seemed hopeless. Listen to me, I actually bawled at her. I'm listening, said Marina quietly. No, you're not listening. You're not listening. I'm listening to you, Marina repeated. What are you hearing, I asked irritably. You haven't said anything yet, said Marina with a smile. I shut up and began kissing her again, biting her, poking her, like some naughty little child. Between the kisses, the nervous, almost desperate kisses, I demanded she gave me the key to her Tartu flat. She became serious, her hands were shaking as she handed me the key, and my hands were shaking and I recited a couple of lines from *A Midsummer Night's Dream*: swift as a shadow, short as any dream, brief as the lightning in the collied night. Our times, as a friend of mine once said: the women have run wild, and the young men recite poetry on their knees. I will never learn to play the violin. I don't know how to make music with it. I can't use a bow. We walked back to the camp along the same path we had come by. I gradually calmed down, the shock of the morning light began to wane, my hopeless state gradually subsided and it turned more and more into an ordinary day. I looked at my watch; it was only half past four. The camp was asleep, the flaps to all the tents were buttoned shut, it was a dead town in the bright sunshine and only a few hours before I had for some reason expressed my opinions and views here. Marina left me waiting at the staff tent, went off and returned with the keys. SWIFT AS A SHADOW, SHORT AS ANY DREAM, BRIEF AS THE LIGHTNING IN THE COLLIED NIGHT. A car was parked behind the tent. SWIFT AS A SHADOW. I got in and wound down the window. Then Marina came to sit next to me. I wanted to kiss her, but she pulled the starter. BRIEF AS THE LIGHTNING IN THE COLLIED NIGHT. The roar of the engine was ear-splitting in the sleeping camp. Luckily, we got away quickly. SHORT AS ANY DREAM. Not one tent opened up.

The whole island seemed to have died. We drove along deserted roads past stone walls. The sky was clear, but the wind had risen, something we had not noticed among the brushwood, ripped at the leaves of the bushes and made the hayfield billow, whistled though the car windows and cooled my hot face. Marina said sweet nothings to me, which was the right thing to do, but I made no attempt to reply, I wasn't listening to her just looked at her brown ARMS, as she clutched the STEERING WHEEL. Something was now gone for ever. Not only out of my life, but out of those of my friends. Something had been left behind. What it was I didn't think about, perhaps there never had been anything. MY VEXATION WAS GRIEVOUS, DEATH COULD TAKE ME AWAY, BUT THEN MY DARLING WOULD BE LEFT HERE ALONE. Shakespeare again, poetry again. I remembered that the critic Rähesoo had once said of me: two potential dangers in my development, one being "the pretence of the reality of ideal idyllic love, the illusion of sentimentalism"; the other being making self-pity heroic as the Host did in his "tragic role" in the play *Cinderella* by Paul-Eerik Rummo. The sky was filled with seagulls, they were fleeing the sea, which could appear at any moment. They were screeching loudly, their cries could be heard above the noise of the car engine, as if they were CRYING my name, but I knew, that there was no point in answering their alien, obscure cries, that would bring mishap to anyone answering. I had never before seen such an open, white sky AS NOW. Going uphill. LIKE A FLASH OF LIGHT IN THE MURKY NIGHT. It really was a sky you could fall into. Marina had fallen silent. I looked at her weary face, the first, early, crows feet at the corners of her eyes, which stood out against her suntan, and an incomprehensible pain pierced my heart. A hundred metres before our summer place Marina stopped the car. I undid the buttons on her dress and we started kissing again. I pushed down her shoulder straps and pressed my lips onto her breasts. The Empty Beach was deserted, the road was empty, the morning lorries had not yet started on their journeys. Over the juniper bushes the sea glittered, the wind had got up even more during our trip and the sea was full of white horses.

The engine clicked as it cooled down. Marina's watch was ticking by my ear, but I couldn't stop or move away. I thought: I must start speaking again: MY ONE AND ONLY DARLING MY DEAR MY JOY MY ANGEL MY LITTLE FLOWER MY LILAC BLOOM MY HOPE MY BLUE SKY MY LITTLE LEVERET MY WOMAN MY POSY OF BLUE FLOWERS PUPPY BEST OF ALL MY MOST BEAUTIFUL ONE HOW I LOVE YOUR HAIR YOUR BREASTS YOUR MOUTH YOUR LEGS YOU ARE MY ONLY ONE I WANT TO BE WITH YOU ALWAYS AND FOREVER BELIEVE ME I HAVE NO ONE ELSE IN THIS WORLD DO YOU LOVE YOU ME AS MUCH AS I LOVE YOU MY JOY MY STARLIGHT, will I have to repeat this as I once did to Helina, now that the wind is blowing and the birds flying. When you go to my place and before I arrive in Tartu, said Marina, then don't turn on the telly. There's something wrong with it, it hisses and there are sparks, it could even explode. You'll find the sheets and blankets, and there's coffee and sugar in the cupboard, and don't forget to lock the door at night. I gave her a kiss and went out to stretch my legs that had grown stiff. The wind blew dust in my eyes. My lips were numb and inflamed from kissing. I didn't know whether I was dreaming or not and whether there was any hope of ever waking up. Marina started the engine, turned the car around and drove away. I didn't want to go to sleep in the loft, but I couldn't find anything to do either. I stood by the corner of the shed, rolled a cigarette, but it made my mouth grow bitter. Then I climbed up the ladder. In the loft, where the wind didn't penetrate, it was hot and stuffy. I watched my sleeping wife. She was alone, and nobody appeared to have visited her in the meantime. Of course I couldn't be sure. Without taking off my clothes I lay down. I tried to remember something, but then gave up. Remembering is childish, a stage passed by. Less memory, less thoughts, less self-torment. My eyes smarted, were full of sand. My wife slept soundlessly, without snoring. I too dozed off. In the morning, my wife reminded me that we ought to leave. Where to in such a hurry I asked her sleepily, lying there on the bed. A sea voyage she said, don't you remember? I still didn't understand anything. The roof of the barn creaked in the wind. I didn't want to get up. Don't you remember that we were going to go to that little island? With Eduard, I asked. She made no reply, I got up and remembered everything. Yes, the little islet, an hour by boat. I put on a thick jumper, I'd grown cold while asleep. We climbed down the ladder. I was surprised how the world around us had changed. Thick clouds were flying low over the yard, the wind pushed me back. You seem to find the time to go on a boat trip, I grumbled. My wife again said nothing. I didn't want to seem weak. My maleness had challenged me to a duel. WE WENT OUT TO MEET THE STORM AND THE SEA. I had to go along with it as it was part of love and LOVE WAS THE REASON why we had gone to the western islands in the first place. We arrived at the main road, took the first bus into town, from there to the port. At every stop the number of passengers grew smaller. In the end, the only ones left were the driver and the three of us. We got out at the port. THE SEA was dark grey and unpleasantly choppy. I couldn't get a clear picture of the waves until we went out onto the jetty. There was a lot of spray, the waves were beating against the posts and the structure beneath our feet kept on swaying. We stood at the end of the jetty. Before me in the mist loomed an iron ladder from the crane, dripping with water. The water dripped down the back of my neck. In the wild waters flapped an absurd poster saying "Swimming prohibited". The larger waves splashed over us, and soon my trousers were soaking wet. Where are we going, I asked and immediately Eduard nodded to me in encouragement and winked, so that I couldn't help feeling embarrassed. We moved into the lee of the harbour building. The window panes jingled loudly. We sat down on a long bench, the only piece of furniture in the room. I couldn't grasp why I was here and what my role was in all of this. OH YES, TO FIGHT FOR MY WIFE. She was here, wrapped in a weatherproof raincoat. We looked outside. There was no one on the jetty. A couple of ships bobbed helplessly on the waves. Almost an hour and a half passed. No one came in. In the end, Eduard went out to look for the bo'sun. The mail boat was likely to be sailing over to the islet. In all weathers, no doubt. The two of us remained. I no longer knew what word I should use with regard to Helina. She was resting her chin on her hands looking at the windows down which the rain constantly streamed. I suddenly remembered my father who had arrived at a noisy wedding party without a tie and how I immediately told him to put one on. He squatted down in the corridor and began rummaging clumsily and uncertainly in an old briefcase which I felt ashamed of. Someone came out of the pantry and pushed the door in such a way that he fell to his knees. My wife sat there looking at the rainy windows. And no woman can stand in front of a beast, when it's all about her. Don't sully yourselves with all this. BECAUSE THE LAND HAS BECOME SULLIED AND I WISH TO PAY IT BACK FOR THE ABUSE, SO THAT THE LAND WILL SPEW OUT THOSE WHO LIVE HERE. Eduard returned unexpectedly, his face dripping with water. The boat will be sailing right away, he shouted. I stood up hesitantly. Hurry up, said Eduard. I moved away from my wife, I really couldn't care less now. Between two large ships a small motor boat that I hadn't spotted before bobbed up and down. A man stood at the prow and beckoned to us. We climbed into the boat, the man released the rope, and our contact with dry land was cut off. Once we were beyond the lee of the jetty, the storm got its claws into us. Now the prow dipped in the water, the straining engine of the boat was pushing through waves a house high. We clasped the rope and didn't go down into the cabin, though the skipper gestured for us to do so on several occasions. Warm water sloshed into our faces. I really wanted us to sail across the waves, but that was obviously not possible given the direction we were heading. As we proceeded sideways against the savage mountains of water, I thought several times that our boat would not be able to right itself. My wife was dripping with water and Eduard had his arm around her. I stood apart, at the other side of the boat and I took no notice of either my wife or Eduard. I wanted to get back to dry LAND. At the time, we didn't know that this was a hurricane, traces of which would still exist in 1967. Few people along the whole coastline knew about it then. The hurricane had knocked down radio masts and so communications were broken. The whole horizon was covered by low cloud and spray and I knew that one fateful wave could swamp the boat, and the last thing I would see in life was two people in an embrace, my wife and Eduard, with their blue lips and staring eyes. I listened nervously to the chug of the engine, every missed beat made my heart grow cold. But you get used to anything. Five minutes later I had grown calmer and was looking out at the mass of water almost with indifference, as if this were a perfectly normal situation. In any case, nothing depended on my will any longer. OH LOVE AS LONG AS YOU CAN, OH LOVE AS LONG AS YOU ARE ABLE. Land ahoy! shouted Eduard after what seemed an endless period of time. Through the rain we could make out something vague: woods, a harbour, a house. Slowly but surely we were getting near dry land. We had reached the lee of the islet, the waves were smaller now, though even more restless. The sea writhed nervously and for the first time I felt seasick. I breathed vigorously in and out, my gaze fixed on the contours of the islet. By now you could make out the harbour, a number of trees on a stretch of open ground behind the house and the remnants of the mast swaying in the wind over the roof of the harbourmaster's cabin. Once INDOORS, I took a bottle of vodka from my bag, offered it to Helina and Eduard, took a swig myself, but the vodka didn't go to my head. Only after a teacupful or so did I get a warm feeling inside. The host family looked at us in wonder, they couldn't make head or tail of us. Their sons had gone off a couple of days before to Tallinn. Along with us sitting in the corner was a TV film director, but he said very little indeed, simply smiled at our story. I slouched on the divan, resting my head against the wall, and shut my eyes. The house swayed under me. Helina and Eduard were sitting on the other side of the table. How on earth did you start out in this terrible weather, asked our hostess eyeing us. Well, we just did, I replied in a non-committal way, we just happened to do so. The TV film director was smiling in his corner. What does a TV film director know of our great summer festival, our great dream of love? No sane person could understand. I shut my eyes once more and ignored the swaying of the house. I could hear snatches of conversation, someone sighed, someone described something. I couldn't be bothered to follow the conversation. Boiled potatoes were brought to the table, along with meat and gravy. We drew our chairs up to the table and I poured out vodka for everyone. I raised my glass first, paying no attention to the rest. The TV film director gave me a crafty look and we drank. Through a small window you could see a hayfield and some hazel trees whipped by the storm. I got the impression that it had grown a little lighter outside and I pointed this out to the others. It'll get lighter after lunch said our hostess, the wind will drive away the clouds. The TV film director pushed away his plate, went over to the window and examined the sky. We'll soon be able to start, you can already see the sun through the clouds, he said rather enigmatically, and I couldn't really be bothered to ask what he meant. Then he yawned, put on his coat and left the room. I lit a cigarette and looked at Helina. Eduard was staring stiffly at the table and now and again he muttered something. How d'you feel darling, I asked Helina. Fine, she replied. Take some more, said our hostess. No thanks, said Helina. It was very nice but I really couldn't eat any more. It was very nice, I repeated. Then the TV film director came back in, in a good mood. Let's start, he said. We rose from the table and thanked our hostess. We put on our coats and went out. The clouds were thinning out, although they still flitted over our heads at the same speed as before. We followed the TV film director through the wet undergrowth. I was walking alongside Helina, Eduard walked behind, snapping off twigs and mumbling to himself. By evening the storm will be completely over, I said to Helina and she nodded. Are you homesick, I asked her. Yes, she said and our eyes met briefly. We climbed up onto a knoll. At that moment the SUN came out and shone from under the CLOUDS that covered the whole SKY. I walked carefully, so as to avoid treading on SNAILS, which were scattered all over the road. Looking down from the KNOLL we could see, against the sun, the evening SEASHORE, the dark blue, almost BLACK sea in its MOVEMENT after the storm, even the GRASS looked black against the light. It was flat and open here, there was only a NET-DRYING SHED down on the beach, the sun was blinding us, it was a DEAD landscape that stretched out before our eyes: windy, strangely lit up, and apocalyptically sombre. This is how it will go, I was thinking, the smooth sea buried under huge clouds, the sun scorching hot. The cameras stood in a triangle by the shed. The director asked us to run and play tag. I didn't argue and we all ran down the hill. My wife ran along shrieking, I behind her. I slipped a few times on the wet grass and fell on my face, got up and ran on after her. Eduard tagged Helina before me, she turned round like lightning and began chasing me. I ran straight to the water's edge, I saw nothing, so bright was the SUN in an otherwise dark landscape. I only turned aside when my feet had reached the wet sand of the water's edge. I ran along the shoreline, my lungs filled with air to the point of bursting, but Helina caught up with me and tagged me. Now Eduard began to follow us, so we had to run back to the knoll. Eduard waited there fairly patiently, till I got near, then he tried to trip me up a couple of times and I might have escaped but he fell with me. I splashed about next to him and lashed out. When he ran after my wife, I stayed put. I lay there, my heart pounding. My wife and Eduard ran along the shore, so boundlessly tiny on the face of the outstretched landscape and the universe, like the first human beings, and from their shadows you could imagine that they were NAKED. In the end, Eduard took hold of my wife, and she broke away and began running towards me. I was happy that the director shouted for us to take a break and gave us the sign that we could go out of shot. I strolled over to the others, because an interview was now taking place with some local people. That little race had now warmed me up. We went over to the old schoolhouse, looked at the new one, and chatted to a local man about the island. In the evening the three of us went to sleep in the hay in the shed. We were sleeping between clean sheets. There was a knot in the wood above my head and I could see out through it. The sky was now completely clear, though the wind was gusting as before. The world seemed swept clean. We lay for a while in silence. Then Eduard said he had to take a leak. I waited for him to descend the ladder, and turned to my wife. Forgive me, I said to her, but I have to tell you something. Well, she replied. It's like this, I said, we ought to get a divorce. She said nothing, thinking presumably, that I was trying to stir her up on account of Eduard. I'm in love with Marina, I told her. What marina, she said, with a small "m", as if she wasn't aware I was talking about a person. The Marina who came to our place once, you remember, it was raining and we lent her our umbrella. Helina kept silent for a good while and stared at me blankly. What's with this Marina she finally asked, rather agitated. I'm in love with her, is what I said. My wife rose up onto her elbow and slapped me in the face. I embraced her and started to kiss her just like any film hero would. It startled me that her lips responded as if there had never been discord between us. Then suddenly she drew away. At that same moment, Eduard's head appeared in the opening to the trap door. He understood everything, sensed that we had kissed. I couldn't summon up the energy to explain things to Eduard, turned my back and lay there motionless. A few minutes later I heard

SATURDAY

that Helina was crying. I thought that Eduard might try and comfort her, but he merely muttered something under his breath. There had been times when I would wait for hours in the rain for my wife to return, in the night, in the darkness. Now everything suddenly seemed boundlessly comical. I strained to suppress a laugh, but couldn't hold it back and burst out laughing. Are you laughing at me, asked Eduard quietly. No, no, I replied, I just remembered something funny. I'd be curious to know what, said Eduard. So I told him: once, when I was still a tiny little boy, some men drove up to our house to bathe in the sauna. Our sauna is in a dale in the woods. They drove right up to the sauna and were already drunk. They had their sauna, but afterwards couldn't get the car back up the hillside. I remember naked men pushing the car and yelling. Then some horses were brought and only then did they pull the car away from the sauna. Quite understandably, no one laughed at my tale. I could hear the soughing of the wind above us in the sky, my lungs were full of fresh sea air. I was seized by melancholy, I got a lump in my throat, as if I had eaten an apple and a piece had got stuck. I thought that we would never regain paradise, we were broken people. I got up and without a word to the others pulled on my clothes. Nor did either of them ask me what I was doing. They were not asleep but daren't move either. I climbed down the ladder and strolled through the wet grass down to the water's edge, across the empty beach. It was clear and cold and once again the END OF SUMMER was at hand. It was AUTUMN that surrounded me now, that penetrated my lungs, wet my feet. The sky was now so high that it no longer existed. I sat down on a rock by the sea and planned how I could get away as soon as possible. By swimming, by boat? Like Leander? Across the Hellespont? It was Saturday already, and they were expecting me back at work on the following Monday, my holidays were over, back to my desk, back to meetings, bad language in the corridors. But in principle everything would be the same and it would make no difference, so there was no point in waiting any longer. It didn't matter what the international news or the weather forecast said – a person's heart can sense very precisely when a war or a storm is in the offing. I sat there a long time, but when I went back to the other two so that I could get some sleep, they were still awake and Helina was crying. Now I felt content. I lay down next to them and soon nodded off. I only woke up once, it was as if I could hear the sound of conversation. As I moved, silence reigned supreme again. I breathed long and deep. A few minutes later I heard Eduard whisper: I can't live without you, I never believed that you could cheat on someone like that, you're not a woman, but Satan, the monks were right to hate women, I feel like that myself now, how could you destroy everything in one instant, just remember how I've arranged a flat for us in Tallinn, everything, everything we spoke about, how we would start living together, what shall I do now, is everything really finished, can a woman manage to destroy everything that's beautiful? Shut up, whispered my wife. The wind gusted as before over the ridge of the roof. I fell asleep again. In the morning I was the only one left in the loft, this scared me – had they really left me behind? I dressed hurriedly and looked out through the door opening. It was cold and overcast. My wife and

Eduard were walking along the village lane in silence. We went to the harbour in the same silence. This time the boat was full of people, the sea was beginning to grow calm, but the boat was still rocking enough for me to get seasick. The spray over the gunwale was no longer warm like the day before, but icy cold. Nonetheless, the danger had passed. I didn't look Eduard straight in the eye, night had opened up a gap between us, we no longer belonged together. Suddenly, I felt sorry for him and I leaned over and asked in a whisper whether he wouldn't mind playing the violin that evening before our final departure. He seemed startled, as if I had hit him. No honestly, I said, play the violin for me. I've never heard you play; don't think I'm joking, it's just that I can't ask in a more natural way any longer: so many days together, and you haven't played for me once. If you're artistic then you ought to do so. Why, he asked grimly. I don't know, I replied, I just feel that's how it should be. He grunted sadly. The boat moored. I'll come for you two later, Eduard said; I'll get a taxi. Don't bother, we'll manage, said my wife. It would be really nice of you, I said. We hitched a lift with the first vehicle to come along and it took us to where we had been staying. We were in the back of a lorry along with some workers and the men eyed my wife and coughed meaningfully and I was thinking that it was now the first of September and that the school term would be starting soon. At our beach one of the men helped my wife down. I stood and watched, hands in pockets. We packed up our things in the loft. Everything happened very quickly. Then I said I was going down to the shore. Did you spend the night with that woman, asked Helina, by the way, I wasn't sleeping when you got back, she added. Yes, I did. Where, asked Helina. At her place. And you're not ashamed, said Helina with surprise. No. I feel no SHAME. What's going to happen to me? Will it last a long time, she asked. I don't know. I DON'T KNOW. I DON'T KNOW ANYTHING ANY MORE. You have to pay the old lady, I said, the money's in your hand, ten roubles. My wife said nothing. Give me the ten roubles. She gave her the money. I went in to where the old lady was sitting among the flowering houseplants. She asked whether we had liked it there. I told her we had. She said that we had been very nice quiet people and that we were just right and she also asked whether we had children. I told her not yet, our accommodation was very cramped. You'll have pretty children, she said. I smiled and shook her bony hand, adding that we would no doubt be back next year. I went straight down to the beach from the house and swam for a long time up and down the shoreline. Evening was approaching, the last evening. When I got back to the house Eduard was waiting with a taxi below the loft hatch. We put our things in the car. We drove back into town. The heat had not gone away, the taxi windows were open, but I was still sweating and wiping my face. Over the shallows of the small bay birds were slowly wheeling in the sky. People were walking listlessly along the streets, cats were prowling in the dust. Sadness seized my heart once more. Eduard took us for the night (the plane wouldn't be taking off until the next morning) to his aunt's abandoned house. It was already growing dark, the heat was abating. Eduard disappeared off somewhere. I sat hunched up on the steps, time stood still, the branches were motionless. My wife went off somewhere, said something. I was thinking of nothing. It grew dark. Someone was talking in the neighbouring garden. Everything, everything stood still. EVERYTHING. I went inside. The walls of the room were covered in yellowed photos. My wife had gone to bed, under an old blanket, in an old bed. All of a sudden, the silence was broken, soldiers were marching past. Then everything stood still again. There was a knock at the door. Eduard entered, holding his violin. My wife turned her face to the wall. Eduard took out a bottle of wine and put it on the table. He picked up his violin and started to play. He played for a long time. Asked something, I answered something. He went out. I went to bed. My wife said to me: let's wait a bit, everything will turn out for the best, we have to come to terms with our feelings, we're both just as guilty, we don't love one another very much, we should have had children, but we are made for one another, remember you yourself said that, and also said that I was your ray of sunshine. She pressed up against me. She was talking and I felt sexually aroused. She was doing everything to increase my arousal. I did what

I had to. I said: MY CRAZY ONE, MY MENTALLY ILL WIFE, MY INCOMPREHENSIBLE ONE, MY HEAD-SPINNER, WHAT WILL BECOME OF YOU. She said, it had never been so good with me as now. She was crying and stroked my cheeks. Then there was a knock at the door. I said come in. Eduard came in, sat on the edge of our bed and said: Helina is in love with me, but she can't decide, do you hear me, Helina is in love with me. That's her business, I said. He spoke, clutching our blanket, do you remember Helina, what we said, do you remember that you said that I'm the only person on Earth that you have ever loved, who has ever understood you. Helina did not

SUNDAY

say a word. He just sat there and said that you should make up your mind, Helina, or everything is over. Helina said nothing. He said: what is LOVE, who can trust it, what is TRUST anyway. Helina said nothing. Eduard went down on his knees beside our bed, his long soft hair spread across the coarse bedspread. He repeated monotonously: HELINA, HELINA, HELINA, HELINA, HELINA. I suddenly felt ghastly. I was ashamed of being naked: by chance it was me who had been picked out today. By what right? He repeated: HELINA, HELINA, HELINA. He repeated the name of his murderer. Helina said nothing. I just couldn't look on, while my wife murdered him. Helina's glazed eyes looked out of the window, a branch was swaying in the black of night, back and forth, as if someone were giving a sign that he would help if he could. Eduard huddled up even more, as if an invisible pneumatic press were squashing him into a ball. A repulsive weeping emerged from his lips. My wife swallowed hard, but did not move, waiting. In that case I'm leaving now, said Eduard in a shaky voice and rose to his feet. I leapt swiftly from the bed, I wanted to be with him. We all have limits to our endurance. MAY THE HEAVENS GIVE US THE STRENGTH TO LIVE, MAY SATAN GIVE US COLD BLOOD. May food give us vitamins. Eduard moved towards the door. I pulled my trousers on and ran after him. Eduard's face was dead. For one of us happiness had sunk, for the other it had risen, both without reason. We went together to the steps. We both stood outside in the dark garden that had run wild. The sky was filled with stars and it seemed that there was a light burning behind the heavens. It was chilly, I was shivering. I offered Eduard a cigarette. He took it, didn't light it, stood there, an unlit cigarette jutting from the corner of his mouth. OH, LOVE AS LONG AS YOU LIVE. Why? What for? We listened to the sounds of town: a dog was barking somewhere, a lone car was driving along. I said: you play the violin beautifully, Eduard. He laughed glumly and gave a sigh. Well, I said. I was embarrassed. I'm going now, he said. Don't go yet, look how beautiful the night is, I pleaded with him. I've got to go, you have proved to be stronger than I am. I could never have imagined that you would be stronger than me, he said. So, do you have to go right away because of that, I asked. I would have said take that woman then, take her, I don't need her any more, she's free to go as far as I'm concerned, but how the hell do I know how you can win back her heart, I simply can't help you. She loves ME, he said. Me too, and she'll start loving YOU again, if you play your cards right, I said soothingly. He sighed once more. It's the end, he said. For me too, I agreed. But I love her, said Eduard. Love her then, I said. OH, LOVE AS LONG AS YOU CAN. A kind of muffled cry emerged from Eduard's breast. He vanished like a shadow into the darkness. The sky was still filled with stars. I went inside, where my wife awaited me with a helpless smile on her lips. I lay down beside her, but avoided touching her. We lay down on our backs, next to each other, in silence. I now remembered that the piece that Eduard had played for us was from a Paganini concerto, maybe his fifth, but I am no music expert. I too am simply a murderer. Don't you want to talk to me, asked my wife, her voice quavering. Sorry, but no. I told you we should try to come to terms with our feelings, she repeated. I didn't reply, I simply couldn't. Everything came back to me. How we said under the trees in the dark park that we loved one another for the first time. How we would go for a walk on winter's nights and knock snow off the branches onto each other's heads. How we made a midsummer's night bonfire. How we made presents for each other's birthday. How we received visitors. How we dreamt of our future together and the best flat available. How we went to Moscow. How we went skiing together. How we were ill at the same time. How we fed a stray cat. How we celebrated Christmas. How we cried when a friend had an accident. How we studied for our exams together. How we saw the university building burn together. How we entrusted everything to each another. How we sold books to the second-hand bookshop when we needed the money. How we danced. How we made love. How we lived. Time was advancing slowly. In the end, my wife fell asleep. I waited and waited, the plane would take off at eight. At half past five I got up and tried to read the book I had brought with me. Enzensberger's article. How on 26 August 1880 Wilhelm Albert Wlodzimierz Apollinaris de Kostrowicki was born in Rome. Time stood still, then started again, then stopped. At half past six I woke Helina. Her eyes were red and swollen. She'd not slept much. We went out onto the street in silence, into an empty, empty, empty Sunday morning. Misty. No buses running. We had to go on foot to the city centre, where the airport bus was waiting, with drowsy people taking a nap inside. We took a seat, they all had their collars turned up, saying nothing, as if they were returning home for some important anniversary. As if nothing had come between us, as if we had woken up from a bad dream, as if it was still 1966. Then we started moving. Our trip to the western islands is over, I said for no particular reason. Helina seemed to smile, smiled gratefully. I took hold of her cold hand. Her hands were always getting cold; she had poor circulation. I looked out of the window, where bushes and the tops of the trees were poking out of the mist. The airfield was already in sight. Now too the border guard seemed quite satisfied with me and didn't pay any more attention to me than necessary. The plane rose into the air and flew low over a corner of the island. The earth lost its substance and turned into a map, and I didn't know whether Eduard was watching the plane rise, and the plane flew very low over the sea, very low beneath the clouds and the whole of the expanse of our native land was cleansed and wet, we descended into pockets of low pressure and rose again and a child began to spew up and I thought nervously about what was going to happen, but my thoughts were tense, frozen, and for a moment I thought the plane had come to a standstill, was falling, but no, it flew on doggedly, even lower in the sky, almost over the treetops, over Estonia, where all that was left to do was love, since any other activity seemed insincere, or a trifle awkward, and with every turn of the propeller, with every metre, we were getting nearer to the seaside resort, which we had left a week previously, and now we were returning and didn't know who was bringing whom back from hell, couldn't be helped, I could already make out the water tower and the white beach hotel near the sea, as choppy as before, standing there like a matchbox, and the plane veered and descended and I expected a crash and an explosion, but then suddenly everything went quiet and the door was opened. I was the first to get off, I helped my wife down, supporting her arm, and I took our things. The long grass rustled under our feet as we crossed the meadow. Outside the airport building I put down our luggage, excused myself and went to look for the toilets. On the way there I stopped, retraced my steps, stopped again, then continued. The toilets were behind the airport building. I stepped up onto the toilet seat and looked out of the window smeared with fly droppings. In the wind, the nettles and willows were swaying. I forced open the window, grazed my hands against the plaster, bloodying them and jumped out of the window down into the soft grass. Luckily, no other window gave onto this area. I broke into a run in such a way that the airport building shielded me from my wife, who had stayed with the luggage. Quite soon I went up onto a hillock, descended into a dale. I no longer needed to run. I went in no particular direction, my trousers covered in burdock burrs, I looked around me, tried to find some landmark. In the distance I could see some telegraph poles and I went towards them. I was not mistaken. Soon the main road came into view. I walked in the direction of what I thought was the town. After five minutes or so, I heard the throb of a lorry engine, and raised my arm, the vehicle stopped and I climbed up into the back and sat under the tarpaulin between some fish barrels. The barrels rocked about and I kept them off with both hands. I had no time to do anything, let alone think. When I peeped out from under the tarpaulin some while later, I saw that we were already in the seaside resort, where I had stayed and walked each summer with my wife. People were quite calm here, no one would have guessed that I was in the back of the lorry. Luckily, we also got past the militiamen. The lorry stopped in front of the bus station and I jumped down and rushed into the ticket office, looking no one in the eye. Here too, no one seemed to recognise me. I was in luck and got a ticket for the bus to Tõrva, which was leaving in fifteen minutes. From Tõrva it was still some sixty kilometres to Tartu, but that was a minor problem. I didn't hang around on the platform but got straight onto the bus. The sun shone in through the window, I grew sleepy. I hadn't taken anything with me apart from my wallet, a ballpoint, and my passport – no, I'd left my passport in the side pocket of my bag. I shut my eyes and everything began to sway, as if I was still drunk, still at sea, or in the air. I had to open my eyes and focus on a fixed point. For the first time I realised what a bus was. I realised that what it represented was what it now meant to me. Had always done so. Its red rear lights had disappeared into the night. Its bright headlights had come out of the night. It was hard to get off. Had been hard to get on. It had lain in the ditch, wheels in the air and I'd climbed out through the window. As if out of the grave. I'd done that. It had meant darkness and I had pressed my wife into a ball on my knee and kissed her mechanically. I have woken up in a bus around midnight, when the moon of the steppe was shining in through the window. I have listened to life stories, from a mouth smelling of vodka. This was the last refuge from the icy sea breeze. This has meant expectation, impatience and worry. And it has also meant wolves, elk and deer. It had meant Estonia. Fleeing, subjugation. Now it meant the bus. I don't know why. This lack of meaning was not significant, far from it. I felt I was standing before something quite ordinary. For several hours. Skin colliding with metal, skin colliding with glass. Glass colliding with metal. Air clashing with metal and glass. Eternal, not trembling. A little bit dead. I was travelling through Estonia. As I was doing at the time. As of late. Sometimes I slept, sometimes not. The bushes were growing out of the ground, buildings were being built on top of their foundations. Cocks were bigger than hens, had combs. Rivers ran in a particular direction. Cars had wheels underneath, most tractors too. On some building flags flew, on others not. Women's chests stuck out more than men's. I recognised my native country. I could say tomorrow that yesterday I saw Estonia. For which people have fought and died, written, haunted, betrayed, got married, made ironic comments, cultivated fields, gone mad, spawned children, indulged in language renewal and film. For what do people live? For which reason have people felt that passion is an invention of post-Renaissance Europe? Why do people think that passion is more basic, even an Oriental phenomenon? Why are women walled up alive, pushed under cars, burnt at the stake, presented with brocade? Anyway, an ordinary bus trip. This time without irony. Ordinary. A completely ordinary bus trip. Then Tõrva, a small town, the bus stopped, I got out, stepped down onto the cobbles of the wide dusty town square, saw some grey sheds in the distance, some bored travellers, a distant food stand. I drank a glass of cheap fortified wine there and bought four pastries for the journey. Then I strolled back over to the bus station and had a look at the timetable in the waiting room which was strewn with fag ends. The next bus would be departing in three hours' time. I couldn't wait that long, I hadn't got that much time. I started off through the town to find the main road. The sun was still shining but there was a rainbow-coloured halo around it and the sky was losing colour. At a kiosk on the edge of town I bought another small bottle of vodka and two hundred grammes of sausage. Then I took off my shoes and socks. The asphalt grazed my untanned feet. At the edge of a brook I sat down in the grass under an alder tree, drank the vodka and ate the sausage. I didn't get intoxicated, it just became hard to look up into the hot hazy sky. The urge to move on battled within me with the urge to go to sleep. A couple of little boys were running along the road, the new generation, conquerors of the Earth. It was past three, but I just couldn't walk on any longer. I lay face down in the grass, and remembered a childhood dream: to be tiny, the size of an ant, and walk through the grass as if it were an alien jungle, amongst new, infinitely large plants, in the shade of the dandelions, with the cloying fragrance of the clover, walk there with a small dark-headed schoolgirl, Reesi or Kristiina, someone I had to protect from the earthworms and the huge hens. As a little boy I already had a clear idea of distance, I knew that distances could change and become insurmountably long. Now in this instance walking from an un-familiar river to my home town could take a lifetime, and only if I were not crushed by the farmer, or if ants didn't dragged me into their ant-hill. I would, in the end, arrive home old and grey like Peer Gynt, still perhaps capable of remembering middle-age near Rõngu and my first signs of palsy in the pine woods at Elva. Wading through sweet wrappers and spent matches, I approached a house whose key a woman had recently given me, someone who was trying to capture my soul. When I awoke, everything had changed yet again. The shade of an alien forest fell upon me, the absolute silence frightened me. I looked anxiously at my watch, but now it really had stopped. And when I earlier, with a still functioning watch on my wrist, had experienced time coming to a standstill, now the actual stopping of the watch made time rush on ahead like an express train. I leapt to my feet, as if someone had been spying on me expectantly for ages either through the bushes or from the sky, and ran from the riverbank to the main road. The dusk was thickening, there were no lights visible anywhere. Not one single one. I stood there a short while, sat down at the kerb, then knelt on the asphalt and talked to myself in my head, like a schoolboy kneeling on a handful of peas as a punishment: where are You now, wherever are You now, now I'm in a foreign country and I cannot go anywhere. I am asking You, come here, come to me, a candle in your hand, come so that I can recognise You from afar. Forget all the black days, all quarrels and pain, all lunar eclipses and earthquakes, all grey afternoons, all nights spent weeping, all fears, forget the orbiting of the Earth and the approach of comets and those hurling away from us, forget the sewage system and taxi ranks, headaches and tears, come so that the Earth will grow light. LET THE SUNSHINE, LET THE SUNSHINE, LET THE SUNSHINE, LET THE SUNSHINE IN. But my cold hoarse voice sounded so inappropriately alien in the darkness, on an alien main road, so that I forced myself onto my feet again and began to walk along the road. I hurried forward like someone out of his mind, and looked back into the darkness now and again, as if there were someone following me. I must have walked three or four kilometres, then began to hum a made-up song, but that didn't help either. Finally, I heard the sound of a car engine and lights could be seen over the trees. I stopped and looked into the approaching lights appealing for help. I raised my arm, stepped somewhat more into the path of the vehicle than the highway code allows one to do out of propriety and the car came to a screeching halt. The driver yelled at me above the noise of the engine, wondering what the hell I was doing wandering about on the road when I was drunk. I replied that I wasn't drunk, and begged him to take me to Tartu, it was a question of life and death. He muttered something more under his breath, but agreed to take me, adding that I should sit in the back. The driver opened the door to the small space and I now realised that it was an empty bread van. I climbed up into this uncomfortable space between the shelves and the driver shut the door from the outside. Pitch darkness and shaking, I gripped hold of the metal shelves and no longer understood where I was. How long this all lasted I do not know. But gradually my spirits fell, and my back began to ache from crouching. I suddenly began to worry that he had forgotten about me, because who was I after all? A refugee from the western islands, an outlaw. Someone you were no longer allowed to love, no longer hate. Someone you could not ask about his income and expenditure. Someone who could be summoned by the ring of the phone. Now everything was ahead. Everything a blank sheet. Like the snow on Linnamäe, where my skis broke when I was a tiny little boy – the only ski tracks on the slope. A nowhere man in a nowhere land, as the song puts it. Everything was ahead for me. I could still buy a car. I could still commit patricide. Begin as a butcher or a sexton. Draw up a new moral codex for myself. Write a poem. Demolish graves. Buy a new suit. Turn the unruly banks of the river into a park. Enter a ballet dancing competition. Invent something. DO SOMETHING NEW. START FROM SCRATCH. After an endless space of time the van came to a halt. The bolts and bars rattled and the back of the van was opened. I was in Tartu; it was late summer. The street lamps were lit, leaves rustled. I gave the driver a rouble and walked down a long street. I looked neither to the left nor right, I saw my dark shadow, shortening then squashing up before me, and I hurried on as if someone were waiting for me. In the end I stopped in a side-street in front of a dark two-storey building. I looked around me, went in, up to the first floor, unlocked the door, stepped inside. The room smelt as rooms always do when they have stood empty and not been aired all summer. I immediately opened a window, sat down on the sofa and looked around me. Suddenly some moths flew in and began beating their wings against the wall. At the railway station someone was speaking in a metallic voice. I leafed through a paper from June. The lamp shone, steadily, without blinking. I wanted to know what each moment held in store, why time and life and memories were so concentrated. I sat and sat and sat. Tears hide the beauty of the Earth, as the song says. Even in childhood I had always been grown up – will this ever come to an end? It occurred to me to start looking in the cupboards, but I didn't need anything. I had more or less everything I needed. I lay face down on my pillow. The pillow did not smell of human contact. The end of summer was at hand. Moths flew in. I lay face down on my pillow. At the station someone was speaking in a metallic voice. Moths were beating their wings against the wall. The newspapers were from June. The moths were touching my pillow. I didn't want to look in the cupboards. The moths were speaking in a metallic voice. The pillow did not taste of human contact. The railway station had fallen asleep. The station had fallen silent. I fell silent. I went to sleep. The moths beat their wings against my pillow. They neither smelt nor tasted of anything.

Tartu – Tallinn – Pärnu, Winter 1971/72

The Collector

Rein Saluri

You could see through the woods. Each tree stood out, stark, leafless and bare, having shed its leaves in a heap at its foot, covering the roots with a sodden dark brown layer. Summer, which had held the crowns together, plaited the branches in a jumble, had broken up in the autumn storms. The woods no longer served as a windbreak, a shelter; all that remained were isolated trees, trembling in the north-easterly gusts. You could see through the woods – during the summer, you could only find this abandoned barn if you knew where to look, now the damp wall of logs chased away any hope of finding a dry place to rest.

He had not walked in the autumnal woods for some time, all that he remembered was how the misty silence had once calmed him down, moved him somehow, and the memories caused him to feel guilty, looking for the reason for this within himself, he had to understand that seasonal changes took place in the woods, he wanted to find peace there occasionally, but was unable to.

I've devised this withdrawal for myself. I can't see the wood for the trees. I know that in the shadow of what once seemed a joyful party, a grand race is being held, where the stronger conceals all light from the weaker, where everything flourishes on its own. At present, the woods are peaceful, tamed, submissive, and this is irritating.

On reaching the hay barn, he tried to find a somewhat drier spot, but the mossy stone, which would be emitting heat during summer, felt cold and clammy when he tried to sit down. He leant against the wall of the barn, nudged it a couple of times with his shoulder, but the logs held firm, and this made him feel better. So what if, between the logs, you could see wet bunches of hay – the wind came through the cracks and the decay had not yet got to the walls, the logs were knotted and would burn well. But even in the dry conditions of summer, if he struck them with an axe the logs would resound with an eager ringing sound, as proof of their suitability. He would not have begun to demolish this old abandoned structure for firewood, he wouldn't allow himself to derive an easy warmth from the efforts of others.

He was used to stocking up for winter on his own, even keeping his wishes in check when busy working rapidly in the woods. He would walk around in the area where he was allowed to fell trees and pick out trees that neither stood out for their beauty or their ugliness, the wood for his stove had to be something in between, leaving the long and slender ones to embellish the woods. Even during the busiest time, his eye would fall on really odd trees, and he would suppress his joy at finding them, raise his axe almost in embarrassment and somewhat stealthily, as if regretting his find. He would saw down the tree or cut off the strange branch from it, root out some stocky stump of a tree that the wind had brought down, and take the whole lot back to his yard, to add to his pile of oddities. Right from the start – as far back as he could remember, he had been taken over by such a collector's urge when in the woods – he had never dared to admit to himself that he had enough material for the rest of his life, bits and pieces from which he could make attractive objects, to whittle and carve clothes-racks or stools, knife-handles or juniper walking sticks, gable vent decorations, or simply amusing wooden sculptures, to be displayed where he felt, simply for fun. Proud guardians would stand at the entry to his sauna cabin and over time everyone would get used to them – besides, he made the best spade handles in the village and joined in any kind of work to be done wherever he smelt wood.

At the entrance to the sauna he could place elves and witches, an idiot with a face like his neighbour, and other characters, about which he himself couldn't say what or whom they represented.

He had always roved about in the woods with anxious expectancy, knowing that he would never return entirely empty-handed. So far, as long as the thicket behind the sauna, where the oak branches blackened in the bog water and the gnarled juniper roots stuck out, provided him with the solace of ownership, and he would brush aside any realisation that the spirit was willing, but the flesh too weak for his hands to reach that far. A good steward would even pick up a rusty nail from the ground, and all the more such remarkable creations of nature that only he could spot.

In previous times, he had been content with himself, feeling he was rather special: on account of his sharp eyesight and skilled hands, he would have been able to reply in good part, or banter back at every question posed about why he did all this, and what sort of game he was up to.

In actual fact, he wasn't playing any game, had never even started to play one, and sometimes he felt joy at the thought that his dreams had luckily never come true, and he had become resigned to the fact that both dreams and embitterment lived peacefully side by side within him, and he consented to such cohabitation. But when wandering about in the woods he was always on the lookout, kept his eyes open, touched approvingly the gnarled knots of the birches, though he did not believe that touching them would fend off illness, and fingered the windfall and took some of it home with him to make a witch, or use the wood for her broom. On returning home he would always be excited; even when bent double by a heavy burden, he would explain to his neighbours at great length why he had picked up and lugged along just that particular stump or root, and would then leave them with the rest, in a heap behind the sauna, and then think what a joy it would be if he could ignore all his other duties and sit on the barn porch, pick up a clatteringly dry branch and really make something out of it. He always remembered whether he had picked up the branch in the spring or the winter, in the woods, on the beach, in the marshland, or by the lake, what the weather had been like that day, and from which angle the light had been falling onto it. He had noted these oddities of nature and had to remember how he had got hold of them.

He leaned wearily against the barn and thought that in his life he too had worked with logs to construct a wall, had collected and dried moss and filled in the cracks in the walls with it. He had rolled rocks along to form the foundations and when the rafters were in place, a wreath was made to celebrate this, but all this serious work had not been anywhere near as pleasing to him compared with the pleasure he felt sitting on the barn porch, or even when sitting in front of the stove on a footstool; all those houses, benches, tables and roofs were nothing compared with the figures that could be standing at the entrance to the sauna. Once, it would actually have been nice to take a picture of him at the sauna entrance – holding a black alderwood Old Nick, next to him a huge wooden spoon the size of a man, a real giant ladle which he would present to a couple of newly weds at a village wedding, and his gift would be accepted with gratitude and admiration.

Why couldn't he carve wooden spoons the size of himself, and make tractors, as small as cigarette packets?

He ran his hand over the logs, smooth with rain, sighed and left the woods. In the leafless woods, your eyes tend to close even when walking, ears grow deaf and fingers numb as if with rheumatic pains.

When he reached the space behind the sauna, it began to sleet. The wet flakes stuck together and fell on his random collection and he didn't want to see how it was again getting covered with snow, so he went into the shed where the firewood lay in stacks next to his dry wood for carving. He took a piece of juniper, one of alder and a snake-like one of birch, dragged them after him into the house, scoring a track through the first snowfall of winter.

He had managed to keep his old bread oven, which took up half the kitchen, and had argued with the members of his family and the village folk who had wanted to demolish it, as any child could see that the stove used up too much wood and did not generate sufficient heat, and no bread had been baked in the village for decades. But he needed that stove. The vast quantity of firewood that he was prepared to let go up the chimney was his own business, he would saw the wood and work it all by himself. He brought the wood out of the forest, chopped it up into sticks of firewood, stacked it up and dried it, using the same effort with the firewood as with wood for carving. Only now would both become equals in the stove.

Those gnarled branches from under the shed immediately caught fire, such twisted pieces of wood had strange bumps and hollows, where the flames of the fire quickly took hold, while they would initially slide over the smoother logs. He sat by the door of the stove, his gaze filled with the fire and his head empty. Could anyone achieve such peace as he did when sitting at his old stove – such empty peace? He had no urge to think that there were many other people on this Earth huddled devotedly around fires, and that they could now be, at the very same moment sitting at their luxury stoves, bonfires or fireplaces – what did he know of their thoughts and feelings, and whether they had anything valuable to throw on the fire, something kept for a long time and treasured.

The juniper hissed, the alder crackled, the birch burnt steadily.

There was always some reason why the odd, unusually shaped pieces of wood had ended up as they were: branches of a more vigorous tree could have pushed their way in, causing a branch of the weaker tree to bend double to reach the sun, or some disease could have entered the tree, some fungus or something even smaller and more damaging, which then twisted the branches of the tree. The roots could have been squashed up in dense parts of the woods, and grown in such a way that a passer-by like him would put the tree out of its misery and would enjoy it himself.

You should live in the desert for a while to understand trees.

Once he had found a birch that had grown a crust around the sap-tapping spout – the gnarled knot around the protuberance sticking out of the trunk resembled the face of an old man with pouting lips, a slightly barmy old man with a surprised expression on his face. This piece of wood inserted into the tree three decades ago had not disappeared until he had come along with a saw and an axe, as happy as a sand boy, looked at the old pouting man from the front and the side, spat on his palms and sawed the birch down. One thick log went into the shed to dry, the rest became firewood, and he could not be bothered to fetch all the branches from the woods. Once, he had wrestled with a yew, but he didn't want to think about what he had gone and done, and the trunk ended up somewhere behind the woodpile. He did not feel himself to be a criminal, as the people who had invented rules for the conservation of nature could not understand the passions of a poacher, and he could have hidden the stripes of the yew tree by making a yew beer mug, as he used to do long ago, and no one would have noticed anything. And yet he did feel equally guilty with regard to all trees, including an old alder stump, and the nobility of the yew did not intimidate him any more or any less. A tree is a tree.

When however, his booty behind the sauna consisting of the oddities of nature had finally to be stuffed into the bread oven, could it be true that all that would be left was ashes to take away by the bucketful, or was there something in these trees, some trace of human guilt, which was the root of their degeneration? Was there among all those knotty stumps some branch or twig and root with a broken axe head or a shard of saw blade inside, and that the tree was now concealing, or perhaps even hidden explosives that got stuck in the tree long ago waiting to burst out among the flames of the stove, in order to utter its ultimate "no" in the name of thousands of fallen trees? Always when some branch suddenly gave a crack in the stove, or on a bonfire, in the pain of the flames he remembered how he, when still a boy herding cattle, would throw cartridges into the fire while crouching behind a nearby rock, and the fire would crackle and the bullets whined all around. Grown men had pointed the barrels of their rifles at one another, had sent bullets flying wherever they were needed, while boys had this urge for play in their blood.

He got up to poke the fire in the stove – a round hunk of alder wood had been broken in two by the flames like a ripe turnip; he hit at it with the poker, knocking the charred layer off. A merry flame leapt out of the mouth of the stove; this tree had stood at the top edge of the old trench, stubbornly gnarled like an insistent memory.

1977

The Rococo Lady

Maimu Berg

She passed under our window again, wearing a dark brown waisted costume, whose jacket sported two flared flounces at the hips. Her hair was of a peculiar shade – a greyish white, parted neatly at the forehead and hanging in two coiled locks over her cheeks and back. She had a small brown handbag over her shoulder and her high-heeled shoes were brown as well.

"The Rococo Lady," said my mother, noticing my look of fascination. The word "Rococo" was new to me, but suited this mysterious woman, so different from the others, all the more. "The Rococo Lady," I repeated, unable to believe in the existence of such an odd word as Rococo and that it would apply to such a being as this beauty in her brown costume. I didn't ask my mother what Rococo actually meant, didn't even want to, as wasn't there a slight note of mockery in my mother's words?

The beautiful lady lived two blocks down from where we lived, in a flat on the first floor. There were mysterious curtains at her windows, different to any others I had seen, and in their case my mother had uttered another strange, unfamiliar word – *Jugendstil*. So this lady was also associated with another word that belonged to her alone.

I rang the bell of the girl next door in order to ask her to come out with me. Our neighbours had arrived in our block of flats after the war and another epithet was attached to them – Pechory. And they lived up to this name completely, as they were different to everyone else in our block. They spoke Russian together, but an idiosyncratic form of Estonian with me, not quite the same as we spoke at home.

But I certainly understood what they said. The Pechory people had two daughters – Anna and Yevgenia, but these names were hardly ever used. Anna was mostly called Nyura, and Yevgenia was called Zhenya. Their father, a grim man with light thinning hair and a red face, was a ship's captain. He wore an officer's uniform, drank vodka and when he had drunk a good deal you would hear a revolver being fired in the garden. This was exciting, except that his wife Marushka would always distract me as I stood watching. After the first report you would hear a scream from the flat next door and she would storm into the garden and throw her arms round us, while my father would start arguing with the captain in Russian. Then the captain would turn the revolver on us, yell, and his face would grow bright red. He would be positively glowing, looked terrible and proud, but the revolver was no longer fired.

Marushka had a small shed in the garden that the captain and his men had built. In this hut lived the goat Katya, an intelligent and friendly animal, that understood everything. When Zhenya and Nyura were not in the garden, I went over to Katya, turned over her water bucket, climbed up on it to reach over the edge of the pen and tempted her with bread, took her by the horns and spoke to her. Katya would nod her head and roll her eyes. Katya especially liked it if I pressed my nose against her nose, and murmured quietly.

Nyura and Zhenya had had a third sister Lyusia, but she died. We would sometimes go and visit her grave in the cemetery. Lyusia was buried in what was called the children's row, and this was filled with small graves. Lyusia too had her own little grave with cement edging, and covered with small pebbles. There was also a nameplate. Some of the letters were familiar to me, I could read a-d, m-I, k-d. Zhenya said that what was actually written on the nameplate was Lyudmila Popkina, as Lyusia's real name had been Lyudmila.

When we were by Lyusia's grave, just the three of us, and there were no strangers around, Nyura would dance for Lyusia. She would perform whirls between the graves, arms outstretched and lift her delicate feet, humming a tune to herself. Zhenya and I would sit on the cement edging and play with the pebbles. Then we'd all go and visit the Bride. The Bride had dropped dead at the altar, before she had even had time to say "I do". The bridegroom had had a statue made of her. This was placed in a small mausoleum, with barred windows, and the statue was at the head of a grave, presumably hers. There were two other graves, and I wondered how they had had room to get the coffins in. But Zhenya said they had dug the graves first, then built the mausoleum on top.

I liked the Bride a lot. I peered and peered in at her through the window, and wished she had been alive... When alive her skin would be pure, almost white, like the marble statue, but on her living skin, and on her nose and soft wrists there would be freckles. She has greyish white hair, almost like the Rococo Lady, but lighter, and in the hair is a white flower. The pleats of her dress are floating around her legs, and her white shoes are decorated with silver roses. She approaches me, holding out her hands through the window bars and strokes me, while I turn the key which has appeared from goodness knows where in the padlock to the mausoleum to let her out. We walk, hand in hand, with the others behind us, marvelling at the white beauty of the Bride.

When I rang the doorbell, Marusha opened and asked me in. The flat was filled with the smell of frying. Marusha was frying plaice, but as she came from Pechory, she didn't use fat but oil called *poslamasla*. This smelt better than fat, margarine or even butter. It was obvious from my expression that I liked the smell, and Marusha took a few of the fish from a large platter, pushed a smaller plate in front of me and told me to eat. Nyura came into the kitchen. Zhenya was not at home, but Nyura was nicer, younger than Zhenya, the same age as me, and didn't tease you like Zhenya did. We ate the fish with potato pie. In my home we never ate potato pie, and when I once asked why not, my mother said that was what Russians ate. I didn't bother telling her that Marusha also made potato pie.

Nyura and me went outside. I suggested we went to play in the yard near where the Rococo Lady lived. Nyura wasn't so sure, we would be scolded if we played in someone else's yard. But I promised Nyura that if she came along, I would tell her a word she had never heard before. Nyura of course imagined that I would teach her some swearword and came along. I wanted to play by the steps, not on the lawn behind the building or in the garden, where it was in fact nicer to play. But from there we wouldn't have been able to see when the Rococo Lady came home. So we played by the steps, where there was nothing but grey soil, and soon our clothes, hands and faces were covered in it.

"Tell me that word," said Nyura, remembering. I raised my chin, conjured up a look of mockery on my face, and said: "Rococo!"

"That all?" said Nyura, disappointed. "And what's it mean?"

"I don't know."

"Where did you hear it?"

"Mum said it."

"What was she talking about?"

I didn't want to tell Nyura. "She said it just like that."

"Funny," said Nyura and repeated: "Rococo!"

At that same moment the Rococo Lady came in through the small gate. I was startled, as she could well have heard Nyura saying it, and would no doubt think we were talking about her. But she didn't seem to have heard anything, in fact she didn't even notice us. Once on the steps however, she turned round, looked at me and said: "Why are you playing here? Go home, have a wash and change your clothes! You'd do better reading something." She had a quiet, somewhat mournful voice.

I felt so ashamed of myself, that I even had tears in my eyes. Nyura, however, felt insulted: "She said nothing to me. So much for Rococo!"

"I'm going home," I said, but didn't have time to start off before a man entered the yard, whom we recognised since me and Nyura had often seen him following the Rococo Lady and sometimes speaking to her. He was a tall man, wore a grey suit and looked quite presentable except for the fact that his jaw was too prominent and angular.

The angular-jawed man entered the Rococo Lady's block of flats. "Let's follow him," whispered Nyura. We quietly opened the entrance door and peered into the corridor. We could see the man climbing the stairs and ringing the bell at the Rococo Lady's door. We sneaked up the stairs and peeped through the banisters. The door was opened by an old, evil-looking woman who lived with the Rococo Lady. People said she worked as a maid, but no one knew for sure, as people no longer had maids in our country.

"Is Ella at home?" asked the man with the big chin. "No," replied the alleged maid. "She isn't home."

"She's lying," whispered Nyura.

"Shush," I said.

"When will she be home?" asked the man, and whispered something else, which we couldn't hear.

"I really don't know," said the old woman and slammed the door shut.

Nyura and me ran all the way back to our own yard as fast as we could. Marusha then asked Nyura to come in, and I went to the shed to visit Katya the goat. I discussed everything I knew about the Rococo Lady with Katya. That she was Rococo. And a lady. That her skin was nearly as white, delicate and fine as the Bride in the graveyard, and she didn't even have any freckles. That she had whitish grey hair, but her face wasn't at all wrinkled. I myself didn't understand whether the Rococo Lady was young or not, she was too peculiar for things like that.

On one occasion, I heard my parents speaking about the Rococo Lady; my mother uttered some odd words about her. "She was once the mistress of some politician," was what my mother said. This had to mean something connected with men. But once my mother had noticed my presence and asked what I wanted, I slipped outside. In the yard there was a piece of furniture, someone was moving house, and a coffee table was standing on the lawn, and Nyura and me ran around it, singing a song we had heard somewhere or other: "We don't need no more clocks, Moscow'll give us the time!"

This move affected our lives. A boy called Vello moved in, the same age as Zhenya. He soon became curious about the Rococo Lady, but even more so about the evil old woman who lived with her. "She's an old witch," said Vello, quite convinced he was right and spat.

"Don't be daft!" said Zhenya, growing angry.

"You're daft yourself, you're from Pechory!" yelled Vello. "You're not only daft, but a liar too. People who lie also steal and stare down into Hell!"

Of course, none of us, not even Vello, actually believed her to be a witch, but we pretended we did as this made the game more exciting. We followed the woman, and yelled after her: "Old witch! Old witch!" And then made the sign of the cross, if she appeared.

"They should put her in a grotto," said Vello one day. "We have to find out what she eats and whether she can cast spells." A shudder tingled down my spine. "You're coming!" said Vello, pointing at me. "You'll have to see what kind of nest she lives in."

The four of us were standing in the hall of our block. I was just going to argue against it, just for the sake of appearances, when the outside door opened. We ran down the stairs to see who had come. Downstairs, a young woman we had never seen before was standing, a headscarf on her head, holding a roll of paper under her arm. Out of this she pulled a large poster, then took a box of drawing pins from her pocket and fastened it near the entrance door. "Well, children!" she cried cheerfully. "Everyone's got to vote!" And she left, and the door slammed behind her. There was now a poster hanging by the door, with the photo of a man. The man had a curly head of hair, a broad face. His gaze was stern and alert.

"The politician," said Vello.

"Can't be!" I replied. I knew the word politician.

Vello gave a superior smile. I went up to the poster and spelt out the word politician.

"Who is this politician?" I asked Vello.

"Doesn't have a special job, he's just a kind of man," said

Vello evasively.

"Is this man in the picture the politician?" I asked in a whisper.

"Exactly," Vello confirmed. "The politician."

And the Rococo Lady had been the politician's mistress. That meant that she liked the politician, and that this was the man that she was in love with. For my part, I thought this man even more horrible than the man with the angular jaw, someone the Rococo Lady clearly didn't like. What would the Rococo Lady think when she saw his picture all over town? The roll of posters under the woman's arm had been quite thick. But then I thought I should enter the witch's grotto. I will indeed go there. I'll have a look what it's like. I wasn't in fact that frightened of the old woman, and I really wanted to see what the Rococo Lady's flat looked like, how she lived, the mistress of that stern politician with his crinkly hair. Besides, I had nothing against showing others how brave I was.

"I can go there now," I said to Vello.

"Where to?" he asked.

"Into the witch's grotto," I said proudly. Nyura and Zhenya gasped. "And I'm going this evening!"

I went home washed my ears and neck, put on a silk dress which my mother had made for me out of an old dress of my aunt's from the days of Estonian independence. The dress had a beautifully embroidered belt, and matching collar. I put on white tassled socks, so I didn't need to bother to wash my feet, and fish-skin shoes. My aunt had been married to a Baltic German and had gone abroad a long time ago ("she went when Hitler invited her" was what mother had once said, and I was surprised that Hitler had known my aunt, and could have been so horrible). I put on a pearl necklace that my aunt had left behind and also put my mother's ring with a green stone on my finger. The ring was a little too large, so I put it on my thumb, just to be on the safe side. I sprinkled plenty of "Red Moscow" scent onto the front of the dress. The light beige pure silk front became a kind of bluish lilac, it was exciting to watch, but the scent soon dried and the beige returned. Then I took a book from the shelf. There was a whole row of them and the series was called *Novels From Scandinavia*, they were all different. I pressed the book to my chest and left the flat.

Nyura, Zhenya and Vello were waiting in the corridor. When I came out, the girls began to twitter about me and my jewels, while Vello simply told them to shut up. And so we started on our way. I walked in front, clutching my Scandinavian novel and enveloped in a cloud of sweet perfume, then, at a respectful distance, followed Nyura, Zhenya and Vello.

"You lot shouldn't come into the corridor," I told them when we had arrived at the Rococo Lady's block of flats.

"We're coming inside," said Vello. "Otherwise, how do we know that you're not bluffing."

I didn't really know what bluffing was, but I had the feeling that Vello didn't think I'd dare.

"I'm not bluffing," I said haughtily. "You lot stand under the window with the *Jugendstil* stuff, and I'll come to the window."

"You're bluffing," said Vello uncertainly, because he, for his part, didn't know what *Jugendstil* was.

"What sort of window?" asked Zhenya.

"Under their big window," I said, and stepped inside. In the Rococo Lady's block there was also a poster of the politician. For a moment I hesitated under his stern gaze, but I had no choice. I went up the stairs.

Outside her door I pressed the Scandinavian novel closer to my chest and rang the bell. The old woman opened the door. As she didn't immediately see me, she unfastened the chain and opened the door wide.

"Is Ella at home?" I asked ducking under the old woman's arm and into the vestibule of the flat.

"Yes, what do you want?" asked the old woman in amazement.

"I've brought a book," I replied and held out the Scandinavian novel under the old woman's nose.

"Mum sent me."

"Well then, come in," said the old woman and escorted me into the living room with its *Jugendstil* curtains. There was also a large oval table, some attractive chairs, a sideboard and a small bookcase. Maybe a few other things, because I didn't take everything in, just went over to the window and looked out. There stood Vello, Zhenya and Nyura down in the yard, looking up at me in dismay.

"Who's there?" cried the Rococo Lady's voice from somewhere.

"A child!" the old woman cried back.

"What does she want, let her come through!"

The old woman showed me into the other room, where, on the huge bed, with its white satin bedspread and two pillows was sitting the Rococo Lady. Around her sparkled white cupboards, mirrors and vases with flowers. The Rococo Lady herself was dressed in white too, silk pyjamas with shortish trousers. Over her shoulders was draped a close-fitting cape of swan down, on her head a silk turban, on which swayed an attractive peacock feather. In her hand was a large matt glass jar of skin cream, and she was applying the cream to her thighs. I can remember her long, shiny, though unvarnished, fingernails as she rubbed in the cream. During the brief silence during which we eyed one another, I understood that the Rococo lady was not all that young. She smiled, and her jaw, as well as the line of her mouth, looked weary. I could take no more, ran out to the vestibule, stumbling against a cupboard, upturned something on my way out. I saw that the door was on the chain, removed it, and ran into the outside corridor. Down at the entrance door I bumped against someone. It was the man with the angular jaw, wearing a grey suit. He grabbed me by the shoulders, shook his head, and asked where I'd just been. "At Ella's place!" I yelled and as the poster with the politician was right in front of me, I pointed to his photo, and said "and he's her lover". The angular-jawed man gasped and ran up the stairs. I could see how he wrenched Ella's door open, as the old woman had presumably not managed to put it back on the chain. I started to run. Somewhere I was joined by Nyura, Zhenya and Vello, and they quizzed me as we ran. Suddenly I felt that my hands were strangely empty. I had left the Scandinavian novel in Ella's flat. I was afraid of returning, but even more afraid that losing the book would cause trouble at home.

"Wait a minute," I cried to my companions, "I've got to go back." I went back to the Rococo Lady's block. The man with the angular jaw was coming towards me from the entrance, but he took no notice of me. I ran up the stairs and carefully tried the Rococo Lady's door. It was open. I stepped into the vestibule. The light was on, and from far away I could hear someone crying and wailing. I grew afraid. I sneaked gingerly in the direction the weeping was coming from. The large room was deserted, but in the bedroom the Rococo Lady lay on her back on the bed and her pyjama jacket, the bedspread and the pillows were bloody. She was lying awkwardly, her head back, her gaze towards the corner of the room. Before her on the floor sat the old woman, and stroked the hand of the Rococo Lady with its long nails and was weeping loudly. On the floor lay the matt jar with the cream and my Scandinavian novel.

For many years I dreamed of someone loving me as passionately as the grey-suited, angular-jawed man had loved the Rococo Lady. Only later, when the old story of this murder came up in conversation, did I get to know that the man in the grey suit had been a dangerous psychopath.

2005

Chance Encounter

Eeva Park

My whole body was sore, raw somehow. My skin was hot and my lips cracked. It was still very early morning.

On the market place next to the bus station there seemed to be more sellers than buyers. I stood there hesitantly and counted my money once again. It was now clear that I wouldn't get away from here before evening as no bus would be leaving, and that my only hope of getting home by seven was to hitch a lift at the roadside, so I now had plenty of money over to buy some pears. The day ahead was so long, evening so far away, that the information about the buses did not make me particularly depressed.

I had begun my journey back early, had risen after two sleepless nights into a morning floating in the mist of dawn, in order to make the first bus travelling in the direction of Tartu. I was not tired, in the same way that someone starving is not hungry after a long fast, but I did have the feeling that the boundary between waking and sleep had become blurred. For two nights I had only slept deeply in snatches and had woken up again, afraid of missing any part of the short weekend. Even when he was asleep, I lay there trying to touch him with the whole of my body. At some point, it got quite dark, I could hardly see him, then the moon had begun to shine faintly between the planks of the wall and everywhere was filled with a playful, brittle light. As he slept, I thought I loved him more when he was asleep, but when he woke and looked at me with his slow gaze, pulled me towards him and touched my hot tender lips, I felt that somewhere in my brain tiny sparks were flying, that flashed and burned through all my body. It was like a little death, yes, really!

I ceased to be and was no more. Then I came back to this strange loft where the hay smelt and prickled everywhere on our perspiring skins.

We had almost separated before, during late winter. I think that he too had understood how alien we in fact were to one another, that we thought in completely different ways and felt differently. In order to calm myself, I had thought that he simply didn't come up to my level, where I hovered in my imagination. Petty everyday life tired us both. Making meals, doing the washing, the child's illnesses, the cold and damp rented room, money, which there never was any of, and the fact that every hope was postponed for years, into the future.

When he went to the other end of Estonia for the summer, I felt relief, liberation, the chance of a hundred opportunities, though after two weeks all I could think of was him. He sent me amusing letters, sensible ones and then suddenly wrote with a childish, clumsy kind of tenderness. His scrawl was terrible, hasty, and I carried the letters with me everywhere, and would sometimes stop in the street to read a sentence over again by the light of the street lamps. With one letter, snapshots had been included, blurred and slightly out of focus, where he was standing on an unknown country road, thin, bearded, his hair bleached. I would have followed him, but I had to go to work and I couldn't find anyone to look after the child at the weekend. She was still too small to take along. Only this midsummer weekend, mother had agreed to look after her from Friday lunch-time right through to seven o'clock on Sunday evening. Till seven exactly, not a moment longer. She had something important to do, and before I had left home, I heard the words "seven exactly" at least ten times.

Taking into account that fateful hour, I was already on my way back very early on Sunday morning.

It had been so distressing to lie there and watch the night as it grew light. Leaving, tearing myself away, had initially been almost a relief. Better like this, better to leave at a dewy cold-morning hour than saying a long goodbye in the middle of the tepid day, when he would already be thinking of work that coming week.

I stood there, money in my hand, looking in the direction of the market place. It was actually not yet the season for pears, but the warm spring had come early, and the hot summer weather had ripened everything early. I really wanted those pears, wanted them still to be a little unripe, a yellowish green. I could even smell them on this as yet dustless summer's morning.

A bus drove by and I saw faces at the windows. It was quite incomprehensible that so many people from this sleepy town would be travelling to Tallinn, and there was no place for me. If I hadn't been haunted by that "seven exactly", I would have walked all day, with my sore face and cracked lips, visiting familiar places, stopping to watch the sluggish flow of the river, wandered the streets. But now I went to the market place, walked among the stallholders and felt they were staring at me long and hard.

Sore, was what I was thinking. "I'm sore all over from the two nights and one day." It could be seen from afar, you could smell it, like pears or over-ripe strawberries.

When I stopped, I smelt it myself too. I raised my arm to my face, the fine golden hairs were erect and shining, the skin against my cheeks was cool.

A man who was selling new potatoes, had leaned in my direction. He leaned so hard on a full bag, that it fell over and potatoes tumbled to the ground. They bounced in every direction and as I walked by, I trod on one. It burst with a squelch. On both sides, flowers were being sold and their overwhelming beauty caused me to quicken my pace. I began to worry that there were no pears to be found on the whole market, all that would be for sale were at best hard green apples, but as I turned back to leave, I saw them from afar.

I came to a halt by the pears and asked how much they cost. Actually, the price no longer mattered in the least. I wanted to eat some immediately, although even as I looked, I could see that they were not yet ripe, that they were hard and a little bland. They didn't, in fact, even smell of anything, but I enjoyed the thought of biting into one. Eating them called to mind a poem about unripe fruit, which was to be eaten by moonlight, when the clocks were wrong and you could see paths you could not cross. Trying to remember the words, I walked towards the bus stop. The chill of morning was beginning to turn into the heat of a summer's day.

I stood for several hours by the roadside at the edge of town, watching how the shadows on the other side, under the tall trees, gradually vanished. There was hardly any traffic, everyone seemed to be in bed on this Sunday. A couple of family cars, filled with passengers, passed by, one black Volga and several rattling lorries from the local *kolkhoz*, then the road was deserted again for a while. But it was still early morning, and seven o'clock in the evening was a long way off. I would have liked to walk out of town along the verge, but flagging down a car later on, when vehicles would be travelling at full speed, would be much more difficult. I strolled back and forth near my bag that I had put at the roadside; I still had some pears, but was saving them for my child. I grew hungry.

Then I heard the bass tones of a large approaching vehicle. It was driving fast, over the speed limit, no doubt. The lorry had a large, shiny orange cab, and a substantial space for goods behind. The air brushed my face as it passed then it braked with a squeal and came to a standstill at the kerb. I grabbed my bag and ran to the lorry. I heaved myself up, wrenched open the door and was almost left swinging on it.

"Are you driving to Tallinn?" I asked.

"Yes."

My politely imploring smile became a happy one, and I heaved myself up onto the high seat. The lorry engine roared, it moved off slowly at first, then ever faster along the road, baking in the sun.

On both sides there was a forest of pine trees with smooth trunks, and as always I was happy to see the bright light that is characteristic of such forests. I had only looked straight at the driver immediately after asking for the lift, and for the first several kilometres I felt uncomfortable, as always with a stranger you are indebted to and in whose company you will be obliged to spend several hours. Sometimes the driver tells his "guest" interminable stories, and you have to listen to them and make the right noises. Sometimes, and this is to be preferred, they remain silent, whistle to themselves, watch the road and ignore you.

This one was driving at a fair speed, keeping silent and I could judge by the mileposts how quickly I would arrive. Sat up in this high cab, the road below seemed far away, and when the lorry overtook a smaller vehicle, it seemed as if it would disappear under its broad wheels. The speed caused me to think excitedly what I would do for the free hours I would have after I arrived, and it was some while before I noticed that the lorry had slowed down. The trees at the side of the road that had been whizzing by, seemed to have come to a standstill and several cars passed us. I tried to look at the speedometer, but it was too far away. Leaning back lazily on his seat, the lorry-driver said:

"You in a hurry to get anywhere? I'm not. I've got loads of time on my hands."

He wasn't even thirty years old, with rolled up sleeves which revealed muscular and hairy arms, he looked at me, as if measuring me up and said: "Tons of time."

He turned towards me and I could now see his eyes. They were an indistinct colour, greyish and yellow. His gaze was old for his years, and his mouth expressed a mixture of mockery and mirth. He was enjoying himself, imagining that I would recognise him, knowing that I would be shuddering with fear inside and would cry out for help. Evil. I had seen enough of him to look him in the eye, searching for words that would least irritate him:

"My time is in the hands of others... so I was glad you were hurrying."

"Your time is now mine, since you climbed up into my lorry."

My legs were bare under a short skirt, my skin, sore from tenderness, slowly covered with sweat, my neck ached and was stiff, as if someone's fingers were already gripping it.

"But as you are not in a hurry and I am, then perhaps you

could let me get out so I could wait for another lorry." My lips hurt as I said this, but I dared not lick them.

He laughed.

"Oh no. Now you're going to travel with me, unless you want to go for a stroll in the woods right away. Look, there's a turning there."

He fell silent for a moment and looked in my direction: "Do you want to? Right now?"

"No," I said, feeling the pressure on my neck increasing. I tried to think, rather than imagine, what was going to happen not seeing myself struggling, until the fist, still resting on the wheel would hit me on the temple. I could see myself lying there in the grass, ripped apart, the flies buzzing round me. I would be their prey and by winter there would be precious little left of me...

"No," was what I thought, "I will go mad if I concentrate on such things. He has no reason to hit me..."

I pressed my bag, which was slipping to the floor, closer to me, and felt the round lumps of the pears. I thought about their taste, they were hard and unripe, good. I thrust my hand into the bag and took one out.

"It's going to be a hell of a hot day, and a long one. You have the choice whether I turn right now..."

He was now driving leaning against the back of his seat, speaking with certainty, enjoying himself.

"No thank you," I said, squeezing my pear. In the past, when travelling, I had a sheath knife in my bag, a real Finnish *puukko*, and although I knew I could never actually use it on anyone, it gave me a feeling of security.

"You don't seem to be worried. You don't seem to believe I can do anything I like with you. Anything."

I stared at the road, as it slipped with painful slowness under the lorry. Nevertheless, the vehicle was moving at such a speed that if I had jumped out I'd have broken all my bones. The road was quite deserted, so he could easily stop and come over and look at what was left of me. I could see him bending over me, his animal curiosity, something that can be seen in people's faces when they gather at the scene of an accident. A swarm of flies.

"He's getting an orgasm from my fear alone, the fucking bastard," I thought to myself, "he doesn't even need to turn off the main road."

"It won't be that easy to get me out of the cab..." I forced myself to look at him, to meet those eyes. "Pushing," I played for time, "won't be easy and pulling me down will be very difficult."

I would have liked to shout: "I'll beat your face in!" but I hoped he could already read that from my face. Maybe I could pretend to be brave and furious, at first fool myself, then him, so that we both ended up believing it.

"Oh," he said, "what guts. Nice you haven't started blubbering right away. I like it, the weak ones are boring. You're unable to cry and you're too proud to plead. We're going to have fun with you..." He gave a short, barking laugh. "My own woman, you know, used to think that if she needed something she could simply burst into tears. Later, she simply hissed, painted her nails red and sharpened them as I was watching every evening. You can even see the scars, here and there."

He pulled open the neck of his shirt and around his collar bone a blue scar of a knife wound could be seen.

"Those weren't made by fingernails."

"You should have seen how she sharpened them, then you'd believe me."

He pulled his shirt tails out of his trousers and opened the front. "It's fucking hot. Do you want to hear how I got these scars?"

I nodded. I wanted him to keep talking, keep on talking.

"In prison."

"Why?"

"Why was I inside, or why the knife?"

"Why the knife."

"I wasn't a good boy, you know, baby. So that answers both questions in one go. Do you know how I got beaten up the first time? You think I lifted something or walloped someone too hard? No, I was getting on the tram and got in someone's way. Someone was running, someone was struggling, some youngsters were up to no good and I got hit, before I got on the tram, with a rubber truncheon. I grabbed the truncheon and before I realised what I was doing, I'd landed one on the bastard."

While talking, the driver had accelerated, his shirt tails were flapping from the breeze coming in through the window and the heavy vehicle nearly reached its earlier speed on the quiet and deserted Sunday roads. My tense arms, legs, and back weakened from relief.

"And then?" I asked.

"Then..." He noticed the speed and began to drive more slowly. "The bastard grabbed hold of me and began blowing his whistle, they clustered around me and let me have it. He wasn't wearing a uniform, I couldn't make out who he was and why, I was on my way back from technical school... They wanted to nail me on some charge. Some stupid children's charge! That crowd of snotty nosed children! Me! But I laughed at them and got it in the teeth. I've been through thick and thin, and if you heard more about it, my sweet, you'd fall on your back with sheer fear, but that sort of rubbish I'd never heard before that first time. Me and you, baby, are Estonians, they made sure I knew that."

He barked out a laugh. I had never heard such an angry laugh before. The sound of joy and merriment became distorted in his mouth into mockery against everything and everyone. His childhood had no doubt been one long hell. All sorts of horrific scenes flashed through my head. I was no longer afraid.

He turned into the old road, which wound past a copse, then back onto the main road. The vehicle moved towards the kerb and came to a standstill. Suddenly, it had become very quiet, you could hear the buzz of insects and the distant sound of machinery. A tractor was chugging between fields. On my side of the road there was dense undergrowth, the branches were touching the cab. I took hold of the door handle and wondered what to do. If I jumped out now, he would catch me at the side of the road. The cab was so wide that he couldn't reach me. The plastic flowers that had been trembling in a mug when we were driving, were now motionless. It became more and more difficult to bear the silence.

He stretched, slouching there on his seat, scratched his chest, then his throat. It was two o'clock and we were about halfway. I wondered how much time I had lost, I thought about late winter and about how I hated my love, and how I'd fallen into this trap because of it. All my big dreams had come to nothing and I shrunk every day, becoming ever smaller and less significant.

"I've driven a hell of a long way," he said, and glancing in his direction I saw that his eyes were shut. "I'm going to get a little shut-eye."

The main road was within running distance. You could see that he wasn't a bit tired. He was waiting.

"Where've you been?" he asked, and when I made no reply, he opened his eyes. "Come on," he said irritably. "Open your mouth."

"I was visiting relatives in Otepää, and I've got to get home to my child. I couldn't get a bus ticket, not even for a minibus..."

What I didn't tell him was that in the past, I used to hitchhike everywhere when I had no money. Sometimes there were two of us, sometimes three, occasionally I was alone. Then, when the driver of a milk lorry had turned into a familiar stretch of woods and raped a friend of mine, such journeys came to an abrupt end. The pot-bellied middle-aged man had seemed so safe and calm, that my schoolfriend hadn't understood what was happening even as he was turning off the main road. She told me that she spewed up for days on end afterwards, and even as she was telling me, she got up and staggered to the lavatory.

"You're lying. You've never been visiting some old aunt, even a blind man can see that. Who were you staying with? And have you really got a kid... You probably think that sort of talk will make me take pity on you... I've got all the time in the world..."

"Tons of time," I thought. "And so heavy too."

"In prison I understood, that there are tons of time, you

can't chase it anywhere, just have to sit it out, then it'll all fall on top of you unless you make a move at the right moment."

He spread his fingers, then made his fist into a ball.

"I never got caught for anything big, just for the little things I did. Do you want to know what I actually did. If I do, I would have to shut you up for good."

He laughed again.

"OK," I replied.

"That's what I thought. You have that sort of look on your face that you want to break the bank. Looks as if I can't rape you in the woods quietly, so I'll have to do you in." He sat there looking at his hands, which were resting on the steering wheel. A couple of flies had flown in through the open window. They circled around us, flew against the windscreen and carried on buzzing there.

"Fuck," he said. "Can't stand it when they buzz around when I'm driving and get inside my shirt. Open the window on your side, so they'll fly out again as we drive."

He started the engine and we drove along the old potholed road back to the main road. We were moving, but slowly, creeping through the bright, sunny Sunday. When we approached a village he sped up. A couple of times, as we neared some houses, I was on the point of opening the door and jumping out, but he then said, without even giving me so much as a glance: "Don't try anything, I'll back up and you'll end up under the back wheels so that even your mother won't recognise you."

When we got to Saint Anna's Church, the smell of melting asphalt wafted in through the window and there was heat haze on the road. Everything was distorted by the heat: the church beyond the low wall, a closed shop and the houses on the edge of the woods. Everything was so familiar, in its right place, and yet so different to before. I had become very calm, I no longer thought about keeping him talking, outwitting him, making him feel sorry for me. I was so tired, that all I wanted to do was press the accelerator so we would race along and the huge vehicle would crash into something, and become a wreck. But everything proceeded slowly, hour after hour, as he weighed up what he would do with me at every new stretch of woodland. Tons of time.

As we passed through Vaida, it was already late afternoon. As the sun was going down, it shone into the eyes of those approaching Tallinn. I could hardly see the road, but that didn't seem to bother him. The traffic had become more dense. A number of cars overtook us, I could see their tail lights if I screwed up my eyes. Would it be possible to cry for help? Would the sound not be lost in the rumble of traffic, the speed, the blinking of tail lights?

"You are capable of shutting up and listening," he commented. "My wife is a real cow in that respect, but I've had a two-year-old boy with her, and she's quite a decent cook."

He drove the lorry to the side of the road, jumped out, came round to my side and took hold of the door handle. I kept the door shut from the inside and he gave his brief laugh. Then he turned round and peed at length into the ditch at the roadside. He did this calmly and I briefly thought that if I suddenly opened the door now, I would hit him on the back or the shoulder and would have the opportunity to run away. If there had been another car in the vicinity, I'd have tried this. Not so much out of fear, but out of an angry weariness at the slowness of the journey.

He seemed to sense my intentions. Taking his seat, he said: "Hatching plans, eh? Don't start struggling too soon. You'd like to knock my teeth down my throat, wouldn't you?"

"No," is what I said.

He laughed, barked as if choking on his own joke.

When Tallinn came into view, I could not even feel relief. A plane had risen into the air, its lights rose and moved away.

"You think you're nearly there," he said, as we turned off towards Järve at the roundabout near Lake Ülemiste. "It'll be half-past six soon, I'm driving over to the empty depot at Hiiu and I'm taking you with me. On Sunday evening there's no one there. Don't you believe me? Do you think I'd let you go, just like that?"

"You're playing a dirty game," I said.

"A game? You imagine it's just a game. I've told you more

about myself than I ever have my own woman, I've brought you here, although I could have left you in the first clump of bushes, and no one would have noticed. Get out! Now! Get going! What are you waiting for!"

His face was one mask of rage, if he had been able to reach me, he would have hit me. The large vehicle continued forward for some distance, even though he'd applied the brakes. I opened the door.

"Wait," he said. "I don't know why I'm letting you go..."

I looked him straight in the eye, and he barked his laugh one more time. "If you'd have yelled or started crying just once... but you just sat there like a fucking... Wait!"

I jumped down from the cab, slammed the door shut and began to walk towards the level crossing nearby. He drove past me before I had reached it. I looked at my watch, and broke into a light run. If the bus came along now, I would perhaps make it home by seven.

In my bag I had three half-ripe pears for my child.

1993

Stomach Ache

Peeter Sauter

I woke up. The room was dark. I was alone in bed. The light was on in the hall. Splashing could be heard from the bathroom. I rolled over. Let myself sink back into sleep.

I awoke once more. It was dark, the light was on in the hall, splashing from the bathroom. Maybe it's started, is what I thought. Should really get up and go to have a look how things stand. Couldn't be bothered. It was nice sleeping. I'll get a bit more sleep. I put my hand under the pillow. It was cool there.

I woke up. It was dark in the room. Jo Jo was standing by the bed. She wanted to tell me something. I looked at her and waited.

"It's coming on rather a lot." She was agitated and wasn't thinking about her voice. "Look, it's simply running out. I was sitting on the toilet. Then had a wash. Thought it'd pass. It started coming again. Look."

She was standing with her feet slightly apart. Her hair and her thighs were moist. I felt I ought to get up. I pushed my hand out from under the covers and held her leg near the knee. Jo Jo stood there motionless and looked at her wet cunt and legs. Then looked at me.

"Labour pains as well?"

"Are you asking me if there are pains?"

I blinked my eyes in agreement.

"No pains."

I wriggled down into the bed, lifted the corner of the covers and looked her in the eye. Jo Jo opened the door of the wardrobe. She opened a drawer within, pulled out a pack of sanitary towels and took one from the packet. She pushed it between her legs and held it there by squeezing them together. She found some knickers in the wardrobe and put them on. She straightened the sanitary towel inside them.

Jo Jo shut the wardrobe door and slipped in under the covers next to me. I hugged her. I stroked her back with my right hand. I let my eyes fall shut. I wouldn't get back to sleep now, but could doze a while. Jo Jo pressed her head between my shoulders and neck. Her hair fell onto my face, and tickled, so I eased back my head. Jo Jo moved hers, so that her hair was no longer in my face. I blew up into my face and the last hairs flew away from it.

I felt her big stomach. It felt soft. I thought, still half-asleep, that when Jo Jo stood before me the shape of her stomach had been normal, that the baby was not yet in position. But perhaps I didn't understand, how many pregnant tummies had I seen, only one before this one. And if the waters break early and the labour pains do not start, the birth has to be induced artificially. Does Jo Jo know this? Doesn't matter. The less she worries, the better. Her first birth. The kid could be climbing out through the neck of the womb for an entire day. The later she's taken to hospital to mope around there, the better.

Jo Jo curled up and tensed up for a short time. Labour pains? Should maybe look at the clock. I looked. It was dark and I couldn't see the hands. Is it some time after one?

Have to get up. I stroked Jo Jo and got out of bed. Went to the next room. Susa had pulled the covers up to her chin. Her breathing was barely audible and she was beautiful. I was naked and felt how cold the room was. I stood by the window and peeped out at the street lamps through a chink in the curtains. The street lamps were on and the street deserted. I could see three blue street lamps, the asphalt they lit up, and a little snow. I stood and watched for a little while, everything remained the same. I then thought that Susa had opened her eyes and was watching me standing naked by the window. I turned towards her. Her eyes were shut. I went over and gave her a kiss. Susa did not move. I began to feel cold. In the other room Jo Jo was in exactly the same position as before.

I rinsed out my mouth in the bathroom and looked at myself in the mirror. I had a pee and flushed the lavatory. My head was empty of thoughts, and not even that fact sprang to mind.

I could hear Jo Jo moaning quietly and looked at the clock. Twenty past one. I farted.

I sat on the edge of the bed and held Jo Jo's hand.

She was looking at me.

"Labour pains?"

Jo Jo nodded.

"I'll go and phone an ambulance soon."

Jo Jo frowned and shook her head.

"Do you want to go immediately?

She shook her head.

"You don't want an ambulance?"

She shook her head vigorously.

"Shall we take a taxi?"

She nodded.

"You got any money?

She nodded.

"I'll get a taxi soon."

Jo Jo indicated the back room with her eyes.

"Yes. Not sure. If I drop you off at the hospital and come back right away, she can maybe carry on sleeping here. What do you think, can you manage there on your own?"

Jo Jo shrugged her shoulders. I thought she might say something more. She was staring blankly into space. She pulled her hand out of mine and put it on my leg. She rested it there quite lightly.

"Jo Jo," I said.

She looked at me.

"No point in rushing. Let's wait an hour and then go."

She nodded.

"Do you want anything to eat?"

She shook her head.

I liked her hand on my leg, but thought that if I mentioned it she would take her hand away: I waited a couple of seconds, I had goosebumps, then said nevertheless: "I'll go and make some coffee."

She took her hand off my leg.

I got dressed. I went to the bathroom and had a shave. I thought I could hear her moaning, but I didn't look at my watch. I had taken a new disposable razor for sensitive skin and tried not to cut myself.

I went into the kitchen. I switched on the radio and put some water on the stove. I switched off the radio and took the kettle off the stove. I added water and put it back on the stove. I made some sandwiches. Five with liver pâté. I spread the pâté on the bread and watched my hands doing the spreading. There were large lumps of carrot in the pâté. Should I measure the intervals between the cramps? No, I won't, nothing's going to happen anyway. Three salami sandwiches with pickled cucumber slices, bread with margarine and honey (I switched on the radio again), two cheese sandwiches (I put the honey sandwich into my mouth) and two cottage cheese sandwiches. The water was sizzling in the kettle. I looked at the sandwiches on the table and waited for the water to boil. There was a very faint sound coming from the radio. I couldn't tell whether it was speech or music. The water was on the boil. I put some coffee grounds into the coffee pot, poured the water on top and put the pot on the heat for a moment. The coffee frothed up to the top and I switched off the gas. The froth came out over the edge of the pot and ran down onto the stove. I put the coffee pot on the table, lifted the grille of the stove and wiped the stove top clean with a kitchen cloth. I rinsed the cloth under the tap. I looked for the thermos flask in the cupboard, put in five teaspoonfuls of sugar and squeezed in a little lemon juice. I blew on the coffee so that the dregs would sink to the bottom, then filled the thermos. I glanced at the clock: one fifty.

I could hear the sound of a zip-fastener in the hall. I put a slice of lemon in a cup, two teaspoonfuls of sugar and poured out some coffee. The coffee was still too hot to drink. I should have to wake Susa now, dressing her could take some time. Jo Jo can dress her while I go after a taxi. In that way she won't have to sit there with thoughts going round and round in her head. I tasted the coffee, it was still too hot. The sandwiches were spread out across the kitchen table and I laid them in a row in the middle of the table. On the table was a large knife, a butter knife, white bread, brown bread, margarine, cottage cheese, pâté, salami, cheese, the sugar bowl, a lemon on a squeezer, a flower vase with some willow twigs, the salt cellar.

I had no appetite. I ate three liver pâté sandwiches and one with cheese. I don't remember how they tasted. The coffee could now be sipped. The coffee was good. I sipped, and sipped some more.

I put the cup down on the table and went into the room. Jo Jo was dressed. She had made the bed and was busying herself with some bags and bundles.

I went into the back room. Susa was asleep. I put on the light. I stroked her cheek. Susa was fast asleep. Jo Jo muttered something in the other room and I went in to see. She was standing at the edge of the bed, bent over the bed with her hands resting on it, rocking back and forth. She was frowning, had clenched her teeth, and was muttering. She sank down on all fours onto the bed and rested her head on her arms. She stayed in that position and groaned.

I went into the back room and lifted Susa out of bed. I put a bedspread over her and took her to the kitchen. Jo Jo was still in the same position, her face pressed into the bed. I couldn't work out whether Susa was asleep or not. I said: "If you want a wee-wee, just say."

I drank up my cup of lemon coffee and rinsed the cup under the tap. I took the milk and some yogurt out of the fridge. Clutching Susa with my left arm, I moved around the kitchen. I poured some milk into my coffee cup and put the milk carton back in the fridge. I poured out a cup of coffee and added a spoonful of sugar. I stirred the sugar. Susa screwed up her eyes and I said: "If you want a wee-wee, say so right away."

"I don't need a wee-wee."

"OK then, but when you do, just say so. Do you want some yoghurt?"

"Don't want any."

"I'll put you down on the chair."

"I do want some."

"In a cup or a glass?"

" In the green cup."

I poured the yoghurt into the green plastic cup and sipped my milky coffee.

"Daddy, but it's dark outside."

"That's right, it's night now. Take whichever sandwich you like."

"Am I going too?"

"Do you want to?"

"Yes I do."

"Then you can come too, but it could take a long time."

"I want a wee-wee now."

"Well, hurry up, then."

"But I haven't got anything on my feet. I can't go with nothing on my feet. Don't you know that?

"Oh, all right."

I picked Susa up and took her to the toilet. In the hall she said: "Wait," and switched the light on in the toilet. In the toilet she said: "Daddy, guess who put on the light in the toilet." I lifted her down onto the floor. "Daddy, guess!"

"Now sit quietly on the pot and make sure the tinkle goes in the right place and wipe yourself afterwards." I lifted the toilet lid and wanted to seat her on it, but Susa wouldn't let me and said:

"I can do it myself."

"OK, I'll be in the kitchen."

"Will it be a boy or a girl?"

"I don't know yet."

"Wait," I could hear her peeing. "If it's a girl, then we'll call her Bunny. Bunny, or Marta, won't we daddy?"

"We'll have to wait and see."

I went into the room. Jo Jo was sitting in an armchair, wearing a coat, and looking at me. Next to the chair was a sports-bag crammed full of things, the zip pulled shut, and her handbag.

We looked at one another.

"I'm going to finish eating, then we'll go and find a taxi. Could you dress Susa?"

Jo Jo gave a sign with her fingers: are you and Susa coming too?

"Yes, we're both coming with you."

She indicated: will you and Susa be there when I give birth?

"Yes. I hope they let us both in. Maybe they'll let Susa sleep somewhere. You OK?"

"I'm OK. We must go soon."

"Very well. Susa's having a wee-wee right now. I'll put some sandwiches in a bag for us. Do you have the phone number of the reception?"

Jo Jo bent down, took a diary from her handbag, plus a blank slip of paper and a biro. She wrote the number down for me. I wondered, is she upset or just very concentrated.

"You've got your health insurance card and all the necessary papers?

Jo Jo nodded.

"What sort of taxi do you want?"

Jo Jo made a sign: go now.

I took a plastic bag from the kitchen drawer, pressed the sandwiches together – one of the cheese sandwiches got completely smeared with pâté, and I put them in the bag.

I took the bag of sandwiches and the thermos. I went quickly into the back room. I put the thermos and the bag of sandwiches into a shoulder bag, and glanced at the shelf. I took a book and shoved it into the bag. I put on my jacket while walking and unlocked the door.

Out in the corridor, before shutting the door to the flat, I had realised that I had my bag over my shoulder. I thought for a moment, then pulled the door shut.

Once outside, I lit a cigarette and strode towards the taxi

rank. The street lights were on. The street was deserted and I had an easy walk. I inhaled the smoke deep into my lungs. The air was chilly and I hardly tasted the smoke at all.

In the distance I spotted a state taxi approaching. I didn't hail it. I bounced my way across the snowy street. The food kiosk lights were on. I wondered whether to get a bottle from the kiosk, I slowed down. Then sped up again. I tossed the longish fag end far away in an arc.

At the taxi rank one Opel taxi was standing, one state taxi, and one private one. I got into the state taxi and said the address. The driver repeated the address. The car turned round.

"Hang on, drive back to a phone box for a minute. I've got to ring."

"To a phone box," said the taxi driver. He had crammed a thick brown book between the front seats, one he had been reading. The book was pushed down in such a way that I couldn't see the name of the author or the title on either the front cover or the spine. I looked to see whether the price was written in Cyrillic or our alphabet. I couldn't see.

I lifted the receiver. I waited a short while and then dialled Susa's mum's number. The telephone rang and I replaced the receiver. I looked for the number that Jo Jo had given me and lifted the receiver. I thought. I phoned. They replied immediately.

"Hello. I'm bringing in a pregnant woman about to give birth within half an hour. She's twenty-years-old, the waters have broken and the labour pains started at one o'clock, this is her first birth, she's called Jo Jo Laht, I'll spell that: jay, oh, that's one name, then the other, jay, oh, then the surname – ell, ay, aitch, tee. She's deaf." I felt I was speaking a bit oddly. There was silence at the other end.

"First birth?"
"Yes."
"What time did the labour pains start?"
"One o'clock."
"And her waters have broken?"

"Yes."

"We're expecting you."

"Goodbye."

I put down the receiver and waited a further couple of seconds, with my hand on it. The phone booth had aluminium walls, no windows. I lit a cigarette and took a few quick puffs. I threw the fag end on the floor and trod on it.

I got into the taxi and gave the address. The taxi-driver put the thick brown book between the seats and repeated the address. I couldn't make out whether he had an accent or not. The book was placed so that I couldn't see what book it was or what language it was in. Won't get to know, is what I thought.

"Here?" said the taxi-driver.

"Yes. Stop and wait a while. I'll be bringing down two ladies."

I waited for him to say something. He said nothing. I looked at the taxometer. It was already showing eleven kroons and I wondered how much the hospital trip was going to cost. Sixty or seventy. And if he drove us back too, it would be over a hundred. The taxi-driver had his hand on the book, but didn't open it. I opened the door of the taxi and got out.

Jo Jo was pulling up the zip of Susa's jump suit and looking in my direction. She pulled the zip up halfway and put on Susa's scarf. Susa grabbed the scarf herself and tried to wind it around her neck.

"Do hurry up," I said.

"Is Jo Jo ill?"

"No. She's going to have a baby."

"Her tummy hurts. That's why it hurts," explained Susa.

I put my bag down on the floor, did up the last button on Susa's jump suit, straightened her scarf and pulled up the zip right to the top. Jo Jo stood there motionless. She had her handbag in her hand and the sports-bag was on the floor near the door. I eyed my own bag.

"But my mole's got to come too."

"Bring him along, then. Now put on your wellies quickly."
Susa's hair was a mess. I went to the bathroom. I took a comb from
the shelf and two hair bands.

"Did you eat your yoghurt?"

"Didn't eat any more. Only before, when I went to the
toilet."

"Are you going down to the taxi," I asked Jo Jo and she
shook her head. I went into the kitchen without taking off my shoes.
I took an unopened carton of yoghurt out of the fridge and put it
in my pocket. I took a teaspoon from the drawer and put it in my
pocket. I looked round the kitchen. The gas had been turned off. I
looked out of the window. The taxi was standing there in front of the
building with its sidelights on. I took the brown and the white bread
from the kitchen table and put it away. I put away the cottage cheese,
margarine, cheese, sausage, pâté, gherkins. I put the lemon squeezer
near the edge of the table. I could hear Jo Jo groaning. I washed
the cutlery and put them in the drying rack. Jo Jo was groaning. I
went into the hall. Jo Jo was standing, leaning her head against the
electricity meter, one hand clutching a coat hook, the other a balled
fist. The electricity meter was ticking very slowly. Susa was still
putting on her wellies. She looked at Jo Jo and at me.

"Hurry up," I said to Susa.

Jo Jo stood there without moving. I wanted her to go and
sit down on the hall stool. I stood a while and went back into the
kitchen. I wiped the table with a cloth. I shook the crumbs out of the
cloth into the sink. I wet the cloth and wiped the table again. I shook
it out again under the tap and let the running water wash away the
crumbs. My shoes had left marks on the floor.

"Mittens!" said Susa in the hall.

I wound up the white kitchen clock and put it in the
cupboard. I switched off the kitchen light.

Jo Jo was pale and was holding Susa's mittens. Susa was
standing opposite her, holding out her hands stiffly in front of her. I
took Susa's mittens out of Jo Jo's hands and Susa turned towards me
like a robot. I put on her right mitten. Susa straightened her thumb

at the right moment. I checked, whether her thumb was in the thumb hole.

"Right,"said Susa.

I put on her other mitten. Susa turned like a robot towards the door. Jo Jo took her keys from her handbag and hung them on the hook. I touched her shoulder: "I'll take your big bag." Jo Jo went out. Susa moved her stiff moon-robot legs in the direction of the door.

"Beep-beep," said Susa and came to a standstill.

"Get a move on now."

"Don't push me," she said, emerging from her moon-robot act.

"What is it now?"

"Mole!"

I went into the back room. I looked to see if my shoes were still leaving marks. They weren't. Susa's nightdress was in a heap on the chair. The mole could be seen between the mattress and the bedframe. I folded up her nightdress and put it under her pillow. I folded up the blanket and threw it on the bed. I pulled her pet mole out from under the mattress.

"The mole's going in the bag," I said to Susa.

"Beep-beep," said Susa and started walking.

I locked the door and wondered whether everything was OK in the flat. Susa stood on the stairs, her arm up in the air.

"Waiting!" said Susa. I gave her my hand and we went downstairs.

"Do you want to sit in the front or the back of the taxi?"

"Who else is sitting in the back?"

"Depends on where Jo Jo's going to sit."

"In the back."

I opened the taxi door and Susa crept in next to Jo Jo.

While sitting in the taxi, I couldn't help looking at the brown book between the seats. The book was pushed in so I couldn't see what it was. I had hoped that there would be music playing in the taxi.

I looked out at the streets and whistled quietly. I turned

round towards Jo Jo and put my hand on her belly. Susa put both her hands on Jo Jo's belly. Jo Jo was looking out of the window. I got the feeling she was afraid of getting her next wave of labour pains. That she was tired of the pains. Didn't want any more. I withdrew my hand, looked out of the window and whistled: "The answer, my friend, is blowing in the wind, the answer is blowing in the wind".

"I hate ambulances," said Jo Jo. The taxi-driver's head jerked a little to the right when he heard Jo Jo's voice.

I carried on whistling and had a good feeling that nothing bad was about to happen. Have to do everything step by step. And I wanted to be doing that.

"Stop whistling", said Susa.

"Why?"

"You don't whistle in cars."

"Why?"

I carried on whistling.

"Stop whistling!"

I stopped.

Jo Jo was resting her arms on the back of my seat. Another contraction had come. She tried to groan as quietly as possible. I wondered what to say at the hospital so that Susa and me could stay with Jo Jo. Dunno. I'm saying it as it is.

The taxi-driver knew where to go. He drove round a large building. We turned into some yard or other and stopped outside the door. All the windows were dark and the door seemed to be so tightly shut that it seemed not to have been opened in years. There was a notice: "Maternity Reception". I wondered whether to check the door before letting the taxi go.

I looked at Jo Jo. She was OK now. She handed me her purse. I paid the taxi-driver and took my bag and Jo Jo's.

The door was locked. I pressed the bell. The taxi drove out of the yard, its headlights shining onto the yard and the surrounding bushes. There was a weak light by the door, the rest of the yard was in darkness. Jo Jo signed to me that she could spread her legs in the middle of the yard, that that was a good place to do so. I pressed the bell again.

"Aren't you sleepy?" I asked Susa.

"No."

I thought that if Susa and me had to go back home, I'd have to ask Jo Jo for the taxi money.

The door opened.

"Hello."

"You phoned earlier."

"Yes."

"Got everything you need with you? Your health insurance card?" The nurse asked Jo Jo.

"Yes," I replied.

"Got your child with you?"

"Yes, the child has come along."

"She's not intending to stay here?"

"I don't know. She hasn't got anywhere else to go."

"Why didn't you leave the child with someone? Come in, anyway."

The nurse led the way. I moved only my lips to say to Jo Jo: "At least they've let us into the warm."

The nurse continued along a corridor. Jo Jo went to the corridor window, leaned forward and took hold of the sill.

The nurse opened a door at the end of the corridor and looked behind her. "I'll leave the door open," she said.

"Mmm," said Jo Jo and looked fixedly at the radiator under the window. I caressed her back. Susa had a blank look on her face.

"Nice sister," I said. "Really nice."

"What sister?" said Susa. "Haven't got a sister yet."

"The one who let us in, she's a sister, that's her job. The word has two meanings. You can have a sister. And you can call a nurse in a hospital a sister."

"Mmmmm," said Jo Jo and bent her knees somewhat. She gripped the windowsill tightly. She was white around her lacquered fingernails, as was the windowsill. I spread my fingers and took a firm grip of her hair, near the roots. That's what I sometimes do when

I fuck her. Jo Jo took hold of my left wrist and said once again: "Mmmmm."

"The baby wants to come out," said Susa.

"Yes, I think so."

"Are we staying here?"

"Let's wait and see."

"Otherwise Jo Jo will have to stay here all on her own and she'll get sad."

"Yes."

Jo Jo stood up straight and was panting. We went on down the corridor.

A nurse was sitting at a desk in reception. She had a newspaper in front of her and a biro in her hand. She was solving a crossword puzzle. We went in and stood there. The nurse was just writing a word in the squares and she wrote the whole word before looking up at us. I was beginning to like her.

"Take off your clothes."

"Can I stay here with my child?"

"I don't know. All the same to me. I don't know how you're going to cope with her in the maternity ward. Isn't she sleepy?"

"Not right now she isn't. Maybe she can snatch some sleep in some bed or other. If there's a free bed."

The nurse took a key out of the pocket of her smock and unlocked the wardrobe. There were a lot of clothes hanging there. A whole cupboardful of women giving birth had come in before us. The nurse handed us a clothes hanger. "I'll take you up to the maternity ward and we'll see what they tell you." She gave Jo Jo and me a smock to wear. "Do you have slippers?"

"We do." I saw how we could have been given some green slip-on museum slippers too.

It would have been fun to give birth in such footwear. Susa watched how we put on our smocks.

"What's your name?" the nurse asked Susa.

"Susa."

"I see. I'm Sister Aino. I'm afraid I haven't got a smock

small enough for you to wear. If you want to go to sleep, Susa, then you can go and lie down on the bed over here." There was a bunk bed next to the desk.

I tied the tapes of Jo Jo's smock behind her neck. Jo Jo signed with her fingers that she didn't want her cunt shaven.

"Yes, I know," I said.

"You can come to the next room," said the nurse to Jo Jo.

They went into another room and the door was left open.

The nurse fiddled with some equipment. "Please lie down here."

"Please speak slowly so she can see your lips. She's deaf," I said to the nurse.

The nurse turned towards Jo Jo: "Please lie down." She indicated the bunk bed with her hand.

The bed was high. Jo Jo climbed up onto it.

I helped Susa out of her outer clothes.

"Can I go up there too?" asked Susa.

"Don't." I looked for Susa's slippers in my bag. They weren't there. "Keep your woolly socks on." I took off my smock, took off my jumper and put the smock on again. I tied the tapes behind my back and went to sit on the bed.

The nurse stuck some leads on Jo Jo with medical tape and switched on her machine. An electro-cardiogram could be seen on the oscilloscope. The curve swung up and down on the screen and it was like in a film. I was exhausted and slow thoughts were crossing my brain. If I saw someone being killed it would also be like in a film. A birth isn't really like in a film. Is this Jo Jo's heart or the baby's? Must be the baby's, if what they've got is some kind of ECG. Susa leaned against me and I took her up onto my knee. When should I mention the shaving? Jo Jo was groaning on the table and was trying to curl up. The nurse patted her hand and nodded to her. Strange that everything is as it is. Well, it's like that now. I didn't want to think this thought. I sat next to the nurse's desk and turned her open newspaper towards me. I was looking to see what I could add to the crossword. I found something. I saw the biro on the desk. I didn't pick it up. I read through the crossword again. I tried to visualise which squares I had filled in and to match them with those words crossing them.

Susa was getting too heavy for me. Her head was nodding down. I lifted her cautiously onto the bunk bed. She touched the cool plastic and put her arms round my neck. I stroked her head.

"I'll put my jumper over you." I took her arms from round my neck. She put her hands together and put them under her cheek. I spread the jumper over her and returned to the crossword.

"I've got to fill in some papers," said the nurse from the adjoining room.

"Yes," I said and thought about a word in the crossword puzzle.

"How many births has she had?"

"This is her first." I couldn't guess the word.

"How many pregnancies?"

"Don't know."

"How many pregnancies?" the nurse asked Jo Jo.

"This is the third," said Jo Jo.

"First birth?"

"First birth. One was an abortion, the other a miscarriage."

"What diseases have you had? Which diseases has she had?"

"Don't know," I said.

"Don't know," said Jo Jo. "Ordinary ones. Mumps and something else. Haven't had jaundice."

"Venereal diseases?"

The Estonian author in the clue was 'Teet Kallas'.

"Trichomoniasis."

"When?"

The vegetable was 'cabbage'.

"Two years ago."

"That all or is there anything else?"

"That's all."

Do, re, mi, fa, so, la, ti, do. Ra? Or fa?

"When were you expected to give birth?"

"In two weeks' time."

"And what time did the contractions start?" The nurse got up off her stool and looked between Jo Jo's legs.

"One o'clock," I said.

It was cosy sitting here. Sit here a bit, have a natter, then go home. The curves on the oscilloscope were making an even pattern. A needle was describing this same pattern on a roll of paper. The nurse was doing something at the sink. Jo Jo lifted her head.

"She doesn't want to be shaved, if that's possible."

"I won't take much off. Have to take a bit from below, but I'll leave it all above. Your child's asleep now."

"She fell asleep." I signed to Jo Jo: she'll shave you a bit. Jo Jo lowered her head back onto the pillow.

The nurse shaved Jo Jo's cunt. I couldn't remember the words I'd thought of for the crossword. I slid the newspaper round to its original position.

The nurse turned a knob on the machine and the picture vanished from the screen. She ripped off the printed sheet of the ECG and stapled it to some other papers. She got up and had a look at Jo Jo. She patted Jo Jo's wrist and removed the leads and medical tape from her belly. "Get up now," she said very clearly.

Jo Jo came over to me. I held her hand and stroked her belly. The nurse picked up our clothes from the chair and put them in the wardrobe.

She gave me a green oilcloth bag: "Put your shoes in the bag." I put my shoes in the bag and pulled the drawstring shut.

"You're not married then?"

I looked the nurse in the eye. "No, we're not."

"That's all right then. I didn't think you were."

"I trust you haven't been drinking?"

I looked the nurse in the eye. "No I haven't."

She hung the oilcloth bag on our hanger and locked the cupboard.

"Take your Susa onto your lap now."

I did so. She did not wake up.

"Second floor," said the nurse.

We stood there in the corridor, in the maternity ward, by a desk and watched the nurse examine our papers.

"Sit down, you needn't stand." We sat down. The nurse looked at Susa sitting on my knee and back at the papers.

Across from us the door of the ward stood open. A woman was lying on a high delivery table, her bent legs open towards the wall. She looked at me. Next to the delivery table a man was standing, with his back towards me. The man watched the woman watch me, then turned around. We looked straight at one another. The man didn't like it that I was looking.

"Why..." said the man, looking at me. "Aaaa," said his wife and grabbed his hand, so he turned towards her. I got up and sat down further away.

Two young girls came in. "Girls," said the nurse, "take them along."

"Come this way," said a student. We got up.

"Are you the husband?" asked the nurse.

"No." Susa was heavy to carry.

"I see," said the nurse. I thought she'd say something more. She didn't.

The student stood at the door to the ward. Jo Jo walked in and I followed her. It was a large room with a high ceiling and many beds. There were high nickel-plated delivery tables, and low couches covered in sheets and plastic.

"She should lie down now," said a girl. "The doctor will be here soon. Is the child staying here?"

"Yes."

"Put her on a couch. I'll bring her a blanket."

The room was brightly lit. I lay Susa down and put the bags in a corner. Jo Jo stared at the ceiling. She was tired.

I touched her hand. "Do you want a sandwich and some coffee?"

Jo Jo shook her head. "Drink of water," she said.

There was a tap in the ward. I found a plastic mug and brought her some water. She let me support her head and hold the mug. Some of the water dribbled down her chin.

"Hold it yourself."

Jo Jo took the mug and drank on her own. She took my wrist and looked at the time.

"I'm fed up with all this," said Jo Jo.

"OK, then let's go home. Leave giving birth till another time." Jo Jo looked aside and tears rolled down from the corners of her eyes. I took the mug back to the sink.

"Jo Jo," I said, "do you want me to read you something from a book? It could still take ages. Be strong."

"I can't take it any more."

"If you try, it'll be easier on the baby. Then it won't have to flounder about so much in that narrow neck of the womb."

"I'll try then."

Someone came in quickly and authoritatively. She had a perm, a fat peroxide blonde.

"Hello. How many's she had?"

"This is the first."

"Not had an abortion?"

"Yes, she has."

"What time did the contractions start?"

"At one."

"We'll have a look right away." She pulled a rubber glove out of a packet and put it on. "This is going to hurt a bit." Jo Jo looked at me and I nodded. The doctor pushed her fingers into Jo Jo's cunt. Jo Jo frowned.

"Don't know," said the doctor. "Could be here soon. I'll be in the observation room. But there's a nurse in the corridor. So the gentleman can call me if necessary." She stood up and removed the rubber glove. I wondered whether to stand up too or stay put and I stayed seated. The doctor left immediately in the same business-like and matter-of-fact manner as she had arrived. I noticed that a student was following her around everywhere.

"She's like a good car mechanic."

"I'm not a car."

"Not such an enormous difference." I went and pulled Susa's blanket up to her chin. "I wonder whether a doctor finds it more difficult to give birth herself. She knows what can go wrong." The young girls came in with some trays and bundles. One of them placed a small pile of faded hospital sheets by Jo Jo's head. Jo Jo closed her eyes and let her head fall on one side as if going to sleep. I walked up to the girls, though I didn't really need anything.

"I'd like to put out a few lights?" I noticed that I was speaking quite quietly. Susa was asleep.

"Sure." The girl went to the light-switch herself. She flicked the switch. She switched some lights off then a few on again. The room was now in semi-darkness. The girl looked at me, with interest I thought.

"That all right?"

"Yes." Anything more to ask? No, there wasn't.

Jo Jo began to groan and I went to her. The students went off. I thought that Jo Jo wanted to curl up, and I supported her neck. She held my hand so tight that it hurt, looked at the ceiling and groaned. At first she tensed her stomach muscles, then completely tensed up.

"Aaaa," she said, when it subsided.

"Breathe deeply." She was panting, even so. "Going to push more, are you?"

She pressed her nose against my wrist. I felt she was trying to keep control of her voice.

"Yell, if you want to." She wasn't watching my lips. She tensed up and groaned loudly and then went slack on the bed. She shut her eyes and opened them again a short while later.

"I can't take any more. I don't want to."

I looked at her.

"I won't be able to cope, if it comes again. Isn't there anyone else here on the ward?" She turned her head and looked around. "Susa's over there."

"No she isn't. But there are others giving birth in the next ward."

"I don't understand. Say it again."

"Others giving birth in the next ward."

"Oh, I've got to have a shit. Do you know where it is?"

"I don't know. Shall I go and ask?"

"Yes. No, wait. I'm coming with you." She heaved herself into a sitting position and searched for her clogs under the bed with her weak legs. I pushed the clogs towards her feet and helped her up.

There was no one in the corridor. Moaning sounds were coming from the next ward and the door stood ajar. People were moving about in there. The wooden heels of Jo Jo's clogs clacked impatiently on the stone floor of the corridor. From the half-open door of the ward came a loud shriek. This was still like a film – couldn't see anything but you could hear it all right. A shriek of a newborn child as background sound was very much like a film.

Jo Jo was clacking onwards and I trotted after her. The corridor was in semi-darkness. We were like spies. Another door was standing half-open. It was some kind of rest room. Some knitting was on the table. Jo Jo was increasing her pace. She reached the end of the corridor. There was nowhere to go now and there were no signs on the doors. Jo Jo pushed open a door. A nurse appeared from somewhere.

" 'Scuse me, where's the toilet?"

"Here. But the man from the other ward went in just now, I think."

"Jo Jo," I said. "It's a bog, but it's occupied."

Jo Jo's eyes widened.

"Isn't there another toilet?" I asked the nurse.

"Not here. What's wrong with her?"

"She has to go to the lavatory."

"She'll have to wait."

There was a flushing sound coming from the toilet, the door opened and out stepped a man. Jo Jo rushed into the toilet. I waited.

I went back to the ward. The neighbouring one was silent. I looked through the half-open door and could see the woman was still there on the delivery table.

Susa was asleep. I took the mole from her bag and put it by her head. I screwed open the top of the thermos, pulled out the cork and poured out some coffee. I took a sandwich from the bag and pushed it into my mouth. I picked up the book. I sat down on a chair, opened it in the middle and started reading.

"As the old man spoke, I became aware of a loud and gradually increasing sound, like the moaning of a vast herd of buffaloes upon an American prairie; and at the same moment I perceived that what seamen term the chopping character of the ocean beneath us, was rapidly changing... " (I munched the cheese sandwich and drank some coffee without stopping reading.) "Even while I gazed, this current acquired a monstrous velocity..."

Jo Jo opened the door a little and peered inside. She came in and lay down on the couch.

"Do you want some coffee?"

Jo Jo nodded. She took hold of the thermos mug, took a sip, and handed it back.

"Oh dear," she said. "I shat in my knickers." Another contraction began. She took my hand.

"Try to do it quietly. Susa's asleep."

"Oh dear, I've shat my knickers full and couldn't wash them. I didn't know where to put them... oh dear... I removed the shit with some toilet paper and put them in the bin."

"Maybe you'd be better on all fours."

"Help me."

She supported herself on her left arm and went on all fours. I had the coffee mug in my right hand and a book on my knee. Jo Jo groaned and moved back and forth. I put my left hand on her back and looked at my watch. It was ten past four. I drank my coffee up.

"Oh, oh, oh, oh. Tat-tat-tat-tat," said Jo Jo.

I read quietly to myself. "Here the vast bed of the waters, seamed and scarred into a thousand conflicting channels, burst suddenly into frenzied convulsions – heaving, boiling, hissing – gyrating in gigantic and innumerable vortices, and all whirling and plunging on to the eastward with a rapidity which water never elsewhere assumes except in precipitous descents."

Jo Jo's contraction passed. She eased herself onto her elbows and then gingerly onto her side. Jo Jo's eyes were shut. I looked at her. I poured out some more coffee. I wasn't following what I was reading, but read on:

"The general surface of the water grew somewhat more smooth, and the whirlpools, one by one, disappeared, while prodigious waves of foam became apparent where none had been seen before. These waves, at length, spreading out to a great distance..."

Jo Jo sat up. She leaned on her arm and looked around. Her eyes were darting hither and thither. She put her left hand to her mouth and her eyes stopped wandering.

"What is it, Jo Jo?"

"Going to be sick."

I got to my feet and looked around.

"The sink," was what I said and saw a bedpan under the white-metal working top. A wide, flattish bedpan, in white enamel, with a black edge. I thrust the bedpan in front of Jo Jo on the couch and she spewed up. After the first wave of vomit, she rested a little and shut her eyes. The puke coming from her stomach gave her body a wave-like movement, sprayed out of her mouth and splashed down into the bedpan. Jo Jo was holding the bedpan handle. It was about to slip down onto the floor. I took hold of it. My right hand was still holding the thermos mug and the book. Jo Jo lay on her side on the couch. Her cheek was pressed against the edge of the bedpan. I looked at the floor. Some of the sick had dropped down onto it. The bedpan was still pressed hard against Jo Jo's cheek. I reached out for a small cloth and threw it down onto the vomit on the floor. Jo Jo raised her head a little and spewed up again. There was less vomit coming up now and it was entirely liquid. Jo Jo spat several times. She no longer had the energy to spit and allowed the saliva to run down from the corner of her mouth. She lay there panting, eyes closed.

I touched her shoulder. She looked at me. "No more coming up?"

She shook her head and leaned back.

"Want some water or coffee?"

She shook her head.

"Then take a rest." She shut her eyes.

I wiped the floor clean. I went to the toilet with the bedpan and the cloth.

The nurse was sitting in the corridor. She looked questioningly at me.

"She puked up."

The nurse stood up. "Give them to me." The nurse took the bedpan.

"You don't have to." I kept hold of the handle of the bedpan.

"Give them to me. It's my job." I let go of the handle.

The nurse went with the bedpan and the cloth to the toilet. I sat down on the sofa in the corridor.

I wondered why I was so sure everything would go well. I'm either sure or indifferent. But what if the child were to die? Well, I don't know. It'll die one day anyway. I was born, live and will die. No, it's not that. I know nothing of my own birth and death and never will. I know some odds and ends. Would things be different in the case of my own child? Don't know. What would be different? Something would. Something would be different, if any number of details were different. If I had seen the taxi-driver's book, if I'd bought a bottle, if the weather had been different. But what? If a fly flew down the corridor. That's what it is. It's this. This is what it is. And the next moment is what it is. What next moment? Time doesn't exist. I yawned. Time doesn't exist, but what does? What does? Susa is my own child, and I don't know who was there when she was born, what her birth was like, or how she was born, now I am here, but I can leave Jo Jo and the child won't see me and won't know that I was here when it was born. Neither will it know the room, or the thermos mug or the cloth. Of course. I yawned. Where do they go to have a smoke? Why did the other man go to the toilet? And what thermos mug will be present at my death? Doesn't matter. Doesn't of course matter. Did she carry on doing the crossword or lie down on her side on the couch? What does matter? How you are dealt with. There are good motor mechanics. How you relate to people. So that you feel good about it. An ordinary act can be perfect. An ordinary existence can be perfect, if anything at all. Don't use such words. It damages. Does it? I wonder why. Let there be perfection, immortality, timelessness. It doesn't mean anything nor damage anything. Nothing is obligatory. I yawned. Felt for my packet of cigarettes. The nurse came back. She handed me the bedpan she had cleaned.

"Do you still have any of those cloths?"

"Yes. Thanks."

"You're going to have a girl."

"I see."

The nurse sat down at the desk. I put the bedpan by my feet under the sofa.

"When will she be born?

"When she's born."

"She's tired."

"That's natural. Is the child asleep?"

"Yes."

The nurse started to fill in forms. I left the bedpan on the floor and went to the toilet.

I raised the lid of the pot and opened my flies. I wasn't in a hurry to piss, but it just kept coming. The pissing ended with a small spurt and I felt good, as if I'd achieved something important.

I put a fag in my mouth and pressed down the pedal of the rubbish bin with my foot. The knickers were in there. I pushed the cigarette back into the packet and removed the knickers from the bin. The little bit of shit that there was disappeared under the water running from the tap. I rubbed some soap in and rubbed again. There were small butterflies on the knickers and I liked them. I wrung out the knickers and looked at my face in the mirror. I needed a shave.

I walked down the corridor holding the knickers in my fist. I picked up the bedpan on the way and went onto the ward. Jo Jo was standing by a small metal table. She gripped one of its legs and squatted down. When she tried to get back up, the table came with her with a clatter. I managed to support her, otherwise she'd have fallen on her back. The enamel bedpan fell out of my hand onto the floor. Jo Jo stood up, turned towards me, smiled grimly and took my arms. Her eyes were now focused and her nostrils flared. She gritted her teeth. Jo Jo leant on my arms, eased herself down to a squatting position and then stood up again. Susa mumbled something. Jo Jo's nose was sharp, her eyes squinting, her teeth clenched. She breathed noisily through her nose. She leaned on my arms, squatted and stood up again. She glanced at the knickers in my hand.

Jo Jo let go of my arms, held her big belly and staggered through the ward. A small piece of shit fell from between her legs. She headed for the delivery table and held onto its edge. I went over to Susa. Susa had turned over onto her side and was clutching the mole. I picked up the bedpan off the floor and put it under the edge of the couch.

Jo Jo was wandering about the ward. On the floor near the delivery table was a small piece of shit. I draped the knickers over the radiator and looked to see whether Jo Jo would tread in the shit. She saw the shit on the floor and stepped past it. She touched things as she passed them: she touched the wall, the sink, another couch, a white metal cupboard, a small high white table, the weighing scales for the babies.

Jo Jo took hold of the edge of the sink, leaned forwards and said: "Tat-tat-tat-tat-tat". She waved her left hand, I didn't know whether she was beckoning me. I went over and held her hand. She pressed her forehead against the edge of the sink, half-squatted and whimpered. I put my other hand under her armpit. I looked at Jo Jo's hair in the sink.

Jo Jo slowly heaved herself to her feet and waddled over to the couch. She lay down on her back with her bent legs apart. I looked between her legs. The bottom of the smock was covered in shit. Her bared calves and thighs were thin, slack and tired. I took a piece of cloth from the top of the couch. Should I wipe the floor with it? I patted Jo Jo's thin thigh. Her cunt was now bulging, shining, bluish. Her arsehole was turned outwards.

I carefully wiped her buttocks and the cleft in between. I ran the cloth across her bulging sphincter and Jo Jo grasped my hand. I screwed up the cloth and looked for somewhere to put it, then threw it under the couch. The book was lying open on the floor. I took another cloth from the top of the couch and put it under Jo Jo's bottom. I looked at the floor of the ward and the traces of shit. Jo Jo's hand was clamped to mine. I took a look at the book.

"...but no particle of this slipped into the mouth of the terrible funnel, whose interior, as far as the eye could see, was a smooth, shining and jet-black wall of water, inclined to the horizon at an angle of some forty-five degrees, speeding dizzily round and round with a swaying and sweltering motion, and sending forth an appalling voice, half shriek, half roar, such as not even the mighty cataract of Niagara ever lifts up in its agony to Heaven..."

The door opened. A woman stood there who I had not seen before.

"How's it going?"

I looked at her and couldn't find anything to say.

The woman looked at the floor. She stiffened and took a cloth from the head of the couch. "Whatever have you done here?" She picked up small pieces of shit from the floor. "You don't do that sort of thing at home." She took more cloths and cleaned up the shitty patches.

She threw the cloths into the bin. "No harm in wandering around, but don't do that again." She came up to Jo Jo. "Show me what you've got here."

Her soft hands opened Jo Jo's cunt and then let go again. She stroked her stomach. "Anyway," she said, "don't go around messing up the floor." She spotted the book on the floor.

"No," I said.

The woman left.

I stretched my legs while sitting and then stretched my back. I picked up the shitty cloth from under the couch, rose to my feet and threw it in the bin. More shit had come out from her bum and onto the couch. I wiped it away and put another cloth under her bottom.

Jo Jo was lying on her back, staring vacantly. She no longer seemed tired.

I pushed the soiled cloth into the bin, it was beginning to fill up, and I washed my hands under the tap.

Jo Jo groaned. I went over and sat by her. Her cunt had grown more bulging, more shining, more bluish. Jo Jo's throat swelled up and she said: "Ot-ot-ot-ot-ot-ot-ot." She thrust, her anal sphincter pushed outwards and shit came out onto the cloth. I stayed calm. The longer things went on, the calmer I became. Jo Jo's face made her look as if she were weeping, but she wasn't. She said: "Ot-ot," held her breath, then panted. I took hold of her hand.

I looked at the book on the floor.

"The mountain trembled to its very base, and the rock rocked. I threw myself upon my face, and clung to the scant herbage in an excess of nervous agitation. 'This,' said I at length to the old man: 'this can be nothing else than the great whirlpool of the Maelström.' "

Jo Jo squeezed my arm and I looked up. Her face was red and her knees rose upwards. Her heels were now clear of the couch, her toes were still touching the oilcloth. She looked at me, her eyes wide: I smiled at her. In her bulging cunt was a small split, and when I peered inside, something red and blue could be seen. It didn't look like a head. I wondered whether some stuff would come out first.

Jo Jo leaned back on the couch, slackened off. Her cunt contracted.

"Breathe!"

Jo Jo panted for a few seconds then began to groan again.

"Push downwards! With your stomach muscles!" Her cunt swelled up and the split became wider still.

What could be seen? A piece of the foetal membrane?

"Push!" Jo Jo couldn't push any more and slackened off.

I picked up the book from the floor with my right hand.

"Sixty seven," I said the page number to myself.

Jo Jo was resting. I turned back a page and read:

" 'You must get over these fancies,' said the guide, 'for I have brought you here that you might have the best possible view of the scene of that event I mentioned...' "

It started again for Jo Jo. I shut the book with my right hand and tossed it into my bag. I was wondering when to call the doctor. I didn't want to call her too early. I wanted to get things just right. Jo Jo stared into space and her mouth made a silent : "Tat-tat-tat-tat-tat." It seemed as if she had lost contact with her surroundings. She squeezed my hand harder and groaned heavily. And groaned again. And again. Her bulging cunt widened. Through the split, now one and a half finger's width, a red mass with bluish stripes could be seen. Jo Jo gave a shrill yell.

"Come on out, little Maelström, we can see you." Should I call them now? Or not yet? I felt easy and calm. Shit was coming out of her bottom. I wiped her arse and changed the cloth under it.

Jo Jo groaned in a low, raw voice. I removed her gripping hand from mine, put it on the edge of the couch and went into the corridor.

The nurse was filling in papers.

I wondered what I should say.

"Maybe it's starting to come out. I can see something there."

The nurse glanced at me, then returned to her papers. "Ahah, well, the midwife'll be along soon." She carried on writing.

I turned halfway round. Should I? "Ahah, ah well."

I went onto the ward. Susa's eyes were open. She was clutching her pet mole tightly. Jo Jo was gripping the edge of the couch and groaning loudly. The groaning subsided, she slackened off and slumped back onto the couch. If they came now, would it be a false alarm?

"You don't want to go for a wee-wee, Susa?"

Susa looked at me and did not answer.

The door opened and several people entered hurriedly. One of them switched on all the lights. A wheeled stretcher was pushed in. Someone was lying on it. People bustled around. Talking at one another.

"Get down. Where's she to go? Let her lie on that table over there. The other one's giving birth here as well. Doesn't matter. Get off the stretcher! I'll help you. There's a man here too, let's go over to the other table. Hang on! OK, get down now. Get up over there. Course you can. Come on, come on. Your third birth, is it?"

"Yes," said the woman from the delivery table, "poo coming."

I went over to Susa. "You getting up, or are you going to lie here a bit longer?"

Susa put her arms around my neck.

"Lie here a bit and hold your mole."

Jo Jo started up again. I wiped her arse and changed the cloth under it.

"Well, there we are," someone said near the delivery table.

Jo Jo gurgled. I looked at her bulging purple cunt. Jo Jo's lips were moving. She developed a double chin and there was a grimace on her face. Then her lips moved again. She thrust. Her heels and her neck had lifted themselves up from the couch. Her breasts flopped down on either side of her body and she was wet between them. I stood there, wishing to do something, not knowing what. I wrapped the smock around her breasts.

"Done," came from the delivery table and there was the sound of a baby crying.

Susa hugged her pet mole.

Jo Jo gurgled. A woman came towards her quickly, looked at Jo Jo's cunt and went away again. I stood there not knowing whether to go over to Susa or stay with Jo Jo. Two women came swiftly up to the couch.

"Push," said one of them, "push now."

"She's deaf. Speak so she can see you, she'll read your

lips."

"Push." The woman bent over Jo Jo and put her hand down on her groin. "Push, down here. Push! Push! Push. Breathe. Breathe calmly. Push. Push hard! Push."

There was the head anyway. And the rest came out quickly with a plopping sound.

A woman held the baby above Jo Jo. "Look. Ready?" The child was covered in white membrane, dark red clots and bright red blood. A tube was pushed with a slurp into the baby's mouth. The tube slurped in its nose. The baby shrieked.

"Is it breathing?" said Jo Jo very loudly with her uncontrolled voice.

"Course it's breathing." The woman looked Jo Jo in the face from close to and said loudly: "It's breathing. A daughter. Everything's OK."

The baby was placed on Jo Jo's chest. Jo Jo looked at her chest. Her hands were in the air near the baby. Her palms were ten centimetres from the baby. She wanted to touch it but didn't dare. "Little," she said, controlling her voice.

I went over to Susa and stroked her head. Susa stretched out her arms towards me. I picked her up. A white umbilical cord stretched from the baby into Jo Jo's cunt. The woman put two clamps on the cord a few centimetres apart and nipped them shut. And cut the umbilical cord between the two clamps. One clamp lay there on Jo Jo's stomach, the other dangled between her legs.

"Bowl!" said the woman. "Under the lamp now and we'll weigh it. Did you note the time?"

"My watch is slow," I said clumsily. She got her bowl, put it down by Jo Jo's cunt and tossed the clamp into it.

"Go and have a look, the clock in the corridor is right."

The child moved awkwardly on Jo Jo's chest and blinked its eyes.

"It's not bawling," I said.

"Doesn't have to."

I went with Susa to the other side of the couch. Jo Jo raised her eyes from the child, looked at me and smiled. A red mass dribbled out of her cunt. The woman massaged Jo Jo's belly towards her cunt. Jo Jo was screwing up her face.

"Want to wee-wee," said Susa.

"We're going to have a wee." I mouthed to Jo Jo.

I walked quickly down the corridor.

"Did you have a good sleep?"

"Yes."

We opened the toilet door.

"Can you manage?"

"Yes."

I unbuttoned Susa's jump suit, folded it down, took off her knickers and lifted her up onto the pot.

"Sit on your own."

"Hold me."

I squatted and supported her under her armpits.

"Where's your wee-wee?"

"Wait." I heard the tinkle.

"Did the baby get born?"

"Yes. You saw it happen."

"Jo Jo's got no more tummy ache now."

"Still has now. The foetal membrane still has to come out. Then, that's it."

"What's a foetal membrane?"

"Where the baby was in her tummy."

"Like a bag?"

"More or less. Ready?"

I lifted Susa, softened the hard toilet paper and wiped her little cunt. Her crack was pink.

"Does it smart?"

"A little bit."

"Remind me when we get home. We'll put some cream on it."

I put my finger under the tap and washed her crack. I pulled up her knickers, then her jump suit and buttoned it up. Must get the

265

yoghurt out of my jacket pocket. And the spoon. I opened the door.

We walked down the corridor. Susa gave me her hand.

"Are you tired, daddy?"

"No. Come on."

Jo Jo was lying on the couch, her eyes shut. There was a folded blanket spread over her upper body. Between her legs near her cunt was a bowl. It was almost filled with a red mass which went right into her cunt.

The student gave me the baby which was wrapped up in a sheet and a blanket. The baby's eyes were wide open and she was staring calmly into space.

1998

Nuuma Aljla

Madis Kõiv

A Testament

I probably met him on more than those two occasions outside Daniel's yellow house at the crossroads, with me rushing from Pekri to Viirapää, and he coming from somewhere out Juudakäpa on his way home to Nuuma. Those other encounters could amount to about ten or more, but on these occasions there were others present, sometimes several men, and they were doing the talking, not me. But he himself was certainly doing some talking, because it wasn't in his nature to stand there with his mouth shut listening to others. He just had to talk; you could see it in his face – his eyes, his mouth, his chin. And how well he felt about talking, and how much pleasure he derived from doing so, even a deaf man who happened to be there would see, though it might also have seemed that he had a tasty morsel in his mouth, so sweetly were his jaws moving around, so that even a little froth appeared at the corners of his mouth as his rather large and handsome white teeth (as with old Nuuma, who still had a whole mouth of them, and healthy youthful ones too, at the age of eighty; in his younger years he allegedly chewed glass on occasions – eating a wine glass, as people said) were grinding away, whether with words or on a sandwich.

His father was hunched up, with his heavy hands and shoulders, when I saw him for the last time – his beard grey, but his teeth as healthy and white as before, and he said: "Well, you know, if only my Aljla had finished school and had gone to university."

267

This was five or six years after the two conversations with Aljla outside Daniel's yellow house.

That was the extent to which I knew Aljla and ever spoke with him, but they were extensive and boundless conversations, which only ended when we could no longer see each other's face in the dusk, and the words began to float past each other and get lost in the darkness. But the late afternoons, they were long in July and August when the twilight only gradually imposed itself on our conversations, and put an end to them and we began to think of dinner, to which I had to tramp quite some way: through Daniel's hazel copse and skirting the edge of the woods all the way to the marsh at Emma, where the road turned up towards my house. His home was nearer, in Peldamäe itself, a few hundred metres up the road.

And now, when I saw him again unexpectedly, or actually his name on a marble plaque in the small birch grove in the Kähri church graveyard: "Aleksander Nuuma 1927-1945", and realised who Aleksander Nuuma had really been (but it took some time). I did not immediately understand the truth of what was written on the plaque, that it was a full sixty years ago, that I broke off the conversation there outside Daniel's house, and we ran all the way to the marsh until a light and an open door became visible to us up on the slope.

It couldn't have been sixty years between us, it could only be entirely imaginary time, non-existent in reality – as McTaggart has said about time in general (he was at least right with regard to those sixty years).

Or was it the other way round, the whole of that time was instead filled with our conversation, filled to the brim and bursting at the seams, sixty years being too short. So that time may not be a "one dimensional line" and the time for conversation perhaps simply spilt over the edge, and now I'm standing here in front of this stone and wondering why this stone affects me nonetheless, because if time spills over the edge, the stones themselves will begin to speak, not needing to shout, merely talk, as people do, now louder, now more quietly, but at length and in depth, starting out from in front of Daniel's house and continuing in a small graveyard under the birch trees, where there were only a couple of dozen graves and gravestones or a few crosses standing thinly spread, listening eternally to our never-ending conversation. If only they bothered to do so.

I did not however find my own stone there, had I not yet been brought there, or had I ended up somewhere else by mistake, or was I nonetheless here, but didn't see myself only because who sees himself anyway when not exactly looking in the mirror.

This was therefore our third longest meeting and the conversation continued, as if I were still thirteen, he fifteen as we were then, and that explains quite a bit.

What it doesn't explain is how two conversations, whether at the crossroads by Daniel's house, can be drawn out for so long, for years (if you estimate their duration using this unreliable measure), whereas there have been other, even longer conversations, more frequent and more profound – with Arthur there in the rainbow wigwam or elsewhere, when we met unexpectedly and unplanned.

But there was something entirely different and unique in the way Nuuma Aljla spoke, something you would never hear again, whatever the topic (topics, as we talked about everything under the sun, principally about books and school – his grammar school in Võru, and mine in Valga), and thus the conversation was stretched out over years. Or maybe our departure in the evening twilight plays a role here. The darkness came and cut the talking in two and that's how it remained. And endless darkness, which is recalled here in the writing on the stone plaque in the birch grove.

But the conversations tend to end midway and are rarely (if ever) brought to a conclusion; nonetheless the conversations with Aljla seemed to have been cut in two in mid-word, so that the last syllable would remain buzzing in the air and in your head and still buzzes to this day. As if someone had come and cut it in two with scissors. And it really was cut when the NKVD men came in the spring of '45, surrounded the bunker and shot every single one of them down while they were still half-asleep, among them the seventeen-year-old Aljla. They had stood so close together around the bunker that they even managed to shoot down one of their own number (or at least wounded him).

I only got to know this later, when I matriculated from school in Rapla and went to the countryside, and Emma told me.

This murder had probably not yet been committed before I left Rapla and I arrived during half term via Tallinn and Tartu in Viirapää for the first time after the war. While leaving Tartu on foot – across the river by the Möksi mill – I wandered off the road at Kiuma, as it was already pitch dark, and stood there in the slush of the meadow thinking, this is the end, this is where I'm staying, I can't go on any further; but I did and got to Viirapää by midnight, where Emma and Andres had already been asleep a good while, so I knocked on the window... Emma was shocked on seeing me as she had thought I was as good as dead.

But I wasn't, only my legs were stiff and weak the whole of the next day. At that time Aljla and his brother Oss and others who had dodged the mobilisation, were still alive and in hiding in the bunker along with some Forest Brethren, and it was only after the war had ended in May, that an amnesty was declared for all those who were in hiding. Oss went home, to test whether the amnesty was holding or whether this was yet another Russian lie. But someone had betrayed the location of the bunker and the men left in the forest were shot down while still half-asleep.

And that was what Emma told me after I left school – as far as she knew.

What this "half-asleep" actually means, no will ever know, whether someone awoke just before death only to see the flashes from the rifle barrels approaching his face and managed to think something during that brief moment. And how Aljla himself met his end is something that no one told, not even Aljla himself with his big mouth and its slightly drooping corners and the froth there. So it has been left for me to figure out, until I reach his gravestone and begin gradually to realise that Aleksander Nuuma is in fact Aljla himself.

Emma had been particularly angry at Oss, that he had dragged along the boy to the Mereoone forest (Oss was hiding in the forest even during the German occupation!) and left him there, although he himself came home after the amnesty. But you can't really blame Oss, as he only went home to find out what would happen, and left Aljla in hiding only to keep him safe. Who could have known, that someone would betray their hiding place. Who had actually done so was something that Emma didn't know, and I don't know what good it would do to know anyway.

Aljla is no more, he's dead and that's all there is to it.

I can't put into words my feelings when I heard the news, even if I tried to describe them really well, but perhaps this feeling simply cannot be described. The simple words: sadness, shock, anger, etc., don't reach the mark, don't hit the mark, at least not in the heart, although all were present, but other things are more important.

There may have been regret, if to understand the concept correctly, or I could say, according to my usual practice – the sense of the inevitable. Nothing could be changed, Aljla was dead, had been shot and nothing could alter that fact, although my gut reaction (where even the word "my" is out of place), independent of any psychological state, was to try to do just that. There was no longer anything you could do about what had already happened. All the conversations and meetings with Aljla (emanating from this failure) were not real from this time onwards: if Aljla had still been alive, then... and despite such logic, I still found myself asking: is Aljla really dead and buried? It just can't be true.

And this must be added: I had never seen the place where he is buried, nor even knew where it was located.

Did Emma know? She did and perhaps told me, but the information went in one ear and out of the other, for otherwise how could I have known it was Aljla in that grave, some sixty years later? We never called him Aleksander, nor did it ever strike anyone that Aljla was an abbreviation of his name. Only a rather vague feeling of having heard or seen this before came to me the first time I read it, and it was only after this first fleeting moment that Emma's story about Aljla came to mind and something about the Russian Orthodox graveyard in Kähri, where I was now standing for almost the first time in my life.

To be precise, the graveyard did seem familiar even before I remembered Emma's tale of some sixty years ago. And only when I was trying to smooth out the wrinkles of my brain, did I manage to recall the story that Emma could have told on that occasion. However, it could just as easily be something born out of fragments of memory that had stayed with me.

How come I did not know this graveyard, that is to say, its precise location, and even the thought that I had never been there before – although for a long time I did think that I had, and only now, under the birch trees, I am sure that I was wrong, I had not been there, I thought it was somewhere completely different. And since this tale has to be told some day, and it must, because it cannot slip back into oblivion without first being set down in black and white, even in sometimes illegible handwriting.

The strange thing is that I only seem to remember (wrongly?) having been in this graveyard once as a boy, although it was actually near Pekri, about one to one-and-a-half kilometres from the church. But the area behind the church remained unknown to me, even during the time that the Russians left, returned, and left again. And not only that sandy heathland, but the whole village beyond the Kanepi road remained alien to me, not to speak of the houses and land across the stream. I had only crossed the stream to the road to Meemasküla near the old parish hall, and had a swim near the bridge. A few times I have been to Risu farm by the road across the stream, threshing.

But never further than that, except for that once when I walked to the graveyard behind the church, which stuck in my memory as if crossing the border. (By the by, I will have to say that I'd been many times beyond the Kanepi road, on the land belonging to the Kähri manor, but via the Juudakäpa crossroads at Puskaru, where the village of Tännasilma ends.)

For my mother too, who had grown up in Pekri (not born

there, but been brought there as a small child), the land beyond the church was only known to her inasmuch as she knew there was an Orthodox graveyard out there, but where exactly was something she'd forgotten.

What were we looking for that time in the graveyard anyway? For the grave of some acquaintance of my mother's? In which case whose? I don't remember. The name probably meant nothing to me anyway.

I remember the early evening of late summer and the sandy-coloured sun and me and my mother approaching the church and she saying: "There must be a graveyard out there, let's go and see."

And so we arrived at the sandy bit of heath scorched by the sun and this is how I remember the graveyard – sand and a sandy depression, a couple of birches but not one grave or cross. Or were there crosses there nonetheless with the names of priests on them, ones who had served there and been buried right behind the church?

And was this the graveyard I thought I had remembered?

Did I remember it correctly or not? I have no idea because now I could find no trace of crosses or names – there had probably not been that many in the first place, nor any trace of those who had been here – this was, after all, an ordinary small area of an Orthodox church, as had been built here and there in Livonia during Russian times, fewer than a tenth of which now served as churches. Their span of existence had been too brief for them to have collected more than a few crosses around them.

It is nevertheless possible, I am now thinking, that we walked all the way out to the graveyard and saw it as it could have been sixty-five years ago. Because the surroundings have changed a good deal and distort one's memories about it. The houses, the outbuildings, the gardens, even the meadows, which now dominate, are recent, some built during the last years of the *kolkhoz* system, some since then. Everything here is different, and there is nothing left that is old apart from the church itself (even this has been rebuilt to become a Lutheran church and consecrated as such too) and next to it (looking towards Põlva) the Tännasilma primary school,

273

painted red at some point, and from where we collected the post in summertime. The dairy from across the road to the church has gone, as have the Orthodox priest's dwelling house and the large orchard – instead there are two-storey terraced houses, just as there are right behind the church. Even the land has been changed around and improved, so that you can no longer get to the graveyard from behind the church, unless you want to cross a meadow.

All of this wasn't there in those days, instead there was the sparse sandy heath beyond the church with autumn dry grass, sandy depressions here and there right up to the edge of the forest, and that is specifically what I remember: sand, the autumn evening, the sun, the dry and woody hay on the heath, a grove and mother, with whom I had come, looking for the graveyard – at least that is what mother said. There could well have been wooden crosses, weathered and grey under the birch trees (if there were any birches here in those days), and these defined the atmosphere and the essence of the place that evening in late summer, when I perhaps really did reach Kähri graveyard with my mother.

And again I think, why did mother want to go there in the first place? To find the grave of some old acquaintance or other? I no longer remember mother actually saying so – the heath, the sand and the evening sun overshadow everything else in my memory. Did mother find the grave she was looking for, some distant friend, with whom talk had ended abruptly, as did mine with Aljla, did we too perhaps find him there?

But the disrupted conversation of mother's could not have been from so long ago, as my mother wasn't even fifty in those days, far from it; my "distant" conversation was further back in time and more profound than my mother's, if my mother ever had one at all. My "distant" conversation was as long ago as that summer's evening walk to the church at Kähri and beyond.

This time, I went to look for the graveyard alone, after I had seen from the Kanepi-Põlva road through the bus window a gravel path winding off to the right, and a sign saying "Kähri Graveyard 1.5 kilometres".

I broke off my journey to Põlva, got off at the church bus-stop, and trudged back to the fork in the road. I was trying to rediscover that walk I had taken back then with my mother, on that lost early evening. It was again late afternoon and a birch grove could be clearly seen over the fields "full of ripening crops", just the type that should be standing by every graveyard, whether large or small.

As far as I knew, there was no acquaintance of mine to be sought there – apart from perhaps Peetso Saamo, who I had seen once or twice, and heard talking once with my mother over the garden fence at Viirapää when he said: "You know, I have such a strange profession, halfway towards being a doctor." However, I had heard his name used at least a hundred times, more than the name of anyone else in the village, to scare the boys: "Peetso Saamo will cut off your balls!" Anyway, I had now forgotten him, that is, I didn't remember if it was there in Kähri that he was supposed to be buried. It was only when I had more or less arrived that I suddenly recalled that the boys who were snooping around here during the shooting of a film, had indeed told me that Peetso Saamo wasn't lying in the graveyard at Põlva, but was here next to the church at Kähri.

Once I was under the birch trees I saw that everything had changed compared with that early evening long ago, nothing reminded me of what it was like before, there was not one visible sign of what the land beyond the church had been like – no heath, nor sand dunes, all that was left was the meadows and, further off, the houses with their gardens. The gravel road made a bend by the birch grove and then continued towards Kähri manor, but I didn't go looking there.

A small path wound off to the left of the birch grove up to a small house and a gate, and that was all that was left of the graveyard gate.

I stepped in through the gate and there they were – graves and gravestones, plaques and crosses under the birches and right there a grassy hollow between the gravel path and the graves – maybe this was the former sand quarry, a remnant of the previous landscape. But that was something I thought later, as on arrival nothing brought to mind the old one.

Except the names on the crosses, plaques and gravestones. They did not bring to mind that visit from long ago, but they were definitely from the past, memories of those last years of normal farming before the deportations to Siberia and the collective farms, of people who lived round here and whom I knew, personally or had heard about, through stories that were circulating at the time. I wondered if I could distinguish them all by name: Kiuselaas, Jostav and others, had I seen them in person and heard their voices or simply heard about them in Viirapää from Emma's lips, or at the lunch table in Pekri – that the Kiuselaas'Juhan had done this or that, or was the man who...

I wandered between the gravestones, read the names of familiar and half-familiar names (there was not one name that was completely unfamiliar to me), until I stopped in front of an iron cross, on whose brass plate were written the names Gustav Orff and Elisabet Orff. So this is where the composer of *Carmina Burana* is buried – and in my head I suddenly heard motifs from the wheel of life humming away, and I wasn't even surprised that this composer was buried here in Kähri, and only I realised the stupidity of my thoughts and a hubbub of other voices now rang in my ears – the Orffs' Elli saying to me: "Listen, Madis, do come around and tuck in, won't you?"

And on another occasion I was round the back of Elli's house digging up potatoes using a two-shared plough. I had never seen her name in print, and the double-eff of her surname is so alien to these parts, and that's why my mind immediately wandered off to faraway Germany and it took some time for it to return to the correct place – to Naadimõtsa village, near to where Emma lived. But my mind is not fully back home, and I wonder: so Elli Orff is here already, such a young woman... And yes, then I realise how old I myself already am and how long ago it was that Alli took me, the cart and plough all the way round to Elli's place to dig the potatoes (to pay off some old vodka debt, as Elli, though young in those days, was already a widow, and to make ends meet had in some way or other to increase her income and had started being an agent for what was termed "Hanseatic trade").

Finding the right place has always been difficult for me. I'd been a little boy for all those years and then suddenly, and God knows how, I had become an old man – my prime years had somehow never existed. And now *Carmina Burana* is really beginning to turn in my head blotting out Emma and Alli and even Andres, who are all in their place, have ended up in the graveyard on a hillside at Põlva; the skirling tune of *Carmina Burana* passes them by, leaving aside my non-existent years as a grown man and then comes to a halt, allowing objects, times, people to slowly settle into place.

And so Elli approaches me along the furrow "as she then was" and asks me to come and eat, saying among other things "you've left the reins loose" and so I had, I must have been too confused, forgetting to fasten them and it was sheer luck that the horse hadn't snapped them. But it had been an embarrassing moment anyway, that's why it had stayed in my memory and came into my mind as I stood there by Elli's grave. And Alli too, who isn't here, who used to go on a bender every year or so. He would vanish from home for days at a stretch, wander about getting hold of vodka from various places he knew, because although he didn't have a kopeck in his pocket, he always managed to get some, wherever the Hansa system (smuggling spirits) was in place, because he would never leave any vodka debt (of honour) unpaid.

With that, as if following a string of thoughts, a blonde in red tracksuit trousers springs to mind, one who was seen around in Porila one summer, and whom I only saw face to face once or a couple of times, when she brought the post and gave it to me, if I happened to be the first person she saw in Pekri.

But I was not, unfortunately, always the first, very rarely in fact.

And then the other embarrassing incident involving a load of rye, when, during the threshing season in Porila, the same blonde in red trousers was present. While tossing a sheaf up onto the

277

machine, the load fell wide, so that the two halves of the sheaves split
and fell off the machine. Liisa from Porila, bless her, had to come to
my assistance to haul the sheaves back again so that I wouldn't get
in the way of others and have the machine running idle. The accident
had happened and she must have been somewhere nearby and seen it
all or even if she had been in the kitchen all the time, she must have
heard about it, as such incidents were always talked about for quite
some while.

Occasionally, I saw her blonde hair and red tracksuit
trousers flash between the houses in Porila, or I caught a glimpse
of her behind the Pekri stables traipsing barefoot on the other side
of the stream, which was dry in summer, but I never got near her
and would not have dared to approach her. And then suddenly she
had vanished from Porila and I waited for her the next summer in
vain, but she never came back to these parts – she had probably been
deported to Siberia in the meantime.

Mikk had better luck, he even managed to talk to her a
couple of times, but Mikk was always there in Pekri while I, like a
dog with two masters, would be in Viirapää now and again helping
Emma, sometimes for a long time, until Alli invited me back, as the
"hay had to be done".

But I have digressed, and it is high time to get back to the
main matter at hand. This was all about Orff's Elli, and everything in
between is extraneous.

There were others I had seen under the birch trees, people
I had talked to and who wielded a pitchfork during threshing. All
unexpected encounters. There was also the wife of the one-time
teacher (and headmaster) of the Tännasilma primary school, Urgart,
who I've not thought about for decades – Nathalie, the mother-
in-law of the poet Paul Haavaoks, and who now makes me think
immediately of her family, as Andres is already there, although
in fact on the Põlva hillside along with his mother next to Emma,
saying: "Viira and Aala and friends!". This is his second well-known
utterance, that became part of the family tradition and which was
repeated hundreds of times. (Another being: "The Peldamäe's Anni

sewed me a new shirt and braces!")

    Viira and Aala are Urgart's daughters and Andres has just been to see them with his mother (bringing some flowering plants) and Viira and Aala have played with him, or shown him their toys. This has stuck in Andres' mind for ever, although he no longer mentions to everyone that passes by, about his friendship with Viira-Aala. The reason this phrase got so well known is because Andres left Pekri with Emma (when Elfriide, Alli's wife, became mistress of the farm after the death of old Jakob) and went to Viirapää or maybe the word combination Viira-Aala reflected the place name Viirapää, because although one of Urgart's daughters definitely was Aala, the other one's name only approximated to Viira, and was in fact Viivi, or God knows what else even further away from Viira (of course the name could well be Viira, I didn't know those daughters of Urgart and only saw one – which one? – once) in fact there were three daughters altogether, but the oldest, who was already attending the grammar school in Võru, was someone whose name I didn't even know – only now did Ants say that her name was Virve.

    How long the Urgart family lived in their flat in the schoolhouse I do not know, but I do know that the school itself was soon closed down, so that Mikk, Mall and Toomas matriculated there and then went to Kiuma, but the school didn't last long after their departure. It is probable that after "old" Urgart's death and after the daughters had got married, the mother went to live with one of them, so that in the graveyard she is indeed one of those who "returned".

    There are a lot of other very familiar names, but names to which I cannot put a face (I simply don't remember). Among them Kiusalaas, a name that is bothering me a lot right now, so that I am already thinking that it might just be his grave that my mother went looking for "behind the church" in the sandy depressions on the heath that summer's evening long ago.

    Anyway, there near to Kiusalaas I finally saw him, under a row of birches at the back of the graveyard. And although the whole graveyard was under the birches – a little birch grove on the other side of an overgrown sand quarry – it was there that the birches caught my eye especially, as if they were the only ones in the vicinity.

ALEKSANDER NUUMA 1927-1945

As I did not realise at first glance what I was seeing and reading, but presently something inside me said that "that's him" before the "he" even revealed himself: so Aleksander was his full name, like our Alli, which I might have guessed all those years ago at the crossroads, but it never occurred to me, as he was simply Nuuma's Aljla, and no other name would cling to him.

In the evening sunlight of late summer, falling through the birch leaves, the grey stone motley of light and shade, once again reminded me of the tale that Emma had told back in the late spring of 1945.

"When Aljla had been killed, old Nuuma demanded the body of his son so he could be properly buried and a wake could be arranged for him. How he actually managed this, and how much he paid them is something I do not know. But he did eventually get the body, although was not allowed to bury him in the graveyard. Old Nuuma then talked to the sexton at Tännasilma, and Aljla was buried secretly behind the Russian church, although he was not of the Russian faith, none of the Nuuma menfolk were. So Aljla was buried in the sand at Kähri, but his name was not put on the little white cross. There he slept and his family brought flowers to the grave, but he was finally left alone there, as all his relatives were later buried elsewhere, in Põlva."

Yes, they have their place in Põlva, father and mother and grandfather and grandmother and other relatives too, only Oss has not arrived there yet. And Aljla is far away under the birches in Kähri, and now has, instead of a small cross without a name, a large grey gravestone with his name and dates, as is fitting, so that everyone who had known him would now recognise who it was, would stay awhile and remember those times long gone – the war and what happened before, during the heyday of the farms. The silence and the noise of classrooms.

But who knows, whether there still is a schoolfriend, who will come here to Kähri, look at the grave, and say: "Ah, he was one of my school chums." And why shouldn't someone come, when, a mere stone's throw away, is the (now empty) old Tännasilma school and just as near is the former (now demolished) Kiuma secondary school, where the children from these parts had received their education. As for those from the Võru grammar school, I really don't know whether any will chance to come here or not.

I, as neither relative nor schoolfriend, who only had two long conversations with him at the crossroads outside Daniel's house, am standing here, and if I still have the strength to do so, will come again, and when I no longer have the strength to visit, will perhaps come and stay here for good.

This is the third summer's evening that I have come to see Aljla, once along with Ants.

And the fourth time, when that time comes, if I don't fit into the plot by my grandfather or grandmother, or near my great-grandfather's grave behind the chapel, then I'll stay here. There's room here. There is a large open space by the birch grove near to Aljla's grave. And close by there are also the ruins of old Pekri, which was once almost a home to me – if I have ever had a home, then it is there.

So after a short pause, maybe we can have a third conversation, and this one will last well into the late evening, and for all eternity. We will have the time for this, that is to say we no longer need time, once we ourselves have stepped out of it.

31st March 2004, 13:52 hours

Aspendal the Rainmaker

Mehis Heinsaar

Five hundred years the drought did last
Then the child came in crying

Mummy I could no longer hold
Lake Peipsi in the palms of my hands

Time of Drought by Mari Vallisoo

One summer long ago, the area around Noarootsi and Dirham suffered a severe drought. It had not rained a drop for several months, the hayfields and the crops withered, wells dried up to a trickle and the surface of the earth cracked, forming a hard crust. The grass in the pastures shrivelled to such an extent that the sheep and cattle did not even get a moderate amount of feed and just kept growing thinner and thinner. Around Bysholm alone, three heifers had ended up with their legs sticking up in the air in the middle of the day. They had simply starved to death. People too became weak and listless. Their faces grew thin and their skin wrinkly, their lips cracked and their will to work ebbed. The old crones of Hosby sat gasping around the one wireless set, twirling the knobs as they wiped away the sweat and tried to find out, above the crackling and surging signal, what the next day's weather had in store for them. But for ten weeks now, the forecast had been exactly the same: a ridge of high pressure over Estonia with sunshine, the possibility of storms, sharp showers and thunder locally in southern and south-eastern Estonia, while western Estonia would remain windless, clear and hot. The crones would switch off the wireless with a sigh and disperse, worry on their faces.

How would the inhabitants of the Noarootsi peninsula be able to cope with the autumn, where would they get their potatoes and bread from when the whole countryside had been turned into a desert, and the woods threatened to burst into flame on account of the drought, and the last drops of water had dried up in the wells? In order to feed their families, the menfolk had been forced to go and work on construction sites in distant towns, or even work as farmhands on inland farms. Misery and hunger knocked more insistently each day on people's doors.

On one of these dire days, the parish elder of Birkas, Olof Larsen, invited the oldest and most respected people from the four villages to his house, in order to discuss what should be done next. The discussion went back and forth, as they asked themselves whether to apply for a state subsidy or bring in barrels of water from afar on carts, or to send out their children as day labourers on farms in distant parishes in the autumn. But in the end, people found that none of these suggestions were quite right. They had always managed on their own, so would they now have to send around the begging bowl? No, that was not how it was going to be. Could absolutely no one come up with a decent plan?!

They sat there in silence, sucking at their pipes and scratching their heads.

Then all of a sudden the very oldest crone from Hosby remembered than in her youth there had been a rainmaker living in a nearby village, by the name of Sture Aspendal. And on a couple of occasions when the land was suffering from drought, they had obtained help from him to solve the problem.

"Are you seriously trying to tell me, Ingebor, that this man conjured up rain?" asked the parish elder Olof, with a wry smile on his face.

"Well, you can think what you like," said the crone from Hosby, "but either way he did bring on the rain, and saved the fields from drying up completely."

"And if he did manage to do so," interrupted the

representative from the village of Paslep, Erik Karlsson, "what good would he be now? Sture Aspendal died long ago and not a trace of his art of rainmaking has survived."

"Don't say that," snapped Ingebor from Hosby, "you see Sture had a son called Pelle, who was admittedly a quite ordinary farmer in every way and didn't know a thing about rainmaking, but he in turn had a son called Leif, about whom people have said this and that."

"And what sort of things did people say about him?" asked the parish elder, creasing his brow. "You, Ingebor, stop beating about the bush, and say what you've got to say."

The Hosby crone raised her eyes to the ceiling, crossed her arms in her lap and began to speak, twiddling her fingers: "It's not quite so easy to tell as you might think. Leif Aspendal resembles his late grandfather Sture both in appearance and temperament. He loves to stay in bed for days at a time, and keep himself to himself. And just as if some strange disease or depression had seized hold of him. He wanders around the village hunched up and groaning, as if he has a great burden to bear, though he is a strong young man. But what is even more important – the iris of his left eye is black, but his right one is blue – just as it was with his grandfather Sture. If you don't believe me, ask my neighbour Kaarup or old Ove Lindvall. They'll confirm my words."

Ingebor's story did seem somewhat dubious to the parish elder, and under any other circumstances he would have regarded it as the ramblings of an old woman, but as the situation was now grave, he was prepared to try anything, however odd the measures may have seemed at first glance.

"Very well, Ingebor," said Olof the parish elder, turning to the old woman from Hosby after a little thought. "You go and visit Leif Aspendal and have a word with him. If he wants paying, let him state an amount and we'll take it from there."

At this, the old woman from Hosby began to chuckle.

"What are you laughing at now?" asked Olof, with furrowed brow.

"Well, if it were only a matter of money, things would be much simpler," replied Ingebor, "because look, Olof, Sture didn't actually ask for money for his rainmaking, but for a woman. And if Sture was like that, then I reckon that Leif will be no different."

"What's this got to do with women?"

"It has and it hasn't, but at any rate old Sture did have need of a woman. And not just some clapped-out old maid of ripe years, but a sprightly nubile young thing, who also had to be a virgin. And once Sture had managed to get such a woman behind closed doors, there'd be rain a day or two later."

"Did it really work like that?" asked the Österby village elder.

"Yes, like that, like that. And it's the same with Leif Aspendal. Or do you still think that me, an old woman and the mother of three drowned sailors, would sit here telling you fibs?"

In order to do things properly, Olof Larsen put it to the vote, as to whether to believe the old crone's story or not. Twelve were in favour, four against.

In other words: it was believable.

"Well, it looks as if it'll have to be tested," sighed Olof the parish elder. "But bear in mind, Ingebor, that if things don't turn out as they should, then there's going to be a severe punishment waiting for you."

After that, the old crone from Hosby didn't utter a word, all she did was give a chuckle and started filling her pipe with a knowing look.

A couple of days later, Olof Larsen invited all of Noarootsi's eligible young girls of marriageable age to meet up in front of the parish hall. And about forty of them turned up: some from nearby villages such as Paslepa and Lyckholm, others from as far afield as Vööla and Harga, and even a couple of girls from Dirham and Riguldi on the mainland. And as this event had been announced as a great festival and competition, musicians had also been invited and a long table had been laid with food and drink. Older people did, admittedly, think that having such festivities during a serious drought was rather a stupid thing to do, but as the council had agreed to everything, all they managed to do was grumble quietly and shrug their shoulders in wonder.

The girls were assembled on the square, then straws were drawn and it was announced that the one that drew the longest straw would be the winner and the chosen one. And so, when the straws had been drawn and finally the winner was announced, it turned out that the winner was a young pauper girl, Ingeland Eskilsson from Birkas: this rosy-cheeked and pretty girl was very pleased at her victory, hoping that she would now win some honour or prize.

And in truth she was not disappointed. She was solemnly presented with a smart new set of clothes: a white blouse with embroidered edges, a pleated skirt, a blue and yellow top and a headscarf. And she was quickly helped into these garments in the back room of the parish hall. Furthermore, Ingeland was adorned with silver necklaces and bangles so that when the girl had been dressed up in this way, she did indeed look the prettiest girl in the village. The rest of the young women, the ones who had lost, looked on with great envy and anger. Then the girl was offered tasty morsels and good things to drink, after which she was asked to step onto a horse-drawn cart.

Ingeland was short of stature and thin, but had clear blue eyes filled with an enormous joy. She had perhaps never been so happy in her life. Blushing, she thought of how proud Ainar would be now, a young man from faraway Võrumaa, who had worked in the local forests last winter, and whom she had met at a village fair. That same autumn, yes, in a couple of months' time, Ainar had vowed to take her away with him, and so she would flee this land of poverty and sorrow.

So glad was Ingeland thinking about all this, that she didn't even bother to ask why three burly and surly old women plonked themselves down next to her, nor whither they were all bound. And so the lucky girl, with glowing cheeks and her plaits floating on the wind, vanished from view on the cart along with the old women.

After an hour's drive, they finally arrived at a small, low house situated about a kilometre to the north of Hosby. The building was run down, the shingle roof had holes in it, and all around there grew wild golden rod, burdocks, orachs, and hogweed.

When old Ingebor from Hosby had gone up to the front door and heard loud snoring coming from inside, she returned to the cart, exchanged nods with the other women, whereupon two burly women, specially chosen for the task, took Ingeland by the arm and started to walk with her towards the house. Only when they had finally arrived at the door, did the girl get a peculiar feeling, that things were not quite as rosy as they seemed. The happy smile vanished from her face, she tried to struggle free from the grip of the old women, but did not succeed.

The old crone of Hosby opened the door and an astonished Ingeland was led into the dark, stuffy room, which smelt of sweat and filth, and whose air was moist and sticky. From one corner of the room rose a sickly odour. On seeing what was there, fear seized pretty Ingeland. Her face grew pale, and terrified, she began to stamp the floor beneath her and scream wildly, but the old women only laughed at her attempts to escape, pushing her towards the bed in that corner, where there groaned, as if in pain, the vague outline of a snoring being, his face completely covered by his red beard, smelling of pipe tar and sour piss, a huge bear of a man. And when one of the women did something with his trousers, and pulled out something large, red and wet looking, Ingeland could no longer contain herself and fell into a faint.

But the old women now acted all the more calmly. In a manner that betrayed the ways of the world, one of them rubbed the club of the giant sleeper until it grew warm and stood neatly erect like a red fence post. The other was busy with Ingeland, took off the clothes and underwear of the unconscious girl, massaged her body until it was warm, stroked her limbs and her privates so that the juices started flowing and her sex became moist.

Old Ingebor from Hosby watched all of this frowning, and when she felt that the hour was at hand, she gave a nod that the

287

weather-making could commence. And so the blissfully unaware Ingeland was lifted gently onto the sleeper's large cock, allowing the girl and the rainmaker to gradually become one.

The sharp pain that surged through Ingeland like a bolt of lightning brought forth from the girl's mouth such a savage cry, that even the old women covered their ears. The women were ready to pull Ingeland off the rainmaker, otherwise the girl might actually die, but then they saw with amazement that all of a sudden the tone of her screaming changed, her chest was now arched, her head thrown back, although she was still screaming like an animal, eyes tightly shut. Only then did the old women realise that the cries of pain and fear had now changed, in the course of a long breath, into a yell of enjoyment and bliss.

Suddenly, on awakening and realising that her own body, writhing in ecstasy, was impaled on a slimy eel-like cock, the girl could not stop the powerful flood of joy. The flood had totally devoured her, filled her tiniest cavities and immersed her coyness in powerful strange waters. And when presently a dull sigh was heard from the corner and the sleeping giant woke up and opened his reddened eyes, Ingeland no longer felt fear at the huge body of the man on whom she was dancing, but in the eyes belonging to that body, there was a painful and heavy weariness, but no evil. Two strong swarthy arms now reached out towards Ingeland, embraced the thin girl, and she let it happen without resisting, eyes closed – let another wave of desire issue forth and flow through her.

On seeing how the thin girl was now truly at one with Leif Aspendal, the faces of the old women broke into laughter, and blushing and giggling they made a sign of the cross, as a precautionary measure. Because it was, after all, a great sin to watch such obscenity going on in the middle of the day.

Then Ingebor from Hosby nudged the other old women in the ribs, giving them to understand that their task was at an end, and stifling their laughter all three fumbled and stumbled their way out of the room. One of the women then sat by the front door on a chair, the other under the window at the back of the house, while the third,

Ingebor from Hosby, got back onto the horse-drawn cart and drove off to report to the village council that Leif Aspendal had accepted their sacrificial victim.

For two whole days and nights the old women sat outside Aspendal's house and all the while, swearing, shrieks, laughter, things falling over, the noise of a chase, as well as sometimes a brief pause, could be heard by turns, then it would begin all over again.

 The weather, however, grew all the hotter, the air shimmered and the old women were struck by the heat, letting the sweat run in rivulets down their bodies. And when, on the third day, the weather grew even hotter, the old women watching around Aspendal's house, and all the other people involved began to wonder whether this wasn't all nonsense, and a figment of the confused senile imagination of old Ingebor from Hosby. But just as the parish elder Olof Larsen was ready to give the order to have the luckless Ingebor taken away from Aspendal's house, well, just as a plan had formed in his head to crucify Ingebor from Hosby publicly for having made a complete fool of him before the whole parish, at that very moment, from the north-west, a rumbling was heard over the sea. At first, everyone thought that it was an illusion, but the rumbling continued and was coming ever closer.

 And verily, verily the people of Vööla, Paslepa and Kudani, those living closest to the shore, saw a large black expanse of cloud moving closer. A cooler breeze was already coming off the sea, the crowns of the trees were already beginning to sough and rustle and gusts suggested the coming of rain, and blew into people's faces, so that the menfolk gripped their hats, and the women pressed down their wafting skirts. And whether to regard this as a great miracle or not, everyone clearly saw that a huge and mighty shower was approaching the Noarootsi peninsula.

 And when at length the first heavy drops of rain fell to earth, a mad cry of joy left the mouths of all the people – rain, heavy, warm and so long awaited was here at last! It fell in bright showers onto the dry and cracked earth and the people stood, their mouths agape as they watched the sky, weeping and laughing at one and the same time, heifers ran about the pasture, their tails up, dogs barked and howled and the whole of the small peninsula of Noarootsi and beyond experienced great joy.

The rain festivities, great ones, made even the elderly jump for joy and begin to shout! With these unending rains, the muddy stream and the flooded gardens, the wall of rain that eyes could hardly penetrate, suddenly all these things seemed more beautiful and proud to the inhabitants of Noarootsi than any Christmas-tide and Easter taken together.

Parish elder Olof Larsen, who was standing along with the others in the rain, did for a while rack his brains as to whether Leif Aspendal really was such a powerful individual that all he needed was a woman and rain would come, or whether this was, after all, a mere coincidence, but then he shrugged his shoulders in happiness, opened a bottle of moonshine and knocked it back along with the men around him who were doing a roundelay. The men – and not only the men – drank and laughed as their joy at the plentiful rain needed some release.

The wild downpour lasted a whole night as well as the following day, and there seemed to be no end in sight. There were indeed a few breathing spaces, but then the rain would become even heavier. And when the roofs of a couple of houses had been swept away under the buffeting wind, and lower ground, including whole fields had been inundated, and in Enby village lightning had struck down a bull, only then did it strike the inebriated parish elder that the enterprising girl Ingeland and the rainmaker Aspendal were still making love. And so the three women of the Birkas region were once again given orders to get on their wagon and go immediately back to Hosby.

"Please tell the good man," said Olof loftily, "that he should let the girl go, that we're wet enough now. I'll settle up with him later for any further costs."

And when the old women got to Hosby and had travelled the remaining couple of kilometres, it had to be said that the sky seemed to be especially dark above Aspendal's house, they managed to shout through all of this that it was enough now and the girl should be allowed to go.

"Leif, oh, Leif!" they yelled under the windows of the hovel. "Be a good chap and let the girl go, there's been enough rain and maybe you have had enough now."

But all such yelling was to no avail, so there was nothing left to do but for the women to go in after the girl. When they entered the room, they saw the thin and exhausted Ingeland in the huge Aspendal's embrace just like a child. They were lying in the corner of the room and the rainmaker's steaming member was embedded in the girl's vagina. Ingeland's fair and heavy head of hair was spread out over the two of them like a carpet, and both of them seemed to be lying there in a peculiar kind of lethargy. Between the girl's half-open eyelids, only the whites of her eyes could be seen and she had a silent and a mindless smile on her lips. Water was dripping from various parts of the ceiling and the lovers and the surrounding floor were completely wet with rain.

When the old women, thus found the two of them, wet and sweaty, and still in one another's embrace, they could think of nothing else to do but simply heave Ingeland off Leif's glowing member, cover up his exhausted body, and lug the girl to the cart. And so they travelled back towards Birkas, the trembling Ingeland between two of them, who was doing nothing but raving and laughing to herself, as if she had seen goodness knows what kind of wondrous visions.

And it turned out that the women's arrival in Hosby had indeed helped, because as they were on their way back to Birkas, the downpour was beginning to ease, the sky had become somewhat lighter, and patches of blue could be seen here and there between the clouds. On arrival in Birkas, the sky was completely clear, and the dark clouds in the sky had dispersed.

A week or two passed, the earth began to green again, the potatoes, the crops, and the grass began to grow furiously and it could be assumed that there would no longer be a crop failure that year. A miracle had occurred and people put a couple of barrels outside Leif Aspendal's house, containing salted meat and rye. Yes indeed, Aspendal the rainmaker was now one of the great and the good.

But the man himself was indifferent to all of this. Once Ingeland had been taken away, he slept the sleep of the dead for a whole week, day and night, and on awaking was struck again with a desire for the girl. During the days spent with Ingeland he had felt for the first time in his life that a great burden was being lifted from his heart, and that he could now breathe freely. But now his head was once again filled with dull thoughts, his breast with heaviness as if the sky had fallen down upon him, and his feet felt chained to the earth. No, he had to get the girl back! He had to get back the girl who had brought relief to his body and soul, otherwise his life would become hell!

At night, wailing and gnashing of teeth could be heard coming from Aspendal's hovel as if the man was at his wits' end; during the day he could be seen yelling and bawling as he walked the country roads. The giant's melancholy was like that of a hundred men, as was his desire and mental anguish. The old women already guessed that by yelling on the road in this way, he was calling the girl back.

And Ingeland's own lot was hardly any better. When she was brought back to her home farm, her foster parents looked after her in every way they could, they put compresses on her, smeared vodka and honey on her fatigued body, fed her with the tastiest morsels and drink, but she continued to writhe and rave during the night, her temperature rose, and nothing but strange disjointed words were heard coming from her lips. It was as if she were suffering some sickness for which there was no cure, and which was greater and stronger than Ingeland herself. As if she were hearing the voice of the tormented giant or even the enticing sound of rain, as if the rainmaker, by way of his cock, had launched a thousand suns and moons, and a whole shimmering giant lake had entered her.

Poor Ingeland found no rest for even the briefest of moments and every day her suffering was more and more in evidence. The girl could be seen wandering around the house, wide-eyed and in the manner of someone suffering from lunacy, laughing to herself, as if she were out of her mind. She would look straight into the sun with a peculiar expression, without shading her eyes, and would sometimes sit in a dark room, her head cocked to one side, as if listening for something... Nothing and no one pleased her and only made her mood ever more sombre.

One morning, Ingeland was nowhere to be found. The girl had vanished. They looked everywhere for her, but couldn't find her anywhere. Then, a few days later, there was a series of claps of thunder and a wall of dark clouds came in from the sea towards Noarootsi, and each shower was more violent than the last. The parish elder Olof Larsen thought he knew where this was all coming from.

He immediately ordered the three old women of Birkas to drive over to Aspendal's place and bring back the girl. But on arrival in Hosby they found the house empty and abandoned.

Now Olof Larsen let it be known throughout the parish of Noarootsi that Leif Aspendal and Ingeland Eskilsson were fugitives, but a first, then a second, and a third day passed without them being found.

The rain had already flooded streets and pastures, flattening the crops, which had been growing well up to then, the stormy gusts had already loosened the thatch of the roofs of houses, blown apart haystacks and done much other damage, when a young cowherd from out Vööla way came running into the parish hall, and recounted that a passionate pair of lovers had been spotted on the dried up bed of the Lake Kudani.

Olof Larsen and the three old women involved in this matter rushed to get onto a cart, letting the boy guide them. And when they finally reached Lake Kudani, they indeed saw Leif and Ingeland romping about on the muddy lake bed.

Like beasts they were writhing in the mud, filthy and wet from the rain, laughing loudly and biting one another. Ingeland, with her pale skin, was dancing and shrieking on the end of the rainmaker's eel of lust, her head thrown back in bliss, while a great whirlwind danced around them, as if trying to communicate that no one else was welcome there. And when the three strong old women did try, on Olof Larsen's orders, to reach the lovers, a wicked wind whipped up and hard rain lashed them from head to foot, so that they were obliged to splash their way back to the river bank.

Covered in mud and full of impotent rage, those standing on the bank now watched the abominable lovemaking. It was no longer possible to get anywhere near them. The tempest and rain merely grew stronger above the heads of Olof Larsen and the old women, so that they could hardly make out the two human forms.

In the end, Olof and his assistants could think of nothing else to do but shrug their shoulders and go home and see how it would all end.

For four whole days the rain and the storm continued to lash Noarootsi, whipping itself up ever stronger, flattening all the crops and flooding fields and pastures. People again feared crop failure, this time even worse than the drought could have wreaked. Some people had been forced to move into their attics, as the water was pushing its way over their thresholds, others constructed a barrier of sacks containing sand and sawdust. Even dogs climbed onto the roofs of kennels in desperation and started to howl piteously.

Nearly half of the peninsula was already under a layer of water, when the rain suddenly stopped.

Days later, when the water had, for a large part, been soaked up by the earth or run into the sea, and the people had begun to go back to their usual tasks, Olof Larsen, as well as Ingeland's foster parents who were sick with worry, and a few other people, decided to travel out to the River Kudani to see what had happened to Aspendal and Ingeland Eskilsson. They also took heavy ropes with them in case they needed to tie up the mad lovers in order to pull them apart. But on arrival at Lake Kudani, they found nothing but silence and the quiet lake waters, which, thanks to the heavy rains had returned to their normal proportions. But where had Leif and Ingeland disappeared to?

They searched for them all around Hosby and Paslepa, Einby and Österby, the woods and undergrowth were combed, but no one was found. Only ten days later did a fisherman find in the reeds of Lake Kudani the couple bound together in an embrace. Like innocent children, they rested there, beneath the clear water.

2007

Afterword

As Jan Kaus has already intimated, Estonia has undergone quite a few of what he terms "upheavals" over the past century or so, in stark contrast to countries such as the United Kingdom and Sweden, which are also located in Northern Europe, but have enjoyed centuries of life uninterrupted by invasion and occupation however often they have been threatened by such. Nor has such a small country as Estonia ever been a colonial power.

I would like to pick up on Jan's comment that many Estonian authors had an international outlook. The authors represented here are mostly ones that have looked outward, beyond the borders of a country of only around one million native-speakers of the Estonian language even today. Especially Friedebert Tuglas, a volume of whose stories I translated a number of years ago under the title *The Poet and the Idiot*, travelled to a large number of European countries, lived for long periods in Finland and Paris when fleeing the Russian Czarist police as a dissident, and even visited the Maghreb. Another author who was outward-looking in a different way is Mati Unt, whose novella *An Empty Beach* is published here. Even in Soviet times Unt staged many modern foreign plays for the Estonian theatre including ones by Pinter, Genet, Weiss, and Gombrowicz, as well as the classics. Several Estonian authors, including Eduard Vilde, Jaan Kross and Maimu Berg, have all either lived for some time in Germany, or had a good grounding in the German language. Even Anton Hansen Tammsaare, who hardly ever left Estonia, was influenced by the German language on account of being married to a native-speaker of German. Eduard Vilde lived for a long time in Copenhagen, as well as Berlin.

Eric Dickens

Author Biographies

Maimu Berg (born 1945) Her major works are the novels *I Loved a Russian* (*Ma armastasin venelast*, 1994) and *Away* (*Ära*, 1999). In these works which are set in Estonia during the last years of the Soviet Union, the author raises a subject that was taboo at the time: personal relationships with partners from a different ethnic background. Her short stories are about fear, desire and attempts at self-realisation. Berg captivates the reader with her subject matter which she enhances with colourful episodes from Soviet life.

August Gailit (1891–1960) was a writer of exuberant imagination, a late neo-romanticist, whose entire output focuses on the eternal opposition of beauty and ugliness. His most influential work is the novel *Toomas Nipernaadi*, (1928). It is the story of a man who leaves town in early spring, at the time when the ice starts to melt, and sets off to wander around, from one village to the next. Wherever he turns up, adventures and trouble ensue. Nipernaadi enchants the village girls with his tales who then all fall in love with him. Toomas Nipernaadi has become a classic figure in Estonia. In 1944 Gailit emigrated to Sweden.

Mehis Heinsaar (born 1973) is one of the rising stars of Estonian literature. Although Heinsaar has only published three collections of short-stories and a novel, he has enjoyed unprecedented success amongst critics and has been awarded several prizes. Heinsaar is an ironic and somewhat melancholic suburban bohemian, whose ideal, according to his own admission is a normal middle-class existence following the principle of "seeing the world through the eyes of someone living his first day there".

Karl August Hindrey (1875-1947) was in his fifties before his work was published in Estonia. In the next fifteen years Hindrey made up for lost time by publishing novels, short-story collections, travel books and children stories. His short stories are considered quite eccentric, avoiding the structure of classical storytelling. At the same time Hindrey's view of life tended to be quite conservative. His usual hero is an older good-natured man, travelling around the world and observing life from a distance.

Madis Kõiv (born in 1929) is a remarkably versatile man: a nuclear physicist by profession, he writes fiction, plays, philosophical and literary essays. He is also a fine painter. In the 1990s he became one of Estonia's most important playwrights and won many awards. Kõiv's highly praised plays, essays and short stories remained in his desk drawer for almost 30 years, before his friends convinced him to send them off to literary magazines and theatres.

Jaan Kross (1920-2007) is Estonia's best known and most translated writer. He has been tipped for the Nobel Prize for Literature on several occasions for his novels, but in fact started his literary career as a poet and translator of poetry. On his return from the labour camps and internal exile in Russia where he spent the years 1946-1954 as a political prisoner, Kross renewed Estonian poetry, giving it a new direction. Kross described his fiction as psychological character studies. They are set against meticulously observed historical backgrounds, whether the work is in the 16th or 20th Century.

Juhan Liiv (1864-1913) His poetry is scorched into the consciousness of the Estonian people. Liiv's prose has had a significant influence as well. A newspaper journalist, Liiv began by writing happy stories which he thought would appeal to his readers, but quickly abandoned pseudo-romanticism for social realism, writing some of the most important short stories in Estonian Literature.

Eeva Park (born 1950) began as the author of atmospheric "nature" poems. Her fiction combines nostalgia, shards of memory vividly remembered, with the anxieties and vicissitudes of life in the Soviet Union. Eeva Park's latest novel *Trap in Infinity* (*Lõks lõpmatuses*, 2002) describes one of the less attractive aspects of modern life, human trafficking.

Karl Ristikivi (1912-1977) was one of the first writers to deal with the urbanisation of Estonia. He also wrote the first Estonian surrealist novel *Souls' Night* (*Hingede öö*, 1953). His most impressive work is a cycle of twelve books which embraces European history over two millennia. His work is rich in myths and symbols but always has an ethical dimension. He left Estonia during the Second World War and died in Stockholm.

Rein Saluri (born 1939) is one of the most important storytellers of the 70s and 80s, but since then has written little and has mainly worked as a translator. Saluri can be considered one of the chroniclers of the second part of the 20th Century – he focuses on the war and its aftermath. His psychological stories map out the inner world of his characters and explore the labyrinths of their memory. Saluri's introvert heroes are searching for some fixed points in the past and peace in the present, with the national tragedy hiding behind the author's modernism.

Peeter Sauter (born 1962) came to the fore in the 1990s. He is one of Estonia's most important contemporary novelists. His books mark a new direction for Estonian fiction. Sauter's work depicts the mundane. Metaphysics, tragedy or great conflicts are replaced by the trivial details of life which are not generally considered worthy of literature.

Anton Hansen Tammsaare (1878-1940) is Estonia's most famous writer, whose masterpiece *Truth and Justice* (*Tõde ja õigus*, 1926-1933) has been read by almost every Estonian. Although Tammsaare took his subjects from the history and life of the Estonian people, his novels are influenced by the works of Bergson, Jung and Freud, and the novels of Knut Hamsun and André Gide. Tammsaare's writing seems as fresh and original today as when it was first published.

Friedebert Tuglas (1886-1971) was an author, scholar, critic and a highly influential cultural figure in Estonia. He was one of the founders and the first chairman of the Estonian Writers' Union. As Tuglas lived until 1971 he experienced great changes during his life, he saw the Estonian republic come and go, and experienced being a persona non grata during the Stalinist years after World War II. Friedebert Tuglas made a major contribution to Estonian literature with his short stories, essays and aphorisms.

Mati Unt (1944-2005) is considered one of the most influential modernist, and latterly postmodernist authors in Estonia, as well as being a playwright, theatre director and producer. Unt will be best remembered for revitalising Estonian fiction. His writing is rooted in everyday life, personal relationships and urban living – although the national trauma of the Soviet occupation always lurks under the surface. To this he added the deadpan humour of the eternal observer, someone who never quite succeeds in getting fully involved with other people, and yet is always present amongst them.

Arvo Valton (born 1935) began his career as a writer in the 1960s and his work has been translated into many languages. He has tried his hand at all genres, from voluminous novels to the briefest of aphorisms, and has also written literary criticism, plays, film scenarios, travel books, poetry and non-fiction. In the 1960s he first made his mark as a writer of grotesque and strange short-stories. Valton criticises absurd aspects of the technological revolution and its deleterious effects on beauty and art.

Eduard Vilde (1865-1933) was the first Estonian prose writer to achieve classic status, and is generally regarded as one of Estonia's most eminent authors. Eduard Vilde's collected works run to 33 volumes and include novels, short stories, plays, travelogues and humorous pieces.

Recommended Reading

If you have enjoyed reading *The Dedalus Book of Estonian Literature* you should enjoy reading the novels featuring Estonia's near neighbour Finland and the William Heinesen novels set in the Faroe Islands that we have published:

The Dedalus Book of Finnish Fantasy – Johanna Sinisalo
New Finnish Grammar – Diego Marani
The Good Hope – William Heinesen
The Black Cauldron – William Heinesen
The Lost Musicians – William Heinesen
Windswept Dawn – William Heinesen
Mother Pleiades – William Heinesen

Novels set in the former Soviet Union that we have published which might also be of interest:

The Zero Train – Yuri Buida
The Prussian Bride – Yuri Buida
Made in Yaroslavl – Jeremy Weingard

These books can be bought from your local bookshop or online from amazon.co.uk or direct from Dedalus, either online or by post.. Please write to **Cash Sales, Dedalus Limited, 24-26, St Judith's Lane, Sawtry, Cambs, PE28 5XE.** For further details of the Dedalus list please go to our website www.dedalusbooks.com or write to us for a catalogue.

The Dedalus Book of Finnish Fantasy – Johanna Sinisalo

"These stories have two common denominators: nature and war. As Sinisalo explains, Finland is a sparsely populated country with enough room for its citizens to form close ties with nature; and, throughout its history, the country has been torn between the empires of Sweden and Russia, both of which took their turn to dictate the language in which fiction was written. These excellent stories share an edginess that's quite distinct from the quirkiness many contemporary English writers prefer to celebrate."

Tom Boncza – Tomaszewski in *The Independent on Sunday*

"This wonderful anthology is a fine addition to Dedalus's range of fantasy literature in translation, and is every bit as diverse and challenging as its predecessors. Markku Paasonen's prose poem, 'Punishment' begins 'I have seen an author's head', and in a mere half-page he creates a gruesome, dreamy fable that is startlingly memorable. Every entry left me wanting to know more about these eerie authors." S.B. Kelly in *Scotland on Sunday*

£9.99 ISBN 978 1 90351729 1 337p B. Format

New Finnish Grammar – Diego Marani

"It was, naturally, the flatness of the title that attracted me: it bespoke, in its quiet confidence, a deep, rich and eventful inner life. And besides, I have some inkling of what Finnish grammar is like: fiendishly complex, basically, and related to no other languages on earth save Hungarian and Estonian (I simplify). Deep and rich, did I say? That isn't the half of it. I can't remember when I read a more extraordinary novel, or when I was last so strongly tempted to use the word 'genius' of its author. The story is simple, as the best stories are. A man is found on a quayside in Trieste during the second world war, having been clubbed almost to death. A tag inside the seaman's jacket he is wearing bears a Finnish name: Sampo Karjalainen. When he regains consciousness he has no memory, no language. He is simply a consciousness devoid of context. The doctor on the hospital ship riding at anchor, though, is Finnish, and, with nothing else to go on, starts teaching his gradually recovering patient Finnish, in the hope that memories will be triggered, and he can rediscover who he is. Eventually, when Karjalainen is well enough, he is sent to Helsinki, where perhaps he can find more fragments of his identity."

Nick Lezard's Choice in *The Guardian*

"It has taken 10 years, the dedication of a small UK publisher and a perfect-pitch translation to deliver Diego Marani's first novel in English. When it came out in Italian, reviewers called it a masterpiece and it won several prizes. Since then Marani has written five more novels and become a Euro-celebrity."

Rosie Goldsmith in *The Independent*

"Judith Landry is to be congratulated on her seamless translation from the Italian, and Dedalus for introducing English readers to a fascinating writer." Gabriel Josipovici in *The New Statesman*

£9.99 ISBN 978 1 903517 94 9 187p B. Format

The Lost Musicians – William Heinesen

"*The Lost Musicians* builds towards a crescendo of farce and tragedy in which nothing less than 'the cosmic struggle between life-asserting and life-denying forces' is played out."

Laurence Phelan in *The Independent on Sunday*

"Marooned in the north Atlantic between Iceland and Norway, the Faroe Isles are famous for little besides dried mutton and twice drawing with Scotland at football. Indeed, the thinly fictionalised island of this new translation by W. Glyn Jones of William Heinesen's 1950 novel often seems as much a prison as a homeland. The pursuit of happiness is hardly helped by the local Baptists, headed by tactless Ankersen, the spearhead of the prohibition movement. Set against his priggish faith are a colourful crew of musicians and layabouts: Sirius is a frustrated poet, the Crab King a mute dwarf, Ole Brandy a belligerent pillar of the community and Ura the Brink a cliff-dwelling fortune teller. One of their glorious but destructive drinking sessions is the stage for the novel's key incident, in which money is stolen and a young cellist blamed. The result is a tale of stereotypically northern European sensibility, in which merriment is bright, brief and viewed through the fug of booze, and desperation chips at the hardiest of souls. Heinesen's intriguing novel walks a fine line between a fable and a social document."

Jane Smart in *The Guardian*

£9.99 ISBN 978 1 903517 50 5 320p B. Format